THE CHEROKEE HIDEAWAY

BOOK ONE

Wheeler Pounds

Bluewater Publications

Bluewater Publication
Killen, AL 35645
Bluewaterpublications.com

Published in the United States by Bluewater Publications.

This work is based from the author's personal perspective.

Editor – Sierra Tabor
Cover Design – Scott Campbell
Interior Design - Maria Yasaka
Managing Editor – Angela Broyles

SECRETS OF THE CHEROKEE HIDEAWAY

The Cherokee Hideaway
BOOK ONE

The Cellar Vault
BOOK TWO

The Spy Sanctuary
BOOK THREE

Acknowledgements

Thanks to Ricky Butch Walker for his guidance, historical information, and insistence that I do something with my manuscript. Also to Sandra Stricklen, my Cordova High School classmate who has taught high school and college English and creative writing, for proofreading and correcting my mistakes.

And thank you to my daughter-in-law Jennifer Pounds, who was the first to read my manuscript and proclaimed that it was "better than a lot of those other books that I have read."

And to other family and friends who read a partially handwritten rough draft and proclaimed it worthy of publication. And especially thanks to my wife, Judi, who puts up with me in spite of my shortcomings.

CHAPTER 1

Raleigh Walker was born to roam. His Native American ancestry subtly hid any additional Irish lineage which might have crept in. He claimed an ample amount of Cherokee blood flowing through his veins—that it was diluted at all by the white man had very little impact on his appearance. The contamination had failed to deny him the dark skin, high cheekbones, and black hair that distinguished his great-grandparents, who were both full-blooded Cherokee. It was also clear in his love of the wilderness and his distaste for stagnancy. The thrill for action shone in his brown eyes that had a hint of green, successfully highlighting his handsome face.

His good looks rivaled some of the big names in Hollywood, but Ralcigh's personality was quite different. He was too much the outdoorsman to be a slave to schedules and deadlines. The untamed genes in his body vetoed any attempt to corral the wild instincts that he had inherited. It was this love of the outdoors that motivated his dogged persistence to remain committed and to complete the outing he had planned for the coming weekend. It was considered by him to be a great challenge, and he was eager to face it.

It was an undertaking he would have liked to have taken years before, but would have been impossible before his university education had been completed. Through the insistence of his parents, Raleigh had reined in his adventuresome spirit long enough to earn a college degree. He probably would not have endured the demands required to receive his diploma had his major not been in a field in which he had an interest. Criminal justice offered an appealing vocation that suited his risk-taking ways—it offered excitement. His vision of outsmarting the criminal mind presented a challenge that appealed to him.

Although unaware of it, Raleigh was about to enter into an adventure that would satisfy his appetite for excitement. His physical and mental abilities would be totally challenged, and his life would be forever changed.

Raleigh was at home in the woods, the abode of his ancestors whom had occupied this land long before the arrival of the white man. He considered his forages into the forest to be a means of communication with the spirits that had once guided the red man before the intrusion of those who would later lay claim to his homeland.

"Hike in and you may get a free flight out!"

Kurt Marshal's attempt to discourage Raleigh's planned backpacking trip was going nowhere.

"Carrion Airlines wouldn't be *my* way of choice to exit that canyon."

"Kurt, what are you talking about?"

"I'm talking about the BBE—the Buzzard Belly Express. Their cargo is excrement—filthy dung. You would be unceremoniously deposited under their roosting limb. If that is your burial ground of choice, go for it! Funeral home charges are mighty expensive anyway. You could just cut out the middle man and the expenses of a burial plot and let the vultures do the work for free. I would think, however, that you might want to stay around a little longer and have a more decent burial when Saint Peter calls your number. I know it's crude to say, but I'm trying to talk some sense into your thick head. The old timers claimed that many who were crazy enough to go into that canyon never came out."

The Sipsey Canyon in Northwest Alabama was the topic of discussion. Raleigh was determined to make the hike, and Kurt, as a close friend and experienced forester, was attempting to change his mind.

"Ain't no search party going to go in there to pull a dumb knucklehead out of trouble! Most everyone's got enough sense to stay out of that place. If something happened you probably wouldn't be found, and you know there's not a cell phone signal around that wilderness. You will be completely on your own."

Kurt offered sound advice. His extensive knowledge of the area dictated that he strongly discourage anyone who wanted to backpack into the canyon.

"As you know, I once thought that I wanted to make that trek. I didn't get far before I realized it wasn't the smart thing to do, to say the least. Granted, I have never been compared to King Solomon, but I do have enough wisdom to know my limitations. It didn't take long for me to reach them and realize that it was time for me to swallow my pride and call it quits. I think that you should do the same before you get into more trouble than you can handle. Don't go into that place!"

The warning would go unheeded.

CHAPTER 2

◆

"Rattlesnake kisses can pack quite a wallop! I'm not convinced that you are man enough to handle that kind of affection," Kurt persisted further.

"Don't worry, Kurt. It can't be that difficult. Good weather is forecasted for the weekend; that should be in my favor."

"You will get wet. *And* you will get cold!"

"Beats wading through rattlesnakes."

Although Raleigh did not consider cold temperatures to be a major negative issue for the weekend, snakes were a different story. He harbored a strong dislike for the creatures. He was aware that snakebite in the remote wilderness could be fatal. A warm, sunny day could lure the snakes out of their dens to absorb the warmth of the rock ledges through which the traverse must be made into the canyon. Raleigh wanted no part of that possibility.

Kurt responded, "Believe me, you'll be singing a different tune before you get out of that hole. Go ahead! Be a macho red man. Learn the hard way. You're not going for a stroll in the park."

"That bad, huh?" Raleigh's reply did not indicate that he was convinced by Kurt's warning.

Kurt, still pleading, continued, "Listen, Raleigh, I know what I'm talking about. It's that bad! I only started in, and it didn't take long for me to have all the adventure that I could enjoy."

"I'm going anyway!"

"It's your call! I wish you the best," Kurt finally gave in with a sigh, seeming to resign himself to the fact that nothing he could say would sway Raleigh to cancel his plans.

Never the one to back away from adversity, Raleigh was seeking high adventure.

"With luck, my Indian blood will help me survive. I suppose that I'm about to find out just how tough I am."

"Indians had sense enough to stay out of that canyon. So did the early settlers—and for a good reason! They didn't want to be a feast for buzzards."

The canyon to which Kurt referred was located in the Bankhead National Forest. Before it got its title from an influential congressman who worked to have the expanse designated a national forest, the original inhabitants of the wild territory called it the Black Warrior Mountains.

The forest claims a sizable portion of land in two Northwest Alabama counties: Winston and Lawrence. In the heart of the 180,000 acres comprising the whole of the forest, there are 26,000 acres of rugged terrain which has been designated a wilderness area. The Sipsey Canyon cuts a deep gorge through the heart of the wilderness.

Should medical attention be needed, one would not want to be deep in this remote environment. Raleigh planned to hike alone, and he wanted to minimize his risk for the need of assistance. The reality that he might require help forced him to consider his weakness—that inability to resist the forces that pulled him toward the unknown. He normally was receptive to sound advice given in a constructive way, but at times, in matters pertaining to nature, he allowed untamed spirits to trump sound judgment.

The backpacking trip had been two years in the planning, but it seemed that Mother Nature had plotted against such an excursion. She had allowed Raleigh to make a number of lesser treks into the Bankhead but had prevented the hike that he most wanted to make by serving up foul weather at times when he had scheduled the hike. When she threatened, Raleigh knew not to venture far from the traveled paths that coursed throughout the forest. It would be inconceivable that he should consider the canyon trudge when storms were possible. Flash floods and slippery conditions could prove disastrous.

There are few remaining areas in Alabama that have been left untamed by the presence of man. The Sipsey Canyon, however, can lay claim to this distinction. The canyon remains the domain of the elements—with an abundance of rattlesnakes. A number of people have attempted to wrestle this isolation away from nature, but all have failed.

Raleigh recognized and respected this fact, but he now felt that at last it was time to make the journey that he so wanted to complete. The good weather forecast had convinced him that the stars had finally aligned in his favor, and he was determined to take advantage of the opportunity.

"Let's face it, Kurt. I am well aware that this ain't going to be no Sunday stroll, no matter the season. If I wanted easy hiking, I would hit the trail at the city park. To be truthful, the thought of meeting a challenge where others have failed—uh, no reflection on you, Kurt—is a powerful motivation for me."

Raleigh was not seeking Kurt's approval as he continued the conversation. His intent was to explain the rationale behind his dogged determination to complete his plans for the weekend.

"It's now or never. I will probably not find more favorable conditions than now. I'm feeling well, and I'm anxious to get started. I also have the time off, so now is the time to go."

"Go for it, Raleigh. It's your decision! Stay in the canyon, and you can't get lost. Come out the same way that you went in, and we won't need to send in a search party. Not that one would even go into that hole."

"Getting lost is the least of my concerns. Those who get lost in the forest are guilty of not doing their homework before they go in. A person who enters the wilderness not knowing what it is all about only invites trouble."

Serious hikers understand the importance of adequate preparation before leaving the forest roads. After the boundaries were established for the wilderness area, all roads had been closed. This allowed the forest to return to its natural state. Consequently, there are no roads and few trails within its confines. Seasoned hikers ignore the trails and bushwhack the creeks and ridges of this vast domain.

Raleigh had used his acquired knowledge of the forest on previous hikes, but he wouldn't need it on this excursion. In the canyon, there would only be one way in and one way out. Sheer canyon walls would prevent him from altering his path. The meandering confines of Hubbard Creek would dictate his course.

It is not difficult to find the Bankhead National Forest on the maps of Alabama. In the northwestern section of the state, the parcel can easily be distinguished by the large green section on the map, which outlines its boundaries. Only a few roads traverse this isolated area, which surrounds only one small town. Only those individuals interested in wilderness matters give this area a second glance.

Forest devotees, such as Raleigh and Kurt, see the locale differently. A gigantic lake fingers up in a northwestern direction, invading the heart of the forest. Built between towering rock cliffs, an earthen dam impounds waters of the Sipsey River, which flow from the forest, creating over five hundred miles of shoreline. The lake covers 41,000 acres, with depths reaching almost three hundred feet. The water is cold, pure, and as green as the surrounding vegetation. Crowding its banks further downstream from national forest property are houses, cabins, marinas, and other commercial enterprises.

Moving upstream from the dam, the congestion on the lake banks gradually gives way to uninhabited federal lands, breeding a notable change in scenery. Modern development yields to the beauties of nature at its finest. In this setting, Mother Nature has created a dazzling display of her best works. Creeks and streams channel the spring-fed water through lush vegetation and over more than a thousand waterfalls. Creatures that flourish in this environment are numerous and have made it their habitat for eons. Some are found nowhere else.

Numerous sandstone overhangs provided shelter for the original inhabitants of this area. The first inhabitants were the creatures of the forest, who were later joined by primitive humans. It is not known when these new settlers arrived to lay claim to the land, but they began to leave their marks on the surroundings. Generations of use have been documented by the relics that they left behind. The grinding of acorns and grains and the cracking of nuts formed "mortar rocks" and "nutting stones," which were deserted after centuries of use. Tools, weapons, petroglyphs, jewelry, and other artifacts left an account of their presence.

On the lake, only a few individuals today who live, vacation, and play on this man-made impoundment of water are aware of the treasures so near to them. Even fewer have enjoyed their beauties. They delight in their boating and swimming activities on the pure water of the lake but are oblivious to the wonders of its source and the volumes of history written within its boundaries.

It was to the core of this rugged creation that Raleigh was drawn. The entire forest is a treasure chest, but the wilderness is its crown jewel. Service and log roads that at one time existed have been barricaded and reclaimed by the forest. Many of the human imprints have disappeared, and the wilderness has regained control. Now, only the brave dare venture beyond its marked borders.

Originating in the pristine environment of the Warrior Mountains and the surrounding wilderness section are numerous creeks, branches, and small spring-fed streams, which feed the headwaters of the Sipsey River. From the western reaches, Hubbard Creek flows through a relatively placid terrain over a beautiful cascade waterfall before reaching a deep canyon. Water in the creek is then ushered into a wild ride over a rocky creek bed before being expelled into the peaceful flow of the Sipsey River. The water then continues its long journey, where it will eventually be introduced to the salt water of the Gulf of Mexico.

Before beginning the salinization process, however, it must make many stops; the first of which is the nearby dam. It will take many years for it to reach the Gulf. Locks and dams on the Black Warrior and the Tombigbee Rivers impede the flow, while towns, cities, and industries add pollutants to the once pure spring

water. Further downstream, it is joined by the waters
of the Alabama and Mobile Rivers, where it begins to
pick up its salt content. Along the entire expanse of its
journey, numerous small rivers and creeks have made
their contribution to increase the volume of its flow.

The water in the canyon through which Raleigh
would be wading would make a long flow as it made its
passage downstream. In one long weekend, he would
complete his planned adventure. He was unaware,
however, that the water through which he would be
wading would be salty long before the consequences of
this trek would be over. He was about to begin a wild
ride that would take him in many directions.

CHAPTER 3

◆

Jim Manasco is a product of the forest. Being one of the few who were privileged to have grown up in the Warrior Mountains, on which the lands of the Bankhead Forest lie, he has more knowledge of the area than almost any person alive today. It is only natural that he wrote a book that is considered to be the bible of the wilderness. *Walking Sipsey* chronicles his extensive knowledge gained from a lifelong love affair with the Sipsey. It is a store of information on the many options of a forest experience. Jim provides detailed guides to the places and activities available in the forest.

Above all, he advises those who enter the Bankhead to enjoy it, yet to respect and protect the treasures stored within its boundaries. There is also the warning that much caution must be taken for safety reasons while enjoying its beauty. Potential dangers dictate that one should be alert to the surroundings when entering its domain.

In addition to the maps of the forest, Raleigh read and studied the messages contained in the book authored by Jim. It had been instrumental in his development of a strong attachment to the Bankhead Forest and wilderness area. Using this book as a guide, he systematically began to explore the adventures detailed in *Walking Sipsey*. Gradually, he was able to cross off as completed the varied activities that were headlined in each of the book's chapters.

- ☑ Borden Creek Trail
- ☑ Saltpeter Furnace
- ☑ Turkey Foot Canyon
- ☑ Thompson Creek Trail

Raleigh enjoyed the challenges offered up in completing the adventures detailed by Jim in *Walking Sipsey*. Many of them served up multiple days of hiking before a successful completion could be registered.

There was one exception. After discussing the vegetation found in the forest in chapter four, Jim Manasco offers up another adventure in chapter five, to which Raleigh had no check mark.

- ☐ Kinlock Falls

Even the casual visitor to the forest would question why Raleigh had not completed this part. Kinlock Falls was perhaps the most visited place in the forest. The gravel road hugged the bank of Hubbard Creek at the falls. A wide shoulder of the road provided parking where the roar of the falls could be heard below. Even the non-hiker can find it quite easy to descend to the falls.

Jim, however, pitches a curve in this chapter. He begins by introducing the reader to the Kinlock District, which includes a rock shelter formation, a spring of pure water, a history of a covered bridge, an old plantation house that was converted to a CCC camp during the recovery from the Great Depression, a watermill, and the impressive cascade waterfalls. All of these attractions are easily accessible. He teases the reader with this sentence:

"Smiling faces, fish, and standing on a rock in the middle of nowhere—that is what wilderness is all about."

In the next paragraph, however, Jim swings the ax. To soften the blow, it begins innocently enough, but he wastes little time in getting to the point.

"While the head of the Sipsey Canyon is scenic, it is also primitive. The vista will quiet an appetite for natural beauty, but from the little falls on downstream, it is a different story. Take heed; there are no trails in this canyon, and it is no place for the tenderfoot. The bluffs are high, and the ledges are slick and narrow. It is dangerous—one slip and you've had it. To bypass the bluffs, you have to bushwhack through laurel thickets, and that is hard traveling."

The next paragraph becomes even more sinister.

"If you have spent any time in the wilderness, you may have noticed that the old timers shunned this part of the area, and with good reason. The rocky crags and thickets are the home of numerous canebrake rattlesnakes (Velvet Tails), some of record size."

And it concludes with a warning.

"To bushwhack this type of terrain, you have to watch every step and never drop your guard."

A portion of this information is repeated for emphasis.

"OLD TIMERS SHUNNED THIS PART OF THE AREA. THE ROCKY CRAGS AND THE THICKETS ARE THE HOME OF NUMEROUS CANEBREAK RATTLESNAKES, SOME OF RECORD SIZE."

This warning never failed to attract Raleigh's attention as he read the book. He had a strong dislike for snakes. The Sipsey Canyon was well deserving of its reputation. Snakes consider it their domain and resent any intrusion. Knowledgeable hikers did not bicker with their claims. It had been this way since anyone could remember.

The remembering dates go back a long time—much longer than the white man had laid claim to these mountains. The snakes got there first—likely before the first human made an appearance. Native Americans considered the canyon a forbidden place, respecting the claim of the serpents.

Nature had cooperated with the snakes to declare the canyon off-limits to other intruders. There was no visible place where the surroundings had allowed a welcome sign to be placed at the entrance to the canyon, thus declaring it a sanctuary for the rattlesnakes. The dense jungle was practically impenetrable. Canyon walls and rock outcrops provided the nooks and crannies that housed the snakes and provided ledges for their sunbathing. They had the freedom to roam as they pleased.

Raleigh's philosophy was that ever since the days of Adam and Eve, snakes and humans didn't mix. The reptiles cause nothing but trouble. If they stayed in their place, he would stay in his. If the snakes claimed the canyon, he had no business there, unless they had retired for the winter.

Facing reality, Raleigh knew that in order for him to complete the requirements outlined in chapter five, he must choose between warm weather and rattlesnakes or weather cold enough to put them in their winter habitat. The decision was difficult.

In the summertime, the water in the creek would be cold, yet refreshing for wading or swimming. Wintertime created enormous problems in the canyon. The water would be too cold to wade or swim for any period of time. Canyon walls blocked the sun, preventing it from penetrating to the bottom and deterring it from melting the ice that covered the slick, narrow ledges. This made hiking very difficult.

In his book, Jim Manasco cautions that a hike into the canyon in the summertime would lead directly through an active rattlesnake den. Kurt had documented this fact on video. Rattlesnakes of record size, in large numbers— hostile and undisturbed by man... thanks, but no thanks! The decision was obvious. The rattlesnakes had to be in their winter dens when Raleigh trespassed through their territory.

The window through which Raleigh could make his hike through the canyon was drastically narrowed. If it were to be too warm, the snakes would be out in numbers. In freezing weather, ice would make the ledges even more slippery. Rain might cause flooding, making the canyon impassable.

Mother Nature had to place her blessings on this adventure. Patience punched the ticket to a successful completion of this escapade. The time had to be right; otherwise, the outcome would be disastrous.

It seemed that finally the stars had lined up on Raleigh's side. The weekend weather was forecast to be perfect, and he had an extra day off work. He was feeling well and eager to get away for a few days. The time had arrived for him to go where no tenderfoot would dare to venture. He would even make Jim Manasco proud.

Raleigh savored the days when he could get away from everything. The State of Alabama required their field officers to be on call at all times. Telephone calls in the late hours of the night frequently summoned Raleigh to come to the jail to make a decision regarding the possibility of a bail bond for a parolee who had been arrested. This was a requirement of his chosen profession, one which sometimes consumed a lot of his off time. The forest provided an escape from this requirement. There are no communication towers in the forest; they are only located where there is enough population to be profitable.

This, however, presented a problem of its own. If there is a time when outside communication is needed, a solo trek in a dangerous environment would qualify as a prime example of one. There is a high degree of risk when one enters this territory alone, and it would be needful to summon assistance should there be an emergency. There would be no phone service. No safety net. Raleigh would be on his own in the woods.

Kurt had pointed this out and cited it as a reason to discourage the hike. Raleigh reasoned that the Indians and old timers hadn't had cell phones, and this increased his urge for the challenge to prove his stamina.

He had always been an independent sort—doing what he wanted, when he wanted. He had not married yet because he had not wanted to be restricted by the limitations that a spouse might place upon him. However, if he should meet the right girl, one who shared his love of the outdoors and was not afraid to enjoy it, he would then consider marriage.

In the past, there had been females who had made it obvious that they considered him quite good looking and sought his attention. He had dated occasionally but had not met one whom he considered to be that special girl. There was still more forest to explore. Starting a family could wait. He was nearing his twenty-sixth birthday—still young and spirited—and he was ready to get on with this adventure.

CHAPTER 4

◆

The U.S. Forest Service had not provided a suitable space for overnight parking at the head of the Sipsey Canyon. The shoulders of the road were wider at Kinlock Falls to accommodate the visitors there. To leave a vehicle at this location overnight, however, would invite theft or vandalism.

Accommodations for long-term parking were not available at Kinlock because of the lack of need for such a service. It required only a short amount of time to see and enjoy the falls and its surroundings. Some enjoy swimming in the small pool below the falls, but an extended hike was not usually in the plans. Backpackers and overnight campers usually begin their forages into the forest at more hospitable locations.

Raleigh arranged to have Kurt drop him off at the head of the canyon on Friday morning where he would start the trip. The plan was for Kurt to return on Sunday afternoon to transport Raleigh back to Kurt's home where Raleigh would leave his vehicle. This would allow enough time for him to explore the canyon and exhaust some energy.

It was Kurt who had introduced Raleigh to the Bankhead. When he was young, Kurt enjoyed occasional forages into the forest. He and a group of others were instrumental in completing the necessary groundwork required to have a portion of the forest designated a wilderness area. He had grown up on the fringe of the forest, not in its bowels as did Jim Manasco. He was near enough, however, to be introduced to its wonders as a youngster, when an elderly neighbor had filled his young ears with haunting tales of the wild. The forest was packed with adventure, and Kurt was eager to plunge into this enchanted kingdom.

During his school years, while his friends were spending their time on sports fields, Kurt explored the forest. While his peers went to college to prepare for careers in electronics, coaching, and other varied fields, Kurt excelled in science and botany. As an adult, he had become one of the most beloved science teachers in the region. His reputation as a devoted teacher and forest disciple had led to an eventful summer. A leading nature magazine even enlisted his expertise in producing a documentary video of the Sipsey wilderness and of the most popular sites in the Bankhead.

Having seen the video produced by the magazine using footage shot by Kurt, Raleigh was drawn to its beauty. He had not realized that there was such a place in his native Alabama, and it was no more than a two-hour drive from his home. He had always assumed that beauty and adventure on this scale were available only in the Smokies or the mountains and deserts of the Southwest. He now considered the Bankhead Forest to be a worthy rival to these distant destinations. Noting the credits on the video, Raleigh had contacted Kurt for more information on the Bankhead.

Kurt had simply put a copy of *Walking Sipsey* in his hands and said, "Start walking."

Raleigh had periodically updated Kurt on his adventures and his progress in fulfilling his aspirations to make all the hikes that Jim had so capably described in his book. On occasion, Kurt would accompany him on day trips to some of the more accessible areas. Most of the time, however, Raleigh was alone in his explorations.

While planning his current canyon adventure, Raleigh was initially hopeful that he could persuade Kurt to make the weekend adventure with him. He had not been able to persuade Kurt to make the hike with him, but neither could Kurt persuade Raleigh to cancel his plans. Both had seemed determined to get their points across.

Fearing for his safety, Kurt decided to try one last time to change Raleigh's mind. He looked through a rack of video tapes, removed one, and placed it in the player.

"This is some footage that I shot while making the documentary for the magazine. They wanted a good wildlife segment, and I wanted some snakes in the work." He fast-forwarded the tape while talking. "I had always been told that there was an abundance of snakes in the canyon, so I went in."

Kurt reached the portion of tape he was seeking and began to let the picture play. Filling the screen were scenes of snakes—huge rattlesnakes. Rattlesnakes that gave the appearance that an intruder was not welcome in their territory. They were certainly in a foul mood, as if they were not pleased that pictures were being taken of them. Only a small portion of the footage that Kurt showed Raleigh had been used in the documentary. The parts that were used were the most docile scenes of the whole segment, as if the editors wanted the snakes portrayed as being peaceful.

"I did not go far into the canyon. I got my pictures and came out alive. I will not go back!"

This was the end of the conversation. Raleigh would go in alone. He thought of the warning that Jim had given in his book. There was undeniably an abundance of rattlesnakes where he wanted to go. He did not doubt that there weren't any paths and that the ledges would be slick and dangerous. It would be his final test to pass the challenge outlined in his textbook, *Walking Sipsey*, and it would be his opportunity to prove that he was no tenderfoot.

CHAPTER 5

◆

Shortly after sunrise, Kurt dropped Raleigh off at the wide shoulder of the road near Kinlock Falls. Raleigh rechecked the weather forecast, and a perfect weekend was still promised. His backpack and other gear were unloaded, and Kurt left with the single admonition, "*Be careful!*"

That was it. Kurt was gone, with an agreement to return around 5 p.m. on Sunday to pick him up. The adventure had begun.

Jim Manasco had been right on target in his description of the upper canyon. The head of the canyon was scenic and primitive. The vista was surely still an appetite for natural beauty.

I can't even see the mouth of the canyon, Ralcigh thought to himself. *I thought a trail would at least lead a short distance!*

There was no hint of a trail. It was immediately obvious that there would be no easy section through which to hike on this trip. The laurel thickets of which Jim Manasco had warned were there and appeared to be impenetrable. Although Raleigh had been cautioned, the extent of this obstruction was unexpected.

Raleigh slithered through a blanket of tangled mess—mountain laurel, saw briars, hawthorn bushes, blackberry briars, and devil's walking sticks—anything that seemed to grow a sharp point. Even animals had not succeeded in establishing a path through this jungle. His backpack was constantly snagged. His clothes seemed to attract briars and thorns like a magnet.

"Tenderfoot." Raleigh recalled the words used in the book.

He soon realized that this was no place for anyone, tenderfoot or no tenderfoot. This was no place for anything, man or beast. It occurred to him that the reason there were so many snakes in the canyon below him was because they could not get out. Maybe that was an exaggeration but possibly not that far from the truth. It was as if the powers that be had planted a wall to keep intruders from entering the canyon. The entanglement stretched to the cliffs on each side of the creek as they narrowed to form the throat of the canyon. There was no alternate route.

Hours into the hike, Raleigh realized that he was getting nowhere. The thought of admitting defeat and getting out while he could entered his mind. However, he was forced to face reality. He was alone in the forest and Kurt was not due back before Sunday afternoon. He had no transportation available for his return.

I am not a quitter! Raleigh continued to repeat this thought to himself as he inched himself away from the area of the falls.

He had expected difficulty further on when he was deeper into the canyon, but he had not even reached the narrow section where he had assumed the difficulties would begin. The sun was moving faster than he was. This early delay was not in the plans.

Kurt's earlier attempts to discourage Raleigh from making the hike were now making a whole lot of sense. With each step, it became more obvious why Kurt had rejected Raleigh's invitation to accompany him on this excursion. He had been there, done that.

Why did I not listen to him? This is more of a challenge than I bargained for! Raleigh internally shouted at himself as he pulled himself away from yet another saw briar as it dug into his flesh.

This tangle was unreal. A razor fence couldn't have been much worse than this.

Pausing to consider his options, Raleigh reasoned that Kurt had penetrated the canyon far enough to reach the rock ledges further downstream. In doing so, he would have traversed the same terrain that he was now battling. It became quite clear to him the reason for the warning Kurt had given him, but it also strengthened his resolve to succeed in this challenge.

If Kurt can do it, so can I! Raleigh continued the conversation with himself. *It's too late for me to change my plans now. I have set my course for the weekend, and there is a lot of canyon to explore. In a man's world, sometimes one must prove his manhood. I suppose this weekend will certainly do that.*

This reality became more apparent with each step.

The afternoon had arrived far too soon. Raleigh was eventually successful in putting the thickets and briars behind him. From the start, every step had reminded him that he was in the midst of the ultimate endurance test. The snarl that he had left behind had given him a thrashing; scratches from the thorns and briars seemed to have covered his entire body. All of his mental and physical resources had been required just to keep going in the direction leading away from the security of civilization.

Entering the narrow part of the canyon, it became evident that ledges were largely nonexistent, making it necessary to wade the creek. His hopes of staying dry had to be tossed, and the wading led to yet another challenge. The rocks in the creek were covered with moss and slime, which made them extremely slick. It was difficult for him to keep his balance while carrying forty pounds of equipment and food in his backpack, but it had to be kept dry if at all possible. A wet pack would further complicate matters.

The water was cold and quickly filled his boots. His clothing was saturated up to his hips. He was constantly readjusting the backpack up on his back to keep it above the waterline. Wet boots and clothes added even more weight to his burden, continuing to make every step difficult.

Jim Manasco's warning had been right on target. *"To bushwhack this type of terrain you have to watch your step and never drop your guard."*

This had been the case from the get-go; there was no relief in sight. The effort was requiring a lot of energy, and Raleigh began to notice that his stamina was rapidly draining. Realizing that hypothermia was a real possibility, he knew it was necessary that he find a place to camp, build a fire, and rest. He needed to warm himself and dry his clothing. His slow progress was a concern, as it was becoming more obvious that the canyon offered no accommodations for camping. There were no sandbars or ledges large enough to provide a camping spot.

"Maybe around the next bend..." Raleigh reasoned aloud to himself.

The water had not yet been so deep that he could not continue his wade downstream. He had to carefully choose his course, requiring frequent crossing from one side of the creek to the other, avoiding the deep pools. He relished the stretches where ledges widened sufficiently for him to walk the narrow banks, but they were slick.

Occasionally, he would glance at the crevices and overhangs where he knew that rattlesnakes were taking their long winter's nap. He also knew that a warm, sunny day would bring them out to absorb the warmth of the rocks. His thoughts, however, did not dwell long on the things that he could not see. There were more than enough challenges in simply being able to make decent progress down the creek and finding a fit place to camp before nightfall.

The steep canyon walls towered above the narrow creek. Periodically, Raleigh searched for a passageway that might lead to higher ground. While in the creek, he had not passed a suitable camping site, and he realized that he must find one soon. There was nothing to do but continue going downstream and maybe say a little prayer!

In one area, the bluffs descended almost to creek level where a small branch of water flowed into the creek. The bushes and briars formed such an entanglement that what had appeared to be a passageway to a possible camping area outside the banks of the creek proved to be impenetrable. Time continued to pass without any sign of a possible escape route from the canyon.

It was as though the cliffs above him were making their own statement.

You asked for this, big boy! You have set your course downstream; now go. Let's see how tough you really are. You were determined to prove your manhood by challenging this domain; now enjoy it if you think you can!

Raleigh was not having a good time. He was miserable. He wanted an adventure, and he was getting it—in grand fashion. He had two more days to enjoy this nightmare. Although Raleigh had not yet pushed the panic button, he had certainly located it. The sun was beginning to hide behind the high canyon walls, and there was still not a hint of hope in locating a place suitable for nightly accommodations that were level and dry.

He had no way to calculate the distance he had traveled, but he knew there was still a lot of canyon ahead. His plan had been for him to be much further in his hike by this time of the day. He now realized that this miscalculation might result in there being dire consequences affecting his safety. His body temperature was dropping, and he had exhausted most of his energy. To endure, he had to keep moving, not only to prevent his body from cooling but also to locate a place to spend the night. Without a fire, survival would be difficult for him in wet clothing.

Raleigh simply had not covered much territory during the day. The forest maps did not show the canyon to be exceptionally long. On paper, it appeared to be easily navigable in one day; unfortunately, he was not hiking on smooth paper. In reality, it was rough. The old timers had known it; Jim had reported it in his book and warned against entering the canyon. All of this was beginning to make sense.

Raleigh had initially reasoned that this warning was for others—the greenhorns—not Raleigh Walker! After all, this was Alabama, not Arizona. On two different occasions, he had hiked the depth of the Grand Canyon from one rim to the other. Surely this qualified him to challenge the lowly Sipsey Canyon.

In retrospect, Raleigh now considered the Grand Canyon hikes a cakewalk. Possibly it was because he was feeling the effects of the harsh demands of the day, but the Grand Canyon experience now seemed tame compared to what he was experiencing in the Sipsey Canyon. The Sipsey had nothing but entanglements, slick rocks, and steep cliffs that lead to the unknown.

Raleigh was not at all sure that he would find a suitable camping spot for the night; and right about now, he would be willing to pay double for that bottomless bowl of stew that he ate in the Grand Canyon! The twenty dollars he had paid at Phantom Ranch seemed like a bargain. He had eaten nothing since breakfast and was not only tired but hungry.

As Raleigh continued his search for a possible escape route, he spied what he thought might be a place where he could make an exit. Just ahead, there appeared to be a narrow ledge originating from the canyon floor, continuing upward where it appeared to join a larger ledge. From a distance, this rock outcropping blocked his view of the lower ledge as it descended toward the creek. He wished for a change in his luck; it had been bad all day.

The excitement almost caused Raleigh to slip and fall into a deep pool of water. While searching for that passageway out, he had stepped on a slippery, moss-covered rock, and it was with great effort that he regained his balance. He reminded himself that it was imperative he use caution with every step.

He recalled again the warning that Jim Manasco had given, "*Watch your step, and never drop your guard.*"

Coming closer to the vicinity of the perceived exit from the creek bed, he was once again disappointed. The narrow ledge did not descend all the way down to the bottom. There were approximately twenty-five feet of cliff wall below the terminal point of the ledge. A V-shaped formation, however, had been created by a crack in the sandstone rock and ran vertically up to the base of the narrow, descending ledge that he had noticed from a distance. The crack extended in a gradual slope upward toward the ledge, but it was too steep to climb.

All I need now is to fall and break my leg, Raleigh thought as he vetoed an attempt to climb the wall.

Exhausted, he leaned back against the rock. The day was not going well. Raleigh needed to rest and consider his options. He took advantage of the V-shape in the rock formation to lean back and attempt to relax. He braced his backpack in the depth of the crease to remove pressure from his aching back.

Stretching his arms above his head, his left hand brushed against a collection of accumulated dwarf ferns that had grown in a small recessed area in the rock face. It was an odd looking fern, one that Raleigh had not seen before. He was no expert in botany or plant identification, but he was no novice either.

This must be a variety unique to this locale, Raleigh reasoned to himself as he examined the fern. *I should take a sample back for Kurt to identify for me.*

The Sipsey contains a large variety of ferns and other plants, some unique to the state. He prided himself in his ability to identify a majority of them, but this variety was new to him. He placed the specimen in a zip lock bag, which he had packed for just such a purpose. He made a mental note of its source, which he reasoned might aid in its identification.

As he examined the small, recessed area from which he had removed the fern, it occurred to him that it might not naturally belong there. Cleaning the remaining fern from the spot, he made a closer examination.

It's a step! This was actually chiseled into the rock! Raleigh almost shouted the words.

His eyes began to search higher up the rock face. A similar pocket of ferns grew above the first, and another above that. The coloring of the fern blended in so well with its surroundings that the carving they concealed was virtually invisible. Reaching up, he removed the second collection of fern. Just as he had anticipated, this exposed another step. The third batch of ferns was beyond his reach, but he reasoned that it too must conceal another step. Long ago, someone must have chiseled out their own escape route from the canyon floor!

But was it a way of escape from the canyon? It appeared that the steps did lead to the narrow ledge, but did this ledge provide a route up to the larger ledge above it? He could not be sure, but it appeared to connect, creating a way to ascend to the top.

Years of exposure to the elements had worn the edges of the steps as smooth as the surrounding rock, and it was apparent that they had not been used in recent times. They had long been forgotten, their origin and destination forever lost in the passing of time.

Even with the steps, the rock face would not be an easy climb. The steps had been cleverly designed to maximize the natural crease in the rock's structure. With the steps carved on the right side of the V-shape in the rock, the opposite side provided support at the back. The backpack, however, effectively negated this advantage; it extended beyond the edge of the rocks, throwing him off balance. He quickly realized that he needed to make the climb without his backpack.

For this hike, Raleigh had packed a hundred foot roll of nylon twine. Removing it from an inner pocket of his pack, he began unwinding it and tied the exposed end to a strap on his backpack. Making a few adjustments to get a good balance, he was satisfied that he could lift it properly. Unrolling the twine, he began to climb.

The climb without the backpack was quite easy. He marveled at the ingenuity used in the construction of the escape route from the canyon. The steps had been carved in such a way that the V formation continued to add support for his back all the way to the top. He was able to easily step onto the narrow ledge he had seen from the creek. As he climbed, he removed the moss from each step where it had accumulated over the years.

This slowed his ascent, but he was cautious that he did not make a misstep and fall.

The shadows of the higher cliffs had started to dim the lower elevations by the time Raleigh reached the ledge. Nightfall was fast approaching. He was now above the creek and unsure where this path might lead, but he had no other option. Pulling up his backpack, he strapped it on and began to follow the faint trail along the narrow ledge. He was aware that he was not the first to travel this course, but it had been a long time since it had last been traversed. He wondered who came before him and how long it had been since the steps were last descended.

The path led upward to the larger ledge, which had been visible from the creek. Finding the steps had been the miracle for which he had prayed when he was facing his dilemma. Climbing the steps had been the right decision. At the top he found ample space to camp and build a fire.

Creeping darkness had commenced to obscure the view beyond the ledge. Further exploration would have to wait for a new day. Removing his backpack, Raleigh first retrieved his headlamp. He would need it in order to set up camp. The ledge provided plenty of rocks with which he made a fire ring, a practice he was faithful in using before building a fire in the woods. Gathering dead twigs and tree limbs, he soon had a roaring fire. Warming by the fire, Raleigh said a little prayer of thanks to the higher power that had led him to safety. He would survive the night after all.

After heating water and removing a pouch of freeze-dried Wild West chili from his pack, it was time to address the hunger pangs which had now pushed to center stage. He opened the pouch and poured in the required two cups of boiling water. After stirring the mixture, he waited the ten minutes for the food to "cook." He reasoned that the chili would warm him inside as he sat by the fire. The "cooking" time offered him enough time to unroll his sleeping bag and get ready for bed. The chili was no bottomless bowl of stew, as was served at Phantom Ranch, but it certainly hit the spot. The pouch advertised, "*Serves two.*"

He ate the whole thing.

Before crawling into his sleeping bag, he placed all his wet items around the fire to dry. Removing his wet clothing, he climbed into a pair of dry thermal underwear that he had packed for sleeping purposes. He was pleased that he had managed to keep his backpack out of the water. The warmth of the sleeping bag was also inviting, and he was soon asleep.

It had been a *long* day.

CHAPTER 6

◆

The sun was up and announcing another beautiful winter day when Raleigh awoke. He could remember nothing after zipping his sleeping bag to his neck and snuggling into its warmth. The fire had consumed all of its fuel and died out sometime during the night, but not before doing a pretty decent job of drying his wet clothing and boots. The night's rest had reinvigorated him. This trip may not end up so bad after all. He was certainly experiencing high adventure.

Sunlight enabled Raleigh to see the area that he had used for his campsite. What he thought to be a ledge was actually no ledge at all. He had camped on a limestone outcropping that extended above the surrounding terrain. It ran from the bluffs that fronted the creek back to an even higher cliff at the rear of the canyon, forming a long fin of stone. It reached a height of some eighty feet above the level of the creek. Looking in a downstream direction, the fin dropped vertically, encompassing a large cove.

The cove appeared to be an interesting place. Looking down, it resembled a large bowl formed from rock, with a flat field at the bottom. The level field was completely encompassed by surrounding steep, stone cliffs. The bottom of the formation did not appear to be much higher than the level of the creek, but a canyon wall separated them. It looked as if the creator had constructed a limestone wall to completely encircle the cove.

"I sure would like to see what's down there!" Raleigh spoke to himself as he began a search for a passageway down to the floor of the cove.

He quickly decided that if there was a way to get to the bottom, it would have to originate somewhere along the length of the rock spine on which he stood. Time and the elements had worn the top of the rim down to a narrow, flat surface. It was only five or six feet wide in places, but Raleigh could walk its entire length to the rear of the cove where it joined a higher cliff. He traversed the distance but found no obvious passageway that descended to the cove. Higher cliffs around the remainder of the cove offered no hope that an entrance would be elsewhere.

There must be an access into that field here somewhere, he reasoned to himself.

Surely those steps were cut into that bluff to lead to more than this narrow rock trail.

He slowly retraced his steps back along the elevated ridge above the cove, searching for any sign of a passageway which might descend into the space below. He had traveled almost halfway back when he noticed a slight break in the rock that created a drainage leading down toward the cove. He followed the rock downward a short distance before reaching a vertical drop that extended to the bottom.

What at first appeared to be a way to the bottom had ended with a sheer drop of forty or fifty feet. He searched for steps, but this time there were none. He had reached the end of this line.

Dejected, Raleigh stood for a moment looking into the space below and wondering if there was indeed no way to go down.   As he turned and started back to the steep hogback ridge, he noticed a collection of large rocks to his left. He also noticed that they were positioned in such a way that an opening had created a small tunnel through them.

Ages ago, an earthquake had probably hit the area, making a slight change in the landscape. Large chunks of rocks had broken loose from the cliff and rolled downward. At the spot where he was standing, protruding rocks had caught some of the tumbling boulders and stacked them on the side of the bluff. An earthquake could also have been the cause of the crack in the rock through which the drainage flowed.

Rocks had been moved downward, creating the ditch for the water to drain. The space between the boulders was not huge, yet it was large enough that one could crawl through it. Raleigh explored the opening. Making sure that he did not exit over space, he determined to see what was on the other side. The tunnel was not long, maybe eight feet, but the angle was moderately steep, in a downward direction from where he stood.

He went in on his knees and cautiously moved through it. He reasoned that he could back out of it if there was danger on the other side. He certainly did not want to go down into something from which he could not return. He reminded himself that there was no escape valve should he get into trouble. He must be cautious at all times.

Emerging on the other side, he was relieved to see that he could stand on gravel that had washed there, carried by water which flowed down the drainage ditch from higher elevation. The drainage ditch had diverted water to flow through the tunnel and continue downward to the bottom of the cove. Over eons, this had deposited a trail of sand and gravel to the bottom, thus creating a path that was easy to follow. This was a surprise, as none of this could be seen from the upper side.

He easily walked to the bottom.

What a sight! He exclaimed to himself as he stepped into the field. *This place is really protected from any would-be intruders.*

It was incomprehensible that he had stumbled upon the combination that opened the way for him to be standing in the hidden cove. First there were the steps and then the tunnel. Luck had surely turned in his favor.

The field appeared to consist of approximately a dozen acres. Bluffs completely concealed it from the creek. The few who might venture up or down the creek would have no clue that it was there. One who might be bushwhacking the terrain above the canyon would only consider it an extension of the creek with an inlet and outlet through it. They could not know that it was completely sealed off from the creek. Realistically, there were not enough people entering the area to give it a thought.

"Old timers shunned the area."

Raleigh could have added another short sentence to the book. *"And so do present-day hikers."*

Raleigh visualized that he was entering a whole new world. Small—but to him it was an enchantment. There was no yellow brick road to its entrance, no colorful playgrounds or grand castles, but it was still the enchanted forest—a semi-circle of mystery. A stone bowl to be explored.

He considered his next move. His guardian angel had led him down here. He must now rise to accept the challenge and fulfill the mission that he now encountered. His first concern was to make sure that he could find his way back on the route that he had discovered. Using his pocket knife, Raleigh cut the tops from a few bushes. He took a washcloth from his pack and tied it to the top of one so that it would be visible from a distance, thus marking the spot where he had entered the field. The trail down was also hidden from below, and he wanted to be sure that it would not take a long search for him to find the exit when he was ready to leave.

He now focused his attention on the cove. He reasoned that whoever had taken the time to chisel out the steps up from the creek had surely also used the path down through the tunnel to gain access to the field in the cove. Logic would suggest that at one time someone had occupied this place. Using this logic, the path that he took down to the bottom would be the same track that others had used.

Perhaps, upon close inspection, he could find some sign of a trail that might lead further into the enclosed territory. He searched for any sign that might have been left by human habitation. He had traveled only a short distance before he realized that he was indeed following a faint trail that had been abandoned long ago. It did not appear to be in current use, even by animals.

Bushes and weeds had grown in the trail, but there remained the faint depression that appeared to have been worn by footsteps. He followed it as best he could, sometimes having to stop and search to correctly distinguish its course.

Raleigh was able to follow the path through the field as it led in the direction of the back portion, which was abutted by the high cliffs. He estimated that they rose the approximate length of a football field—straight up! There was no possible place to enter or exit the cove there.

As he walked along slowly, following the path, he kept his eyes to the ground so as not to lose his connection to the faint route he was following. He was expecting the trail to lead to the canyon wall. He had traveled a distance before looking up to see how near he was to the cliffs. He was surprised to see that he was nearing a deep gully instead. The view of this ditch had been blocked by bushes and was not visible from any of his previous vantage points. The gully seemed to lay claim to the entire swath of land around the base of the cliffs surrounding the back of the cove. These cliffs formed the blunted side of the semicircle shape of the cove, like a metal pan flattened on one side.

The route he followed led to the gully. As he descended, the cliffs above him seemed to grow even more massive than they appeared from a distance. He again felt the sensation that he was in a land of enchantment. There was no sign of any animals in this land, however. They were effectively fenced out.

The trail continued to the depth of the ditch; at the bottom there flowed a small stream. Water slowly trickled over a smooth gravel bed. It was a meager flow, but the water was cold and crystal clear. After reaching the lowest point, the path turned toward the source of the water. It was not a long hike upstream before the purpose of this trail became apparent.

There, flowing from a small crevice in the base of the stone cliff, was the pure water of a mountain spring. A basin had been painstakingly formed in the rock at the mouth of the spring in order to form a small pool. This collected the water for a short time before allowing it to escape to make its way toward Hubbard Creek.

Raleigh stopped at the spring, leaned down, and lowered his lips to the surface of the water. He took a long, refreshing drink.

With the passing of time, gravel had collected in the rock basin. Raleigh began to clean it out. It was deeper than he had at first thought it to be. There was no doubt that the rock had been chipped away by the hands of man. The basin had been carved by man and polished by the constant flow of water in and over its edges. The large amount of gravel that had collected in the bowl was testimony to the fact that it had been a long time since it had been cleaned. Raleigh was the first to enjoy the water from this fountain in many years. He wondered just how long it had been since another had enjoyed this refreshing treat.

Man, improving on the works of nature, had formed a most inviting place to rest. Raleigh could visualize past summers when those who dwelled in the cove had gathered around the spring and, with dippers made from gourds or turtle shells, enjoyed a cool drink. For some reason, this seemed to him to be more appealing than a plastic bottle of water. Surely this had been a popular place on a hot summer day.

The trail had obviously led to the spring, but it did not end there. It unmistakably continued up the gully, which was dry above the spring. Raleigh followed it, as it now claimed the bottom of the ditch in the absence of flowing water. The gully curved around the edge of the field and continued in the direction of the spine from which he had descended.

As a larger section of the cliff bottom gradually came into view, he realized that he was approaching a large rock shelter. There were many such shelters in the Kinlock district, yet he was surprised that he would find one here. It was not that it shouldn't be there; it was just unexpected.

Raleigh had made numerous trips to the Kinlock shelter. It was no further than a mile from the place from which he had started yesterday morning.

Jim Manasco had labeled it as "a winter sunrise ceremonial site of prehistoric man."

Other descriptions have labeled it simply as "a neat place." It was more than just a neat place. It was considered to be a sacred place by those whose descendants once regarded the mountains as hallowed grounds. It has been described as a "premier petroglyph site of prehistoric Indian occupation" and was still used annually by Native Americans for their religious ceremonies.

Raleigh surveyed the shelter that he had located in the cove. The one at Kinlock had nothing over this one. This was quite large and offered adequate primitive accommodations.   The nearby spring provided a dependable water supply. The floor was quite level and free from large, fallen rocks, which provided   excellent protection from the elements.

Raleigh reasoned that if this shelter had been known and accessible, the current authors of Warrior Mountain material would certainly describe it in glowing terms. This surely was a lost domain, perhaps even from most of the Native Americans.

But at one time, it had been well-known to someone. Hand-chiseled steps and a water basin had been left as testimony to the presence of human inhabitants. Someone had made use of the spring water and had surely escaped the rain and weather by dwelling under the shelter. Someone had descended the steps for the last time and left the place deserted, or perhaps their bones remained somewhere in the cove.

The passing of time had erased the majority, if not all, of the clues that would answer the many questions that Raleigh wanted answered. He was interested in the *who, what, when, where,* and *why* of this mysterious place. If he could find the answers he would be pleased, but he was not hopeful that he would be successful.

CHAPTER 7

———◆———

Although not on his travel agenda when he started the hike, Raleigh wanted to make a quick search of the cove. If lucky, he might find something that had been left behind. The person or persons who had abandoned this site long ago could not have taken everything with them, but they probably had not brought much to begin with. If a clue could be located as to who they were and why they were there, it would be amazing. This was a situation where he could put all his acquired investigative skills to work.

On Friday morning, Raleigh had left Kinlock searching for adventure. His trip had hastily developed into a nightmare. Now, abruptly, he found himself at the center of a baffling mystery. Two hours into the hike he would have turned around if transportation had been available. He now wished that he had more time to explore in the cove. Kurt would be waiting for him at 5 p.m. the following day. If he did not show, he knew that it would cause alarm. He had to meet his only transportation out of the forest. He decided that he would take the remainder of the day to see what he could find in his land of enchantment.

One thing was certain—Raleigh would not see the lower end of the Sipsey Canyon on this excursion.

When he had departed the Kinlock area, he was determined to go all the way. His discovery had now erased all desire to conquer the Sipsey. He would be fortunate just to make it back upstream to meet Kurt at the appointed time.

Raleigh formed a mental map of the terrain as he made a quick survey of the territory. He crisscrossed the field, lowering his estimate to ten acres for the field area. The gully, which had not been visible from above, claimed some two acres of the cove. Facing south, Raleigh looked at the bluffs along Hubbard Creek. Turning northward, the taller cliffs rose from the rear of the cove. The remarkably level field lay between.

Raleigh was puzzled as to what happened to the water flowing from the spring, as there was no apparent outlet to the creek. Following the water downstream, he reached a fissure in the rock bottom of the gully which swallowed the meager flow of water. He reasoned that it would be spit out, thus creating another spring somewhere along the creek bank.

Beginning his inspection of the cove, Raleigh tried to imagine how the area would look from the air. Flying overhead, the rock fin and the gully must effectively blend into its surroundings, creating the perception of impenetrable peaks and ravines that run the length of the canyon. Surveying this section from the air, it would be deemed to have been "*too far and snakey*" to consider it a hiking destination. No one would look down from an aircraft and say, "Hey, let's go there!"

To the contrary, it was apparent why it would be a place shunned by both old-timers and modern explorers. With a very limited amount of time available for most hikers, a more established marked trail is the hike of choice. Raleigh was in the midst of a "no man's land" in Alabama.

And then there were the snakes. Raleigh had not forgotten about them. While larger animals may have been effectively blocked from the cove, this was not the case for snakes. They could slither through the smallest of spaces. He once again considered his decision to come when the snakes were in their winter's hibernation to be a wise one.

Sometime in the past, someone had apparently attempted to snatch the small enclosed space away from its isolation, or maybe they had lived there *because* it was isolated. It was a perfect place to hide away. Raleigh pondered the possibilities. Could it have been a place of imprisonment—or to quarantine the sick? Perhaps someone had used it to conceal loot—or whatever. Maybe someone just wanted to get away from it all for a short time.

He could not imagine that anyone would voluntarily live permanently in such an isolated environment. He was willing to acknowledge, however, that people back then had lived in a totally different world than the one that we now know.

Raleigh took a second look at the large, flat area of the field through which he was walking.

"What in the world?" he suddenly said.

Looking out through the overgrown field, he could see small mounds of dirt. He first thought them to be large fire ant hills but immediately discounted that thought, as they formed a straight line in both directions and were larger than any fire ant hill that he had ever seen. He could look in both directions in front of him and see a straight row of the small earthen mounds spaced about three feet apart.

"Hilling!" Raleigh uttered to himself. He repeated the word with an explanation to himself. *Hilling—this land has been farmed.*

The "hills" covered a fairly large area, enough to grow a decent garden. Considering the probable use of hand tools in cultivation, it was evident that much effort had gone into the project. The plot was now overgrown with trees, weeds, and bushes, but the unmistakable signs of past land use remained.

Raleigh was familiar with the ancient farming method where crops were grown by the method of "hilling" the soil. Small mounds of dirt such as those that lay before him were hilled up a foot or more in diameter where the seed was planted. This method of farming was used primarily by the Indians but was duplicated sometimes by the early settlers. In each hill, the farmer made about a half dozen holes, one or two inches apart, and a grain of seed was dropped into each hole. Over each group of holes, a little dirt was piled, and the land was then worked to control weeds and unwanted grass.

Normally, corn was the main crop planted by this method. Pole beans were usually planted after the corn began to grow so as to allow the vine to use the corn stalk as a climbing pole. In between the hills of corn and along the outer edges of the fields, there would be squash, pumpkins, or gourds planted to utilize this space.

Maybe it was not as long ago as he had first thought since the last tenants of the cove had departed. His first impression was that it had been occupied by persons of the Woodland or even the Archaic Period of human occupation in the region. He now reconsidered and guessed that it had been more recent than that, perhaps as late as the Mississippian or even the Modern era.

There was no way he could really tell, however, as this was also the traditional method of farming which was being used by Native Americans before the arrival of the Europeans. The land had not been tilled as is common in the agriculture of today, so Raleigh felt that the last people who tended crops in this field had done so a long time ago.

Returning to the rear section of the field, Raleigh entered a grove of trees.

"Wild pecans," he mumbled to himself. "I wouldn't have guessed this."

Approaching the grove, he had first thought the trees to be hickory, as they are quite common in the forest. A closer examination caused him to realize that they were pecan trees. The only places in the forest where he had ever seen pecan trees were where the old settlers had planted them.

They were considered to be a species that would not normally be found growing in the wild environments of the forest. They were usually associated with the habitat of man. After a grove is established, however, it is capable of repopulating itself from the sprouts produced by fallen nuts. It was not possible to tell how long the grove of pecan trees had been there, although man had almost certainly planted the original ones.

In another section of the field he found the live, gnarled remains of an old apple tree, but only one. Most of the tree had died away; only one limb was hanging on. He had no way of knowing what variety it was—maybe just an old crabapple—but it was an interesting find.

This was evidence that fruit had once been introduced to this isolated place. Maybe the cove had been inhabited within the last two hundred years.

Raleigh wondered who could have been there. He also wondered when and why. This was the puzzling part, and he found himself compelled to try and figure it out.

Who?

Raleigh wondered if it was the Native Americans or maybe early white settlers who had located this place.

When?

He calculated that no one had been there within the last one hundred years, but maybe less than two hundred, as was evident by the area that had been cultivated.

Most intriguing to him, however, was *why*? Why would anyone, especially those developing the frontier, choose this place as a habitat? There were plenty of wide open spaces available to homestead. The West was open to all who were adventurous. Whoever had stopped here either had adventure in their veins, or they were in trouble.

Raleigh continued his search for anything that might be of interest, covering as much of the enclosed territory as possible but finding nothing more. The sun had almost disappeared in the evening sky before he realized it. His attention had been focused so intensely on the search that he had lost track of time.

He hoped that his luck would hold out one more day. This had been one of the most intriguing days of his life, but it was also one of the most frustrating. He had piled up questions and found no answers. Time was expiring.

It's been like one of those game shows, Raleigh told himself as he headed out of the cove. *Questions are asked, and the buzzer sounds before one can come up with the answer.*

It was time for the buzzer to sound. He had to get back to Kinlock before dark tomorrow.

Feeling a bit frustrated that he had found no additional clues to assist him, he crawled through the tunnel and walked up to the narrow ridge above. Looking down into the gathering darkness of the cove, even the trees seemed to be turning into question marks.

Nearing his campsite, Raleigh's mind was still racing, trying to use logic to understand the place better. It could accommodate a small number of people, for a limited period of time, under the right circumstances. He reasoned that trips away from the cove for supplies would be necessary. The small cove area could not have supplied all basic needs. Meat, clothing, salt, weapons, and other items would be needed. There was an adequate water supply, perhaps garden produce in season and limited fruit and berries, but it was a sparse existence at its best and not a place of excesses.

There were some positives. The absence of trash was remarkable. It was obvious that the place had not been entered during the age of aluminum and plastic. He found no empty cans or bottles, no discarded containers. All trash that may have been left by the ancient residents of the cove, if there had been any, had been covered or reclaimed by the passage of time.

Again, Raleigh had failed to eat lunch. His hunger had not expressed itself sufficiently to disturb his intense search for clues. As he neared camp, he gathered wood for his fire. When he arrived, he built a fire. Rummaging through his pack, he realized that he had only one choice for his evening meal—stroganoff with beef.

He then remembered that a ringing phone had interrupted his packing. He had chosen the chili and stroganoff with beef meals before having to leave to interview a probationer who had been arrested. When he returned home, he forgot to continue his selection of food for the hike. Consequently, his backpacking pantry was almost bare. The chili had been his meal last night. Tonight it would be stroganoff with beef.

His failure to pack more was now an insignificant factor anyway. He had originally planned to rest at noontime each day and eat a good meal, but the circumstances of the trip had altered those plans. The two packs of backpacker's food would be enough.

No one had ever accused Raleigh of being a master chef. Heating water was a challenge; however, sometimes he prided himself on throwing together a fairly decent breakfast. He had no problem reading instructions and following directions. This was the beauty of camp food. Remove beef. Add 2 ½ cups of boiling water to all contents. Stir thoroughly. Squeeze zip lock together and let stand for ten minutes. How hard was that?

This is too easy, Raleigh thought as he followed directions and waited the required ten minutes.

He began enjoying the two servings of beef stroganoff he had "cooked." Not Mother's cooking, but satisfying nonetheless.

As Raleigh settled into his warm sleeping bag, he reasoned that if people could survive as the ancients did with their meager provisions, and do this for a lifetime, his three days in the wilderness should be no problem.

He had started his complaining when he was only a few hours into the hike. He was to be only a weekend away from modern comforts, and he had questioned his survival the first day. He had now enjoyed hot food and slid into the warmth of a modern sleeping bag. He would be home in a couple of days, and he would sleep on his posturepedic mattress.

CHAPTER 8

◆

Raleigh's sleep did not go uninterrupted. It was not the sounds of the wild that had awakened him but a scream of fighter jets. They flew low and fast. He counted only four, but they were loud.

Raleigh lay in his sleeping bag, wide awake, his thoughts on the past day's activities. He actually had not made a thorough search of the rock shelter in the gully. His broad search of the cove had prevented him from making a close inspection of any one particular spot. There could have been something of interest in the shelter, and he wanted to take a closer look.

When he had crawled into his sleeping bag, he had planned to get a good night's sleep and then get an early start on his trip back to Kinlock. He wanted to be waiting for Kurt when he returned to pick him up. He had no intention of reentering the cove.

The planes made another pass over, louder than ever it seemed.

No need to think about getting any more sleep tonight! I might as well get up and do something.

He resigned himself to the fact that he had gotten all the rest that he was going to get for this night. He decided to try to salvage some of the night by going back into the cove and making a brief inspection of the shelter.

Fumbling through his backpack, he located his headlamp and some spare batteries. He crawled out of the warmth of his sleeping bag and rekindled the fire. After warming a few minutes, he soon had boiling water for his breakfast of oatmeal. Hot chocolate helped the situation, and it was not long before he was ready to head into the darkness. He wanted to reach the shelter by sunrise so he could take advantage of as much sunlight as possible in the short time that he had to make the search.

Raleigh had always honored the laws of the forest. This commitment dictated that he have respect for the early inhabitants of the land.

"Take only time. Leave only tracks."

This was a motto he had heard many times before.

He would never dig for artifacts. It was illegal; it was wrong. This practice only desecrated the land of his forefathers. But he could make a search and see if there might be something visual that might shed light on some of his unanswered questions. He had no intention of coming this way again and was now well aware of the reason that Kurt had refused another opportunity to explore the canyon. It was certainly not a tourist attraction, and it should be left just as he had found it. He could not deny that it was a fascinating place, but he felt that he was trespassing in a forbidden realm.

Fate had led him to this place, however, and he felt entitled to learn as much about it as possible. Using his headlamp, Raleigh descended to the cove and followed the trail to the gully. He continued past the spring and made his way on to the shelter. Dawn was approaching, but there was still not enough light to be able to see anything without using the lamp. He sat down on an elevated rock to wait for more light.

The approaching daylight slowly began to reveal his surroundings. He became aware of the rock that he was using as a seat. It seemed as though it was not there by accident but had been placed there at some time in the past. It was about the size of a small desktop and had smooth, rounded edges. His first impression was that it had been used as a seat, but he changed his mind after inspecting it and wondered if it had been used as a low table. This did not quite seem to fit either. It was too high for a seat and too low for a table.

On the top, there still lay a small bunch of dried flowers—wild flowers—the stems still wrapped together by a small vine. There were a variety of different types, all brittle to the touch. They had surely gone undisturbed for a very long time. This "table" was located in a protected place, sheltered from the elements. After an initial touch of the flowers, which caused a petal to crumble, he did not disturb them any further.

Why were they there? Had they been used as a centerpiece for a table? Were these people given to the excesses of flower centerpieces? Surely not! But there appeared to be a woman's touch in the whole scene. Interesting.

Underneath the table was a solid foundation of rocks, supporting it to a height of some two feet. There could be something stored underneath, but Raleigh suppressed a desire to peek. He did not want to disturb the stone and the dried flowers resting on top. He would have to investigate without disturbing. If he found nothing, so be it!

As light began to illuminate the depth of the shelter, Raleigh, having little time to spare, began his search. He was conscious of the fact that he was borrowing precious minutes needed to make the trek back to Kinlock before nightfall. The return trip up the canyon would be no easier than the one down— maybe harder, as he would be wading against the flow of the creek.

He dismissed this from his mind quickly. He would worry about problems only when confronted with them. Presently, he was interested in what he might find in the shelter, and he began a hasty inspection. If there had been anything left behind, with the exception of a bouquet of flowers and the table upon which it laid, time had successfully hidden it. He systematically crisscrossed the sandy floor but found nothing of interest. If there had indeed been a woman there, she must have been a good housekeeper.

Realistically, Raleigh knew that housekeeping had little to do with his inability to find anything lying around. The passing of time would have successfully concealed small items which might have been left on the floor of the shelter. To find anything, he knew that he would have to probe or dig—illegally—even in this secluded spot, because it was still within the boundaries of the protected wilderness area.

He had seen evidence of this unlawful activity throughout the forest before, and he strongly condemned the practice. He would not yield to the temptation of disturbing the floor of the shelter.

His time had expired; the countdown had reached zero. It was time to go. Raleigh would have to hustle to get back to Kinlock before dark. Kurt would be waiting—and perhaps even worrying. The trip back down into the shelter had been non-productive. He had found nothing.

Turning to leave, Raleigh noticed that light had begun to penetrate a back corner of the shelter, which had previously been hidden in the dark reaches of the protruding rock. He couldn't resist taking a second look.

He was amazed to find a rock shelf extending further back into a dark recess near the bottom of the shelter. Sunlight was insufficient to reveal its size or if there might be anything stored there. Raleigh, still wearing his headlamp, switched it on and directed the beam into the darkness of the shelf. His heart almost skipped a beat. A dark object lay on the shelf, although he was unable to tell what it might be. There comes a time in everyone's life when it is impossible not to yield to temptation.

Take only time. Leave only tracks. A worthy motto.

DO NOT DISTURB! A noble goal.

Leave everything as you find it. A practice that he had always followed in the forest—until now.

Raleigh reached with both hands into the shelf and grasped the object. He pulled it toward himself.

A block of firewood?

It took a moment for Raleigh to realize what he held. It was not firewood but a box. It would measure about ten inches wide, eighteen inches long, and eight inches high. It was completely covered by dust.

Brushing away the dirt, Raleigh could distinguish a joint where the lid sealed the box. The cover fit so perfectly that there was no crack left between the two. The box and its lid had almost become one.

But, unmistakably, it was a box. Tapping the box produced a hollow sound. It did not have enough weight to be a solid piece of wood. He shook it slightly but could not tell if it held any contents.

Temptation won another round. Raleigh's initial intention had been to examine the object and return it as he had found it; but it was a sealed box, and the cover wouldn't come off easily. He was in a hurry now.

Finders keepers had suddenly crept into his vocabulary.

He decided to take the box out with him. As he started to leave, it occurred to him that he should double check to see if there might be something else on the shelf. He had seen only the box, but there could be other objects behind it. The box was not large enough to fill the entire shelf space by itself. He focused the light back into the space.

This time his heart did skip a beat—maybe two. In the far reaches of the rock, his light caught the reflection of eyes.

"*RATTLESNAKE!*" He shouted to no one.

Raleigh instinctively jumped backward. It was as if he had just seen a monster. From a distance, he refocused his light back into the opening.

"Lots of rattlesnakes—a den of them," he whispered to himself.

They lay in rock crevices that lined the rear of the shelf. One—the first one that he saw—lay directly behind the dirt outline the missing box had left behind. The chill of the morning prevented their fast movement, but it was clear that they were aware of the intrusion. They obviously did not approve. It was as if the snakes had been stationed there to guard the box, and Raleigh had caught them at one of their weaker moments.

The box had been taken. They had fallen down on their job. There had been a breach in their security. Raleigh had successfully stolen it from them, and they had allowed it. The snakes had an excuse; they were cold-blooded by nature.

Their alibi could be imagined. *If only it had been warmer, things would have been different.*

Raleigh had waited until winter so as to avoid snakes. He had just seen eyes and tongues and massive bodies and velvet tails—and trouble. There was no temptation for him to disturb this discovery any further. He did not shine his light back into the dark recesses of the shelter. He had seen enough.

Carrying the box, he hastily left the shelter and started his return toward the spring. The snakes had unnerved him. He wanted to leave them behind as quickly as possible. Had he known they were there, he would not have had the box. He did not have the courage to knowingly reach into a rattlesnake den to remove, or return, anything. The deed was done.

Now *there* was an excuse that he could use. He could now rationalize a reason not to have returned the box where he had found it. No amount of money could persuade him to reach back into that snake den. They did not prevent the removal of the box; they prevented its return. If he had been bitten—he shuddered at the thought—he never would have been found in this hideaway.

Raleigh made his way back toward the campsite. Stopping at the spring long enough to enjoy one last drink of its refreshing water, his thoughts returned to the problems facing him. He had complicated matters first by getting a late start.   Now, he had added to his burden. He would be packing out with a box, and this would not be easy.

He wondered what could be inside. Maybe nothing. It didn't feel heavy, and he could hear no rattle when he shook it. He questioned, however, why anyone would stash an empty box.

Was it really worth the additional effort? If he was going to pack it out, he was pleased at least that the lid remained sealed. He would not have to worry about losing the cover, and any content would be protected from loss. Maybe it was a waste of time and effort, but the box itself fascinated Raleigh. To him, it was an item of interest that created more questions. Who had made it? What did it contain? Why was it there? He hoped that something inside might answer some of his questions.

Arriving back at the campsite, Raleigh hurriedly shouldered his backpack, tucked the box under his arm, and headed toward the creek. He took a few steps and stopped.

Scatter the rocks, he reminded himself.

He walked back to the fire ring and double-checked to make sure that the fire was completely out. He then returned the rocks to the vicinity of their original locations.

The irony of the scene did not escape him. He was careful not to leave signs of this intrusion, yet he was leaving with the forbidden fruit. He would leave only tracks, but he would take more than time. He again lifted his pack, tucked the box back under his arm, and headed toward the steps. It was time—past time—to go home.

Again using his twine, he lowered his pack and the box to the edge of the creek and descended the steps. At the water's edge, he picked up his load and stepped into the cold creek. It was a long way back to civilization.

Raleigh had hoped that his guardian angel that had joined him in the canyon would, by some miracle, make his return upstream easier than the one down.

He was quickly disappointed. He was again challenged by the effort, and the going was rough. Carrying the box prohibited his use of both arms needed for balance while walking on the slippery creek rocks. He considered other options in transporting the box but could not come up with an easier way to haul it out. It was too large to fit into his backpack. There was no way to fasten it to his body. It was simply an added burden.

This lack of balance almost proved to be disastrous. Stepping on a slimy rock, Raleigh slipped and lost his balance. He instinctively spread both arms in an attempt to regain stability, and the box dropped into the rushing water.

It was too late! Raleigh fell face down into the water. The creek was deep enough to give him a good soaking but not so deep that his pack was submerged. The splash had wet the exterior, but its contents stayed dry—that was the positive. The negative was that he was wet—and the box was gone. The rushing water had swiftly swept it downstream. Raleigh recovered from his fall just in time to see it disappear around a bend in the creek.

He hastily considered his dilemma. The box was somewhere downstream, and he was headed in the opposite direction. Was the box really worth the time and effort to try to retrieve it? Could he even catch it if he tried? He was already behind schedule; he must be out of the canyon before dark. He needed to go upstream to get out, not down. Time was of utmost importance, and it was quickly passing.

Raleigh made his decision. He would return far enough downstream to look around the bend where he had last seen the box. If he could locate it, and it would not take a lot of time to retrieve it, he would go after it. If it was not visible, he would go on without it. There would be no other choice.

As he rounded the bend, he expected to be disappointed, but he was not. He saw that the box was caught, less than fifty yards downstream, on an overhanging vine that extended low above the water. The swift current was trying to tear it loose, but it held on.

Nearing the box, Raleigh recognized the vine to be that of a saw briar. Its sharp briars, such as those that had clawed at his flesh at the beginning of the trip, had grabbed hold of the box and held on tight. The character of those briars had switched, and they now took on the role of a savior. Retrieving the box, he resumed his trudge upstream. He slowly made his way toward Kinlock Falls. It was getting late, and Kurt would be waiting.

The laurel thickets and briar patches were still ahead. On the way into the canyon, Raleigh had illusions of making the trip without getting wet. The dream had lasted only long enough for him to fight the entanglements and reach the creek where the canyon narrowed. There, it immediately became evident that it would be necessary for him to wade in the creek.

Keeping dry was out—he was already soaked. Water was not an issue at this point. Why leave the creek? He questioned the wisdom of going back the way he had entered. It was not necessary that he fight the briars and thickets again. He would stay in the creek until he reached an established trail.

The decision was a good one. He had traveled only a short distance after the canyon widened before the rocky creek bottom gave way to sand and gravel. In a lot of places the bank was wide enough that it was not necessary to wade. The walking was easy, which allowed him to speed up his pace. The sun had set behind the Warrior Mountains. He had hoped to be out by this time. It had already been a long day—thanks to the noisy jets.

Kurt was waiting when Raleigh emerged from the canyon. He had been waiting for some time. His truck was running, lights on.

"I was beginning to worry," Kurt commented as Raleigh walked up, sat down on a rock, and removed his backpack. "I got here a little early. I thought you might be anxious to get out of that snake den."

"Tough hike," Raleigh grunted.

"What are you doing with that block of wood?" Kurt inquired.

"It's a box," Raleigh corrected him.

"Looks like a block of wood to me." Kurt eyed the object from a distance.

"It's a box," Raleigh repeated.

"What's in it?"

"Don't know."

"If you don't know what's in it, why do you have it?"

"I don't know. I suppose because it was there."

"There? Where? Where did you get it?"

"That's a long story, Kurt."

"It looks wet."

"It *is* wet! *I'm* wet! *Everything* is wet! And I'm cold! That's all part of the story. Let's get into the truck and get the heater going. I'll tell you the story on the way back."

Raleigh threw his backpack into the bed of the pickup truck. He climbed into the front, clutching the box. Kurt climbed into the truck and turned up the heat. They headed out of the forest. The cab of the truck began to warm, and Raleigh was enjoying the comfort. He was glad to be safely back in a civilized world.

At last he could read chapter six in *Walking Sipsey* with satisfaction. He could put his check mark in the completion box. Even though he did not actually travel all the way to the end of the canyon, he had gone far enough and had seen all he wanted to see on that assignment.

He had met the challenge and survived. Not won, but survived. He did not come out via Carrion Air but was forced to admit that the canyon was still the master.

Tenderfoot, he admitted to himself. *I'm still a tenderfoot!*

Raleigh wondered if there had ever been anyone who had really conquered the Sipsey Canyon. Those who had apparently lived there for a period of time had certainly made more progress than he, but were they ever the masters?

The fact that old timers stayed clear of the place pointed to an answer. There were no trails and seldom were there intruders. Rattlesnakes claimed the territory for their own. Raleigh was one of the very few today who would even attempt the challenge. The canyon was still the victor; it always has been. Its continued dominance was secured.

"Don't let me forget to have you identify some fern for me," Raleigh broke the silence. "I've never seen any like it. I have a sample."

It was time for Raleigh to tell his story. Kurt invited him to spend the night at his place.

"Chestnut," Kurt spoke as much to himself as to Raleigh, who was looking over his shoulder.

"Huh?" Raleigh responded.

"Chestnut. This is chestnut wood." Kurt now agreed that he was indeed holding a box.

He examined it as he sat at his kitchen table. "Interesting." His comment was directed as much to himself again as it was to Raleigh as he continued with his inspection.

"Yep, it is definitely chestnut! It's very old." Kurt's words were uttered in fragments. "It's a well-made box, but it's not ancient. Maybe a couple hundred years old. Looks like something the early settlers would have made. Wonder what's inside."

Kurt had his complete concentration centered upon his examination of the exterior of the box. Obviously, however, he was also interested in what might be inside.

"It's been a long time since chestnut trees grew in the forest." Kurt now directed his comments toward Raleigh. "At one time, there were large groves of chestnuts in the Warrior Mountains, long before the forest was called Bankhead. The chestnut blight wiped them out."

Raleigh was not totally ignorant about the fate of the chestnut trees in North America, but he didn't want to interrupt.

"The chestnut blight killed most of the trees. The blight entered into this country from Japan in the 1890s. By the 1930s, almost all of the big trees were dead, or dying, and they covered the landscape like skeletons. Before the blight, there was a stand of trees that was equivalent to approximately nine million acres or more in the Southeast. The dead trees were harvested for many years after they died because of their ability to resist decay. There is nothing left now from the remnants of the original giants but a frail sprout that returns year after year."

The teacher in Kurt was beginning to show. "Chestnut wood lasts indefinitely! It's the perfect wood to use for something like this box. It resists rot as well as any wood, maybe with the exception of cedar, honey locust, hickory, and 'bodock,' also called mock orange. I wish we still had chestnut trees. It makes the best fence post..."

Kurt would have continued talking about chestnut trees all night had Raleigh not interrupted.

"How do we get the cover off?" Raleigh was anxious to see what might be in the box.

"Good question." Kurt thought for a moment. "Depends on what's sealing it. Whatever it is, it works!"

"We don't want to damage the box if we can avoid it," Raleigh suggested. "We've got to figure this thing out."

Kurt examined the box again before answering. "We won't open it until we can do it right. I would hate to mess this up after you made the effort to haul it out of that canyon." Holding the box, he studied the joint separating the box and its lid. "I've got to figure out what's sealing it. It has to be a forest product."

Kurt smelled the box, running his nose around the sealed joint. "Hmm..." He continued to sniff the seam. Moisture from the soaking in the creek had activated a faint scent. He was in deep thought. "Pitch. Pine pitch. Rosin. Resin. Whatever it is, it has a pine smell." Kurt seemed uncertain of his identification of the possible sealant.

Raleigh felt a need to respond in some way. "I'll lay odds that it is not sealed by something from Elmer."

Kurt chuckled and responded to Raleigh's quip. "Elmer had never heard of glue when this was closed. As I said, it has to be a substance from the forest; it has a pine smell. I have seen scrub and Virginia pine in the forest. They are the source of rosin, or resin, which is used for a lot of things. When I was growing up, we even chewed it for gum. Damage to the tree by woodpeckers or storms causes the sap to run. It's collected commercially to make varnishes, plastics, turpentine, pine torches, printer's inks, and even medicine. Of course, today they have a synthetic to replace it, but it had a lot of uses, including glue. If it was collected before it became brittle, it would make the perfect glue for something like this. It is a soft, sticky substance when it first comes from..."

Raleigh interrupted again. He was in no mood for another botany lesson. He wanted to get the lid off that box. He had already asked the question once.

"So how do we get the lid off?"

Kurt again pondered the question, waiting a while before he spoke. "Well, water won't do it! Ether or an organic solvent could possibly work, but I don't have any, and I would hesitate to use it anyway. It could cause damage to the box." Kurt was silent as he pondered the question for a while. "Heat!"

Raleigh listened. He knew that there was more.

"Yeah. Heat. In the summertime, rosin gets soft and sticky. I think that if we heat it, the lid will slip right off. It is certainly worth a try."

"Heat it with what?" Raleigh responded. "A blow torch certainly won't do the box any good."

"Hair dryer." Kurt countered. "Let me get my hair dryer and turn it on maximum heat. I hope it will work."

Kurt went to the bathroom and got the dryer. Turning it on, he began to direct heat to the sealed joint.

"This is taking longer than I thought it would." Kurt had been working for fifteen minutes in his attempt to break the seal. He slowly worked the heat around the joint. "I really need two dryers, one for each side of the box. One side cools while I heat the other."

He once again tried to coax the lid off by tugging at its edges, but he had no luck. Raleigh had been sitting silently while observing Kurt's attempt to open the box. He felt compelled to offer a suggestion.

"Why don't you try tapping it?" He handed Kurt a hairbrush with a wooden handle. "I'll heat it while you try tapping it lightly with the brush handle. The wood shouldn't damage the box."

It was now a joint effort. The work continued. Raleigh held the blower, directing the heat on the joint, while Kurt tapped with the hairbrush.

"Stop a second!" Kurt shouted over the noise of the dryer. He placed the box between his legs and, using both hands, pulled up on the lid.

The tapping was working; the lid began to loosen. Kurt rotated the box while gently lifting on the cover. With each rotation, the crack became wider.

It was a well-built box. The lid had been expertly carved so that it fit snugly inside the box. An exterior lip matched the outside of the box, but inside, the wood extended about an inch downward to complete a perfect seal.

Raleigh, with the hair dryer in his hand, bent over Kurt's shoulder. The crack in the joint became wider.

Kurt gradually worked the inside portion of the lid upward until he finally saw an opening. Raleigh had never experienced a more suspenseful moment. The secret that had been sealed inside the box was now about to be revealed. He would soon know whether his efforts to lug the thing out of the canyon were justified.

Holding the box between his legs, Kurt made one last turn of the box and tugged again at its lid.

It opened.

CHAPTER 9

◆

"It's empty!"

The disappointment showed in Raleigh's voice. "Just a few leaves—and looks like some hair!" He was still looking over Kurt's shoulder while viewing the box at an angle. He could see nothing else but a black and white pattern at the bottom. "The bottom is painted."

Kurt sat with the box between his legs. He said nothing but continued to hold the lid with both hands. His eyes were focused inside the box. Laying the lid on the table, he kept his attention on the newly-exposed interior. Now that his hands were free, he reached into the box. With his fingers digging at the pattern that covered the bottom, he began to lift, removing what they originally thought to be the bottom of the box.

What Kurt and Raleigh had thought to be a painted bottom was instead the top cover of a book or document. As Kurt removed it, he realized that he held an old notebook. It had fit so perfectly inside the box that it appeared to be part of the construction. Kurt handled it with caution.

Holding the book in his hands, a further examination revealed it to be in remarkably good condition. The seal had effectively preserved the contents, while the storage space in the shelter protected the box from the harsh elements of the canyon. The paper showed little deterioration. The black and white pattern was common for such notebooks dating back to the early 1800s. It was 8x16 inches and about an inch thick. It was bound on the side, with no holes for a binder.

On the cover was printed the word: RECORDS. Hand printed, underneath this machine-printed word, were two additional words: MISSION RECORDS

Kurt had taken control of the box and its contents. His attention was focused on the new discovery, completely oblivious of Raleigh's presence. The suspense had so captivated his attention that he was unaware of anything, or anyone, outside his field of vision. His eyes were fixed on the record book.

He opened it to the first page. The paper was off-white in color, with a noticeably inferior quality to the fine, slick whites that are produced today. It was rough in texture, with none of the ruled lines as is expected among modern writers. Recorded at the middle of the sheet, hand printed in black ink, with large bold letters, the two words were repeated with additional identifying information.

MISSION RECORDS
JOSEPH B. STONE
METHODIST MISSIONS
ALABAMA CIRCUIT

Raleigh continued to look over Kurt's shoulder. Kurt slid the box lid back to make room on the table for the record book. It was directly in front of him as he began to read silently.

Reverend Joseph B. Stone called to minister unto the lost...

Before he could read any further, Raleigh realized that he was being left out of the picture and felt that he was being treated unfairly. After all, he was the one who had found the box and hauled it out of the canyon. By rights, he should be the one handling its contents. Nevertheless, his thoughts were not on fairness but on the experience of the moment. His immediate hope was that this document would be a chronicle containing answers to some of his many questions.

"I never expected this," Raleigh said. "It's a missionary's record book!"

Kurt did not respond. He began reading the first page to himself. Raleigh read over his shoulder.

> Reverend Joseph B. Stone called to minister unto the lost souls of the Cherokee and mixed blood of the Black Warrior Mountains and to convert them to Jesus Christ.

Personal Information:

BORN: 20 February, 1808

BAPTIZED: 1821 - Age 13 - By Hamby Crowe - At the large camp meeting in Cane Ridge, Kentucky.

ORDAINED TO PREACH THE GOSPEL: 14 August, 1828 - At French Lick Methodist Assembly, Tennessee.

ASSIGNMENTS: Assigned, by my request, to the Northwest Alabama Circuit of the Black Warrior Mountains and their environs.

DATES: Starting date - 2 March, 1834

MISSION: Appointed to minister to this circuit as has been the custom of the Methodist Mission - to spread God's kingdom throughout the villages and settlements from Brown's Village to Flat Rock. Appointed to ride the circuit along the old Corn Road, the Leola Road, the Ridge Path, the new Byler Road, and the Doublehead Trace, from the mountaintop to Haleyville and Flat Rock, traversing the divide of the waters of the Tennessee and the Black Warrior Rivers. Sent to be an angel of comfort to the hearts of those who are being forced to vacate their ancestral homeland and to direct them to a new homeland, an eternal home in God's Heaven - a home from which no one will face the fear of removal.

PREVIOUS ASSIGNMENTS: Traveled in Kentucky and Tennessee, conducting camp meetings and preaching at churches (mainly Methodist but any denomination) before receiving the call to minister to the Cherokee and those of mixed ancestry - all God's people! Taught and preached to the Cherokee Indian Nation in Georgia at the Hightower and the Carmel mission grounds.   Moved to Brainerd, Tennessee - March 1831 - due to persecution by the Georgia guard after Georgia illegally passed laws requiring white men to have state licenses to remain on the Cherokee Nation lands - or they were required to leave.

This godless act is a work of Satan. Governor Golmer and the Georgia legislature have no legal right to require the servants of God to be licensed. Our country's constitution guarantees religious freedom. The arrest on 12 March, 1831, at Carmel Mission, 13 March at New Echota, and 14 March at Hightower has proved ruinous to our mission efforts. Several righteous men were taken before Gwinnett County Court, Judge Clayton. Some were released, but others were held in bonds. If Reverend Batrick and I had not been away on a mission trip, we would have suffered the same fate - at the point of guns and bayonets. The missionary posts are unsafe and must be avoided for fear of arrest and persecution.

Kurt finished his reading of the beginning pages and turned the page.

"Whoa!" Raleigh spoke. "Let me finish."

"I'm sorry." Kurt turned the page back so Raleigh could finish his reading.   "I'm a fast reader," Kurt apologized.

Raleigh read a short while longer before saying, "Now you can turn the page."

Kurt did. He still controlled the notebook; he still had not offered to turn it over to Raleigh.

Reverend Stone continued his commentary of the injustices suffered by those who gave aid to the Cherokee. This action obviously had a great impact on him. He put his disapproval into writing.

It made no difference that Elias Boudinot and John Ridge successfully argued against the injustice in the Supreme Court of the United States. It made no difference that in the Supreme Court decision in the case of Worchester and Butler vs. Georgia, the court ruled that the laws of Georgia have no force in the Cherokee Nation. The prisoners were not released, and the persecution continues. Even President Jackson has sided with them. He remarked: "John Marshal has made his decision; let him enforce it now if he can." We have few allies. A nation is lawless when even the presidency refuses to enforce a decision of its highest court.

These hostilities mandate that we leave the Cherokee Nation or be prepared to serve four years in prison. Because of this, we moved across the state line into Tennessee. Working from Red Clay and Brainerd, we continued to serve in a limited capacity with the Cherokee in Georgia.

Georgia was required to repeal its anti-missionary laws - but for how long?

The message continued on the facing page. Reverend Stone had more to say.

April 1833 to October 1833

MISSIONARY EFFORTS MADE FROM RED CLAY AND BRAINERD, TENNESSEE:

Resided in Tennessee by necessity but continued efforts inside Georgia among the Cherokee Nation, but not without difficulty. The Georgia Guards made a regular mission circuit impossible, and no organized activities are safe.

The removal of the entire Cherokee Nation to Oklahoma is almost certain. Many have already left due to the hardships placed upon them by Georgia and the leaders of our country. The white man cannot be trusted. Many are consumed with greed and are determined to steal the lands from the Cherokee and all who claim Indian ancestry. These people are more interested in worldly goods than the love they should have for their fellow man. They seek to lay up their treasures on earth instead of heaven. It is all the work of the devil.

The mission stations at Haweis, New Echota, Hightower, and Carmel have been kept open by the American board. This has been possible only due to the forced repeal of the anti-missionary laws, but the restrictions are so severe that the work can no longer be effective. Teachers and missionaries to these oppressed people are the constant victims of persecutions. Many have left because of the dangers, and there is no one willing to fill the vacancies - nor is there any encouragement for anyone to do so - their safety cannot be assured.

Kurt finished reading the opened pages and then watched Raleigh as he continued reading. Kurt was silent, observing Raleigh until he determined that he had finished the page. He flipped to the next one, and they continued reading.

Because of these restrictions, I requested a transfer so as to be able to minister unto the remaining Cherokee and those with mixed blood who live in the mountains of North Alabama. Although Alabama has passed laws similar to those in Georgia, they are not as strictly enforced. My new ministry begins with a fervent prayer that God will rain his blessings down upon it. Nevertheless, I still remain apprehensive. I can only dedicate myself to do the will of the Creator and his creation - all humanity! It matters not whether they are white, red, or black. Our God made us all, loves us all, and is no respecter of persons.

Records

In keeping with established practices and procedures, a brief record is to be kept of the services rendered to those who are reached in this mission effort. This record uses only the first name and the first letter of the surname of those to whom we minister. In the hostile climate in which we work, complete identification of an individual may place them in danger of being persecuted. I will not place at risk those to whom we minister. The white man uses any reason to persecute those who rightfully lay claim to their homeland. The Georgia Guard seized the records kept by the American Missions in that state, but they were unable to use them to correctly identify individuals because their full names were not recorded. I shall attempt to keep a mental record, and when I can safely do so, I will complete a more permanent record.

3 March, 1834

Departed from Red Clay, Tennessee, to begin my travel to Brown's Village, Alabama. It is with great sorrow that I leave those whom I love in Tennessee and Georgia, perhaps never to see some of them again in this life here on earth - but I am confident of living an eternity with them in Heaven. It is not with sorrow, however, that I leave the Godless rulers and certain citizens of Georgia who covet the possessions of the Cherokee. It is they who have made our continued success in Georgia impossible. There is surely a devil's hell waiting on these unrighteous people. I pray that I will enter a more favorable environment in Alabama.

7 March, 1834

Arrived at Fort Payne. Boarded with Chester W.

8 March, 1834

Traveled to Browns Village, the eastern end of my circuit. I will start here and work my way west to Flat Rock, the Indian boundary line. I boarded with Brother Silas D., an old Christian acquaintance who I had earlier contacted for the accommodation.

Sunday, 9 March, 1834

Cold and rain.

10 a.m. Met for worship services at Brown's schoolhouse. Permission obtained by Silas.

Attendance: 12
Offering: 37 cents
Sermon: The Prodigal Son

Evening Service: 5 p.m. at school building
Attendance: 7
Sermon: Love Thy Neighbor

Comments: Attendance disappointing but not unexpected. Weather bad. Very limited preparation time. Am confident that interest will grow over time and with more personal work in the area. I have been graciously allowed the use of the schoolhouse to present the sermons today. I wanted to emphasize God's love for us in the morning lesson - as the father loved his erring son, and in the evening lesson I stressed the importance that all men love one another. This is a very difficult concept, as those to whom I spoke have been mistreated so badly. I taught that Jesus was also treated badly; he even died for us, yet his love for us is still the greatest thing in our lives if we allow it to be.

The succeeding pages of the journal were filled with similar records. The same simple format was followed: date, weather, time and place of meeting, attendance, offering, sermon topics, and comments. The pages were filled; no paper was wasted.

Kurt remained in control of the book. He scanned the pages as he turned them. Occasionally he stopped to read when he recognized a familiar community.

Sunday, 22 June, 1834

Beautiful day.

10 a.m. Basham Gap. Brush arbor in field of Floyd G.

Attendance: 42

Offering: $2.12, 1 chicken, ½ dozen eggs

Sermon: The Widow's Mite

Afternoon: Baptized Fannie A. and Lizzie T. in creek near Tar Springs.

6 p.m.

Attendance: 36

Sermon: Born Again into God's Family

Comments: God had given us a blessed day. In morning's sermon, I placed emphasis on our stewardship and giving as God has given to us. The Cherokee and mixed-blood souls we reach with this mission are not rich in worldly goods. In the offering, many cannot afford any more than a few pennies, others a nickel, dime, and some even a quarter or food. No gold coins are expected. The morning message assures them that they will be rewarded for their sacrifice, not the amount given, as with the poor widow. The result of the lesson was a generous offering and the baptism of two precious souls. The lesson in the evening service was to assure those in attendance that they can be heirs to the riches of heaven. God promises riches beyond our comprehension. These people are so oppressed that they need all the encouragement that they can get.

Sunday, 29 June, 1834

Weather warming up considerably.

10 a.m. Pinhook. Met under a large chestnut tree

in the pasture of Elias B.

Attendance: 33

Offering: $1.76, 1 mold of butter, 1 pint of honey with comb

Sermon: Rahab the Harlot

6 p.m.

Attendance: 35

Sermon: Two miles to Heaven

Comments: This was another blessed day. God is surely with me in my effort here in Alabama. In the morning sermon, I read the verse in Hebrews 11:31 that lists Rahab, a harlot, as a person of great faith, along with great men of the Bible like Abraham, Isaac, Jacob, Joseph, and Moses. The lesson was that no matter how bad a person may be, God loves you and forgives. The afternoon lesson was taken from the Sermon on the Mount when Jesus, in Matthew 5:41, says that if one shall compel thee to go with him one mile, go with him two. We must do the extra service to our fellow man in order to enter into heaven. It was encouraging that there were two more in attendance at the night service than the morning one. Word spread about my being here to preach the Gospel of Christ, and attendance increased. There was in attendance a very interesting young Cherokee woman who showed a lot of interest in hearing the truth of the gospel taught to her. She is very pretty and well liked in the community. They called her "Sunbeam" because of her radiant personality. It is my prayer that I can convert her to Christianity and baptize her into Christ. If she answers the call of Christ, she should be a good influence so that others will follow her example. I pray that this effort will be successful.

"Sunbeam, that's an interesting name designation. With a name like that I could understand why he would feel she should be converted. That she would be an asset to his ministry," Raleigh said.

"It would be interesting to know whether he baptized her or not," Kurt commented.

And so the records continued. From one end of the circuit to the other, the reverend chronicled his weekly activities. In addition to the Sunday records, he also included some daily activities.

Saturday, 30 August, 1834

Kinlock Community: Performed wedding ceremony of Eve D and Gray Fox. Both are full blood Cherokee as far as I know. I am acquainted with this couple, as I baptized Eve at Kinlock Falls during an earlier stop on my circuit. There was an Indian ceremony after the service of which I took my leave as the festivities extended into the night.

Kurt turned back through the weekly accounts of Reverend Stone's records, looking to see if this had been documented and found his notation of the baptisms at the falls. There were three young girls who were baptized at that time.

It appeared that Reverend Stone was diligent in his record keeping. He also kept records of the funerals which he conducted. There were several. In these entries, he recorded the full name of the deceased, apparently because there was no fear that those already dead would suffer additional persecution.

It was obvious that the missionary work done by Reverend Stone was always intense. Nevertheless, his comments reflected the fact that he never realized the success he had envisioned when he came to Alabama. The Indians and those of mixed blood showed little trust in any white man. Many had gone into hiding in the mountainous regions and were fearful of any public gathering.

Kurt had quickly turned a quarter of the way through the pages. Abruptly, the records ended. There had been no indication that the recording of his missionary efforts would suddenly cease—he had been faithful in keeping a detailed weekly record until this time.

The last recorded entry contained this message:

Sunday, 19 April, 1835

Nice spring day. Warming after a cold winter.

10 a.m. Flat Rock. Met on the front porch of Issac C's house.

Attendance: 21

Offering: $1.44, 1 dressed rooster, 1 mess of poke salad with eggs

Sermon: Heaven, Our Eternal Home

Comments: I am at the western end of my circuit. Tomorrow I start back east. It has been a difficult winter, and I am sick and weary. The efforts in this work become increasingly difficult. It is only by the strength God gives me that I am able to continue. It has been some time since I have felt well, and my condition does not seem to improve. I considered spending some time to rest here at Flat Rock but could find no suitable place to board, as this is a small community. I will return to Kinlock where I will board with Joseph P. I am due to preach there next Sunday.

The facing page was blank. Reverend Stone had recorded his last entry in the journal.

CHAPTER 10

◆

Both Raleigh and Kurt were speechless. The journal that they just read was not what they had expected to find in the box. Raleigh had been standing the entire time, reading over Kurt's shoulder. It was getting late, and Raleigh realized that he was exhausted.

"It's been a long day," Raleigh informed Kurt. "I was up most of the night, and it was a rough hike out of the canyon."

He glanced at his watch. "It's already past two, and I have to be at work at eight. I know that you are required to be at school even earlier than that. I had looked forward to sleeping in my own bed tonight, but I will have no trouble falling asleep anywhere. I just have to get some rest."

"You can sleep in the guest bedroom. You won't have to sleep on the couch."

"Good. I wonder how that box got in the canyon. Surely the preacher didn't take it there."

Raleigh was tired, but he was also caught up in the drama of the whole thing. A weekend hike had developed into an engrossing puzzle.

"We did not read everything that was written in that journal," Kurt responded. "We barely got a quarter of the way through the pages. As I was closing it I noticed that there was more. I believe it is almost full of script. The preacher must have skipped a page and started a new account of his work. We will find out later." He paused. "But you have asked a good question. How did it get into the canyon?"

Raleigh took a quick shower and went to bed. He turned out the light and remembered nothing for the next three hours, until Kurt woke him and advised that he must hustle in order to get to work on time. Leaving for work, he placed the journal back into the box and left with it. He had once again laid claim to his find.

Kurt had one parting request. "If you take it, be sure that you keep it locked up. Let me know what else is in there. You are welcome to come back here tonight if you want to."

One would have thought that Raleigh was leaving with a filled treasure chest. He could tell that it was killing Kurt to see him leave carrying that box. Raleigh had lugged it out of the canyon, though, on the excursion that Kurt had refused to accompany him. Kurt was not there when Raleigh needed him to carry the load, and now he seemed to want to take control. Raleigh took no offense, but he declined the invitation to return for the night.

Arriving at work shortly before eight, Raleigh parked in his assigned space in the courthouse parking lot and locked his vehicle. It was the beginning of another long day. As he walked into the office, his secretary was already on the phone.

"Oh, here he is now," she said. "It's the sheriff." Raleigh went to his desk and picked up the phone.

"Where have you been? I have been trying to get in touch with you all weekend," Sheriff Cole explained. "We have arrested..."

And so Raleigh's work day began. He had reentered the real world. The brief respite from the phone was over; reality had snatched him back to attention. He now had to refocus his thoughts and wade back into the mire which had been created by criminals. In one day, he had come a long way from the isolation of the cove.

The day was a busy one, but Raleigh could not immerse himself completely in his work like he usually did. His thoughts kept replaying the events of the past weekend, the cove, and the journal. He even returned to his truck to check on the box, assuring himself that it was safe. He then plunged back into his hopeless battle against crime.

At the end of the day, Raleigh had given the state fair value for his time, but his heart was not in the work. An old, partially-read journal had controlled much of his thoughts. He not only reflected on the records left by Reverend Stone, but he wondered what else might be written in the remaining pages. There was more to be read, and he couldn't wait to do it.

Leaving work, Raleigh briefly considered calling Kurt to say that he would return to read the journal with him, but he quickly vetoed the idea. Fatigue was beginning to take its toll on both his body and mind. He realized that when he opened the box again and started reading, it would be difficult for him to put the journal down. He decided that he should not even try again until later.

On his way home, he stopped at a drive-through and got a burger and fries for his evening meal. After parking for the night, he retrieved his backpack from the truck bed and threw it loosely over his back. He took the box from the cab, tucked it under his arm and carried it just as he did when making his exit from the canyon. He had completed his weekend adventure and was back into the world of stress, phones, crime, fast foods, and comfort. He was home again.

He slept well on his own bed. Had he known the adventure that remained unread, however, he probably would have had another sleepless night. He could have dreamed of the late radio personality, Paul Harvey, and his daily quote that followed a commercial in the middle of his program. *"And now, for the rest of the story."* Indeed, there was much more to come.

It was Friday night before Raleigh could find enough time to justify the removal of the journal from its box. The week had been an extremely busy one for him. A drug bust had resulted in the arrest of two people who were under probation supervision. Investigations were required, and delinquency reports had to be presented to the sentencing judge. This and many other duties created one hectic week, yet his thoughts were never far from the unfinished reading of the journal.

On Friday, Kurt called. He wasted no words in getting to the point. "What else did it say?"

"I don't know, Kurt," Raleigh answered. "It's been such a busy week that I haven't had time to read any more from the journal."

"Good!" Kurt spoke, and then realized what he had said. "I mean, uh, it's not good that you have been swamped with work, but good that maybe we can get together this weekend and read some more. Can we do that?"

"I suppose so. I really didn't have anything planned except to check out the rest of the journal. I want to stay home though. You are welcome to come over here."

Raleigh had planned to spend a quiet weekend at home, but he was not opposed to having Kurt over to share the suspense with him. It would be quite nice to have company, but this time he would control the book. Kurt was a friend, and he had called on him for help with his hike, but he was not willing to give him the upper hand. The box and its contents belonged to Raleigh Walker.

Kurt was waiting when Raleigh arrived home.

"Have you eaten?" Raleigh inquired of Kurt.

"I stopped for a burger and a shake. I'm ready to read!"

"So am I. Let me get the book."

Raleigh left the room. He returned, not with the journal, but with a metal music stand. He normally used it when he played his banjo. Placing it in the middle of the living room floor, he pulled two chairs up in front of it. He then went for the box, which he had stored in the bedroom closet.

The box itself still held a fascination for Raleigh. He studied the details in the wood as he re-entered the room.

"Chestnut wood. You know, those old rails in the corral shelter were split from chestnut trees. They are as sound now as the day they were split." He referred to a rock shelter deep in the Bankhead forest that had once been used as a corral for horses on the stagecoach route through the forest. The rails had been preserved much the same way as the box he was carrying.

He removed the old journal from the box and placed it on the music stand. He did not want anyone to stand and read over a shoulder as he had earlier been forced to do. They both sat so that they could easily read the open journal.

During the week, Raleigh had speculated on what might be ahead in the proceedings that Reverend Stone had recorded. He was aware that Kurt had promised more as he closed the journal that night.

Once again, they would return to the difficult days when those of Indian ancestry faced the challenge of trying to retain the lands of their heritage. As Raleigh considered the uncertainties these people were facing, their old difficulties were much greater than those he faced. Reverend Stone, and the Cherokee with whom he worked, suffered the loss of all their possessions, their freedom, and perhaps even their lives, all in the name of law and order. These people had a real reason to be agitated. The age of inconsiderate humans is not unique to this century. The missionary efforts of Joseph Stone were made difficult by such people.

The entire land had been the homeland—the hunting fields, the hallowed ground, the burial place of the Native Americans—and now they were facing removal. All of this was being taken from them because of the greed of the white man. Only a few people, such as Reverend Stone, considered that they too were human and should be treated as such.

"I'll turn the pages this time," Raleigh informed Kurt. "You read faster than I do."

He hastily turned through the pages of the journal that they had already read.

As was consistent with everything else having to do with the canyon experience, Raleigh was not prepared for what was to come. The missionary had made his last entry at Flat Rock, which was the western end of his circuit, on the Indian boundary line. He reported that he was headed back to Kinlock when he abruptly stopped writing in his journal. The last entry was written on the top of the last page they had turned. The remainder of this page and the facing page was blank. Raleigh turned the page again. There was nothing written there.

Turning the page again, the sheets were completely filled with script. The handwriting, however, was totally different. Lines that were straight, as written by Reverend Stone, now were crooked. The neat cursive gave way to an amateur's print. Basic writing procedures were ignored. The sentences ran together and there were no paragraphs. The writings, however, were legible, and it appeared that someone had a lot to say.

It was certain that this person was not a missionary.

CHAPTER 11

I spose I mite as well make use of this here papuh seein
as to how I don had it a rite smart while over a year holdin
it fer the preecher which he ant shode back up to git. but
by rites this ant my papuh but I rekun that the revernd ant
got no more need fer it so I took it fer my own as to how
I dont count it steelin whenever you pik up sumpun what
dont belone to nobidy ever since he died. cors I ant seen
him dead but I spose he died him ailin like as to how he was.
word was that he was real off bad with consumpton or
newmomy or someum when he didnt show back up cous
the word now is that them gard men don took and hung
him fer hepin the indian people but that dont seem rite that
they wood do that to a man of god. he done left a pasel of
thangs at uncle joes and I ant got nare bit of it cept the box
and whats in it which ant nothen but this here record book
and 3 pens and a ink jar and ie specks and a song book called
virginia harmony and his bible which nobidy else wanted. i
dont no why revernd stone didnt take his bible whenever
he left caus he never went nowher cepting he had his box
and if he peers back up I take care of it fer him but I dont
spect him too. i ant never ben much count at readin and
ritin caus they wernt no school fer me to go to cept my
sister learnt me a lot an she rites down thangs a rite smart

bit of the time and she heps me whenever we can git some papuh. people say that I am rite smart whenever it comes to books wich is why I took the preechers thangs and I can spel tolably well cept when it comes to them hard words.

xxxx

aint nobidy seen the preecher ever since the last time I rote in his book so I spose he ant comin...

Raleigh paused after starting to read the first sentence of the second paragraph. "I don't see any dates given by this new writer. It's apparent that this second paragraph was written at a later time than the first. It looks like this is not going to be an easy read. The sentences all run together, and the spelling is atrocious."

"Raleigh," Kurt replied, "Let's not be too hard on him or her. There is no date on this, but you can bet that it originates from someone who did not have the advantage of Head Start. This was written during the days of the one room, one teacher schoolhouses, or more likely, no schools at all. The writer admits to having had no schooling. It appears that the key to understanding this new entry is all about paragraphs. This person crams the day's thoughts into one paragraph and then stops writing. Whoever did this writing probably had no clue as to what the date was at that time. But you are certainly correct on one point, the spelling is bad, and the grammar is no better. The author obviously could not write in a straight line. It could well be that he, or she, overstates their writing ability. The thing to do is just keep on reading to see what happened next."

They continued reading. The attempt was not easy.

talk is that some whites out of jawja come here fer to caus trouble. they come down the byler rode tryin to scare off indians by sayin the home gard men are acomin to take them out to oaklahoma or arkansaw. they are tryin to make em leve so as to clame indian land fer their own and talk is that preecher stone stood up to em and said fer em to go back to jawja wher they belong and sez to the indians not to let them scareum off and be Caus he did this they kilt him. now there are some who says that ant what went with him and that he was ailing terribly bad what kilt him. I heard tell that ther ant no prof that he be dead and that we shouldnt berry him till we git his body. i dont know what is rite and he mite come back but I shore dont spect him to and I am gwin to hold on to his thangs in the box fer myself. fox sez he thinks he got kilt like they say and we got to go hide out to keep from gitten kilt ourself but I say I dont want to go hide out. but I dont want to git kilt and I dont wont to go to arkansaw or oaklahoma caus word is people die fore they even git there and it ant home but fox sez we ant got no chois cept to hide caus presdent Jackson dont like Indians nere a bit and he wants all indians gone which ant rite. The Cherokee heped presdent Jackson when he needed hep in fightin them creek Indians down south but then he turns on us whenever he wants us gone so as to take our land and whatever little else we still got left. They tret us indians like we ant worth nothin and they dont want us round here on what is our land and has ben long befor the white man ever got here.

xxxx

"Oh, I think I've got it! I remember that Reverend Stone recorded in his journal a marriage between Gray Fox and Eve at Kinlock. This could have been written by Eve. They were a Cherokee couple."

"You might be right," Raleigh agreed. "The mention of Fox went over my head. I took it to be an animal, and of course that made no sense; but as the name of an Indian it makes perfect sense. We don't know anything about these people. Who are they?"

The writing continued without a clue.

its been a long spell since I rote in this caus thangs keep gitten worse what with all the talk bout removal and fox sez that the gard is bout to start arrestin anybidy what claims to be cherokee and they are gwine to make em walk all the way to oaklahoma or put em on botes and take em away. he sez that trators have signed a treaty givin away our land wich was promised we cude keep fer ever and ever and now they say that we got to go west wich fox sez we ant gwine to do. he sez he noes a place whur we can go and hide and nobidy will find us but it is a place where nobidy goes caus of snakes and thangs. no bidy noes whur it is but fox found it when he was huntin one time and it is a place whur the arme men wont find us. fox says that we can stay there til they get thru takin away the indians. i dont know what to do but I wont leve fox caus I love him and I do what he sez but I dont like snakes and I dont wont to leve my folks but fox sez we could die if we dont hide and the gard is goin to take us and we ant got no chois.

xxxx

thangs ant gitten no better and I fib if I say I ant scared. word is that jawja men are alredy takin Indians down the river on botes and some are made to walk and they are starvin to death and some are ailin from dierea and disintery and measels and newmony and they ant got no closes and shues and the gard men are forcin emsefs on the women in a bad way and fox is rite when he sez we got to go hide but I dont want to.

xxxx

the talk is that the arme men is starten to rondup indians in jawja and thangs is bad and arme men are headed this a way and it wont be long fore they git here. Fox sez that president Jackson got a big fat ole general called winfield scott what he made a Cherokee agent and word is he got a lot of arme men what is goin to make all Cherokee git gone from the land what is ritefuly theres and whur they lived long befor the white man got here. fox sez that jest ant rite to do the Cherokee that a way and ifn he sees any of them arme men round here he is gwine to kill em but I sez that he will jest git kilt caus he cant fight no arme by hisself. I will go with him and hide caus I love him and I dont wont no white man to take me bad like so I tell fox to wate caus we live in the hills and the arme men may not no we are here and maybe they will leve us alone.

xxxx

the arme men wodnt let me brang nothin with me cept preecher stones box and some close caus I sed I wanted to brang my bible wich ant mine but reverend stones but I dont tell em that. i was at the sprang when the arme men showed up on hosses and had guns and sede they were takin me to go to oaklahoma and I sez I dont want to go and they sez I got to go caus this ant cherokee land no more. them arme men sez that they gotta take all the cherokee what they can find caus they got orders from general scott and that is what they are gitten paid 50 cents a day to do. talk is here in camp that them arme men hide up close to whur cherokee a gotta go for to git water and they git em to send em off to oaklahoma and

brang em to this here camp. now ant nobidy done told
me bout that or I would have kep my ie out fer em fore
I went to the sprang. they got a lot more indians side
me and they come from all over and they sez they wood
shoot us ifn we dont go peceful and they had mixed blood
folks that sez they are cherokee and they got to go. they
had some blacks too what were with the cherokee heping
em to make ther crops and thangs. they ant got fox caus
he is to smart fer em to catch him and they brote me to
camp whur there was a heep of indians and nobidy dont
want to be here but ant got no chois caus of the guns and
they will shoot anybidy what runs. some they got here are
old and some sic and one died and may be another one
and babys be cryin and I seen a lot of biggons cryin to and
the food here ant no count. they sez we git a pint of corn
meal and a half pound of fatback hog meet fer to eat fer
a day but I ant seed nothin but corn meal that is mostly
bugs and I miss fox and dont wont to go no wher ifn he
ant with me. talk is they are gwine to make us walk all
the way thru tenesee and ilinoe and misouri and arkansaw
and oaklahoma wich take 6 months and it is hot now but it
will be in the winter time fore we git there and I am scared.
some have left here on botes but I dont know what went
with em and I am scard of gitten on one of them botes.

XXXX

them arme gards done moved us to a bigger camp
what is on the tenesee river what is caled gunters landing.
talk is now that they wont to put us on botes but there
ant much water in the river and it is shalow here at what is
what they call the sholls and the botes cant git this far up
the river. talk is that some of em gard men don told some
of the cherokee that we got to walk down to a place I ant
never hered of called waterloo what is still in alabama but

ant fer from mississippi and it is over 150 miles to git there. they say that the reason we gotta go there is caus it is below the sholls and the water is deeper there and they say that they are going to lode us on botes and take us all the way to litle rock arkansaw and I dont want no part of that. i miss fox and ifn he was here we could go to gather cept I don't think that he wood go. he is to smart to let em catch him but I wish he was here with me.

XXXX

fox is so brave and he came and found me and take me away from the camp and the gards dont know it caus he got me at nite and they was so many Indians that the gards dont miss just one. I had frends that I wunder whatever happened to. I could name a lot of them but just of their indian names. Cors nobody wants to let peeple no what their real name is just like nobidy calls fox nuthin but fox and me nuthin but Eve. Or like my frends possum and bullfrog. I had frends named sparrow and holly and a good frend from pinhook called sunbeem. I hope she got away fore they put her in a camp. Caus she was always so sweet. I hope nun of my frends got sent off from here. we are gwine to hide out whur fox sez nobody can find us caus ifn they git me again they will kill me and I dont wont to get kilt either. I want to be with fox and he is brave and will take good care of me and wont let nothing go wrong so we are gwine to go hide so we wont have to go to oaklahoma and fox wont go.

XXXX

Raleigh paused from reading. "Well now we know for certain that is in fact Eve and Gray Fox. This is the first time she has actually stated her name."

Kurt agreed as they both took a break to rest their eyes.

The printing was not good, the spelling was not good, and the lines still wandered about the pages. It was apparent that Eve had difficulty with the effort of putting thoughts on paper. Many words were started and then crossed through, only to be incorrectly spelled in the second attempt. She did not necessarily spell the same word the same each time she wrote it.

"She seems to be spelling a lot of her words phonetically," Kurt reasoned. "Her grammar leaves a lot to be desired, and her capitalization and punctuation are not good. I notice that most of the time she does not appear to know exactly what the correct way is to write a sentence. Sometimes she does it right; sometimes she doesn't. It is hard for me to go back to Indian days when most of the rural children had a limited opportunity to get an education. Actually, she is doing quite well, considering the circumstances."

"Yeah, a lot of Indians were illiterate, especially when it came to the English language," Raleigh replied. "Most of the Cherokee spoke their own language, and they even had their own alphabet, thanks to Sequoyah. It's a good thing that Eve didn't write this in the Cherokee language. We wouldn't have a clue as to what the message might be that she was leaving in this journal. I guess we cannot expect her to be flawless in her literary endeavors. I certainly would not be the one to complain because every word was not spelled correctly, or even the same, and every 't' was not crossed nor every 'i' dotted."

"There was something else in that last passage that caught me, besides the fact that Eve's husband managed to help her escape from the camp," Raleigh said, looking back at the roughly written words. "All these Indian names she listed. Didn't she mention one of these before? Sunbeam? That sounds familiar."

Kurt frowned, shaking his head. "No, that was from the mission records of Reverend Stone. He mentioned a Cherokee woman named Sunbeam."

"That's right!   He wrote down that she was interesting, and here Eve speaks fondly of her too. If they're both the same Sunbeam that is..." Raleigh's sentence trailed off as he focused on the next part of the journal. He hesitated before speaking. "I think I know where this is leading. The box is about to go into that canyon."

Kurt was already reading the next page. "I believe you are right," was the only response he managed.

fox has gone back to git some more thangs but he sez I gotta stay here caus it is hard to git here and ifn I go back the gard men mite git me. he sez ant nobidy we can trust caus they got a bonty for anybidy who turns in a indian that is hidin but fox noes how to not git caute and it ant hard for him to git in and out caus he walks and hunts a lot. we waded in the creek all the way from kinlock caus fox sez ther is a lot of rattlesnakes on the banks and in the bushes and we seen some and they were a cotonmouth mocosin and I dont like them snakes and they was layin on the rocks and we had to go careful so as to not git bit. I dont wont to go back without fox caus he takes care of me and wont let me git bit but he ant here. I ant gwine no place caus I am scard but fox sez that a snake wont bite me if I be careful whur I walk and a rattlesnake will warn me with his tale before he trys to bite me.

xxxx

i ant saw fox in 3 days and he brote lots of thangs that I dont know where he got but he sez he dont steel it and there is a hepe of thangs the indians had to leave caus the gard men wants to git them fer themselfs and we mite as well git em ifn we can. He sez that the gard men are makin the indians to walk all the way to oaklahoma and they cant take nothing with them cept their close and i am glad that fox got me away from the gard caus I wood be walkin with em to oaklahoma or be dead or the gard men would be on me like I dont want nobidy on me cept fox caus I love him but he ant here enuf. he sez that the gard men are bad to force emsefs on the woman they be watchin and some are gwin to have their babys. the white man is takin all the indians thangs that they left and fox sez we mite as well git some ifn we can but they is hard to brang here but he hides em till he can git them thangs brote to here. we ant got much caus the white men took it fer emself and we git what we can wich ant steelin. all I brote with me when I come was the thangs I had when fox stole me from the camp. fox sez I cant brang the box but I wanted it and he sez that I shud brang sompum worth sompum but I sez the bible is worth sompum caus it is gods book and he sez I can brang it ifn I want to. It was hard gitten up the steps from the creek what ant much and fox sez them steps bin there a long time but nobidy nos abot them and you can fall and git kilt but fox heped me git up. the gard men wont find us here caus nobidy nos how to git here but I miss my folks and thar ant nobidy to talk to and I dont know ifn they had to go to oaklahoma. fox is gone a rite smart and he sez he noes what hapened to my folks but he wont tell me.

xxxx

I cry a lot and I try not to when fox is here caus I love him and I dont wont him to no that I cry caus he sez brave people dont cry but he cant read so I can rite and he wont no. he is bizy gitten redy for winter and it is to late to plant a crop and we dont have a garden yet but fox keeps brangin in thangs he sez was left when they took the indians to oaklahoma which by rites they dont belong to the white man but they stole them and fox gits it back. ther ant but 2 of us and fox wants us to have enuf vittals in the shelter fer to last the winter and he got some seed to plant and we got to clere a new grond. fox got some irn tools to help and the indians wont need em no more caus they are gone and they couldnt take em to oaklahoma so fox got um and a ax and a hoe and some pots and pans and thangs but it is hard here and you gotta keep an eye out for snakes.

fox has ben bizy gitten thangs what we need fer to last tru the winter what ant far away. there has ben some frost and it gits cold at nite. somewhur fox got a bunch of old quilts an blankets and brot em in which will help a lot when it gits cold. i sez to fox that I wanna go home and he sez we ant got no more home caus em white men alredy got it and sez it is theirs now. he sez we got to make the rock bluff what we now live in our home till we can git out and be safe. he sez that he will fix it up like home so I will like it but I wont like livin where thay ant nobide else. he made us a bed so as to sleep better at nite. he took some chesnut trees bout as big round as my leg and made post and bilt it out of strong wood for the frame and split som cane from the creek and wove it fer a matress. he split some white oak to weave in it to make it stronger and he put a thick quilt on it and it makes a good bed. he built it up high enough off the groun to keep the snakes and bugs off the bed. he took some big poplar logs and made some stols fer to sat on and he cut one long one in half and made a table fer to use. fox noes how to do stuf like that and he noes how to make em good and strong. he made me stuf to cook with like a mortar what he made out of a big hickory log over nee high what he cut and burnt a bowl in the top so as I can put corn and acorns and thangs in there and smash them up into meel. he took his ax and cut a hickry tree bout as big round as the top of his leg and as long as he is tall. he trimed the bottom to fit in my mortar but left the top big like he cut it so as to make it heavy enuf to smash stuf. I call it my stomper but I have herd people call it a pestle. it is hevy enough that I can stomp out corn and acorns to cook with what we will need caus we ant got much else. i had best quit now caus I see fox a comin up from the sprang and looks like he is totin a deer.

xxxx

i rote some bout 3 days ago but stoped when I saw fox a comin with that deer. I heped him to cut it up fer to keep fer the winter. fox got some cane from the creek bank and made the ends sharp and I cut the meet in thin pieces and stuck the cane thru the midle of the pieces till I had the cane full. I did this with all the meet that I could and dried it over the fire till it got good and dry. then I got a long grap vine and ran it thru the holes what the cane had been in till I had a long strang of meet what I hug in the back of our shelter house fer to eat in the winter. we got some fish and more meet what we have dried and hung up fer the winter. it keeps me a workin hard but time pases quicker when I stay bizy and maybe we can git outta here fore we eat it all. fox has brote in some wild graps and persimons what I have dried and fixed em fer to eat when it gits cold.

xxxx

It is the cherokee cold season what I have been told was the time of the eagle and fox has ben brangin in a lot of chestnuts and hickornuts and some black walnuts and acorns from the woods. I cracked up a lot of hickornuts and biled em and made some hickornut butter which is reel good. he gits them white oak and red oak and sometime post oak acorns and I bile them to git the bitter out and it makes good meel what will be good in the wintertime. he brote in some wild graps and muscadines what was good to eat and I squzed out some juce fer to keep fer when it gits cold. fox found some glas jars what I can use to put up my stuf fer the winter and some of the thangs what fox brangs in is good to let dry in the sun or over a fire and they will keep reel good. he has brung in a lot of them soft ripe persimons and I squzed out the seds and mixed it up good like and let it dry out in the sun fer a while till it got hard like I did with some plums to. i keep em persimon seeds and dry em out and I can smash em up in my mortar and make meel outta em and then mix water with em and make litle cakes and cook en in the irn skilit what fox brote in. i put the skilit in hot ashes and put the lid on and put em hot ashes over the top of it and let it cook and them cakes can keep a long time after they git dry and they shore are good whenever you git hungry. fox went out and kiled another deer and we fixed up the meet fer to eat. the hide will be good to use to keep warm when it gits cold but I hope that I dont have to stay here and can git to be whur I can talk to somebidy sides fox caus he stays gone a lot but ifn I dont git out we will have someum to eat fer the winter.

xxxx

Raleigh looked up from his reading. "I gotta git-er, uh, got to get me a Coke, Kurt. I'm already trying to talk like her. You want someun to drink?"

Kurt chuckled. "Yea, brang me a Dr. Pepper if'n you got one."

They both laughed. Raleigh went to the refrigerator and returned with a Coke and a Dr. Pepper. He set the drinks on the table while commenting, "My goodness, that's hard to read, but it *is* interesting."

"You said it!" was Kurt's short response. "Turn the page. I can read while I drink."

I hadnt rote in a long time caus fox has been here most of the winter cept when he goes huntin and most times he dont stay long caus it dont take long fer him to kill a deer or a turkee and we have enuf to eat. In the wintertime fox looks for snakes in dens and he gits em and skins em and they is good eaten and snakes dont go nowhere in winter and fox sez he is going to git shed of as many as he can round here so ther is not as many to be careful for. he found a pile of em rite here in the back of the shelter whur we stay and we ate em and he keeps the skins. we eat turkee and fish he gets out of the creek and deer and ther ant many bears left but he fount one and kilt it and skint it and it makes a warm cover fer to sleep under but it ant dried yet. fox sez that he saw where that bear had climbed up in the top of a big holow tree caus it had made some claw marks going up and down the tree gitten ready for cold wether wher the bear made a den fer the winter and he climbed another big tree by it and he throwed in some fire on the sleping bear what causd it to start down the tree wher he kiled it befor it got to the ground. he learnt how to hunt like that which is the cherokees old way of doing it and he is a good hunter and he wont let me go hungry. he got the bear fat first and brote it in and I cooked it in a big pot what fox had alredy brote in and I got lots of bear oil what I can use to cook with. he brote in some big gords what was good to put oil in and I cut off the top of the handle and pored the seed out what we can plant and I clened out them gords and drilled a little hole thru both sides of that handle so I can put a vine thru it and I pore in that hot bear oil and stop up the hole with a corn cob what I shelled seed corn off of and i hang it up whur the bugs wont git it and I can use it when I need to and he dried out the rest of the meet like he does the deer and fish so as to eat it in the winter. it ant to bad here but I miss my folks and I spose they got took to oaklahoma but they may not be gone.

xxxx

It has been hard this winter but we ant gone hungry. fox is a good hunter and he brangs in meet what he gits down by the creek. he noes how to trap coons and possums and rabits and squirls and he kills em and guts em and skins em and I cook em hole over the fire. he keeps the skins and I can make warm coats out of em when they git dried. he gits some beever what is reel good to eat and make close out of and the coon to. the litler animals like rabbits and possums and squirls is easy to cook caus I just take a piece of sharp sourwood bout as long as I is tall and make one end sharp and stick it thru the butt end and roast it over the fire. fox put up 2 forked sticks on both sides of the rock stove pit what he made and the sticks hold up the meet fer it to cook. that sourwood makes the meet taste gooder when it cooks on it. i hafta turn the meet to make it cook rite and it is good eaten. sometime I hafta put biger animals like coons and grounhogs and beever on biger sourwood stiks and cook them longer but we dont go hungry. we are gwine to plant the seeds what fox got whenever it gits warm enuf fer em to grow and we have been cleanin some newgroun fer to have a place to plant a garden.

xxxx

it is the warm season what is the time of the snake and the leves are coming back on the trees and I have done seen some snakes and fox ant kilt them all. we are still clerin new grond and we are gwine to plant some beens and sqush and some corn and he is gwin to git more diferen seeds and fox got some aple trees and peech and plum and some pecon trees. i tell fox that it takes a long time fur trees to grow and it takes a long time for pecon trees to have pecons and I dont want to be here that long but he planted em anyhow and I spose it dont hurt nothin. My blood stoped and I tell fox that I thank that I am gwine to have a baby and he sez that we will see caus I ant gitten big but I sez it ant time fer me to git big yet caus my blood ant been stoped fer that long and I think that I am going to give birth to a baby and I am scard but fox sez that ifn I do he will take care of me but I tell him that this ant no place to have a baby.

xxxx

Turning the page, they noticed that glued to both sheets of the opening was an article which obviously had been cut from a newspaper. In the space left above the clipping was a handwritten note.

fox brung in this what was rote in a newspaper what he sez shows that it ant safe fer us to git outa here caus they wanta git us to oaklahoma or git us kilt so as to take our land from us. i got some of that fish glue what fox makes so as to stick fethers on to his arrows and used it fer to glue that letter onto this book so as not to lose it.

The article read:

> MAJOR GENERAL SCOTT, of the United States Army, sends to the Cherokee people, remaining in

North Carolina, Georgia, Tennessee, and Alabama, this address

Cherokees! The President of the United States has sent me, with a powerful army, to cause you, in obedience to the Treaty of 1835, to join that part of your people, who are already established in prosperity, on the other side of the Mississippi. Unhappily, the two years which were allowed for the purpose, you have suffered to pass away without following, and without making any preparation to follow, and now, or by the time this solemn address shall reach your distant settlements, the emigration must be commenced in haste, but I hope without disorder. I have no power, by granting a further delay, to correct the error that you have committed. The full moon of May is already on the wane, and before another shall have passed away, every Cherokee man, woman, and child, in those states, must be in motion to join their brethren in the far West.

My Friends! This is no sudden determination on the part of the president, whom you and I must now obey. By the treaty, the emigration was to have been completed on or before the 23rd of this month, and the president has constantly kept you warned, during the two years allowed, through all his officers and agents in this country, that the treaty would be enforced.

I am come to carry out that determination. My troops already occupy many positions in this country that you are to abandon, and thousands and thousands are approaching, from every quarter, to render resistance and escape alike hopeless. All those troops, regular and militia, are your friends. Receive them and confide in them as such. Obey them when they tell you that you can remain no longer in this country. Soldiers are as kindhearted as brave, and the desire of every one of us is to execute our painful duty in mercy. We are commanded by the president to act toward you in that spirit, and such is also the wish of the whole people of America.

Chiefs, head-men, and warriors! Will you, then, by resistance, compel us to resort to arms? God forbid! Or will you, by flight, seek to hid yourselves in mountains and forest, and thus oblige us to hunt you down? Remember that, in pursuit, it may be impossible to avoid conflicts. The blood of the white man, or the blood of the red man, may be spilt, and if spilt, however accidentally, it may be impossible for the discreet and humane among you, or among us, to prevent a general war and carnage. Think of this, my Cherokee brethren! I am an old warrior, and have been present at many a scene of slaughter; but spare me, I beseech you, the horror of witnessing the destruction of the Cherokees.

Do not, I invite you, even wait for the close approach of the troops, but make such preparations for emigration as you can, and hasten to this place, the Ross' Landing, or to Gunter's Landing, where you all will be received in kindness by officers selected for the purpose. You will find food for all, and clothing for the destitute, at either of those places, and thence at your ease, and in comfort, be transported to your new homes according to the terms of the treaty.

This is the address of a warrior to warriors. May his entreaties be kindly received, and may the God of both prosper the Americans and Cherokees, and preserve them long in peace and friendship with each other!

Winfield Scott
Cherokee Agency,
May 10, 1838.

"That treaty imposed upon the Cherokee was a product of greedy men, both white and Cherokee. Those who represented the Indian interest were Cherokee leaders, but none of them were full-bloods, and they certainly did not have the interest of the Cherokee Nation in mind when it was ratified." Raleigh felt compelled to respond to the letter they had just read.

"I know a little something about that treaty because I did a study of it and wrote a research paper for a history class I took in college," he continued. "It was an American History class, and I requested to use the subject, which was granted due to my Cherokee heritage. The major players were a handful of wealthy families who rose to the top positions among the Cherokee Nation because they were literate—maybe with the exception of Major Ridge, who signed the treaty with his X. John Ross was only 1/8 Cherokee, having 2/3 Scottish blood. He built a large plantation house at Ross Landing on the Coosa River about a mile from Major Ridge's, and he had vast holdings of land on which he had orchards and cultivated crops. He flaunted his wealth by having peacocks on his lawn. All the Cherokee who were large land holders had slaves, black and captured Creek Indians, who did the work for them."

Raleigh paused momentarily in thought, but he soon continued his history lesson to Kurt, sharing with him the unsolicited information he had gathered in his research.

"Major Ridge's maternal grandfather was a Scottish trader who deserted the family, leaving him to be raised as a Cherokee. First known only as Ridge, he picked up the additional name when he was made a major in the United States Army by General, later President, Andrew Jackson. He was a slave thief, a horse thief, and he was ruthless. He had two hundred and fifty acres of cleared land, a vast orchard of peach, apple, and plum trees, with slaves to do the work for him. He had many farm animals, a ferry, a store, and much wealth. He lived in a large, two-story, colonial-style house with fences and outbuildings—the plantation he christened 'Running Waters.'

"Then there was James Vann, a half-breed, and his son Joseph, who owned eight hundred acres of cultivated farmland and vast peach and apple orchards. They had numerous other assets in Spring Place, Georgia. They owned the finest house of any of the Cherokee. I remember that they had extensive belongings, which included a grist mill, a sawmill, a blacksmith shop, eight or ten corn cribs, over forty cabins, six barns, five smokehouses, and most importantly, at least to them, a whiskey still that produced large quantities of corn liquor. Much of the best was consumed before reaching the market.

"David Vann also played a key role in the negotiations for the Cherokee Nation. The Vann, Ridge, and Ross families, including fathers, sons, and their relatives, all played a major role in signing the treaty on December 29, 1835, at the home of Elias Boudinot, a nephew of Major Ridge and editor of the Cherokee Phoenix newspaper.

"Stand Watie, a brother of Elias Boudinot, was also a participant of the signing ceremony. I could name a lot of names and say a lot about that travesty of justice, but the bottom line is that they all did it for their own gain and did not have the Cherokee Nation's best interest in mind. As I said, those Cherokee leaders were out to get the best deal for themselves. The poor, old full-blood Cherokee who rightfully owned the land and holdings didn't get anything but the shaft. It was rumored that a fifty thousand dollar bribe was offered to John Ross while he was in Washington if he would support the signing of the treaty. He reportedly didn't take it, but it just goes to show the type of shenanigans that were taking place in order to get the land away from the Cherokee."

Briefly pausing to think again, Raleigh had more to say. "I recall that Major Ridge got about twenty-four thousand dollars for his property, which was a fortune back then when a person was lucky to get a half dollar a day for his work. The Vanns received much more! The others who were involved in the ratification of the treaty received comparable compensation and a luxury trip to Oklahoma. The truth is that the illiterate full-blood Cherokee had no idea what was happening until the government started rounding them up to march them on the Trail of Tears.

"To be entirely truthful, however, there was no good choice for the Cherokee, because after gold was discovered by the white man in Cherokee territory, the government immediately sent in an army of surveyors who started dividing up the Indian lands in forty and one-hundred-sixty-acre parcels. The forty were in the gold fields, and a lottery was held where only whites could participate. The whites were then gaining titles to the land and forcing the Cherokee to vacate it before the treaty was even signed. The treaty only served the purpose of allowing the government to justify their actions—and the half-breed Cherokee to pad their pockets. Much of the choice land had already been taken by the government and parceled out before General Scott's treaty was ratified!"

Raleigh paused. "Sorry Kurt, I really got on my stump there. I just get upset every time I think about that travesty. I know you probably know most of what I just spouted off. I need to turn the story back over to Eve and let her writings do the talking."

Kurt said nothing. He turned the page where Eve continued with her writings.

Its been a hot sumer and we work hard and the crop made good and we ant got snake bit but I come close to stepin on one and fox kills em when he can and we eat em cept when they ruin by the hot weather. fox skins em and he has lots of snak skins wich I dont no what he wants them all for but he sez he can make a soft bed for the baby and strech em tween forked stiks and weve em so as to make a matress and he sez this is gooder than usin split cane or white oak strips caus it will be softer fer the baby and jest as strong and he sez that he has saw indians do it but I ant and we need sumpum to keep the baby up from snakes and bugs and thangs. he took some of em rattlers what he had cut off the tale of some of em rattlesnakes and tied em onto a bone from a turkee leg and made a rattler fer the baby. fox dont talk much bout it but I thank he wonts the baby to git here so he can see what it is and he wonts it fer to be a boy. I am gitten big and the baby kicks inside me and fox sez not to worry caus he will take care of me and the baby. he went out and piked lots of berys fer to eat and I put some up fer later when they are all gone from wher they are piked. there was blackberys and gooseberys and rasberys and dewberys and wild strawberys and mulberys and huckleberys and wild cherys and wild grapes and fox noes whur to find em all but I want to git out of this place

but I dont want to have to be made to go to oaklahoma so I
dont no what to do cept stay here and have my baby.

XXXX

fox sez that its alrite that its a girl caus thats what the
spirit wants us to have and she is big and has foxs black hare
and bron ies and dark skin and she is a pretty baby. fox sez
the spirits may wont a boy next time and we can wate but
this ant no place to rase a baby. I sez to fox that we can go
back now and he sez we cant go back caus the soldures will
still git me and take me to oaklahoma and the baby and
he wont go so we gotta stay here whur nobidy cant find
us and they ant yet. we done been here more than a year
but I ant got no calander or clock so I go by the sun but I
wont to see my folks but fox sez I cant see em but he wont
tell me whats hapened to em. I wont fer em to see the
baby and I named her adah caus adah is the first womans
name in the bible past eve wich I reed in genesis 4 and fox
sez he dont like that name and I dont have to name her a
bible name just caus I am named after the first woman so
he sez if I haffta name her a bible name to name her sarah
so I changed the babys name to sarah fer to plese fox and
it is a prety name and I didnt have adah writ down nowher
anyhow so I can change it to sarah ifn I am so a mind to do
which I did.

XXXX

As they finished this passage in the journal, they
realized it was getting late. The journal was hard to
read, and they were both tired.

"Let's get to bed," Raleigh suggested. "If we don't put
this down at some point we'll be up all night, and I have
had a hard week. We can finish reading this tomorrow."

Kurt reluctantly agreed.

CHAPTER 12

◆

Raleigh was not a breakfast person; he had not been since his college days. He preferred the extra wink of sleep in the mornings over an early meal. There were too many late night study—and bull—sessions for him to get an adequate amount of sleep.

Some Saturdays, however, he would cook breakfast for himself. As a bachelor, he considered it his sovereign right to get into his own kitchen and do as he pleased. If he made a mess, there was no one around to reprimand him. His father had stayed out of the kitchen because he could never do anything that met his mother's approval, but Raleigh did not have these restrictions. He considered that there were certain advantages to his bachelor status, and he had no intention of changing it.

This morning, however, he had a guest to feed. He decided to go for the ultimate—his "concoction omelet." It was very doubtful that this recipe would fit anywhere in the omelet category, but it was certainly a concoction. He had prepared this culinary masterpiece a few times previously, but he never used the same ingredients. The secret to this recipe is *what you find is what you cook*. In the end it was more like a scrambled mess.

Raleigh gave the morning meal his best shot. Grits and sorghum molasses with biscuits and butter were even on the menu. He was now ready to reenter Eve's lost world. He cleared the table, placed the journal back on the music stand, and sat down.

Kurt was already seated. They both were ready to resume their reading.

before we got run off from home I liked to get thangs from the tradin post and cook up som differen thangs but now I dont have much to put in whatever I cook. i wish that I could git outta here so I could git some of them thangs that I would like to cook with and to help make the food taste gooder but fox sez that I cant do that now. i told him what I would like to have and he did brang in some thangs like salt and ground peppers but he sez that he cant git a lot of thangs caus he dont want to git caught. weve got a few thang but we ant got no sugar or much of that bought spice what you can get at the tradin post. fox is good about knowin where he can git some wild spice like dill and sage and he has brote some of that in. i used some of it in the wintertime when fox brought in a passle of ratleshaks what he had found dened up. It was cold so he could git em without gitten hurt and he cut off their heads and rattletales and skint em and guted em and brote in the meet fer me to cook. i didnt no what to do with all that ratlesnake meet so I boiled it and got the meet off the bones and it made me thank that I could make some soup or stew outta it. i put some sprang water in a big pot and put some taters and carots and beans and corn and peas what we had growed in the garden and put in some of that sage what fox had brote in and boiled it an put that ratlesnake meet in it what I had alredy cooked. in the sprangtime fox cut some little sasafras trees and brote em in and cut open the stems and got out the soft center part and got the new leves and ground em up fine like and I put some of that in that stew

and it made it to be thicker and helped give it a good taste.
Fox nows how to get thangs like that caus his folks didnt
have no tradin post what to go to get thangs they needed
but they new how to go in the woods and git thangs that
would help em cook with. that ratlesnake stew shore was
good and we ate on it fer awhile. I will make some more
of it ifn fox brangs in some more of them snakes. we don't
git no chicken here and that snake soup tasted just as good
as ifn it was chicken soup what I used to make before I
had to come here. i have learnt to make use of whatever I
have and this helps keep us from goin hungry or eatin the
same thang all the time. i never had give a thought to eatin
snakes before I come here and I still dont like em snakes
alive but they can make some good soup.

i wont to leve here caus it ant no place to rase a kid
but fox sez that we got to stay here a spel longer caus it
ant safe to leve. he sez I shud be hapy and thank of this as
the garden of eden caus it was eve who was in the garden
of eden where god made em and she was hapy till she ate
the aple. I sez that they got trowed out of the garden caus
there was snakes there and I don't like snakes and a snake
is what got eve in truble. he sez that sinse we got snakes
anyhow and he planted a aple tree we got our own garden
and I can call it what I wont to and I sez that I will call it the
garden of eve ifn that is what he wonts. i ask fox how he
noes so much about the bible and he sez he noes more
about it than I thank he does caus he had went to some
camp meetins with some girls and hered what the preecher
preeched but didnt get baptized like some of the girls did.
I sez to fox that preecher stone baptized me and it didnt
hurt me non and I want to go to heven and it might not be

long till I get there seeing as to how we are stuk in this place. i sez to fox that I wont to git out of here caus of the snakes and caus I wont to go home and he sez we ant got no more home cept here caus the white man done took all the land and houses and everthang and we cant leave here caus we will git kilt or made to walk to oaklahoma but I sez this ant no fit place to rase a girl. fox sez there ant no more indians left here what ant hidin and I ask ifn that means my folks are gone to oaklahoma and he wont say and I say for him to tell the truth and he sez I dont wont to no but I do. i wont them to see sarah caus she is growin and she is a pretty girl. We ant got no close for her cept what we made from deer hides and rabit skins and fox brot in some feed saks what had been used to tote corn to the mill fer to git grond up for meal but I cant make no pretty close out of no feed sakes for her to wear. it is hard here and cold and I dont rite much caus I ant got much ink and fox dont no I rite this so I cant ask him to brang me none but revernd stone had 3 pens in the box so I got pens.

I ant rote in a long time caus the inks bout gone but it is summer now and I found some pokeberys and I got some juce out and tried it fer ink and it works so I can rite cept it ant black like the preechers ink but purple like pokebery juce so I got enuf to fill the ink jar.

Kurt read the most recent entry and voiced his thoughts. "I was wondering where she got this different colored ink. I suppose pokeberry juice makes sense. When I was young, my mother was very unhappy when I would come in with pokeberry stains on my clothing. It was extremely hard to remove—from clothing and from skin. I can see how it would make a good ink substitute."

"You learn to do with what you have," Raleigh responded. "The poke juice seemed to do the job. About the only noticeable difference in that and the original ink is the color. We can still read what she wrote."

The writing continued, now in purple ink. Another day's entry began.

I can rite but I ant got nobidy to talk to cept sarah and she cant talk back but she is growin and I talk to her a lot and she is rite smart and a pretty girl. I ask fox all the time bout gitten outta here and go see some more people and he sez they ant nobidy left to go see and the white folks got everthang and he woud hafta go to oaklahoma and we ant gwin to go. He sez that he will let me no when it is safe to leve here and I got to git it in my mind that thangs ant what they use to be. i sez to him that I want to be round more people so as to have somebidy to talk to and he ant here a lot an I cant talk to him. he sez that I got sarah to talk to now but I sez that sarah cant talk back. I got weave that I talk to but weave cant talk back nether caus she ant nothin but a big spider what bilt a web tween 2 rocks and lade eggs and had babys and I dont bother her but named her weave what sounds like eve so I can have copany sinse it gits lonesome sinse ant nobidy else here. I dont much like spiders but they dont hurt nuthin like snakes but black widows which weave ant. I dont have nobidy to talk to cept sarah and weave and fox and fox ant here much.

XXXX

i dont know how long its been sense we come here but it was a long time ago and sarah is a growin and a walkin and a talkin and I am going to start learnin her to read and writ so she will no how when we git outta here but fox sez we cant go caus it still ant safe and I say just how long is it gotta be that we stay here caus we shud of done ben gone long time ago. fox sez for me to read again that letter what was wrote by that general scott and it will sho me that it ant safe to go outa here. I read that hole newspaper and got to thankin that I dont write and spell very good caus I looked at what they spelled and rote and I ant got a lot of my words spelled rite. I want litle sarah to do gooder than what I do so I am a fixin to start readin the bible to sarah and we will rite down bible words so as to practice readin and ritin and I can lern how to beter do it to. my blood has stoped agin like before and I sez to fox that I think that I have another baby comin and he sez that ifn I do he wants it to be a boy this time and I say we jest got to wate and see. i sez to fox that sarah ant saw no people yet cept us 2 and she need to be rond more folks than us and I wont my family to see her caus she is so prety but he sez he noes it ant good but we ant got no chois cept to stay here. he sez I no he is rite but I dont wont to stay hid forever. he sez he will tell me when it is time to go.

Raleigh turned the page. The sheets of old paper took on an entirely different look. Words were written as if they had come from an elementary school classroom. It was an obvious practice session.

"These are words from the Bible. They are the first words found in the Bible—Genesis one and one." Raleigh recognized the source. "Eve had no chalkboard or chalk. She used her precious paper as she turned teacher to her one student."

beginning beginning beginning
created created created created
heavens heavens heavens heavens
earth earth earth earth earth
form form form form form
darkness darkness darkness

And so the printing practice continued. There was no message for the journal; only words filled the pages.

Raleigh turned through several pages of the journal. They all had the new look. It was obvious that the pen was in two different hands as the lessons continued. There were words that were legible and others that were not.

Sarah was now a student. A number of pages were devoted to the learning experience. When Eve resumed her journal message, it was evident that Sarah was not the only one who had benefited from the lessons. Eve's writing had improved. Her spelling was better, and her lines were straighter. She even began to improve on her capitalization of words where needed. The journal was easier to read.

I ben learning Sarah how to read and write and I have learned a lot myself and I can do better now. I guess I werent to good and I still ant caus I got a lot to learn. I have learned to spell ~~write~~ right which I wrote rite which ant right. thats why I have been practicing and to help Sarah learn to. It gives me something to do cept work and I get lonelee with nobide here. I been using reverend Stones Bible to see words wrote right and I read what he wrote in his record book before I got it and he could spell and write good so now I check some words that I write so that I spell them right and I get a lot wrong but I am learning and

Sarah too. I learned Sarah how to put dots after a centence where they belong so thangs don't all run together.

Some of Eve's words were now written, marked through, and rewritten. It was apparent that she was taking her time and was trying to write everything correctly. Her spelling had improved but was far from perfect, probably because she could not find the spelling of some words in order to check their accuracy.

She was making an effort to get everything right though. As Raleigh read the next paragraph in the journal, he made an observation.

"Eve uses the word 'ain't', but it is not a proper word. She cannot find it in the Bible or in Reverend Stone's writings, yet it is a word she commonly uses. She is trying hard to get everything right, but there are some words she just does not know how to correct. She is making progress, although at times, she spells a word correctly only to misspell it when she writes it again. Old habits are hard to break!"

The next paragraph was an improvement over her previous writing efforts but was somewhat of a mess nevertheless. She had spelled some of the words incorrectly, marked through them, and spelled them right the second time.

Sarah ant old ~~enuf~~ enough to learn much but i put the pen in her hand and ~~heped~~ helped her to write. English is hard caus words spell ~~dife~~ different that sound alike like right and write which dont make much cents or sense or however you spell it. Some words are hard to get like cents caus I know that cents means money but it means something else like you spell it sense and it means a whole lot of other things cept money and I dont know how to learn this to sarah. It takes a long time to write and look everything up to get it right to write right and this dont make no sense. Preacher Stones bibles got a concordance in the back and it helps me to find words easy so I can spell them right.

XXXX

Eve was clearly struggling with her attempts to give Sarah a continuing education, but she was diligent. She was teaching and learning, but old ways die hard. She was capitalizing better, and her spelling was improving, but the same words were subject to be spelled right in one paragraph and misspelled in the next.

As they continued reading this, the struggle she was having in her attempt to improve her daughter's education became evident. The teacher was preparing her class of one for an unknown future.

CHAPTER 13

More pages were devoted to the learning process. Raleigh noted that the words now appeared in alphabetical order.

"She is writing down common words from the Bible concordance. It is quite a good way for her to study with the source that she has available to her. It also looked like she used the songbook to get some of her words."

Amazing Amazing Amazing
Grace Grace Grace Grace Grace
Sweet Sweet Sweet Sweet Sweet
Sound Sound Sound Sound Sound

"It's a good thing there are a lot of pages in this journal," Kurt voiced his thought. Reverend Stone had used less than a third of the sheets when his writing ended. More than half the pages were now filled. The most recent additions to the journal resulted from the practice sessions. As a practice pad, it was obvious that Sarah was using her share of paper in her attempt to learn to write. Eve worked hard to get it right."

Eve's practice sessions not only improved her spelling, but she was also making progress in her penmanship. Her handwriting was not yet great, but it was much better than her earlier efforts.

It wont be long before the baby gets here so I tell Fox that its a boy and he wants fer it to be one. I just wish that Fox would take me outa here but he wont and I cant go by myself with Sarah. I dont write in this much no more caus me and Sarah are learning a lot about writing.

Fox is so proud of his boy and I let him name him and he sez his name is Buck caus they are brave and smart in the woods and he wants his boy to be like that. I say I dont want him named after no animal and Fox sez whats wrong with that caus he is named after one. I say that he has a point there but there is a diference in a pretty fox and a ugly deer. He sezs a deer ant ugly and his boy ant ugly and his name is going to be Buck. I say to name him Seth caus Seth was the first boy that dont kill or get killed in the Bible but he sez that he dont want no bible name for his boy. He sez I got to name Sarah from the bible and he can name his boy a real name that means something. Sarah is getting big and I am learning her how to be smart in books. We practice a lot and I say to Fox that I am going to learn Buck the same way and he sez he wants him to be wood smart and not word smart caus that is the red mans way. I say to Fox that Sarah is just as red as Buck and he sez that dont matter caus Sarah is a girl and Buck is a boy and boys have to be brave and take care of girls. I spose he is right caus Fox takes care of me and I would be in Oaklahoma or dead ifn he had not stole me from the gards before we come here but I love him cept I want to be around more people to. Fox sez we still cant go no where caus the white people what took our land would kill us or make us walk to

Oaklahoma and we ant going. I say they done forgot about us by now and he says they dont forget nothing. I keep asking him when we can leave this place and he sez that when it gets time to go he will tell me and I tell him I think it is way past time to go. I would go by myself but I cant get the babys down the steps and up the creek without Fox helping me but he wont so I gotta stay here. Sometimes I wish that somebody would find us and take us away then I would have somebody to talk to but dont nobody come here and Fox was right caus ant nobody knows this place is here it is so hid from the creek where Fox sez not much people go anyway. One time I heared dogs barking on the creek and I thank they may find us but then I thank that they cant climb the steps and that is the only way to get here but I wish they could caus I would like to see some dogs or anything sides snakes.

I call this the Garden of Eve caus it is just us and snakes and the apple tree but it ant big enough to grow no apples like what got eve throwed out of the bible garden. We make a good garden and dont go hungry but if we had apples I would eat one caus I would like to get throwed out of here caus then I could see somebidy. But the baby helps and Sarah is talking some Cherokee and some English and I talk to her and want her to be able to talk to Indians and white men to so as to know what she is saying and she is reel smart to learn. Buck is a growing to and it wont be long before he walks and talks and the babys keep me busy and fox is still gone a lot.

And the lord God planted a garden eastward in Eden and there he put man

Kurt, who was reading ahead of Raleigh, soon realized that Eve was once again using the Bible to conduct a practice lesson. She had begun at Genesis 2:8 and continued through the second and third chapters of the book, painstakingly copying each word correctly. In the fourth chapter, she started with the first verse.

And Adam knew Eve his wife; and she conceived and bore Cain, and said, I have a man from the lord

Abruptly, the copying from Genesis ended.

Virginia Virginia Virginia Virginia
Harmony Harmony Harmony Harmony
Carrell Carrell Carrell Carrell Carrell
Clayton Clayton Clayton Clayton Clayton
1831 1831 1831 1831 1831 1831 1831

"What do you suppose that is?" Kurt wondered aloud.

Raleigh had just finished his reading of the page and replied to Kurt's question. "That is the title of the songbook that the preacher had in his box. It appears that she copied the face sheet one word at a time. The songbook was *Virginia Harmony*, and it was apparently edited by Carrell and Clayton in 1831. Eve must have tired of rewriting the Bible."

"I guess so! Or maybe she realized that her paper was limited," Kurt agreed.

Raleigh turned the page to find that the practice session had ended and that she was once again recording her thoughts on her precious paper.

"It appeared that she had decided that she should end her educational effort after she filled that last page.

I suppose that is why she ended the copying of the Bible when she did. She used the title of the songbook to finish filling that page, and then she decided to use the remaining paper to tell her story."

I ant got that much paper left and I wont practice my words no more so that I can use my paper to write on whenever I want to.

Raleigh flipped through the remaining sheets in the journal. "She still has more pages to fill, but not that many."

More than three quarters of the sheets in the journal had been filled.

"I suppose Eve figured out that there was no need to practice if she had no paper left to use after her practice."

The message in the journal continued.

I practice words but there ant a lot to write about caus everything is always the same cept the babys are growing and I keep busy watching after them and specialy since Buck got to walking everywhere. Sarah is a help to me now but in summer I got to grow the garden cept Fox helps some but he is still gone a lot. I ant freting about not having nothing or knowing nothing much cept what Fox tells me. He sez he goes and listens to what they say bout them making the Indians go to Oaklahoma and he tells me some bad thangs. He sez that a lot of the old folks die and that somebody told him that a gard man who got back from Oaklahoma was a saying that they kept a count of the bunch of Indians that he went to Oaklahoma with and he sez that they started out with 875 Indians and when they got to where they was a going that there was 602 and the rest had died on them and I hope that it was not some of my folks who died. He sez the gard man was a bragging

that they did a good job as to how most of the time a lot
more than that die in other bunches before they get there.
He sez the old folks dont want to leave but the army dont
give them no choice and ifn they are real bad off sick they
still got to go and they make them to walk a long way
every day and lots of them are not up to doing that and
they make them walk through dust when it is hot and mud
whenever it is rainin and the rich Indians from Georgia who
didnt go there by them steamships git to ride on ponys and
horses and the others are made to walk. He sez that the
army men did the Indian women alful and took whatever
woman they wanted and made some babys and that they
shot their dogs when they wimpered to go with them. He
says it is a general Scott who they say is a big fat man and
a General Eustice and the Georgia Governor whose name is
Wilson Lumpkin who is a telling the army men what to do.
I know their name and how to spell them caus Fox brought
in another one of them old newspaper what had the name
of Elias Boudinot on it and it was like the one that had that
letter what I cut out and stuck in this book.

Me and Fox argued about when it is time to get out of
this place seeing as to how we done been here for such a
long spell of time. I dont like to have words with him but
I wantta get outta this place and go see somebody else.
Now Fox sez that he dont want to tell me but he heard bad
things about that bunch of Cherokee what I would have to
go to Oaklahoma with, He sez that there was 1,070 what
started and there was 722 what made it to Little Rock
Arkansaw and they still hadnt got to Oaklahoma yet. He
sez that they were made to walk to Waterloo Alabama
where some children and a grown up died cause word is

that it is a hundred and sixty miles and that is a long way fer to walk. There was not much water fer all them people seeing as to how it was so dry and the river was low and the sprangs was all dried up. It was reel hot and it werent right fer them army men to make them old and sick people do that. He sez that the federal agent knowed that it was not good and that the Indians was tired whenever they got to the camp in waterloo and there was no shelter and they had to sleep on the ground. He knowed that the Cherokees needed to rest but he was made to put them on boats in that shallow water and they were made to go down the river. Now he said that with all them people what was the gards with them that the camps and boats got to smelling alful bad cause they did not have toilets fer em to use and they would not let them get out of sight whenever they had to pee or dodo and there was lots of that stuff what smelled and the people could not bath like they needed to. There was a lot of direara and disentary what made things worser off.

I ant worried about not having nothing to eat caus we got garden stuff and blackberrys and huckleberrys and mulberrys and the apple trees and peach trees and pecan trees ant got nothing on them yet but Fox is good at finding bee trees and we got honey. We ant got no sweet milk from cows and there ant nothing to drank cept water from the sprang but it is always good and cold and fox brings in some sassafras roots and we make some tea which is good ifn you put a little honey in it and Fox still is finding them bee trees and he brings in lots of honey. Buck still sucks milk from me and I let Sarah suck some to caus she needs something to drank beside water. Sarah eats taters and beans and pees ifn I squish them up good and we keeps tators spred out in the back of our rock bluf shelter for to keep for the wintertime and corn and pumpkins too. Sometimes it gits so hard in the wintertime and sometimes I dont have enough milk for Buck and Sarah both to suck so I have to feed Sarah whatever I can find. It is real hard and I think it is time for Fox to say that we can git outta here cept I dont want to die like fox sez all them people do when they are made to go to Oaklahoma so we stay here so as not to die. We grow corn and I grind it up in my mortar what fox made me and make cornmeal which helps a lot and we grow enough to last through the winter and keep seed to plant back. I been writing a right smart long time today caus I ant done no writing in a long time but I got to quit for now caus it is gitting close to dark and I still got plenty of things to do while I can still see how to do them.

I tell Fox that I been here bout 5 years but he says it ant been but 4 but I tell him that Sarah is 3 and close to 4 and Buck is close to 2 and he sez he supose that I am right cept we ant got notin to tell what year it is and he cant read or write so he dont know. All I know is that I been here a long time and I am gitting tired of being here and I tell this to fox and he sez something might happen to us ifn we go out. I say what can happen worse than not being round nobody and he says we could be dead and that is worse. I say that we got to git the babys out so that they can git close and shoes and more food or they might be dead and he says that they ant yet. He says that ifn we go out of here they are more likely to die and says that the army gard will shoot a person for anything and he says that he heared that there was a deaf Indian who couldn't hear what they were a telling him to do so when they told him to turn and he went straight caus he couldnt hear so they shot and killed him dead. Now that ant right but I sez to fox that Sarah and Buck can hear so that ant no xcuse not to get out of here. I say that Sarah and Buck cant suck me always for milk and they ant nothing else but water and he sez he knows it ant good but he dont want to go to Oaklahoma or be dead.

    I have been learning Sarah how to cook cause she is a growing girl and she needs to know how to fix things to eat ifn something happens to me. I got to use whatever Fox can brang in for us to eat and whatever we grow in the garden. I show her how to make hominy from corn and how to make woodash lye so as to make it and soap. Fox made a box to put ashes from the fire in and driled a little hole in the bottom for to let the woodash lye to drain into a pan what is under it when I put the water in the top. I told Sarah that she has to be very careful so as to not get any of that lye onto her skin cause it will hurt her real bad. I try to teach her about being careful about things that will hurt her like snakes and lye and sharp knives and fire so she wont get hurt. I teach this to little Buck too cause I dont want for him to get hurt neither. I showed sarah how to put the dry corn into a pot of cold water and let it soak overnite then pore out the water and put the corn in the mortar to crush it and get the hulls off what has been loosed by the soaking. When the hulls get off they are put to soak in the potash till the corn turns yellow and it make hominy. I also showed her how to make soap from the grease that I have saved from cooking meat and turkee. I put in about 6 gourds full of water in a pot and put in the potash lye. I dump in a can of lard what I have saved and boil it over fire for 2 or 3 hours. I have to put in a little more water so as to get it right like it ought to be. I have to keep stiring it so as to not let it burn but when it get thick enougf that it makes a string when I pull the paddle out of it I let it cool a little and pour it into pans and let it get hard for about a day before I cut it up for to use. Now sarah ant old enough to do this but I show her how so she can do it if she needs to when she get older. I show her lots of other things like how to dry meat and fruit and vegetables so as to keep it for when it is needed and how to cook it too. She listens good and learns easy.

It gets alful lonely round here with Fox being gone a rite smart of the time. I have learned that ifn I keep busy with Sarah and Buck the time passes faster. I told Fox that I needed something to do with my hands and he went out and picked some cotton outta the fields that are planted on land what was stole from us Cherokee so he sez he has as much rite to it as anybody. I take the cotton and make threads and yarns out of it. When I was little I learned how to cord the cotton to get the seeds out so as to make thread outta it course back then my mother had a spinning wheel what I dont have now and I hafta do it with my hands. I cant make it tight like thread that comes on a spool but I can make yarn what I can use to crochea. I make needles outta bones what comes from the heron bones that Fox brings back from the river and use them to knit and crochea. I have started to crochea a piece what I want to make like the face of a fox in the middle of it but I dont know ifn I can do it right. I want to do it to help Sarah learn how to do things what I learned to do when I was little. Fox brote in some possums what we ate and then I cut off their long hair for to use. Fox made me a little loom what I can take it and make little stuff like pouches and sashes outta that possom hair. Ifn I had some of that buffalo hair what daddy got somewhere long time ago I could do better but you cant get that no more cause the buffalo is all gone from around here. I ant got much use for them things that I can make outta possom hair on that little loom but I gotta do something until Fox get us outta here. It give me something to do with Sarah and Fox sez that he is a gonna learn Buck how to hunt and do things that he did whenever he was a boy but Buck ant big enough yet to start that but he is a growing fast and Fox says he is going to make him a proud Cherokee.

I ant wrote in a right smart while caus I dont feel up to writing or doing nothing else either since Buck got snake bit and died. I ant done nothing much else than cry and ask why we even have to live ifn there ant nothing better than this place. It ant fun to live no more and ifn it werent Sarah to live for I ant got no other reason cept for Fox but he stays gone a lot more ever since Buck died. I ant never seen Fox cry caus he is a man and brave but whenever he found Buck after he got bit by the rattlesnake and his little leg swelled bigger than 2 legs and he swelled all over and little Buck cried and hurt bad before he died and Fox cried and I cried and Sarah cried but werent nothing we could do cept hold him and kiss him and watch him die. Fox ant seemed right sence Buck died and he sez the spirits are turned against us and now he dont talk much and stays gone lots more than he is here what makes it more hard on me. Buck was getting big and strong and talking and Fox was learning him the ways of the woods and said he would be a brave warrior and leader one day but now he is dead. I feel real bad caus I didnt watch him and didnt keep him safe from snakes but I thought that Fox had took him with him and I still belive that he did but Fox wont say that he did and it dont matter none anyhow caus ant nothing going to bring him back. I cut off some of his hair and wrapped it in a leaf and put it in the bible box so as to remember him by and Sarah says she wants to put some of her hair in there to so I did that but I dont want for her to die to. I made some burring cloths out of some rabbit skins what Fox had brought in from hunten caus little Buck had swelled to big for him to wear any of his other close and he didnt have much clothes anyway and he went naked when it werent too cold and I didnt want to put him down naked. Fox dug a hole under the rock bluff shelter where we stay and I put down some deerskin and laid him on it looking up and I crossed his little hands and put Reverend Stones Bible under them and I opened it up to the first part where it tells about Eve and the Garden of Eden and Seth what I wanted to name him. He needs the good book worse than me cept I could have used it to help learn Sarah how to read better but the bible is for more than that and it needs to go to heaven with Buck. I put the song book in with him to caus I dont never feel like doing no more singing with Buck gone and he might need it to sing with the rest of them in heaven and Fox sez that he is gone to a happy hunting ground and he made a little bow and some arrows and put side him. It was so hard and I cried and sarah cried and Fox cried some more to. I laid up rocks round his grave and Fox helped me git a big rock which was hard to git and we made it smooth on the edge and put it on top of his grave so nothing will git him. I wish I had gone to Oaklahoma but I still got Sarah and I hope a snake dont bite her and I watch her all times. I wouldnt have sarah ifn I had a gone to Oaklahoma caus Fox wont go but then I wouldnt have had Buck neither and he is dead so I am going to try and be hapy caus of Sarah and it ant easy.

XXXX

"My, that's hard!" Raleigh looked up with a trace of moisture in his eyes. "Eve's teardrops have played havoc on that pokeberry ink."

Some of the words had been smudged so badly from her tears that they were difficult to read.

"It had to be a grim experience for her to suffer the loss of her son in her isolated world. Her children were all she had to live for, and the loss of her baby surely had to be devastating. Can you imagine...?"

Kurt interrupted Raleigh in mid sentence. "When someone values the company of a spider, can you conceive of what it would be like to get a big strong healthy boy and then lose him to snakebite? No one should suffer like that! I suppose one could say that she escaped the Trail of Tears but not this *tale* of tears. People today seem to ignore this sad chapter in our nation's history and dismiss it as necessary action that had to be taken against the '*savage red men*,' as if they had no personal feelings. Regretfully, I guess that not many people cared."

"Kurt," Raleigh said his name and then paused a minute in thought. "My Indian ancestry probably prohibits me from making an unbiased reply to that comment, but Eve made an effort to speak for herself and her people—and she did it much better than I ever could! Who today would want to walk in her shoes? We live as if nothing like this could ever happen, or would ever happen, in this country. Now, I don't want this to sound like I am a crybaby, because I love this great country that we live in, but it has not been without its flaws!

"It might be unfair to compare the Indian removal to the events that took place one hundred years later in Germany involving the Jewish people. Their trail of tears led to a gas chamber, whereas a new homeland was provided for the Indians—for a period of time anyway. There is no getting around the fact, however, that the circumstances were certainly similar.

There was a race of people that was not wanted, and they were dispensable, which was proven by the great disregard for the health and safety of those who were forcibly ejected from their homes. There were around eighteen thousand Cherokee who were forced to leave their eastern homes, and around four thousand of them never made it to the new Indian Territory. And very few of those that made the trip survived long enough to enjoy their new homeland.

"As I earlier proclaimed in my stump speech, almost immediately after gold was discovered near Dahlonega, Georgia, the state confiscated the area that belonged to the Cherokee, and all the rights that the Cherokee had over it were rescinded. There was a lottery held to sell the rights of the mining area, and only whites were allowed to participate. President Jackson and his army troops went about clearing the land of those who were, to them, obstructionists.

"The fact remains that over four thousand died in this debacle, and they were just as dead as the Jews who met their fate at the hands of the Nazis—the numbers were just much smaller. Sadly, little Buck was a victim of this miscarriage of justice. There is no wonder that this chapter in American history has been largely ignored. People tend to dismiss that which would be painful to discuss. There is not a whole lot more that I can add to the message that speaks loudly to us through that pokeberry ink. Even the blotches tell their stories—and Eve is not out of that place yet."

Both read on.

Fox stays gone a lot more ever since Buck died and he sez we are goin to leav this place and then he sez that we cant go caus there ant no place for the Cherokee to go to cept to Oaklahoma caus they wont let no Indians live in these mountains no more but I ask him where he goes cause he ant here lots of times and they ant made hin go to Oaklahoma and he sez that he stays in the woods and gits thangs to brang here. I say that Sarah is growing big and we got to go some place else before Sarah gits snakebit and dies like litle Buck did or I git snakebit and Sarah wont have me to watch her and I tell Fox that he is gone to much for him to watch out for her to keep her safe. I ask him what he thinks will happen to little Sarah ifn I get snake bit and die while he is gone wherever he goes and then there ant nobody to take care of her. Sometime I wish that I still had preacher Stones bible for to learn Sarah how to read better but then I think that Buck needs it worse and it is in heaven with him so I let Sarah read what the preacher wrote before he died and those two newspapers what Fox brung in. Preacher Stone ant got no use for his Bible cause he is dead but I supose he died but I dont know but I still got his box and book. Sarah is learning fast and growing big and now I have somebody what I can talk to who can talk back and she knows how to talk in Cherokee but she dont have nobidy to talk to cept me and sometimes Fox. I dont like winter much caus it is cold but I will be glad when it gits here caus it puts them snakes gone and I dont like snakes caus they done killed Buck but I had rather get out of here no matter what.

Things cant get no worse ever since Buck got killed by
that snake and I stay scared and dont know what to do next.
I need to go someplace else since I done got another baby a
coming and fox sez he dont care ifn we have another baby or
not caus the sprits are against us now and bad things happen
when they turn against people. I say to him that he may be
right and that God may be giving us another boy so as to take
Bucks place and that God is so proud to have Buck up there
in heaven with him that he is giving us another one but he
says that ant so caus there ant no other baby that is going
to take Bucks place and he is dead and is gone to the hapy
hunting grounds and he ant a coming back. I say that we just
gotta wate and see what happens and he dont say nothing
but just gets gone again. Fox sez that maybe we should have
just of gone to Oaklahoma with the rest of the Indians but
he sez that wouldnt be good after what he heared happened
to his folks and I asked what happened to them and he says
I dont want to know. I tell him I do want to know and what
happened to my folks to caus I ant heared nothing. Fox just
says that the world has changed and the Cherokee ant got
no more friends and treatys dont mean nothing and now the
Cherokees are fighting one another caus the white man has
got them so crossed up. He sez that the word is that the first
Cherokees what went to Oaklahoma dont like them last ones
that was a made to go caus they is more of them and they
dont want for them to start running things in their new land.
He sez that them what got there first wont to run everything
and now there is more of the new ones that ant been there
long and they ant got what was promised them when they
made them leav here and that ant much. Fox sez we dont
need to go all the way to Oaklahoma for to starve to death
but I dont know and Oaklahoma is a long way off from here.

Fox sez that it ant no good for the Cherokee nowhere and we are better off ifn we stay here but I say that we are not better off here ifn we git snakebit and die like little Buck already did. I cry a lot and I dont think that I would cry anymore ifn I was in oaklahoma but I might already be dead before I got there or had a baby made by one of them gard men but I dont want no baby that ant made by Fox and I dont want none of those armey men to be on me bad like so ifn I didnt come here to hide it might be worse so I cant say what was right to do.

It is sprang and the wild flowres is a bloming pretty and I picked some and put then on Bucks grave rocks and I cried a lot. Buck was getting to be a big boy and he would be a growing and I would be learning him how to read and write ifn the snake hadnt killed him but Sarah is a learning fast and is a growing big and is 5 years old and she remembers everything good. The new baby is set to be born most any time now and I am scared. It dont seem to be right like the other 2 and maybe Fox is right when he sez that the spirits are against us caus I get sick and I bleed and fox ant here to help me now but he might come back anytime but I dont spect him to caus he stays gone most of the time. I dont know how he spects me to take care of Sarah and have a baby to when he is not here to help me and I need him bad. It had come to my mind about trying to git outta here by myself with Sarah before I had another baby to tote out and before the snakes got to bad but I already seen some since it got warm and I dont know what I outta do. I wouldnt know where to go ifn I got out and I dont know if I could even caus I would have to tote Sarah and she ant big enough to git down them steps to the creek and wade the creek herself and I need Fox and he might not let me go. I am so sick and frail with the baby coming that I dont know ifn I dont need for Fox to tote me instead of me trying to tote Sarah but ifn he would come and tote Sarah I would git out some how. Seems like the only thing for me to do is to birth the baby and see what happens but I need somebody here to help me specially since I dont feel right but I got Sarah and she can be a big help but Fox needs to git back here. I tell Sarah all the time to be a brave girl caus we dont know what might happen next. I want her to remember that she must be a big girl and not be afraid caus things are bad and shes got to be strong so as not to die like Buck did. I made up a saying for myself. One like a bible verse. I tell it to Sarah and say for her not to forget it caus it might help her when she is tired and dont know what to do. This is what I say for her to not forget. I had for her to write it down on this paper so as to help her remember it. I looked up the words so as to spell them right.

Written underneath this entry, in capital letters, in crude, bold print was the following:

WALK WITH WIND AT YOUR BACK
WHENEVER YOU CAN.
FACE IT WHENEVER YOU MUST.
BE BRAVE AND STRONG
HARD TIMES WILL SOON BE GONE.
TOMORROW IS THE BEGINNING
OF A WHOLE NEW DAY.
WE CANNOT KNOW
WHAT THIS DAY MIGHT BRING
BUT THE SKY IS NOT ALWAYS GRAY.
ENDURE THE STORMS
AND SOOTHE THE PAINS.
ENJOY THE SUNSHINE
THAT FOLLOWS THE RAINS.

CHAPTER 14

"It appears that the last two words should have been THE END," Raleigh commented to Kurt as he flipped through the remaining pages.

As he determined that there was nothing else to read in the journal, he had a look of obvious disappointment.

"The end," Kurt repeated. "Wow, was that some adventure, or what?"

"Kurt," Raleigh countered. "That was not signed off as being 'The End,' because there is much more to this story than what Eve has written. Her writings may have stopped, but Eve was unable to record the final outcome of her exploits in that journal. The few blank pages remaining in that journal give testimony to an unwritten proper ending of her imprisonment in her Garden of Eve. Did she serve her time and have a successful release, or was it a life sentence for her and Sarah?

"The same is true of Reverend Stone, as it is not clear as to his fate. Those people did not just cease to exist. I will make the assumption that Reverend Stone died a natural death; it may be a false assumption, but a probable one nevertheless. He was possibly killed by the troops, but if they wanted to silence him, I think that an arrest would have been more likely.

"It is also possible that he may have been captured—taken into custody and removed from the area. But I think that because he was complaining of bad health, he probably just died. I wonder, though, what happened to his body. Perhaps he was buried in Flat Rock by church members there. With the lack of communication at that time, that could well have occurred.

"There are obviously two mysteries here, but I am not going to try to jump into both of them—maybe later. For right now, I want to know what happened to Fox, Eve, Sarah, and the unborn baby. They either died before they left the cove, or they got out safely. If they were able to get out safely, they probably have descendants somewhere today. I suspect that Fox was not in as much danger as were the females. I see no reason why he should have perished in the cove."

"True." Kurt had reopened the journal and was again reading the last paragraph that Eve had written. "The storm passed, but did Eve and Sarah live to enjoy the sunny days that followed? Let's hope that they did and that they had the wind at their backs for a long time afterwards—but how could we know?"

Raleigh was deep in thought. He hesitated before making a reply to Kurt's remarks.

"I don't know the answer to your question, Kurt. A lot of water has flowed down the Sipsey Canyon since the last words were written in that journal. If they did make it out safely, there may be descendants who can complete this story."

"Maybe, but it will probably be very difficult to find anyone who knows anything about this story. If someone had known of the existence of this hiding place or the journal that had been left behind, it probably would not have been left there where you found it. Eve probably would have sent someone back later to retrieve it."

"Well, maybe. And then again, maybe not, Kurt. If you had to experience all that Eve did when she was in hiding, when you got out, do you think that you would be anxious to go back there? I don't think so! There is no way that I would ever want to see that place again—ever! I was there for one day, and I don't want to return."

"You have a point there. But don't you believe that someone would know about the place? If Sarah survived, I would think that she would have mentioned to someone the details of her childhood—especially if she lived to raise a family."

"Interesting thought, Kurt. But it would seem that if she had told her story, the cove would not have remained such a secret place. I tell you, there had not been anyone there for a long time before I found it."

"I don't doubt that, but we can't actually know that there has not been anyone back there. True, it may have been a hundred years ago, but how can we know? Don't forget, Raleigh, it's been a long time since the Cherokee claimed this land. A civil war has been fought since that time. In 1838, the Trail of Tears was in full march to Oklahoma. That was many years ago."

"There are a lot of factors involved here, Kurt. I know that the snakes have kept a lot of people out of the canyon. Those snakes have been there as long as the Cherokee, and they have been a major factor in it being such a forsaken place. Against the greatest of odds, I found the cove—it was strictly by accident. I have no desire to return to the place, and certainly don't plan to. I can understand how that box remained unnoticed until now. If I had not found it, it may have suffered the same fate as the Dead Sea Scrolls. They lay hidden for two thousand years before someone found them in that cave shelter."

"Maybe an exaggeration, but it possibly would have been there for a much longer time. That chestnut box would have preserved its content in a dry, sheltered space indefinitely," replied Kurt.

"Sure enough! Especially when guarded by those rattlesnakes." Raleigh couldn't forget how unnerved those snakes had caused him to be. "But the important thing now is not the box and its contents; it is the people who left it behind. The obvious question is—what happened to that family? Were they killed by snakes? Did Fox leave them to die in that cove? Surely not! Did Eve die in childbirth? Did Sarah survive and leave the cove with Fox? Did they all leave successfully with the baby? Was it a girl or a boy? If they got out, why was the box left behind? Why did..."

"You can ask questions all night, Raleigh. Finding answers is what we should focus on now. Assuming that they did get out, I think I know why the box was left behind. They would have been carrying a baby out of the canyon and would have had their arms full. Fox had no interest in that box. Eve probably didn't want him to know about it, and if anything needed to have been left behind, it would have been that. Eve probably knew that, so she could have sealed it knowing that it could survive there a long time."

"For once, you make a lot of sense, Kurt. The only way that it could have gotten out would have been for Eve to later send someone to retrieve it. But who did she have to send? And, was getting that one box out of that hellhole that important to her anyway? When people move, they usually have to discard some things. The box could have been that 'something' for Eve. If she did get out of that canyon, she probably knew that she would never see that journal again. She would have been so happy to leave that it would not matter anyway.

It contained a record of events that were very painful to her. If in later years she thought about it still being there, she probably would have no desire to relive those painful years anyway. And she certainly would not want to send a child of hers back into that snake den with the possibility that they may be snake bit. She lost one boy there, and that journal was certainly not worth the risk of losing another one. Yep, I am with you, Kurt. I am beginning to understand why that box remained untouched for such a long time."

"All that is assuming that Eve and Sarah, and maybe a baby, came out with Fox. To be truthful, I really have doubts that the women got out. I don't have any doubts that the odds were stacked against them. It is a mystery, Raleigh!"

"And one that we must try to solve." Raleigh had obviously been caught up in the suspense. Now he was ready for action.

"You are an investigator, Raleigh; I am a science teacher. I can give you moral support, but I am afraid that I would be of little help otherwise. I'd probably even be in the way."

"There is no way that I could close this journal and forget about Eve and her cove experience. I have no illusions that it will be easy, but I must try to find some answers. I am convinced that it will be the most difficult investigation that I will ever make."

"And possibly the most disappointing. It will be nothing short of a miracle if you have any success at all. Those people lived before the Civil War. The Yankees had a bad habit of burning courthouses, along with their records, when they marched through Alabama and Georgia. I highly doubt you could enter their names, if you had them, in a computer and get a printout." Kurt's assessment was not encouraging.

He continued, "The reality is that Gray Fox and Eve were trying to remain invisible. They were not going to run to the courthouse to get something recorded. They certainly did not invite a census worker to the cove where they could be counted. Those people were trying to escape the removal process; they had no desire to see what was on the western side of the Mississippi River. If they did make it out of the canyon, they probably signed on as Black Dutch if they were required to identify their ancestry."

"I really don't know where to start in my attempt to solve this thing. This is something that I must give a lot of thought."

"I wish you luck, Raleigh. I have a feeling that you will need it."

The challenge that Raleigh faced was clear even though the results were not. The journey that he and Kurt had taken through amateurish writings, misspelled words, poke juice ink, crooked lines, and never-ending sentences had proved almost as difficult as the trek through the mountain laurel, saw briars, and slippery rocks at Kinlock. Nevertheless, Raleigh had no intention of turning back before completing this new adventure. He was already trying to formulate a plan of action and was not quite ready to put the journal back into the box without a bit more analytical discussion.

"Eve had to have been writing in that journal for a purpose. True, she didn't carry it out of the cove, so maybe she didn't get out. Or, maybe she had to carry a baby instead. But, why did she make the effort to write all that stuff down?"

"It could have been for any number of reasons," Kurt responded. "First off, she didn't have a lot of entertainment in that hole. The cove was the equivalent of being in prison—in solitary confinement. I would think that she had a lot of spare time. Maybe she had someone in mind that she thought she might sit down with to read and reminisce together."

"One thing you can be sure of. She did not have Raleigh Walker or Kurt Marshal in mind as sharing partners. She could have had no clue that the new days would usher in a new millennium before her message escaped the small world in which she wrote," Raleigh voiced his thoughts.

"And what a different world it is! It is almost impossible for us to comprehend a time when a person would choose to endure such harsh conditions. The truth is, I suppose, that there was no free lunch to be found anywhere in the Warrior Mountains at that time. Today we have become so accustomed to our luxuries that we forget that the world of the eighteen hundreds was very hard for a lot of people. The Fox family is a prime example of that."

Raleigh pondered Kurt's statement as he glanced at the clock. "Kurt, we are not going to solve this thing tonight; it is getting late."

The two had entered so deeply into the hardships of the cove that the tranquil land of sleep would not come easily. They were attempting, without success, to mentally write their own happy ending to the incomplete journal.

For breakfast they ate oatmeal—the instant variety. There was no time for the concoction stuff today. Grits were not even on the menu. The one thing that Raleigh brought to the breakfast table was a determination to give his best effort in finding answers to the many questions that had escaped from the box.

"Finding those steps that day immediately raised questions. Locating the passageway to the cove and entering it created more, and finding the box added even more. I thought I would be pleased if I found some answers. Well, now that I know what was in the box, a whole new list of questions has surfaced. These were not answered by merely prying off a lid."

"So what's next?" inquired Kurt.

"I suppose I should start with the *who, what, when, where,* and *why.*"

"Well, start there then—let's talk about it."

"No, wait a minute! Let me get a pad and a pen so that I will be able to make notes. I am going to do this investigation right."

Raleigh returned with a legal pad, a clipboard, and a mechanical pencil.

"Okay. Let's start with the *who.*"

Raleigh wrote, "*Gray Fox, Eve, Sarah, Buck (deceased), and Unborn*" beside the word "*who.*"

"Now I need to learn anything I can about these people. I don't know their full names, so this will be a challenge. Okay, now for the *what.* I need to find out what happened to these people."

Beside the word "*what,*" Raleigh wrote, "*Consequence of the Trail of Tears: the Indian removal to Oklahoma. What happened to these people?*"

"The Indian removal was the trigger that motivated them to hide in the cove. The question is—what happened to them afterwards? I don't have a whole lot now to be able to contribute to each of these categories," Raleigh said.

"For the *where,* I would ask: *Where did they go IF they left the cove?* I suppose my main interest here is where can I look to possibly find some answers? If they got out, where did they go? Surely not to Oklahoma!"

Kurt was listening intently as Raleigh went on.

"Now regarding the *when.* We know from Reverend Stone's journal notes that Gray Fox and Eve were married on Saturday, August 30, 1834. We also know that the Trail of Tears was in March of 1838. If they were in the cove for more than five years, it would be the next decade when they left—if they did. We have no way of knowing right now whether or not they lived."

Beside his *"why"* category, Raleigh wrote the following: "*The greed of the new settlers in tribal lands prompted the problem. Search for happiness by an affected family of that greed. Escape the Indian removal. Fear for their life and safety.*"

"Those people were searching for a way of life that had been snatched from them against their will. They had been married only a few years, and they did not want to be separated. It was Fox's idea—he thought it to be the correct thing to do under such difficult circumstances. If I put this on a personal level, the question might be—how does this affect me over a hundred and fifty years later? Why am I worrying about it, and why do I care? The answer is that I would like to try to find someone in that family to present the journal to. It would be nice for them to be able to keep it in the family, if that is even possible. I could always keep the box, since it originally belonged to the preacher. It could be a keepsake to remind me of my hike."

"Well, I would just like to get some answers. I want to know what happened to that family. Raleigh, we could walk away from this and forget it. That would be the easy—the lazy—thing to do, but maybe not the correct one," Kurt spoke.

"It is not in my nature to back away from a challenge like this, Kurt. When I start an adventure, I don't turn back. I suppose that is evident in the fact that we have this box out of the canyon in the first place. I was determined to make that hike!"

"Tell me about it, Raleigh. I tried my dead level best to discourage you from going. There was nothing that

I could say or do to convince you otherwise. You were fortunate to have succeeded as you did."

"Right you are there!"

"I'm no good at making investigations, but I do know my history," Kurt continued. "There were some thirteen thousand Cherokee still in the Eastern United States when General Scott awarded the contract to force them to go to the land designated for them in Oklahoma. I believe that was in July of 1838. I also know that it was around the first of September before they actually started moving them. Eve writes this whole thing without giving dates, but I would say that she was captured sometime in the autumn of 1838. She wrote in her journal that they got to the cove too late in the year to grow a crop."

"Okay, Kurt. You say that you are big on history. Well, it has occurred to me that Eve obviously was not. She gives no family record, as if anyone reading her entries should already know them. She provides us with no information other than that she had an Uncle Joe. The preacher gives us more information about her than she does. He says that Fox and Eve are full-blood Cherokee—or so he thinks. She was fearful that her Cherokee mother and her sister had been forced to go to Oklahoma. That's not a lot to go on, but that is all we know."

"We are making the assumption that the marriage of Gray Fox and Eve, as recorded by Reverend Stone in his portion of the journal, was indeed the same two who entered the cove. I think that is a pretty safe assumption. How many like names would there have been to marry in the Kinlock area?"

"Yeah, I think that is a given. They had to be the same ones. Hey, wait a second, Kurt; let me check something."

The journal remained in the music stand where they had left it. Raleigh took it down and began to search for something he thought he remembered reading earlier. He read Reverend Stone's record of the wedding. He then commented, "The wedding was on Saturday, August 30, 1834, in the Kinlock community. I think that is a clue to a later entry."

Raleigh turned to the preacher's last journal entry and began to read aloud again. *"I will return to Kinlock where I will board with Joseph P. I am due to preach there Sunday."* He flipped the page. "Now, there is one last thing that I want to re-read."

Raleigh turned to Eve's opening entry after she had claimed the journal for her own use.

He read aloud again. *"He left a passal of thangs at Uncle Joes."* Raleigh reached for his legal pad and began to write, while thinking out loud. "Gray Fox marries Eve D., who has an Uncle Joe—probably a Joseph P." He continued to reason aloud. "Now this would probably be an uncle on her mother's side of the family because they would have different names, as the 'D' and the 'P' would indicate. Now, if we only knew their full names! Reverend Stone was right; those initials don't help much to identify someone." He turned to Kurt. "Now what is your take on this?"

"Your take is my take, Raleigh. You are the investigator. My additional take is that I have very little hope that anyone can sort this out in my lifetime."

"Let's see now, Kurt," Raleigh continued his analysis. "Eve was a full-blood Cherokee whose maiden name started with a "D" as would her father's. Her mother's maiden name probably started with a "P" as did her Uncle Joe. Now, the reality of this is that it leads to nowhere! It will take a lot more than I have now to get our answers. There is one thing that is certain; the questions won't answer themselves. This will be a challenge!"

"You have to find a starting place first. There are precious few clues to begin an investigation into something that occurred that long ago—talk about a cold trail!" Kurt's comments offered up very little encouragement.

"What do you expect me to do? Can I just close the journal, put it back in the box, and let it sit for another one hundred and seventy years or so? I think I know you well enough to know that you would never consider this to be an option. I have too many years invested in criminal justice to ignore the biggest investigative challenge I have ever had and probably will ever have.

"Well, Raleigh, no one with an ounce of curiosity could walk away from this without a desire for answers. Frankly though, this whole thing looks hopeless to me. I don't see any semblance of a button that you can push to kick-start an investigation here."

"It is not going to be easy to find that button, and there are not a lot of places to look."

"I'm just thinking, though, Raleigh—there may be one, but I am not sure that you would want to go that route."

"What is that?"

"Well, I was thinking about maybe going back into that cove to see what else we might be able to find, like maybe the Bible and songbook."

"No, Kurt—absolutely not! That is not an option as far as I am concerned."

"Why not? I'll go with you this time."

"There are some things that I haven't told you. There is more to this story than the box and journal."

"Oh?"

"Yeah. I am quite sure that I know the exact spot where she placed the Bible and songbook—along with her beloved Buck. I did not tell you about the rock and flowers that I found. In addition to the Bible and songbook, we might be able to find some bones, covered by rabbit skins and deer hides, but I am not sure they would provide any answers for us.

"Even if I knew they would, I would not disturb brave, young Buck. He may be in that happy hunting ground taking aim on a trophy deer, and we might scare it away. The Bible would now be in heaven and the songbook well worn from daily use by Buck and his angels. There is no way to know how much game has been killed by that little bow and arrows in his happy hunting grounds. No, Kurt; that would not be an option."

"Do you think you might change your mind?"

"No! What's the deal here? When I first planned to go into that canyon, you said that I would be crazy to do it. I tried to get you to go, and you flatly refused. Now you are saying, 'Let's take a hike in the canyon.' I cannot imagine that I would ever change my mind. The moss can grow right back into those steps as it was before.

"Fact is, I replaced some of it in the lower steps so they would again be concealed should anyone venture that way. It can stay there, because I will never climb those steps again. I would certainly not consider the cave a crime scene. Although, the way those people were treated, I would consider it to be a criminal act, but I left no yellow tape around the place. This does not require a crime scene investigation. That cove is off limits for me. I will not go back there. I trust that you agree!"

"Yeah, Raleigh, I guess you're right."

"This leads to another issue that we need to discuss. I think this is very important."

"What's that?"

"If word of this find gets out, there will be a stream of people going into that canyon to see what they can bring out. That rock shelter will be dug up like a spring garden. They would take everything they could haul out of that canyon. The only thing we would undoubtedly be left with would be a courthouse full of lawsuits against us, filed by lawyers representing those who claim that we are responsible for the injuries, even deaths, of those who will invariably fall or drown in the canyon. That is absolutely no place for the tenderfoot. These people will get into real trouble in their attempt to find an arrowhead or anything else they can get their hands on. Those who might be successful in getting in and out of the canyon will have no respect for the grave or anything else. Buck's bones would be in someone's closet before a proper prayer could be said over them."

"Sad but true. You are absolutely right about that. I will not mention this to anyone. You have my word on that. We are the only two who know anything about this, and it will remain that way. In the future, if you wish to include others, that is your call. You made the find; you make the calls!"

"I might later second guess myself about packing that thing out of the canyon. Right now, I think it was the proper thing to do. Eve made an effort to write that journal, and I think she would want someone to read it. Otherwise, her efforts would have been wasted."

"What do you plan to do with the box and journal?"

"Keep it in a secure place, preferably a fireproof safe. It was in a safe place all these years, guarded by rattlesnakes; now it falls on my shoulders to protect it. We may not have been the ones that Eve would have chosen to gain control over her writings, but we have them now. Perhaps all of this may have been dictated by a higher power—who knows? I am not sure God works in this way, but he may control some power that guides us as he sees fit."

"Interesting thought."

"It would be easy for me to go on a guilt trip because I took the box. I did go against everything that I stand for, as I want everyone to leave the forest undisturbed."

"What's done is done!"

"True enough."

"And as you said, maybe all of this is out of our hands anyway. How are we to know? This could well be the works of a higher power, whatever or whoever that may be."

"Yes. But if that is the case, I hope that this power doesn't have a sudden change of heart and leave me out on a limb."

"If that happens, I will crawl out on the limb with you, and we will face this together. I have the feeling that you are going to need all the assistance you can get—that would be a power far greater than I could ever offer!"

"The journal is where everything starts. There is nothing else. I will have to begin there and see where it leads. If it ends there, so be it. I will give it my best!"

"I'm sure you will, Raleigh."

"I opened this investigation when I touched the box. Now the case will be pending until I can solve it, or until I determine that it cannot be solved. There is no other way." Raleigh picked up his legal pad and looked at it. "Ain't much there, Kurt! I have a gut feeling that I am going to have plenty of paper here to record everything I can come up with in this case."

As an afterthought, Raleigh reached for his pencil and wrote a notation on top of his pad: *U.S.A. vs. FOX.*

CHAPTER 15

◆

Smoke Signals is a publication of the Echota Cherokee Tribe of Alabama. Raleigh held membership in the Blue Clan, one of the seven tribal clans. Membership into the tribe could be granted only through the documentation of sufficient American Indian blood to qualify. This was not difficult for Raleigh to verify, although his family had always claimed to be Black Dutch. This claim had been devised by his ancestors to conceal their true heritage and to escape the removal to Oklahoma.

Raleigh examined the front page of the *Smoke Signals*. It began in its customary way, "*Osy 'yo Echotas.*"

This greeting was followed by the latest news regarding tribal activities. He scanned through the general information section to find what he was seeking. "*Our next meeting will be at the Oakville Indian Mounds Park...*"

He recorded the information on the legal pad he was using for his investigative notes. The date and time of the tribal meeting was given in the announcement. "*Tribal meeting at 11 a.m. with dinner following—all on Indian standard time—so bring your covered dishes, drinks, and other eating implements, and join us in food, fun, and fellowship. We will be making plans for the annual tribal meeting and giving an update on all other tribal activities.*"

Raleigh had to smile at the reference to Indian time. It simply meant that those activities would occur sometime that day—the exact time being irrelevant. The Cherokee were never servants of the clock.

The date was still three weeks away. Although he had been a tribal member for a number of years, he had never been active in the internal affairs of the group. Previously, he had attended only one tribal meeting and did not find the activities to be of interest to him. His interest in this gathering had nothing to do with helping to plan a future tribal meeting.

He considered it a long shot, but he was hoping to find someone that might know a little Cherokee history. He would inquire specifically about a certain family that had refused to leave the Warrior Mountains. He was skeptical that a courthouse search would provide any useful information, but he was determined to give that a try also.

The Kinlock area presently lies within the boundaries of two counties—Lawrence and Winston. He decided to check the Winston County record first. He traveled to the county courthouse in Double Springs only to learn that this was a dead end. He entered the office of the probate judge and made an inquiry.

"Do you have records that would date back to the 1830s and 40s?"

"No."

"You don't?"

"No. We have no records in Winston County that go back that far."

"Did they burn in a courthouse fire or something?" Raleigh inquired.

"No, there has not been a courthouse fire."

"But you don't have those records available?"

"I take it that you are not big on Winston County history."

"Well, I guess you could say that I don't know a whole lot about it. Why do you say that?"

"Because Winston did not become a county until 1850," replied the clerk.

"Oh, really?"

"Really! Before 1850, it was called Hancock County. We have no Hancock County records, or any records, that go back anywhere close to that time."

Raleigh thought a minute before his next question. "When Alabama became a state, in what county would the northern part of what is now Winston County, around the Kinlock area, have been at that time?"

"Well, let me think. It has been awhile since I studied that in school myself. I remember that the southern part of it was in Walker County." Grinning, she added, "I suppose I am not so big on Winston County history either. I think Hancock County was carved out of Lawrence and Walker Counties."

"So I suppose that if I want to see those records, I should try Walker County first."

"No, not really."

"Why not?"

"That courthouse has burned two or three times since then. It has also been wiped out by a tornado. If it is not recent enough to have been put on a computer, they probably don't have it."

"Well, I know that. I just wasn't thinking. My office is in the courthouse, and I know how impossible it is to get old records there."

"Will there be any other way that I can assist you?"

"No. Thank you anyway. You have been very helpful."

The Lawrence County inquiry was no more productive than the earlier attempt had been in Winston County. There were some old records there, but they were only court and legal records and provided no clues as to how he might answer the questions he had.

Raleigh called Kurt to give him an update on the information he had gathered, which was basically nothing.

"If there is any recorded information to be found, it will not be in any courthouse records."

"What's next?"

"I guess I have a lot of questions to ask."

"Who are you going to question?"

"Anybody that I think might have some answers!"

In an attempt to find someone who might know a little history of the North Alabama Cherokee, Raleigh called the office of the Echota Tribe. He had gotten one simple recommendation—"*Ask Cherokee!*"

No one knew this man's real name. He had a handle for every occasion. The family called him "Hugs." His gambling buddies knew him as "Ace." He was "Harley" to his motorcycle friends, and to his Native American tribesmen, he was "Cherokee."

There was no visible space on his body to put an additional tattoo. His gray ponytail reached his waist. He talked a lot and had an answer to every question.

Ask Cherokee! It soon became obvious that this would be easier said than done.

Cherokee was a trucker. The other truckers called him "Kenworth." Raleigh was met with blank stares when he went looking for Cherokee among them.

It was not until he described a guy covered with tattoos, sporting a long gray ponytail, and talking constantly that he picked up on the Kenworth handle.

After some difficulty, arrangements were made for them to meet at a truck stop on I-65 North near Birmingham, Alabama.

The instruction for the meeting was simple. "*Look for a red Kenworth truck driven by a tattooed man wearing* a *long ponytail*." The truck would be marked by his company's logo.

Raleigh arrived at the specified truck stop early and was waiting when Cherokee/Kenworth/Hugs pulled up to the pumps for fuel. Raleigh introduced himself and went into the adjoining restaurant to wait.

Kenworth paid for the fuel with a company card and joined Raleigh at his table.

"How ya doin', Kenworth?" a waitress greeted him.

It was obvious that he was no stranger at the truck stop. He was definitely an individual that one would not soon forget. At this meeting, he was wearing a sleeveless shirt, displaying as many of his tattoos as possible. He had captured his ponytail in a succession of rubber bands.

He was abrupt and to the point in his first remark. "What is it that you want to know?"

"I understand that you know a lot about the history of the Alabama Cherokee. I have a question about an old Indian family."

"There ain't much that I don't know about the Cherokee. My veins run full of redskin blood."

The waitress came to take their orders as they began their conversation. "You want the usual, Kenworth?"

"You got it, darling. You know what I always got to have."

Raleigh ordered and then listened as Kenworth talked.

"Now, you came to the right place to find out what you want to know about us Cherokees. You ain't going to find nobody that knows more about them than Kenworth— uh, Cherokee, that is. You can just call me Cherokee."

"Great, Cherokee! Now, this goes back a long time."

"Put it on me, baby! Just how far back are you talking about?"

"Trail of Tears—to the time of the Indian removal—Early 1800s."

"You some kind of a historian or something? I might want to charge you for this information if you are."

"No. I am no historian. I just want to find out something about one specific family. That's all."

"Guess I can take your word for it. Now, if I see what I tell you gets put in a book later on, you got a lawsuit on your hands, mister. I plan to write a book later myself, and I intend to put all this information in it, and I don't want nobody using my stuff!"

"There's not going to be any book, Cherokee. As I say, I only want to know about one family."

"Well, okay. That Indian removal was the low point in the history of our country—the pits! There was not one promise made to the redskin people that was ever kept. It was all criminal. The white man just stole what he wanted, when he wanted it. A lot of my ancestors were marched to Oklahoma, and not all of them made it there. Their bones are somewhere between here and there—who knows where.

"To the white man, it didn't matter if the Indians made it all the way to Oklahoma or not. It was just another dead savage to them when one dropped. There were some of my people who refused to go. They hid out in the mountains, and when questioned, they said they were Black Dutch. Now, I'll bet you never knew what it was that the Indians called themselves when they didn't want nobody to know that they had the blood of a red man..."

"Well, actually, Cherokee, I knew a lot of those Black Dutch myself. Do you know any of the names of the Cherokee who stayed and survived?"

"Just what names are you interested in, mister? I know most of them, seeing as to how I was raised up being a Cherokee. Give me some names."

The waitress came and placed their order on the table. "Now you enjoy that, Kenworth."

"I notice that around here everybody calls you Kenworth. Are you sure it's all right for me to call you Cherokee?"

"That's who I am to you, man—Cherokee!"

"Okay, Cherokee. Now, giving you the names of who I am looking for is one of the problems. I don't have their full family names. For instance, I don't know your birth name, and I don't think it was Kenworth or Cherokee. I only have first names, or given names—no surnames. I know that is not much to go on, but it is all I have."

"Just where did you get these names? Why are you so interested in them anyway?"

"They were on some old documents that I discovered from that period of time," Raleigh answered.

He had no intention of revealing details about the journal. He was going to disclose as little as possible in order to get his information.

"I found some old documents, and I thought it would be considerate to try to find the family and pass the items on to them. I think they might be happy to have them in their possession."

"Well, if you want to, you can just leave whatever you have with me, and I will look at them and find the people they belong to. I won't charge you nothing for doing it unless I can get them in the right hands. If I do find the people the information belongs to, I will cut you a good deal. I think I can do it. As I say, I know almost all the Alabama people that have Cherokee blood."

"No, this is a little project that I thought I might enjoy doing myself. The documents are of a personal nature, and I don't want to pass them around too much."

"Tell you what, mister. If you want me to get them papers where they need to go, I won't charge you nothing but for the gas I burn looking them up and maybe a little for my time, especially if it takes longer than I plan for it to. I spend most of my time on the road, and when I'm off, I got to make the best use of whatever little free time I have. I would have to charge you a little now; you can understand that. But then you could go on and forget about this and do something else with your time. I am sure you are a busy man."

"I think I will just hold on to those documents myself."

"You can trust me. I help people out like this all the time. People know there ain't nobody that knows the Cherokee like I do. It helps them out, and it gives me a little extra spending money. I want to put a new tattoo on my—"

Raleigh interrupted, "The reason that I contacted you was because someone told me you had this knowledge. If you help me to identify these people, maybe I can get in touch with them. There is a little story behind the items I have, and I want to give them an explanation. I appreciate your offer though."

"Well, if that is all you are worried about, I can handle that! You can just tell me the story like you would to them, and I can tell them when I find them. Ain't nobody that can tell a story like I can!"

"I want to do it myself. They might have some questions that you would not know how to answer."

"Well then, I guess that is fair enough. Just who is it that you are looking for?"

"I have very limited information, actually. There was a female identified as Eve D. who was married to a Cherokee known as Gray Fox—"

Cherokee interrupted, "There were a lot of Gray Foxes back then—and Red Foxes too. It was just about like the name John today. That don't help much!"

"Just let me continue. They were married by a Reverend Joseph B. Stone on Saturday, August 30, 1834."

Cherokee interrupted again, "If that reverend is just now getting those two a copy of their marriage license, he is a little late—don't you think?"

"No, Cherokee, this has nothing to do with a marriage license." Raleigh was beginning to regret having arranged this meeting.

"Well, go on with your story." Cherokee was giving a pretty heavy workout on the food his waitress had served. When she had placed it on the table she had told him to enjoy it, and he had apparently taken that to heart.

"As I was saying, the female was Eve D. The D is the first letter of her maiden name—that's all that I know about that. They had at least two children.

"There was a girl named Sarah and a boy they named Buck, who died young. That's just about all I know about the family."

"That's not a whole lot to go on. Don't you have any more than that?"

"That's about it. I really didn't expect anyone to be able to identify these people with the little bit of information I have. I guess I was hoping for some old family names that might match up or tales about them that have been passed down through generations. Sometimes family stories survive through the years, although I know that is unlikely in this modern age. These people were survivors; they refused to go on the Trail of Tears. I was hoping that their story had been passed down through the years."

"I can't say that I have ever heard of these people. There is a good chance that they are some of my people. I will ask around to see if any of my folks have ever heard of these names. I am the one they come to when they have questions like this."

"Thanks for your time and the information you gave me. I will give you one of my office cards, and if you should learn anything more, just give me a call."

Cherokee examined the card.

"So you are a prohibition man, are you?"

"Probation officer. I work in probation and parole. My home number is on the card."

"Oh, well, if I find out anything, I will let you know."

Raleigh paid for the food and left the restaurant. He secretly hoped that there was no connection between the two families. He had learned his lesson for the day. One can waste good time talking to some yo-yo who knows nothing but thinks he knows everything!

His next attempt to get information would be at the next meeting of the Echota tribe. He hoped that there he would find more sensible people to question regarding Cherokee history.

CHAPTER 16

◆

There was the usual gathering of Indians at the Echota tribal meeting. The numbered membership cards in their possession identified them as such. Ample zeal was displayed in order to identify their ancestry. Proof of their Indian blood was required before their acceptance into the tribe. Many, however, did not have the looks one would expect of a Cherokee. There was a good assortment of pale skin, blue or green eyes, and light or red hair.

This physical look went back to the time in which the Scotch-Irish immigrants began to intermarry with the Indians. Many of the leaders of the Cherokee people were of this heritage and made a significant contribution to the tribe.

Raleigh hastily surveyed the small gathering that had assembled at the Oakville Indian Mound Park in North Alabama. Many who were there had gravitated to a lakeside amphitheater where they awaited the tribal meeting. He began searching the assembly for a likely candidate to field questions about an old Cherokee family.

And then she caught his eye.

Sitting in the upper corner, at the greatest distance from where he was standing, was a young adult woman. She had previously been blocked from his view by a large straw hat being worn by another attendee.

It was as if a dream catcher had snagged her and deposited her in the midst of all those other Indians to show them what a real Cherokee woman should look like. There did not appear to be much interference of the white man's blood in her lovely body. She was a perfect specimen! The true natural beauty of the Cherokee woman was on full display here.

Raleigh caught his breath and swallowed hard. He looked away for a moment, then looked back to make sure that this was not an illusion. She was still there, although the straw hat was again partially blocking his line of sight. He moved his head to one side in order to get an unobstructed view of her.

She sat there, seemingly deep in thought, apparently oblivious to others who were there. Raleigh was able to distinguish her Cherokee characteristics, even from far away. She had jet black hair and dark skin. She was too far away for him to see her eyes, but he knew that they were brown like her ancestors. She had a beauty that had been molded long ago, in better times, before the arrival of the white man.

Although Raleigh observed her from a distance, he knew that it was not necessary for her to show her membership card in order to prove that she belonged in a meeting of Cherokees. Her looks dictated that she belonged to an ancient time with blood that was largely uncontaminated by later arrivals on American soil.

She sat by herself and continued to appear preoccupied in thought. Raleigh moved in her direction, as if being drawn by her appearance.

"Hello," he greeted her as he approached.

She had not seen him coming and was startled by his voice. He sat down in the row in front of her, leaving space for him to talk to her as he looked over his left shoulder.

"Do you attend these tribal meetings regularly?" Raleigh initiated the conversation.

"First one," she replied.

"The second one for me. But it's been a while."

Raleigh paused. He wondered to himself whether or not she had an escort. Was there a jealous "brave" nearby, ready to suggest that he find seating elsewhere? There was one way to find out.

"Are you here with family or friends?"

"No, I came alone," she answered. After a brief pause, she added, "And I don't have a clue as to why I did! Well, I take that back. I didn't really come here for this meeting, but I thought I might stay a few minutes to see what it was all about. And I think I've seen just about enough."

"Why did you come here if not for the meeting?" Raleigh inquired.

"To run a little. They have a world class cross country track here in little old Oakville, and I thought that I would try it out. When I saw in the *Smoke Signals* that the meeting was to be held here, I decided that I would come down and try out the track. That's why I'm wearing this jogging outfit. I came early and did some running, and I was just sitting here resting a little. Now that is a good track! They have state and national championship cross country meets here. If you're a runner, I would highly recommend it."

"Oh really?" Raleigh thought this to be a weak reply, but it was all he could come up with at the moment. "Mind if I come back and sit with you?"

"Come on back! I don't know just how much longer I am going to be here, but I will stay for a little while. Who knows? I just might learn something."

She moved down a little even though the whole row was empty.

Raleigh moved back to join her. He could now get a better look at her. She was even more beautiful than he had first observed. She had a flawless dark complexion and eyes that truly sparkled. The sun accented the sheen of her black hair, and the jogging outfit complemented her full figure. The moisture from her workout had caused her garments to cling more tightly to her body, even further revealing her perfect shape. It was with great restraint that Raleigh avoided staring at her.

"I'm Raleigh Walker." He figured that an introduction was in order.

"Raleigh. I can't say that I know any Raleighs."

"It's an old family name that has been passed down for generations. Our family is big on that kind of thing. I have had it all my life, of course, and it has served me well—I have no complaints. I suppose it was just my time to get that one. They had to name me something when I got here."

Raleigh stopped talking once he realized he had started rambling. All that explanation was totally unnecessary. He was still caught up in the moment.

My, she is a beautiful woman, he thought to himself.

"Well, they named me Jenny Riddle."

"Are you from this area?"

"I live in Huntsville right now, but I grew up a country girl from way back out in the sticks. My folks live over across the river in the corner of the state, real close to Mississippi."

Raleigh smiled. "It appears that you are one of the few who needs no card to proclaim your heritage. I don't want to offend you, but you look as though no white man had ever found this land."

"It has never been a topic of general discussion in our family, but I think my family is mostly Cherokee. I would know a lot more if I had taken more time to talk with my parents and grandparents. I was like most younger people; I didn't have a whole lot of interest in genealogy growing up. What about you? I can tell there's a lot of Native American in you as well."

"Yes, it is obviously there, and I am proud of it. I know what you're talking about. In our family, the Indian heritage was a hush-hush matter. It's only been recently that they have felt at ease while discussing our past. I was like you—other things were more important to me when I was younger."

"What brought you to this gathering today?"

"I don't really know. In retrospect, I think I must have had a mental lapse. I was hoping to find someone who might provide me with a little history of the Cherokee, but it doesn't look promising."

"Who's in charge of this assembly anyway? I don't see anyone who looks like they know what's going on," Jenny said, glancing around.

"I was wondering about the same thing myself. Everyone seems to be doing their own thing. There are some who are fishing at the lake, some who are preparing food, and some look as lost as we are. I don't see anyone else running on that cross country track either. I guess that's too much effort for most of them. I suppose many of them are here for different reasons."

"The *Smoke Signals* specified a time for the events. No one seems to be paying that a lot of attention. It's already past time for this shindig to be up and going."

"This is all on Indian time, Jenny. I have heard that that means things will happen when they happen. Nobody gets into a hurry. The Indian people were not clock-watchers—they didn't even have them!"

Just repeating her name in a conversation gave Raleigh a lot of satisfaction. *Jenny, Jenny—now that* is a *name that I would like to repeat more often,* he thought to himself.

Suddenly the atmosphere changed as a hulk of a man hurried into the park. He wore an assortment of clothing that hinted of a Native American theme; something he apparently thought the Indians wore two hundred years ago. Maybe they did wear a variation of some of that stuff when they dressed for ceremonies, but it struck Raleigh as being just plain weird.

The man immediately took charge and began speaking. "First, let me apologize for my lateness. There were some important issues that needed my attention, which took a little longer than I had expected, and now I'm running behind."

This was a sufficient explanation to the gathered tribesmen. They took their seats in the amphitheater.

"I call this meeting to order!"

And so the meeting began. The first order of business had to do with the status of the completion of an Indian quilt which was to be auctioned off during the next meeting. There was good news: "It's just about done!"

The next question was about a blanket that some had begun to weave that was to be offered to the highest bidder at the same auction. This time the news was not so good.

"We ain't doing much account on that one! That is a whole lot more than we bargained for. Ain't nothing going right on that thing."

"So you don't think you will have that finished in time for the auction?"

"Nope, don't look like it. There is a whole lot of doing and undoing. We can't get the pattern right. Ain't nobody done this kind of thing before. It's a lot harder than we ever expected it to be to get one of them things right the way they are supposed to look."

"Maybe you are trying to get too fancy with it. Do you think you can get some kind of spread ready for auction?

We got one of them down to be auctioned off. Just do the best you can to get something ready in a hurry that might bring a few bucks. The tribe needs the money."

"We'll try," was the solo response, which did not sound very convincing.

Raleigh had his doubts that an Indian blanket would show up at that auction. The meeting went downhill from there. The speaker suddenly realized that he had forgotten something.

"I've been so busy I forgot to bring the material I had prepared—left it at home on the table. I got so much to do that I just can't remember everything. I spent a lot of time on getting that stuff, and it is back at home right where I left it."

There was some discussion about the upcoming tribal meeting, but because the specifics had been left on the chief's table, the men agreed that they would all gather at his house later to hammer out the details and figure out how to pay for it. A tentative date was set for that meeting.

The meeting was short because the agenda had been left behind that morning, but this seemed to please most of the women. They were more interested in getting their food on the table anyway. The chief had really done them a favor by coming empty-handed, although a little murmuring could be heard because he had been so late in getting there, and the food in the covered dishes was getting cold.

Maybe because Raleigh and Jenny were sitting together, some people seemed to think that they were a couple.

One woman commented, "You two have really got that Cherokee look."

Or maybe they just thought the two of them were brother and sister. Even though he had only met Jenny a little earlier, he received great satisfaction in being connected to her by those who did not know them. He was happy that Jenny didn't attempted to distance herself from him, just as he didn't bother to separate himself from her. It was okay with him if people thought them to be a couple, but he was unable to tell how Jenny felt about the whole situation.

Raleigh and Jenny enjoyed the meal that had been prepared, but at the first opportunity they faded behind the bleachers of the amphitheater and walked toward the parking lot. Although they had been together for no more than two hours at the most, there had been an immediate attraction, at least on Raleigh's part, and it seemed only natural that they should leave together.

As they approached their vehicles, they realized that they had chosen the same shade tree to park under. The great oak with spreading limbs provided a dense shade from the hot sun. A gentle breeze created a comfortable atmosphere for them to continue talking. Leaning against their own cars, they seemed to be in no hurry to leave.

Raleigh continued their conversation. "So you live in Huntsville. I suppose you have employment there?"

"Yes, I live and work in Huntsville."

"Let me guess. Are you a teacher?"

Jenny laughed. "Not hardly!"

"Bad guess, I suppose," Raleigh smiled at his remark. "I guessed that because I think you probably have quite a good education—at least you give me that impression."

"Not all educated people teach! I suppose you could say that I am a professional person. I do have university degrees and have been accused of being a workaholic, or worse. But I do enjoy my work very much."

"And that is...?" Raleigh inquired. "Or is it any of my business?"

"Well, since you put it that way, I suppose the answer is no, it isn't any of your business."

Raleigh was taken aback by her response. The only reply he could muster was, "Sorry."

She had not opened up to him like he had wished. Maybe she was not impressed with this stranger she had just met.

"I can tell you *where* I work, but I would probably be in real trouble if I told you what I *did* at work, unless it's just a general explanation. You see, I work for NASA at the Redstone Arsenal there. Much of what I do is classified and has to stay in the lab for security reasons. I do have an interesting job, and I like it! But it's very demanding and leaves me little time to do anything else. This trip today was a great concession to my busy schedule. I try to run some every Saturday and any other time I can get a chance. The track here seemed like a good place to do it."

"Wow! That's quite an impressive occupation for a country girl."

Raleigh then asked the question that was on his mind. "Are you married—or—have a boyfriend?"

He immediately regretted asking the question. He had only met her a short time ago, and he feared that she may consider it to be an awkward question, or an inappropriate time to inquire about her relationship status.

Jenny looked at him and hesitated with her answer, apparently pondering the question.

She answered after a short pause, "No, I am not married, except to my work. I have very little time to mix business with pleasure. I feel comfortable with this lifestyle and have had no regrets so far."

"That sounds interesting," Raleigh replied. "What is the nature of your work at Redstone—or is that too specific?"

"Well, some might say that I am a rocket scientist, but that description doesn't really fit. Let's just say that I am an aerospace engineer. I am involved mainly in space exploration, but that is integrated with the technology used in our missile and defense systems. That's about the extent of what I can say."

"You obviously have more education than what you can get at a country school."

"I went to Auburn. I've always been interested in space exploration. A country girl has lots of time to lie under the stars and dream. I dreamed of getting out of the country. That has been a focus as long as I can remember. Maybe one could label it as tunnel vision, but I can be a very persistent person. All my university work had that aim. My undergraduate and my graduate studies were based on that dream. I got as much education as I could before going to the workplace. But enough about me! What's your story?"

"One thing is certain—I can't begin to match that! I am anything but a rocket scientist. I have a good job and enjoy my work also. I graduated from a private school in Arkansas, Harding University, and I'm employed by the State Board of Pardons and Parole. My work talks back to me, and sometimes I would like to send those who give me a hard time into space. I do get some satisfaction from my work, but often my failures seem to outnumber my successes. I am definitely not married to my work. My passion is found in the forest, where I answer to the call of the wild. I spend whatever leisure time I have becoming acquainted with the splendors of the forest. Unlike you, I find that more appealing than the void we have in space. A dry, desolate blob of rock and sand is better left for someone like you to cuddle up to. Give me the wet, green, floral fragrance of a forest anytime. To each his own—that's what makes this earth we live on such a great place! And by the way, I'm also single."

"I venture the guess that the call of the wild, as you describe it, comes naturally for you. No one can seriously question your Native American heritage."

"Mixed with a tad of Irish; but yes, I have Cherokee in my lineage. My mother is full Cherokee. On my father's side, there was an Irishman who slipped into that bed, somewhere way back when, but that didn't stir up our looks too much."

"And what brought you to the tribal meeting? I answered that question for you, now what is your excuse? Are you bored to the point that you wish to spend this bright, sunny day with a bunch of Indians?"

"That actually seemed to be a gathering of decent people who are proud of their ancestry. On top of that, the food was good—a little cold, but good. When a fellow is young and single, it is amazing what one will do in order to get a decent home-cooked meal." He laughed at the thought. "And, to put the icing on the cake, I just happened to have met a beautiful rocket scientist in the process. Considering it all, things did not turn out all that bad. If I had it to do over, I would do it again. Things always have a way of working out!"

"I suppose so," Jenny replied nonchalantly. "I need to be getting back to Huntsville. I have to make some preparation for tomorrow's work, and I don't want to get in late. I've enjoyed meeting and talking with you."

Raleigh reached for his billfold. "Let me give you one of my business cards. If you are ever down Jasper way and get in trouble with the law, just give me a ring, and I will see what I can do. On second thought, maybe that is not such a good idea. I might make things worse for you. Just don't do anything too bad, and you'll be all right."

"I'll try to hold it down to a manageable offense," Jenny said as she opened the door to her car. "I don't have a business card, but I do have a listed telephone number under J. Riddle. I am hardly ever at home to answer the phone though. Our paths may cross again— who knows?"

As Jenny drove away, Raleigh realized that he had not asked anyone the first question about Gray Fox and his family. That had been the purpose for his attendance there. He thought about going back to see if anyone was still around but decided against it. He left and headed south toward Jasper. Jenny headed in the opposite direction.

Raleigh was determined that somehow, some way, his and Jenny's paths would once again cross. The day had not been a total waste of time.

CHAPTER 17

◆

The morning mail brought news of an upcoming meeting of area supervisors. The place, Huntsville, Alabama, caught Raleigh's attention immediately. The dates were two weeks away, a Thursday and Friday. Attendance was optional but strongly recommended. Raleigh hardly needed encouragement to spend a few days in Huntsville, Alabama.

More than two weeks had passed since the tribal meeting in Oakville. The woman that he met there was never far from his thoughts. She had affected him unlike any other female ever had before.

A self-professed rocket scientist—uh, correction— aerospace engineer, for goodness sake, Raleigh told himself. *What am I thinking about? How many rocket scientists are there in this world? Probably not enough that I would chance to meet one at an Indian meeting. That girl was probably just throwing me some bait, and I swallowed it—hook, line, and sinker. I am getting all excited about a person I know nothing about.*

He did not have to be convinced that she was of Native American heritage. He also admitted to himself that he had no reason to doubt anything that she had told him.

She had not been questioned about her knowledge of Cherokee history, which was the reason Raleigh had attended the tribal meeting in the first place. He justified this as the reason that he should contact her again, although he knew it would be unlikely that such a young person would have any interest in such matters. Nevertheless, she could possibly direct him to someone who might have knowledge of the information he was seeking. Any lead would be helpful.

A call to directory assistance provided him with a number for a J. Riddle in Huntsville. He dialed the number but got no answer. There was no answering machine or voice mail for him to leave a message. He was hopeful that a caller ID would be activated to prompt a return call, but a week passed without any response.

It was Sunday afternoon of the week the supervisors' meeting was scheduled when he finally got a return call. Greetings were exchanged, and Raleigh explained the purpose of his call.

"I have a supervisors' meeting scheduled in Huntsville on Thursday and Friday. I would be honored if you could join me for dinner one of those nights. If you could go, I would like for you to choose the place."

There was silence before she replied. "It's really not a good week for me to go out. I'm deeply involved in a project at work, and I just don't have any free time. I have no doubt that I would enjoy the evening, but I'm afraid I'll have to decline the invitation—maybe some later date."

"I understand. This is just a spur of the moment thing. I just thought that since I would be in Huntsville, I might be able to enjoy your company and get to know you better."

"Later we may find time to meet and become better acquainted; this is just not the week—sorry!"

"I suppose I will just have to settle for dinner with a bunch of parole officers. Good luck with the completion of your project. I'm confident that it will be first class!"

The disappointment was apparent as Raleigh concluded the conversation and hung up the phone. He was hoping that the trip to Huntsville would be an opportunity for him to get to know Jenny better, but it appeared that this was not to be.

Oh, well, he reasoned. *Sometimes things work out the way you would like, and sometimes they don't. That's life!*

He would attend the meeting, but his enthusiasm toward it had greatly diminished.

Raleigh was packing his overnight bag on Wednesday evening when the phone rang. He was surprised to hear a female voice.

"Hi, Raleigh, this is Jenny. Is your trip to Huntsville still on?"

"Yes, it is. I am just now packing a few things, and I will be leaving here early in the morning."

"Is it too late for me to accept your dinner invitation for Friday night?"

"No, certainly not. I would be delighted to see you again."

"Good! I realized that I need a break from my work. I get so involved that sometimes I ignore the fact that I need to get away from my job for a little while. A change of pace on Friday night might be good for me, and I am sure that I will enjoy your company. I can leave from work and meet you somewhere downtown."

After discussing the details, they decided to meet outside the U.S. Space and Rocket Center, as this was a convenient location for both.

The supervisors' meeting was the usual B-Y-E, as some of the old timers referred to it—their acronym for "Big Yawn Event." Raleigh tried to be attentive enough to be able to make his required report of the proceedings to those under his supervision. He was having difficulty keeping his thoughts away from his anticipated dinner date with Jenny. He was excited, yet apprehensive. He did not know what to expect and was worried that he might do something foolish to ruin the occasion. He wanted the evening to be perfect.

Thursday evening, after the meeting was adjourned for the day, Raleigh joined a group of his fellow workers for dinner at a popular Chinese restaurant in town. Although he didn't choose the restaurant himself, he did enjoy an occasional Oriental meal. He had asked Jenny to pick the place for Friday evening, and now he wondered what she might choose. He did not know her taste preference, but he hoped it was not Oriental. He preferred not to repeat this meal of rice, egg roll, and lo mein.

After dinner, the group decided to take in a movie before returning to their hotel rooms. Raleigh excused himself and returned to his room early. He had little interest in the chosen movie, and the day had been exhausting.

Besides all that, he was aware that his anxieties were beginning to affect him, and he wanted to go to bed early. He was accustomed to physical fatigue, but the mental and emotional reaction to his scheduled date with Jenny was a new experience for him. He wanted to start tomorrow as refreshed as he could, and retiring early would help make that possible.

The Friday session ended earlier than expected, and Raleigh had a few hours of extra time on his hands before he was to meet Jenny. Since he had checked out of his hotel earlier, he decided to drive over to the Space and Rocket Center and visit the museum.

He had been there a number of times before when he was younger, but there had been additional exhibits added as space exploration continued. His time was consumed as he checked out the latest additions in and around the center.

So this is what she does. The exhibits took on a new meaning for Raleigh. He had no idea what type of work Jenny did at the Redstone Arsenal, but he reasoned that she, in some way, had contributed to the success of the more recent exhibits. He felt a sense of pride.

He did not want to be late, so he left the museum about fifteen minutes before he was supposed to meet Jenny. At precisely the time they agreed upon, Jenny pulled into the parking lot.

He had to catch his breath as she stepped from her car. He had not noticed that she was as tall as she now appeared. She was dressed in a tan dress suit that was trimmed in a darker brown, which beautifully accented her deep brown eyes. Her jet black hair fell across her shoulders and glistened from the light of the setting sun. Her stylish brown heels matched the trim of her clothing.

She approached in a self-assured manner; a comfortable smile was framed on her lovely face.

Can even God create a creature so beautiful? Raleigh asked himself.

"Hi," she uttered the greeting as she neared him.

"You look beautiful tonight." The remark was spontaneous, and he immediately wondered if that was the right thing to say. It came straight from the heart, and Jenny seemed to be pleased.

"Well, thanks! You don't look so bad yourself."

Raleigh had repacked after Jenny's call and was wearing clothes that had drawn positive comments in the past—he wanted to look his best.

He opened the door for her, got in himself, and started the engine.

As they were about to exit the parking lot, Raleigh asked, "Right or left?" They had not discussed where they were going. "You chose the restaurant."

"Left!" Jenny immediately replied. "Let's go to the Briarpatch."

"Perfect!" Raleigh answered. He was not familiar with a lot of eating establishments in the Huntsville area, but he was no stranger to the Briarpatch.

On a few occasions, he had made the ninety minute trip from Jasper just to eat there. The place was nothing fancy, and the food was not exotic; it was just plain country food. Located between Decatur and Huntsville, the restaurant offered a varied menu that Raleigh considered to be excellent. It was his kind of place, and Jenny had chosen it for their dinner date. He had a feeling that this was to be a special night.

Raleigh was not disappointed. They even made the same menu choice—catfish and iced tea. They talked over the basket of hushpuppies that the waitress placed on the table before the meal was served. Most of them were already gone when the catfish arrived.

He wanted the conversation to be as informative as possible. They hardly knew one another, and he wanted to know more about the delightful person with whom he shared the evening. As they began to talk, it was evident that she too wanted to know more about her dinner date.

They enjoyed their food, eating slowly as they talked. Raleigh learned that Jenny was involved in the design of futuristic spacecraft and held a position of responsibility within a select group. She again cited confidentiality as her reason for not discussing the specifics of her project, which was focused more on design than propulsion and actual space exploration, although various aspects of her work applied to both.

Raleigh let her tell what she wanted to reveal to him without interruptions or questions. He reminded himself that she had said that she needed to take a break from her work, and he wanted to allow her that needed respite from the responsibilities of her job.

After Jenny's inquiry, he briefly explained his duties with the parole board, but he elaborated as little as possible. There was so much to talk about, and the evening was passing much too rapidly.

Raleigh had initially planned to bring up the subject of their American Indian ancestry, but he soon realized that there would not be time to delve into the questions he had wanted to ask. Oddly enough, his personal interest in Jenny had expanded far beyond any answers he might get from her that would help him solve the mystery. He only hoped that she would agree to future dates so that they could become better acquainted.

After Raleigh returned Jenny to her car, he headed south toward home. They had agreed to stay in contact, but made no specific plans to meet again. Jenny had indicated that she would welcome a second invitation from Raleigh, but only after her work project was closer to completion. She said she hoped that it would not be long before they wrapped everything up on her current project but acknowledged that there were a lot of variables involved.

CHAPTER 18

———◆———

Raleigh had been going through the motions at work, but his thoughts were elsewhere. Two weeks passed since he left Jenny in the parking lot of the Space Center, with no additional contact with her. He had thought it impossible that a person could have such an impact on him, but he could not get her out of his mind.

Nevertheless, he was determined not to overplay his hand with her. He subdued numerous temptations to call her, reasoning that she would not be at home to answer the phone anyway. She had been straightforward in her desire to complete her work project before engaging in leisure activities. He would honor her wishes.

In an attempt to occupy his mind with something other than Jenny, Raleigh made a half-hearted attempt to research old Cherokee records. He gave up on the effort after reaching only dead ends regarding the family he was interested in.

On Friday night, Raleigh considered taking a short trip to a local bluegrass concert but decided that he was in no mood for fiddles and banjos. He opted instead to stay home and go online to make one more attempt to find a clue that might help him solve the mystery.

He had sat down to log on to the Internet when he was startled by the ringing of the phone. It was even more startling for him to hear a female voice on the line.

"Hi, this is Jenny. I was hoping I would find you at home. It's Friday night, though, so I thought you might be out."

"I didn't really have anywhere to go tonight, so I stayed at home."

"Good! I was hoping that I could reach you. I was wondering if you have big plans for tomorrow?"

"No, I have no big plans or little plans—no plans at all. That is, unless you had something in mind."

"Well, actually, that is the reason I called. I really need to get away from my work for a couple of days, and I thought it might be nice to go on a picnic. I will provide the food if you can come."

"Perfect! Do you have a place in mind?"

"I was thinking about the park at Brushy Lake. It's a beautiful place, and there are picnic tables we can use. I can tell you how to get there."

"Oh, Jenny, I'm plenty familiar with the park at Brushy Lake. I have been there several times."

"I think it would be nice to spend a good bit of the day there, if it's all right with you. Would ten o'clock in the morning be too early?"

"Ten o'clock it is, but I do want to bring something. Let me bring the drinks and desserts—and cups and plates and eating utensils."

"Okay! Fair enough. You might also want to bring a chair."

"I have a folding lounge chair that I can bring. I also have insect spray, which we might need. I'll see you at ten in the morning."

No more than thirty minutes earlier, Raleigh had removed his lounge chair and insect spray from the closet, while considering the trip to the bluegrass festival. They were still by the door. He was already half-prepared to head to Brushy Lake in the morning. He didn't even bother to turn on his computer.

 An alarm clock was not needed to wake Raleigh on Saturday morning. In fact, he hardly slept at all. He had difficulty believing that Jenny had actually called him and suggested they should meet again. Surely, someone as gorgeous as Jenny did not have to be calling someone to ask for a date—and she had chosen him.

Raleigh was about twenty minutes early as he neared the lake. He would rather wait on her than have her wait on him. As he pulled into the parking area, he was surprised to see that her car was already there.

She had laid claim to an empty picnic table by placing a tablecloth over it with a covered basket on top. Raleigh placed his drinks and other items beside the basket and began searching for Jenny. Her chair was under a large oak, but she was nowhere to be seen.

In a short time, he heard her call his name. She stood in a thicket of mountain laurel that was in full bloom.

"Come here, I want to show you something!" she called to him.

He headed her way after placing his chair near hers, and as he approached, she pointed toward a bird's nest, snugly built in a tangle of branches.

"Do you have any idea what kind of birds these are?" she asked as Raleigh observed the nest filled with hatchlings.

Their mouths were open, pointed upward, waiting for their next feeding.

"Hungry chicks," Raleigh chuckled. "I believe those are mockingbirds. That looks like a mockingbird nest. They build their nests in bushes like these and also in low trees and shrubs. I am no authority on birds, but the mockingbird is one of my favorites, so I know a little bit about them."

An alarmed bird flew close, complaining loudly about the intrusion.

"Yep, that's a mocking bird. She is pretty insistent that we leave. It won't be much longer before this will be an empty nest. They mature quickly."

"I suppose we had better leave them alone," Jenny added. "It's obviously feeding time."

"It's always feeding time for little chicks like this," Raleigh responded. As they walked back toward their chairs, he changed the subject. "I was really trying not to be late; I could have been here sooner."

"Oh, you're not late. I usually wake up early, and I decided to come on down. I have been here an hour I guess. There is nothing more relaxing to me than getting out and enjoying the beauties of nature. I suppose my Cherokee blood is partly responsible for that. I live in the city, but the country lives in me. I imagine that it is a characteristic I inherited from my people, and to be truthful, that is not all bad."

"I fully agree."

Raleigh could relate to Jenny's statement. It was this call that was the motivation behind his adventuresome spirit. It was this calling that had led him into the Sipsey canyon. Now he had met someone who was like-minded. He had no doubts that this would be a memorable day.

They positioned their chairs near enough that they could carry on a conversation. They had chatted only a few minutes before Jenny made a suggestion.

"Let's walk to the dam."

Brushy Lake was created when a rock dam was built during the time of the Great Depression. Work crews housed in a CCC camp nearby had constructed the dam between the cliff walls of a small gorge through which

Brushy Creek flowed. Water now cascaded over the rocks in the dam creating a beautiful, churning spectacle. There were protruding dry rocks that provided seating for Raleigh and Jenny. They sat there silent, with only the sounds of rippling water around them as they dangled their feet in the cascading flow.

Jenny broke the silence. "Sure does beat work!"

"For sure!" replied Raleigh. "Thank you, Jenny, for inviting me to share the day with you."

"Thanks for accepting my invitation. I get so caught up in my work that I think I can go nonstop forever. The pressure builds to the point that I release some of my frustrations when I should have more self control. The project is going quite well, but it does have its moments. Things don't always fall into place just the way that we would like for them to, and our project is quite complex, to say the least. Very complicated! From experience, I know that things click better for me when I am refreshed. But, I didn't come here to talk about my work. Have you noticed how pretty the sky looks today with those fluffy white clouds?"

"Interesting that you should ask. I was just looking at that one there." He pointed to a cloud almost directly overhead. "I see a steam locomotive. Those fine clouds billowing up above it look like smoke puffing from the stack. This reminds me of my childhood. As a kid, I could see almost anything in the clouds. It's sad that as we grow older we tend to lose some of that youthful imagination. Kids today are not into looking at cloud formations. Their time is spent inside, where they play video games, access the Internet, talk on the phone, or watch T.V. Think of all those pretty cloud formations that are going to waste! I think it to be a regrettable thing."

"Times change! Sometimes I don't think the change is for the best, but who am I to say? I spend the majority of my time trying to figure out a way to get above these clouds, even slap out of this planet that we call home! Oh well."

They sat on the dam, saying nothing, listening to the ripple of the water, the songs of the birds, the breeze whistling through the pines, and all the other voices of nature. Raleigh occasionally pointed to the "cloud art" as it drifted overhead. There was an eagle with outstretched wings, a fire-breathing dragon, and Jenny had to admit, a fairly decent space rocket in flight.

Jenny's attention was drawn to a water snake as it slithered up the wet rocks of the dam. It posed no danger to their safety, and they watched it until it disappeared in a rock crevice.

"Let's go eat," Jenny suggested as she noticed that the sun was almost directly overhead.

After walking back to the picnic area, Jenny began to prepare the food and produced a vase of wildflowers for the centerpiece.

It was a beautiful Saturday, and the picnic area began to fill with couples and families enjoying a weekend outing. The park quickly became a beehive of activities. There were a number of children playing and laughing, effectively drowning out the sounds of nature that Raleigh and Jenny had enjoyed at the dam.

Jenny had not depended on a deli to feed them on this outing. There was chicken in the basket, and it was apparent that she had spent some time in preparing it.

"I hope you like chicken," she said as she began placing food on the table. "I prepared some grilled, some fried, and I even made chicken salad."

There was enough food to feed half the hungry kids that were running around the park.

Raleigh had made a mental note that Jenny ordered sweetened iced tea at the Briarpatch restaurant when they had dinner together. He produced a gallon of sweet tea, as well as varied soft drinks and water, keeping it all on ice in his cooler. He had also made a late trip to the bakery, where he purchased a variety of sweets.

They enjoyed the picnic, eating slowly and talking. The pressures of their jobs had drifted away with the moving clouds.

The shade of the large oak had moved with the passing sun. They repositioned their chairs occasionally so as to get the maximum cover offered by the dense branches.

He noticed that she moved her chair closer to him than it had been previously. As they followed the shade once again, Raleigh allowed Jenny to sit down first before reclining beside her.

He was surprised when Jenny reached over and took his hand. She said nothing, just leaned back in her lounge chair, closed her eyes, and lightly squeezed his hand. It was as natural as if they had been friends for years.

Raleigh returned the squeeze and turned his head to face her. She opened her eyes, saw him looking at her, gave him a slight wink, and smiled.

"This isn't half bad," she said softly.

The hand-holding lasted only a few minutes, but its impact on Raleigh was overwhelming.

Maybe she does care for me, he reasoned to himself. *The most beautiful, most exciting, most appealing girl I have ever met, and she's holding my hand!*

He was certain that he would wake up and find that it was all a dream, but a ball smashing on his cheek confirmed that he was indeed awake.

Jenny picked up the beach ball and threw it back to the kids, who had in turn kicked it back to her. She picked it up and threw it toward Raleigh. Her aim was perfect. Raleigh kicked the ball back to the children, and soon they had joined them in their ball playing. The day passed rapidly.

In the late afternoon, the children began to leave, and Raleigh and Jenny once again repositioned their chairs to move with the shade. When they sat back down, their hands moved together to resume where they had left off before the intrusion of the ball.

Raleigh could feel warmth—an emotion—an attached bliss flowing through their clasped hands. It was a feeling that he had never previously experienced. He wanted the day to last forever.

He sensed that Jenny was also enjoying the moment. An occasional gentle squeeze indicated that the hand-holding was more than a token gesture. Still, however, they were virtually strangers, knowing very little about each other.

Raleigh began to speak, "Jenny, tell me about yourself—anything. I want to know more about you."

There were a few moments of silence.

"Where do I start? I consider myself to be just an average person—no exciting episodes to talk about. I entered no beauty contests, so I didn't win any. I didn't try out for group sports or cheerleading. It just wasn't my thing. I *did* study hard, and I made good grades in school. I finished at the top of my class, but I suppose good grades come at the expense of a full social life.

"Parties, proms, and late night activities were never a part of my lifestyle. I grew up a happy child, and I have no regrets. I am doing what I have wanted to do since I was old enough to make a career choice. No one could ask for more than that. I suppose anything I might have to say would be dull—boring, actually. Let's talk about you. I'm sure your story would be more exciting!"

"My job sometimes gets exciting, but I'm afraid that my life is not filled with heroics. I wasn't a quarterback,

I didn't drive a fast car, and neither was I a late night person. I can't honestly claim to have been a straight A student, nor was I at the top of my class. I did make good grades and had little difficulty with my school work though. I also am doing what I long aspired to do and am very content with my life choices."

The sun was beginning to set, and the sign at the entrance to the park declared that the gates would be locked at sunset. Before leaving, they revisited the picnic basket and enjoyed leftovers from the noon meal.

The park was once again quiet, except for the renewed sounds of nature. The frogs had now become the most vocal of the park's inhabitants, calling back and forth across the water. The birds made their final statement before roosting for the night, the crickets and other insects increased their volume of calls so as to be heard above the frogs, and the clouds all disappeared from the sky so as not to obstruct the twinkling stars that were scheduled to appear for their night shift.

It was a perfect setting, but the day was preparing to make way for the darkness. They made their way to their cars, knowing that the park's gate would soon be locked. In the distance, the sound of the ranger's truck became louder as he neared the park to secure the lock.

Raleigh faced Jenny, took her hands in his, looked into her sparkling brown eyes, and then gently kissed her lips—for a very short moment.

"Thanks for an absolutely gorgeous day," he said sincerely. "It was perfect."

They drove out of the gate as the green and white truck of the forest ranger rounded the last curve before reaching the park. Raleigh turned south toward Jasper; Jenny headed north toward Huntsville.

The kiss, though brief, was the crown jewel of the day. The contact had awakened a lifetime of dormant emotions; emotions Raleigh had been unaware that he possessed. And although neither of them could have known, this was the first significant kiss that either of them had ever experienced.

Jenny came to realize there could be things that are more explosive than rocket engines. Of one thing both were certain. They would be together again at the first opportunity.

CHAPTER 19

Jenny was not the woman Raleigh had envisioned for his life. For so long he had been the confirmed bachelor who refused to be tied down to anyone or anything that might threaten his free-spirited ways. He had imagined that if he did settle down, it would be with someone who knew the wilderness and who would accompany him on his hikes. So far a picnic at a forest lake had been the extent of their outdoor adventures together. Jenny was committed to an entirely different lifestyle than his. She got up early every day, worked in a restrictive environment involving secret activities, and rarely saw the light of day.

Raleigh spent the next several days pondering this sudden turn in his life. He had gone out in search of information relating to the old journal, but he had found her instead. He had made no progress in his investigation, and he had not mentioned his motive for attending the meeting of the Echota Tribe. He had now seen Jenny a couple of times, but he had asked her nothing about her knowledge of the Cherokee people.

It didn't make sense to him; this was not the ideal match he'd had in mind for a serious relationship. He had always loved being footloose and fancy-free; she was hogtied and penned up in her work, and yet he couldn't stop thinking about her.

In the past, Raleigh had laughed at those who cautioned him that one day, when he was least expecting it, he would turn a corner and there would be a girl who would change his life. He was laughing no longer. It had happened exactly the way they said it would.

Jenny was someone he wanted to know much better, but he was apprehensive that she might not share the same feelings for him. He hoped that she had left Brushy Lake with a greater appreciation of him and that this would translate into additional meetings together.

Raleigh decided to initiate the next date. He allowed two weeks to pass before calling her.

"Hello, Jenny, this is Raleigh."

There was a slight pause before the reply. "Hi, Raleigh. It's good to hear from you."

"Listen, I know you're a busy person, and I don't want to be an interruption, but I was hoping that maybe we could get together again if possible. The time we spent together at the lake was a delight for me," he said into the phone, waiting hopefully for her answer.

"It was for me also, Raleigh," he heard her say. "I was tempted to call you myself, but I was afraid that maybe I've been coming off too strong. I know I have an assertive nature, so I thought it best to let you have a little say in our contacts together."

He didn't waste any time in responding. "I have tomorrow free. How about you?"

"I had *last* Saturday free, hoping to hear from you. I'm glad it won't be two in a row. What do you have in mind?"

"I have a boat on Smith Lake that needs to be used. What about a day on the lake this time? Do you water ski?"

"I don't ski, but I can ride in a boat," she said cheerfully. "I understand that Smith Lake has about five hundred miles of shoreline, so I guess we could ride as long as we like and not have to look at the same scenery."

"Great! Meet me at Duncan Bridge at ten o'clock sharp this time. My boathouse is only a short distance from there."

"I'll see you in the morning at ten. I'll stop by a deli on the way and pick up lunch. You bring drinks. Will bologna sandwiches work?" she laughed. "Just kidding! I'll bring some lunchmeat and cheese, and we'll eat sandwiches. Is that okay with you?"

"Good enough! I'll bring a cooler of cold drinks on ice. See you in the morning."

Jenny was waiting as Raleigh arrived at the bridge the next day, and she followed him to the lake lot where his boathouse was located. His lot was in a subdivision that was only partially developed. Boathouses were spread along the shoreline, and seasonal dwellings provided a level of security.

Raleigh did not use his boat as frequently as he had first intended. This was largely due to the fact that he did not always have someone to accompany him on the lake. As Jenny followed him from the bridge, his investment in this boating equipment was beginning to feel more significant.

From his boathouse, Raleigh could ride almost all day in either direction. Today, as he and Jenny loaded up their supplies in the boat and pulled away from the dock, he headed east toward the dam.

"So where exactly are we going?" Jenny asked over the sound of the motor.

"Goat Island."

"What a glamorous name," Jenny said with a wry smile. "Why is it called that?"

"It used to be inhabited by a herd of goats," he answered, smiling back. "It has a perfect beach for picnics."

He had an additional reason for wanting to visit this particular spot. During the dry season, with the water at its lowest level, arrowheads and other artifacts could sometimes be found along its banks. During the time that the area was populated by Native Americans, the area was a high strip of land where a tributary joined Ryan Creek, and this elevated land offered safety from flood waters.

There had once been an established settlement there for thousands of years. Artifacts dating back over ten thousand years to the Paleo period had been found there. An abundance of flint chips left by the early stone knappers could still be seen in some places.

Raleigh chose this place to picnic because he felt that it would bring them close to their roots.

He and Jenny traveled at a moderate speed. The surface of the water was as smooth as glass, and they rode for almost two hours before reaching the island. Both enjoyed the ride, commenting occasionally about the scenery or the grand lake houses that had been constructed along the shore.

Around noon, Raleigh pulled the boat up to the island. He secured the boat by tying it to a large piece of driftwood that had been left stranded on the bank.

Jenny jumped to the shore and began to make preparations for their picnic. She spread a tablecloth over the sand and started making the sandwiches. In a short time they were ready to eat. They had brought along the lounge chairs, but they decided to sit on the sand and eat their lunch.

After they finished eating, Jenny retrieved the sunscreen she had packed. After a generous application, she offered some to Raleigh. He declined the offer. His frequent excursions outdoors had further tanned his already dark complexion.

There were few shade trees on Goat Island like there were in the park at Brushy Lake. Raleigh suggested they take a stroll around the island instead of sitting in the sun doing nothing, deciding that wading along the shallow shoreline would be more refreshing.

There had been less rain than normal in the spring, resulting in exposed areas that would normally be underwater. Several fishing lures that had been lost when snagged on submerged tree roots or rock outcroppings were now visible. They left them just as they were found in case a fisherman might later return to look for them.

Holding hands while they strolled now seemed natural for them. As they walked and talked, they were oblivious to the passing boats and water-skiers who were also enjoying the beautiful weekend.

"An arrowhead!" Jenny exclaimed as she stooped to pick up the artifact.

It was quite large and perfectly knapped—an impressive find. She handed it to Raleigh.

"A Pickwick," he identified the projectile after a close examination. "They are rather common to this area but still a good find. This is a classic example of a Pickwick point—and a large one at that. These date back a long time, but not as far back as the Paleo points do."

"That's interesting." Jenny took the arrowhead back and reexamined it. "What do you think we should do with it?"

"I suppose that technically it is illegal to remove it, although the restrictions apply more to artifacts found on federally protected lands. This is Alabama Power Company land here. It was in plain view, and it was there for you to see and pick up, so I suppose that it's yours if you want it."

"I *would* like to keep it, but that might not be the proper thing to do. This was made by our ancestors thousands of years ago and has been here, unmolested, since that time. I think we should just leave it here."

"If we do," Raleigh responded, "let's try to place it where it might stay for a few more thousand years. If we just leave it lying here, it won't be long before it will be in someone's collection box."

Jenny spied a large mussel shell, hinged open, lying at the edge of the water. A raccoon or other animal had probably dined on its inhabitant, leaving the empty shell. Both man and animals have dined on shellfish from local creeks and rivers for as long as the arrowhead Jenny held had been formed. Their ancestors left huge mounds of mussel shells on the shoals of the river, which is now called the Tennessee.

Jenny picked up the shell and held it with the arrowhead. Raleigh could not suppress the urge to give a short history lesson.

"The mussel is one of the major reasons this area was so appealing to the early Native Americans. There was plenty of water here as well as mussels. Shellfish was one of their favorite staples and was available year round. On the Tennessee River in Muscle Shoals, the earlier inhabitants of this region left huge mounds of mussel shells, which had collected over the millenniums.

"There, as what has happened here, the dams were built, and the natural habitat of the mussel was covered with deep water. The shoals were lost to the resulting impoundment, and the mounds of shells still lie beneath the lakes created by the dams. A great number of species were lost forever, but there are a few survivors of certain types—," Raleigh stopped. "I'm sorry. I don't mean to talk so much. What did you have in mind to do with the shell?"

"I am going to put the arrowhead in it and bury them as deeply as possible. Maybe in two thousand years the sand will have washed away, revealing it again. And then, some couple out for a Saturday afternoon picnic will find it, put it in a surviving mussel shell, and bury it again to be found another two thousand years later."

The arrowhead was so large that the shell would not close tightly, but she walked a distance from the shoreline, dug deeply into the sand, and deposited her find.

"For another millennium or two," she said as she patted the sand. "Rest in peace, and may the ages be kind to you!"

The ceremony was over, and they continued their stroll around the island, not mentioning the incident again.

A breeze blew across the water, and the weather was quite pleasant. Ending their stroll around the island, they went to their chairs and reclined under the afternoon sun.

"If we could recall a few thousand years," Raleigh speculated, "we might be in the midst of a hundred or so villagers who would have no clue as to the fate of their beloved settlement. They would probably be going about their daily routines, concerned only about the present. There is no way they could have even begun to envision the changes that our generation has made on the land. Maybe it's been for the better. Maybe not."

"And now we are going for that change in outer space," Jenny mulled over Raleigh's statement. "And maybe that will be for the better. Maybe not."

She thought for a minute longer before speaking again. "And I am smack dab in the middle of it. Sometimes I wonder what the heck I'm doing there! And to think—I have even lost sleep over some of the problems preventing us from doing even more in space. Who knows what consequences our space activities may have a thousand, two thousand years from now?

"Oh well, it's all in the name of progress, and the work pays my bills. Someone will do it; it might as well be me. We've come a long way from stone tools to spaceships; from mussel meals to gourmet restaurants."

"It can be mindboggling actually," Raleigh weighed in. "What may be even more mindboggling is where our world and its people will be in a thousand years. It is impossible for us to even fathom in our minds today what the future holds for this planet and its inhabitants—humans, animals, or plants." He continued after a short pause, "This conversation is getting deeper than that lake out there, so how about a change of subject?"

Raleigh looked at Jenny as he spoke again. "Jenny, tell me something about your heritage. How much do you know about your Indian ancestry?"

He had finally asked the question he had initially planned to ask at their first meeting. It had been a long time coming, and his interests were beginning to shift, but he was still committed to the completion of his investigation into the fate of Eve and her family.

Jenny did not answer immediately. She sat and contemplated her reply.

"I really don't know how to answer that question," she said in a halting manner. "I must admit that it's not something I spent a lot of time discussing when I was younger, and in all honesty, it was a topic in which I had very little interest. My parents and grandparents would occasionally talk about it, but I didn't pay much attention. Our family chose to live in the present and let the past be forgotten.

"I think that's true with most of our people who escaped the removal. Our ancestors believed that if they talked too much, they would be carted off to Oklahoma. Perhaps later, after I think about it more, I can discuss it with you more easily; but I can tell you up front, what

I know about my ancestral family would fit more easily into that mussel shell than the arrowhead did."

Raleigh could relate well to Jenny's statement.

"I understand what you're saying, and you're absolutely right. This is a common reaction among many of the remaining Native Americans who managed to escape the one-way trip to Oklahoma. There were plenty of white people who were searching for any Indian that they could turn in. Then they would jump right in and lay claim to the possessions that might be left behind."

"The memories of the Trail of Tears have certainly had a deep emotional impact on our people, and rightfully so," Jenny said. "A great injustice was carried out on the Cherokee, the Creek—on all the tribes. At the same time, the black slaves were valued only by the amount of work they could be forced to do to satisfy their masters, and then came the Civil War.

"The land was stolen from the Native Americans, and the Africans were stolen from their lands. I suppose that it was inevitable from the time that the first pilgrims began to occupy the land on this continent and the first slaves were imported from Africa that the ownership of the "New World" would gradually change hands. It was new only to the foreign intruders. With fertile lands, labor to produce profitable crops on this soil and rich natural resources, it was inescapable that the strong would suppress the weak. This is the nature of greed. Two hundred years have passed, the transfer of title has been completed, and there is no turning back. There is nothing to do now but to accept reality and go on with our lives."

"So true, Jenny. But that doesn't mean that we have to be happy about it or erase the memories of the crimes that have been committed against our people. Some might argue that we should now just label ourselves as Americans, accept that what's done is done, let bygones be bygones, and find our little niche in life and live it to the fullest.

"There is little dispute that this land has been transformed into the greatest nation on earth. It might even be that if we could be able to spend a short time in the world of our ancestors, with their tribal conflicts, limited food supply, lack of medical care, primitive shelters, and harsh conditions, that we would gladly welcome a return to the modern age. But this does not negate the great injustice that was forced upon them without their consent and against their will. We can always find something to complain about, so maybe we should just give thanks and enjoy what we have. However, it still upsets me to know that we gave the true owners of this land no choice as to what their wishes might have been or where they would like to live."

Jenny smiled. "You got back on your soap box again! Seems like I may have helped you climb up there. But you are completely right in what you said. There is no turning back the clock, and very few would want to. Yet this does not justify the harsh treatment that was inflicted on our people who had their lands stolen from them."

"That has always been the way of mankind. I suppose there has never been a time when there was not some great injustice perpetrated on the weak and innocent. If it happens to be directed against us and our people, it is a big deal. When it happens elsewhere, we hardly give it a passing thought. That's the way it has always been and probably always will be."

Jenny and Raleigh sat for a while without speaking. Jenny reached for Raleigh's hand and held it as she had at Brushy Lake.

Eventually she spoke again. "That was a non-answer to your question about my heritage. We got off on our stump speeches, and I didn't tell you much. But you understand—I don't know much. My grandmother is still living. She's getting very old, but her memory is still as sharp as ever. One of these days I am going to sit down with her and have her tell the story of our people as she remembers it. It should be soon though, because she won't live forever.

"All my life I have been too busy to really stop and hear her life story. Other things have always seemed more important. We're fortunate to live in an era when we can electronically record images and information from those who precede us to pass down to those who will follow—another advantage of living in this modern age."

"There are very few who take advantage of this opportunity. Like us, most are too busy to take the time, and it would be so valuable for future generations. Usually, we don't think about it until it's too late," Raleigh said.

"I'm happy that we had this conversation, Raleigh. This is something that I really do need to do soon and would probably not have realized it otherwise," she said before inquiring, "What about your ancestry? Tell me something about your family."

"Okay, first off, I was not raised a country boy. Sorry, Jenny. I guess you could say that I come from a middleclass family. I never went to bed hungry, but I certainly was not a rich kid. My father has been involved in medical research for many years. His work is in the field of birth deformities and childhood disorders.

"When he was growing up, he aspired to be a pediatrician, but he did research during his studies and was quite good at that. He became so involved in it that he turned his focus toward the field of medical research. Somewhere in his past, he realized that he wanted to be a factor in helping the young overcome early physical adversities over which they have no control. His philosophy is that everyone deserves an equal opportunity in life whenever possible."

"That is a noble aim in life, for sure. I'm impressed! Tell me more about him—and your mother."

"I'm extremely proud of my parents. Both are very compassionate individuals. I suppose I didn't fully realize the extent of their empathetic natures until I became an adult. It was always there, but as we have discussed, young people are too involved in other things to notice some of the most important aspects of life. My father was always willing to help anyone who was ill or down on their luck. His ancestors were reportedly always a very compassionate group.

"There is a saying that has been passed down through our family for generations. I have heard my dad quote it many times when he was bogged down in some research project and needed a little boost to help relieve the pressure he was experiencing. When I was very young, I learned that medical research can be demanding and sometimes very disappointing—maybe somewhat like your work.

"When he would seem to have reached a dead end on a project that he had been working on for a period of time, he would quote that saying and turn his attention toward another possible solution in his research. He quoted it often enough that I learned it also. He even had it hand-printed and framed. The copy still hangs on the wall of his lab office above his desk. I hadn't thought about it for a while, but I can visualize the message as he has it written..."

Raleigh recited the quote from memory.

"Helpless we begin our life
Dependent on a man and wife
Nurtured then by love and care
We must each our burdens bear
Helpful then we must become
Troubles will surely fall on some
With the golden rule to guide
Help is always by your side
Always do unto others as you
Would have them do to you."

Raleigh paused. "My mother took that attitude to heart also."

"Tell me about your mother. Your dad seems like a great person, and I am sure your mother is special too."

"Very special! She was a housewife and mother until I started school, and then she accepted a job as an elementary school librarian, where she had been a volunteer for many years. She gave the job her full attention, and consequently, after over a period of almost twenty years, she has a lot of admiring students. The ones who have now graduated are always anxious to talk to her when she meets them away from the school grounds. She is also a very caring person. I have great parents for which I am very thankful. Maybe someday you can get to know them."

"And I would like to."

"My parents, especially my dad, wanted me to be a medical doctor, specializing in the field in which he researches. This was a dream of his, and I suppose I let him down. There's too much of the red man's blood in me to commit to a lifetime confined in a hospital or lab— no offense to my dad or to you—it's just who I am. I really feel that I was called to work with the disturbed and criminal element in our society. There is no shortage of those in that group who are in need of help."

Raleigh stopped, suddenly taking notice of the light in the sky. "I could talk about this for a while, but it's time we head back to the boat dock. We want to get back before dark."

The return trip took another two hours. There was enough of the day remaining that they were able to complete the excursion at a leisurely pace.

The sun was beginning to set as they neared the dock. It had been another enjoyable day together. Raleigh was determined that this time, before Jenny's departure, a date would be set for them to meet again. He was about to inquire about the possibility of their meeting again the following week when Jenny spoke.

"I think I'm going to spend next weekend with my family. God forbid that anything should happen to my grandmother, but I want to make sure that I talk to her as soon as possible. I'll also check to see what knowledge my parents have about our family tree. If I procrastinate on this I'll never do it. Would it be okay if we got together again in a couple of weeks? My place or yours—your choice. I'll share whatever information I get with you."

"Sounds like a winner," Raleigh replied. "I'll be in touch with you, and we'll decide where we want to meet. I think I'll spend next weekend with my folks too. They may be able to pull a few skeletons out of our family's closet as well."

Raleigh wanted to ask Jenny if she could ask specific questions that might assist him in his quest for information about the family of Gray Fox and Eve, but he decided against it, hoping that maybe someday he could talk face to face with her grandmother.

CHAPTER 20

———◆———

"I had no idea—not even a clue!" Jenny said when she called Raleigh on the Monday night following the weekend with her family. "Grandmother is so full of tales of the past that I spent the entire weekend listening to one fascinating story after another. She started talking, and it was as though she had all this information bottled up and was waiting for someone to pop the cork. The stories came pouring out, and I recorded almost everything she said. I am so happy that I was able to chronicle this before it was lost forever."

"I'm pleased that you didn't let your generation down by failing to keep your family's history alive," he said in reply. "Maybe, by your having recorded your grandmother's stories, there will be a better chance that future descendants of your family will continue passing them down through the years."

"I think I told you that my grandmother has almost pure Cherokee blood. I am told that somewhere, a long time ago, it got mixed a little, but mostly it has been Cherokee marrying Cherokee. My grandfather was pure Cherokee. I definitely get my looks from my grandparents. When I was small, I was somewhat self-conscious about my dark skin and obvious Indian features, but now they give me a sense of dignity. My visit with my grandmother over the weekend seemed to reinforce this pride in my heritage. I am so glad that I went, and I will definitely visit more often while I still can."

"Most of us get so busy doing routine things that we forget, or ignore, things of more importance. Many times it's too late after we finally get our priorities straight. I realized this when I went home for the weekend. Those home-cooked meals weren't so bad either. This ole single fellow still misses his mother's cooking. We have a heritage that is really priceless, but we live too fast to realize it. I want to hear your story. Can we get together over the weekend?"

"I would love that. Would you mind driving up here to Huntsville Saturday to meet me at my apartment? I digitally recorded hours of conversations with Grandmother, and I have the necessary equipment to play it. I could cook dinner for us. I'm sure it won't be like your mom's cooking, so don't expect that, but it will be edible. After that, we can begin watching the recordings. I think you'll be interested in what she had to say."

"It seems like we've already established ten o'clock as our meeting time. Will that be okay for Saturday?"

"See you Saturday at ten. I'll give you my address and directions."

Raleigh carefully recorded Jenny's address and the directions she gave to get there. She had become a significant person in his life in only a short time. He was unsure in what direction this might be leading him, but he was certain that he was a willing participant. He went to bed shortly after they hung up.

Jenny's apartment was not difficult to find. She was waiting and met him at the door, greeting him before he could even ring the doorbell. Although they had not discussed any plans to leave the apartment, she was dressed as if he was taking her out for a special event. As usual, she wore little makeup, but her natural beauty was stunning. Her simple greeting began to arouse emotions he was unaware he possessed until he met her. He spoke a greeting in return and could not resist placing a kiss on her willing lips. With great restraint he resisted showing further affection for her, being very careful not to make a misstep that might cause her to doubt the nature of his attraction for her.

Jenny had a pitcher of iced tea and some sliced fruit on the table for a morning snack. It was a simple offering, perhaps with the keeping of the entire environment of her apartment. The basic pieces of furniture were there, but there was no excess. It was a two-bedroom apartment, but one of the rooms had been converted into a work area with a computer and other electronic equipment. After their snack, Jenny made preparations to view the video of her grandmother.

They entered the room, and Jenny closed the door behind them.

"Now that I have you as a captive audience, I'm going to..." she paused, looked at Raleigh in a seductive way, paused again, and then added, "...start from the beginning." She looked at Raleigh with a sheepish grin, gave him a wink, and then continued. "Have a seat." She motioned toward a chair near him.

She positioned a similar chair next to him and sat down, holding her remote control. She activated the video player, and an image appeared on the screen. Raleigh saw an elderly woman of undeniable Indian heritage seated in a rocking chair.

He was immediately impressed by the similarities in appearance of Jenny and her grandmother. Although the years had taken their toll, it was clear that the elderly woman had once been a beautiful young woman. Her face still displayed the high cheekbones and perfectly carved features that would have made her the prized catch of any brave young warrior. Jenny's grandfather must have considered himself the luckiest man alive when he secured her hand in marriage.

In the video, Jenny began the conversation by having her grandmother introduce herself and say a few words about her family.

"My name is Mattie Jackson. I was a Borden before I married, leastwise that is my English name, or I might rightly say that it is my name now. I was given a Cherokee name when I was born..." And thus she continued. "I was born in 1918, or that's what I've been told, so that puts me past ninety. I never dreamed when I was little that I would make it to see ninety years, but times are different now. They got stuff that will get you well that they didn't have when I was a little girl, not that I have been sick all that much anyway.

"Now Silas, that was my husband, died years back. There weren't much that they could do for him once he was taken down sick. I shore do miss him still, but I get along; and I suppose that it won't be long until I join him in that happy hunting ground, or wherever he might be. It can't be that much longer, cause I am an old woman. I've got the most out of life, leastwise, as much as I actually could, considering the treatment they gave us Cherokee.

"It just weren't right at all the way that they done us, but there weren't nothing nobody could do about it, so we had to do it the way they made us do. Course we were one of the lucky ones. We weren't made to go cross the Mississippi—but they would if they could. Now you know that my family did quite well and we had a plenty, but the white man would have took it if he could."

Mattie paused and looked at Jenny. "Now what was it that you wanted me to say? Something about my family?"

"Yes, Grandmother, tell us your family history as you remember it—maybe some stories you heard as you were growing up—anything you might remember."

"I suppose I got to talking there, saying things you don't need to know, but the older I get the more I think about them things that happened when I was little. Course we couldn't say much about that back then, else they would have come and picked us up and put us on a train to Indian Territory, and we didn't want none of that. We just kept our mouths shut and told people that we were Black Dutch, and they pretty much left us alone. Course now I know they ain't gonna ship us over there to Oklahoma, cause now that land out there is just as important to them as this is here. I still don't feel exactly right talking about this, but as I say, I ain't going to be around here much longer anyhow, and it is only right that those young people know about what our people have been put through."

Jenny interrupted and directed the conversation back to the family aspect of it. Mattie continued her discussion.

"Truth be known, I don't know a great deal about our side of the family. 'Bout all I know is what I heard the old timers talk about when we would be outside 'round the fire talking when we knew there weren't nobody around that would turn us in. I can tell you some of those stories seeing as to how they pretty much stuck with me, my being a little girl and all, hearing them old tales.

"When we would get together as family, I remember the old folks would spend much of the night on the creek bank fishing. They would call it tight line fishing. They didn't use no corks or nothing for bobbers. They would cut that river cane for poles and get a stout line and fishhooks. They had them cotton lines back then; there weren't any of this catgut stuff. They baited the hooks with these big ole worms what we called night crawlers, but some of them men called them fiddle worms cause they would fiddle them out of the ground by vibrations somehow. I don't know exactly how it was done 'cause I never catered to that kind of doings, but some way they took an old dull handsaw and cut off a hardwood sapling pretty low and ran a wood hasp or rough bar across the stump and caused the vibrations..."

Jenny interrupted, "Grandmother, I don't believe that any of us are going worm fishing anytime soon, so maybe it's not that important how they got the worms. Let me hear some of the stories they had to tell."

"Yeah, I guess I'm bad to get off on what I've got to say. I 'spect that you couldn't find any of them fiddle worms about nowadays anyhow seeing that there ain't no more places like what there was when they use to find them. Nowadays, there ain't no land left what don't have a house or a road on it. But back to what I was saying. We could all go down to the creek before dark and tote up some sticks and pile them up and build up a big fire. Then we would go to the cane break and get the biggest fishing canes we could find and tie a piece of that stout cord to it. We would fish that tight line and them big ole catfish loved them night crawlers. We would drag up a big log or two and sit around the fire and listen to the old folks tell their stories. Every now and then we would go and run our lines, and most of the time we would have a wash tub full of fish come morning, and they were some mighty fine eating. You can't get fish like that no more these days. Nowadays they get the catfish out of ponds, and they raise them so fast they don't have that good flavor what once the..."

Jenny interrupted again, "Grandmother," she spoke softly, "you said that you can still recall some of the tales that were told while you were sitting around the fire. I would like to hear some of those stories that you said you remember."

"Lordy, child, there was so many of them that I don't rightly know where to start. I remember one that Uncle Ike—now he was a full-blood Cherokee too, you know—liked to tell. I heard it a bunch of times. It had to do with a pack of huntin' dogs he kept to hunt them wild bears. There was a plenty of them wild black bears in the forest back then. They ain't there no more cause the white man has killed them all just for the fun of it. Now that just ain't right, but they went and did it anyway..."

She explained in detail her Uncle Ike's wild bear dog story. She followed that with other tales she remembered from the campfire days. All very interesting to Raleigh, but they shed no light on the questions he wanted answered.

"We'll take a break from this for a while," Jenny said as she moved toward the video player. "That is about all I have on this memory card, but there is another. If you're not in a hurry, we'll eat and then watch more of it following our dinner, or you might be so bored with this whole thing that you've heard enough. If you're tired of watching, please tell me; I'll certainly understand."

"Oh no! I'm enjoying it—honestly! I want to watch it all. Just kick me out the door when you want me to leave."

Jenny laughed. "I think I'm hardly big enough to do any kicking. I don't have but one operational bedroom, but if you like, we can continue watching this and you could sleep on the couch tonight—that is, unless you have other plans. I spent all of last weekend recording, and grandmother still has a lot more to say. Or we could save the remainder for another day if you..."

"No," Raleigh hastily interrupted. "I have nothing planned, and the couch will be just fine. I've been backpacking many times when a couch would have felt like a feather bed. I like the suggestion. So you don't mind having a man in your apartment overnight?"

"I trust you!"

Jenny headed into the kitchen to prepare their dinner. Her grandmother had not revealed the information that Raleigh was searching for, but she did have a clear memory of her childhood activities, and the stories that she told were interesting.

As they ate, Raleigh thought it would be a good time for him to inquire of Jenny whether she had been able to trace her ancestry back for any length of time. Her initial request to her grandmother had been that she provide some family history, but as of yet, that information had not been disclosed in the video.

"I know there is a lot of video remaining for me to watch, but I was wondering if you were able to climb any family tree with her. Do you know any more about your family, dating back to the time of the removal?"

"I asked her about that several times; she always changed the subject. You will see that this is the first question that I ask her when we start the video again, but she avoids the question just like she did when we started. It seems that she would rather talk about worms and catfish than about Riddles and Bordens—or whatever Cherokee names we may have had then.

"I left with the impression that she just doesn't know a whole lot about her ancestors. I think it might go back to her childhood when she learned that the least said about her Cherokee roots the better it would be. In fact, she said as much when I was talking to her while not recording it. I specifically asked her if she would talk more about her parents and grandparents, and she said that she had already told all that she knew, which was very little. She just would not talk about it."

"Lots of people cannot get any further than the first branch of their family tree. That information would be nice to have, but at least you got as much information as you could from your grandmother. I know you tried!"

"Maybe somewhere down the road I will be able to learn more. You're right—I tried, and that is the best I can do for now. She does have an interesting story that she tells when we start the recording again. I think you'll enjoy it."

Jenny started the video again after they had enjoyed their meal. As she had already explained, she asked her grandmother about the history of the family.

Her grandmother responded by saying, "I've got another story that I want to tell you before I forget it."

She looked directly at Jenny as she talked, occasionally glancing downward as if in thought. She seemed determined to tell her story as she had heard it as a child.

"Now this story what I'm gonna tell, maybe I shouldn't ought to 'cause I never heard it more than twice, and then it was whenever I sneaked around and listened to my dad and uncles talk when they didn't know I was anywhere around. I was bad about doing that till I got caught one time and got a whoopin' 'cause of it. The old folks wouldn't talk some things round those creek fires when all the young'uns was around. It was always them stories like what I already done told you. Sometimes when the grown folks got together at home, they would send us kids off to bed and have some serious talk. I would sneak out of bed and hide so that I could hear what they were talking about, that is until they caught me that time. After that, they would check to make sure that we were where we were s'pose to be. I heard a lot before they caught me, but I never repeated a word of it—still ain't.

"I told you that other stuff because I heard it till I could have told it myself. But what I am going to tell you, I ain't breathed a word of it to nobody—never. I ain't got many years before what I know is going to go in the ground with me, and I am too old to worry about what might happen after I am gone."

"That's why I want to record this, Grandmother," Jenny reassured her of her intentions. "But I hope you will be around for many more years."

"Well, as I was saying, this story ain't one for little kids' ears. Turns out, not all the girls in our family were fair, young virgins or all the boys brave, young, fearless warriors. I guess this was the reason for all the hush-hush when the men used to tell this story. I'm gonna tell this to the best of my recollection, seeing as to how about eighty years have passed since I heard it."

Raleigh sat in anticipation as Mattie began her story. It was indeed fascinating, and Raleigh absorbed every word of it.

CHAPTER 21

◆

"It seems that there was this young Indian girl who matured rather young and was not above making an occasional trip into the woods with a young brave to assist him in proving his manhood. Now, when I heard them men telling this story, they would get more detailed about this part of it and say words that were above my maturity level, and that part never stuck. Course, that's probably another reason why they didn't want young ears to hear what they had to say.

From what I remember though, she was not so much as a whore as it was that she just liked it and was a hot Indian woman who was easily talked into sharing what she had; now, you know how men are. All this stuff happened long before my father's time, and I think that part of it was more imagination and men's talk than what they really knew about it.

Now, what was s'pose to have occurred was that before she knew what was happening, she got in a motherly way. She didn't have no husband, and back then, if'n you got that way, no matter whether or not you were married, you had to go ahead and bring that baby into this world. It ain't that way so much no more, but it were that way back then. Well, when this baby was born, it wasn't right; it was crippled in some way. It was a boy, but it weren't going to be a brave warrior, 'cause he couldn't walk and run like it takes to be an Indian warrior. Now, you can guess that this whole thing did not set well with the tribal leaders. That baby was not only a bastard, but he was a cripple on top of that."

Mattie paused and took a drink from a quart-sized fruit jar she had sitting nearby.

She then continued her story. "Now, when this kid was just a little bitty thing, the council met and decided that the mother and her cripple bastard had to go. The plan was to take the mother and her child outside the village and wipe them out, kill 'em and burn 'em so as to get rid of any bad omen that might exist because of the two. Evil spirits had surely placed a curse on the woman, which caused her to have a handicapped child, and therefore they should be eliminated."

Mattie took another swig from the fruit jar. She wiped her mouth with the back of her hand and then continued. "Now, the kid had to have a papa, right? Well, weren't nobody who knew exactly who that was, 'cept the mother and daddy, of course. The father of that child got wind of what was about to happen and told the mother that she had better high tail it outta there in a hurry or she would be history—and the kid too. He helped her escape before anybody could do her in like they had decided to do."

She hesitated, giving deep thought to what she would say next. "Now, the next part is what them that told the story called the mystery. They would get into some pretty good arguments about this part 'cause nobody knew exactly where they went, but they all agreed that they went somewhere, because the story don't end there.

"Did I mention that this here is s'posed to have happened a long time ago? It was when the Indians could make their own rules and do their own thing.

It weren't no big thing if'n the council thought that somebody might be in the way or have an evil spirit; they got shed of them. That was just the way it was back then. Nobody thought too much when a cripple and anyone connected to it just disappeared. Their fate was not questioned. People like that was just a burden to the tribe."

Another pause, another swig from the fruit jar. "Now, where was I? Yeah, so when the cripple and his mother disappeared, everybody thought this was just another problem that had been taken care of. They all assumed that they had been eliminated, so nobody brought the subject back up. 'Cept they weren't killed. People thought that the one that did the killing didn't want to talk about it, and nobody asked.

"So, nobody knew that the daddy of the cripple had taken them to a secret place to hide. Now, the word had it that this was a place that the young brave had accidentally found and didn't tell nobody where it was. Word is that it was someplace not too far from Kinlock Falls, but nobody could figure out where it was at. It must have been hid awfully good."

Jenny interrupted, "Grandmother, how did anyone know about this at all? If she was hid where no one knew where they were, how could the others know that she was not killed?"

"Honey, that's part of my story. This is the place where the old folks would always have some serious discussions. But I can remember that they would talk about some hidden treasure that would be worth more than anyone could imagine. See, what happened was that when the cripple started growing up, he was hid out and didn't have nothing to do and couldn't go nowhere cause he couldn't walk good, so he started making jewelry from whatever his dad could bring him.

Somewhere he found him some gemstones; some gold and silver and whatever else he could lay his hands on for the kid to work with.

"Now, the reason they are s'posed to know about all this is because one time he brought out some of that stuff his boy had made for to sell. Now, at the time, nobody knew where it came from, but they knowed it was the prettiest work of that sort that they had ever seen. Everybody wanted some of it, but nobody could afford what the asking price was because there was lots of work and precious metal and stones that went into making them.

"See, honey, there weren't no money like there is today; everything was barter—uh, they swapped one thing for another. Now, what the cripple boy's dad wanted was a lot more rubies and silver and gold, or whatever they had back then, in return for the jewelry. The problem, so as best I could get from what was being said, was that nobody had enough of that stuff for him to barter and get what he wanted. Well anyhow, some way or another he let somebody, who said that they were going to get some of those things, have some of the jewelry for him to swap. Well, to make a long story short, he never got nothing back. He started getting people who got some of those things that had been stole a wanting more and wanted to know where they could get them.

"Somehow, and I don't remember if I ever heard how, the cripple's dad was able to get some more stuff for the boy to work with. I think they did say something about him knowing where to find some gold over in Georgia, and he learned where he could find some of the gemstones that were needed. You know that back then the white man had not come and got everything of value that God left lying around for to make the earth a prettier place.

"Well anyhow, he got more pretty stuff for the boy to work with, but he weren't about to let it get away like the first pieces of jewelry did. So the story goes that the cripple kept making the jewelry, and only every now and then would a piece be brought out. The dad was able to keep his boy in material that he needed to work with.

"Now, those old folks that I was a listening to were always talking about where all that jewelry is hid. The word was that most of it was hid in a cave where the boy and his mother were hid out. When I could hear what they were saying, them old folks talked about where they could find the cave and get the loot. They agreed that it would be hard to find 'cause when the daddy would go out to see the boy and his mother he would just disappear and be careful not to leave no tracks."

Jenny interrupted again, "Now, Grandmother, if he left no tracks, nobody knew where he was going, and he wasn't talking to anyone, just how do we know that this story is true?"

"Now you just hold your horses a minute, sweetie. I will get around to telling that. This is what got them all talking in the first place. You see, the cripple's dad later took the boy's mom to another settlement and married her. He got far enough away that they did not know what was going on back where they wanted to kill her. You ask these questions and then get me ahead of my story. I was going to explain all that when I told you what happened to the cripple boy."

"Sorry, Grandmother! You just got me so interested in the story that I started thinking ahead. Go on and tell me your account of what you heard."

"Now that you got me going on that part, I will just go ahead and try to explain what you asked. Now, as I said, the daddy of the cripple child made some excuse to leave the tribe where he was after he fathered the child and went to live some distance away. You know that back then they didn't have all this telephone stuff, and he could get away where no one else knew what was going on. So he married this woman; I guess because he loved her and she was the mother of his child, and they had more children and grandchildren.

"Now, all this didn't happen right off. I have to tell you about the boy some more before you can understand it all. Well anyway, what those old men said was that right before he died, the father of the cripple boy called for a grandson. Remember they were all full-blooded Cherokee—hadn't been no white people around to get the blood all mixed up, so he got a grandson that he trusted, and told him the story that I told to you.

"Now don't forget, this is s'posed to be known only in our family because we are talking about going way back, and this all came down as a family secret. That's why they didn't want anybody to know about it 'cept family that wouldn't talk about it. I s'pose I am the only one of my generation who ever heard this story, and that was because I sneaked around and listened to what the old folks had to say, and I know that I shouldn't have done it. So, they ain't nobody left that has ever heard this story, 'cept I am telling it to you now. I ain't ever breathed a word of it to nobody. Now, let's see. Where was I when you asked your question?"

Mattie reached once again for the fruit jar and took another swallow of it. The contents were beginning to get rather low.

Jenny did not interrupt her this time. There was a moment of silence before Mattie spoke again.

"Now, what I was a saying was that he left no tracks so nobody knew anything about him having the woman and kid hid out. One old timer said that he had heard that they were somewhere guarded by rattlesnakes, but that could just have been part of the talk. Now, the story has it, leastwise they say that this is what he told his grandson before he died, that there was a young Indian that was out hunting and happened to find the place where the woman and cripple was hid.

"By this time, the cripple was grown, maybe in his early twenties. I don't know that part, but since his mother was very young when he was born, she probably was in her mid thirties. That part ain't important anyway; there just ain't no way to know that part. But you got to remember that she was real young when the boy was born, and she didn't have no choice but to stay wherever it was that they were at because she was s'posed to be dead.

"Now, as I was a saying about that young Indian, he found the cripple and killed him. The bad Indian found the boy, but he didn't find the cave where all the jewelry had been concealed. The boy had just made some nice jewelry, and since he was not able to get around good by himself, he did not have it stored with the rest of his valuables. There was still some pieces of good stuff lying around that he was working on, and his killer stole what he could find."

Mattie halted the story and finished off the contents of the fruit jar, draining every drop before setting it back down. She gave a big sigh, wiped her mouth again, and continued.

"That young whippersnapper killed that boy and started back with the loot. He did not know that his mother was around and so he didn't kill her, but he probably would have if he had found her. Now, as luck would have it, before he got far away from the hiding place, he met the dad of the cripple who was going to check on them as he often did. You see, that young Indian was unaware of the fact that the dad knew about them, and he showed him the jewelry and bragged about the fact that he had killed a human freak that lived like a wild animal away from everybody else.

"The boy's dad admired the jewelry and acted like he didn't know anything about the boy. Of course, this didn't go over too good with the boy's daddy because he loved his son and didn't want anything to happen to him. Now, the story was that they were in a creek, and after they had talked, they continued in opposite directions. Well, that young warrior never knew what hit him in the back of the head. The dead boy's dad had turned around and snuck up behind him and crushed his skull with a big creek rock. It weren't until weeks later that his body was found after it had washed several miles downstream by flood waters.

It was naturally agreed that he had accidentally fallen, perhaps from a cliff, and crushed his skull. That happened a lot back then. Now, the cripple's dad went to the hiding place and buried his boy. He had taken the jewelry back away from the Indian that he had killed and put it in the cave with the other things the boy had made. The men that was doing the talking that I heard allowed that after that he sealed up the cave and left the place with the mother, he had kept the place a secret, and ain't nobody today who knows where that stuff is hid out."

"Grandmother, are you saying that there is supposed to be a cave out there somewhere that has this jewelry stored in it that was made by the crippled guy?"

"Well now, honey, that ain't all of the story. I know that this is a lot of stuff that I have been telling you, but as I say, I heard those men talk about it two times, and they would be a long time discussing this back and forth and trying to figure out every little thing about it so as to try to find that cave. Course, they never did, but there was another reason why they wanted to find that cave.

"Now, as I done told you, before the father of that cripple died, he picked one of his grandsons, who was then very young, to be what they called 'the keeper of the treasure.' You see, he didn't want these valuable things to be lost forever, so he trusted his grandson and swore him to secrecy and told him where he could find the cave. He told him how to get there and how not to get caught if he went there.

"He also told him that one day he should pick out one of his descendants, and when he became old, to appoint him as the keeper of the treasure. That descendent would have to swear under oath that the secret would remain with him. There was to be only one person living who had this information. He had in mind for there to be a continuation of trusted family members who would always keep the secret from being lost."

"Is there still a keeper of the treasure?"

"No. That's what most of them old folks were most concerned about. Back when there was a keeper, didn't nobody but that keeper know about it and nobody but him knew where the place was. The last keeper lived back sometimes during when the white man was taking everything from our people. Now there was a whole lot of things that the Cherokee didn't want them white men to get their hands on. They had a lot of prized possessions that had been handed down from generation to generation—all kinds of belongings that the Cherokee were determined that they would not let get into the white man's hands.

"There weren't nothing they could do to keep them from taking the land, but they could hide their jewelry and other valuable belongings. The problem was *where* they could hide it so as to keep it safe from the greedy newcomers. Them old Cherokee saw it a coming, and they started making plans to hide out their important belongings before the white man knew that they had them."

Mattie stopped, reached for the fruit jar, and then remembered that it was empty. She resumed talking. "Now there was one young Cherokee that they trusted. This was that descendent who, at that time, had been made the keeper of the treasure. Them old Cherokee that wanted their stuff hid out didn't know nothing about this jewelry that was hid in that cave because all of this was a secret. He didn't tell them about the cripple or nothing, but he did tell them that he knew of a secret place where he could hide their things until the white men had gone.

"Now all of them thought that one day they would all get their land back like the treaties called for, but of course it didn't happen. Well anyway, weren't nothing to lose by letting him hide those things for safekeeping. It was like a cave bank, and it was better than losing it all to those who were already taking their ancestral lands. So the story is that they all collected their valuables and put it in something so that they all could tell what belonged to who, and the young fellow went and hid it in the cave where the cripple's jewelry had been stored. They did this several years before the Trail of Tears, and it is a good thing that they did, 'cause everything worth anything that wasn't hid was stole from them."

"Did you hear them say whatever happened to those things?"

"Most of them people were sent off across the Mississippi and never got back here. Truth be known, there was probably a lot of those old folks who had left their possessions for to be hid who never even made it all the way out there. As you know, lots and lots of them died between here and Oklahoma. I would think that there were some who survived and eventually got their stuff back, but I would also think that there were very few who did. Most everybody left it right where it was hid because they knew that just as soon as they got it back, it would be stole from them. It would then be gone forever, so they just left it hid till they all died out."

"So what happened then, Grandmother?"

"With all this disruption with the removal like it was, the last keeper of the treasure could never find the right person to trust to keep the secret. So all this that had been passed down for generations was lost forever. Perhaps the last keeper of the treasure decided that it would be better that the secret be lost than for the location of the cave to be revealed. The valuables stored there would have probably been looted, and they would then be in the hands of those who would want them only for profit.

"I have to agree that this was the right decision. At least they are all together for safekeeping. Maybe someday they will once again take their rightful place where there are those who treasure our heritage, not just our worldly possessions. Anyway, I did hear that before the last keeper died, he did confide in a much younger female member of the family, one that he trusted. That's the story I heard from the old timers. Since the keeper of the treasure was always to be a male, she could not carry on as the caretaker, thus ending the tradition."

Mattie stopped talking as though she had finished her story. Then, as if on second thought, she began speaking again. "Now, you know that all them folks that I have been talking about have been dead a long time, so I guess the secret is still safe, and all that stuff is still in a cave somewhere. If anyone could figure out just where it was that they hid that cripple out, I imagine that they could take a little time and locate that hiding place. But you know as well as I do that these things happened so long ago that now no one would ever know where that was. No one even knows this story now, so I am sure that somewhere out there is a cave full of valuables that would make a person rich if he could find it. It is probably sealed so as to be hard to find and maybe it is still guarded by snakes."

Mattie ended her talk with one request. "Now, you be very careful who you show this to! Make sure that it is someone that you can trust to keep this a family secret."

Jenny looked at Raleigh and finished the video session with a simple statement.

"I trust you, Raleigh."

CHAPTER 22

◆

"Had you ever heard any of this before?" Raleigh asked as Jenny stored the recording.

He had listened as the old Cherokee woman recalled a number of tales from her childhood. None of them had captured his attention as did the last story she told about the mother and her child. He was especially interested in the hiding place that the old timers had failed to find. Could he have accidentally found it in the Sipsey Canyon? He contemplated the information Mattie had showered on them. He was not a member of the family, but Jenny had allowed him to enter into their secrets. If he had been a family member, perhaps this was a design of that higher power to appoint him, by proxy, to become the new keeper of the treasure. He was sure that if there was a cave in the small confinements of the cove, an intensive search would reveal it. But as keeper of the treasure, he could never divulge any knowledge of the whereabouts of this hidden sanctuary. It must always remain as past inhabitants had left it.

Only one other person was aware of the cove area, and Kurt had vowed that it would remain their secret. He trusted Kurt and knew that he would be true to his word. Kurt had not seen the video Raleigh had just watched, so he couldn't know the added implication that was possibly connected to his find in the canyon. This would be one bit of information that he would not share with him.

The thought of Mattie's story overwhelmed him, but not even Jenny was aware of its implication. Raleigh had not yet shared his story of the finding of the journal with her. She knew nothing about the cove in the Sipsey Canyon that was guarded by snakes. He assessed the whole scenario to be *mind-boggling*. Could this be an omen that someday he would be a member of the family and thus become the new keeper of the treasure?

Jenny interrupted this trance by answering the question he had asked. "Nope—first time hearing that! She said she had never told most of those stories before. I want to thank you for motivating me to preserve this history while I can. Just think, those tales would have been lost forever if I had not spent the weekend talking to Grandmother. Accounts like this are being buried every day—to be lost forever. We are all guilty of this neglect. I really enjoyed the time I spent trying to preserve this information about our heritage."

Raleigh glanced at his watch. "I guess sleep is irrelevant now. It's almost time for early risers to get up. Do you want to sleep for a little while?"

Raleigh was unprepared for Jenny's next move. She took his hand and led him to the couch. She motioned for him to sit down, and she sat down on his lap. She gently turned his face toward hers and kissed his lips. It was not a long kiss, but it was full of passion.

"Not really," she answered after pulling away. "But I guess we should get a little nap."

With that said she headed toward the closet, where she got a blanket and pillow and handed them to him.

"I guess you can make your own bed."

She entered her bedroom and closed the door.

It was mid-morning when Raleigh was awakened by a kiss on his cheek. Jenny was standing over him, still in her pajamas.

"Good morning!" she greeted before leaving another kiss on his forehead. "Did you sleep well?"

Raleigh blinked. His first thought was that he might be dreaming. Standing over him, in her enticing pajamas and perfect figure, was the most gorgeous person alive, and she had just awakened him with a kiss. He immediately tried to conceal the reaction this alluring moment aroused in him. The desire was spontaneous, and it was with great restraint that he maintained self-control over the occasion.

He reached up, pulled her head down to his, and returned the kiss. Jenny went down on her knees, and they started the morning with a long, passionate kiss. No dream could ever be this good.

Raleigh stood up. Jenny circled her arms around him and pulled him close to her before she spoke. "I have never spent the night with a man before. Even though we didn't share the same bed, it still felt special—I mean just to know that you were here with me."

Raleigh also had his arms circling Jenny's waist. He could feel her silk pajamas against his body. He stammered for words.

"Jenny, I have never known anyone like you. I've never really been a ladies man before, because I never met one that was of great interest to me. But then I met you. You asked me if I slept well. I must admit that our kiss last night kept me awake for a while—just knowing that you were in the other room brought out emotions I was unaware that I had."

Jenny smiled. "Want some breakfast?"

She pulled away from him and went back into her

bedroom. When she reappeared, she was neatly dressed in slacks and a blouse. Entering into the kitchen, she prepared a breakfast of bacon and eggs, and to his surprise, homemade biscuits.

"Would you like a grand tour of Redstone today?" Jenny asked after they had eaten.

"Can you do that?" Raleigh responded. "Will they allow you to take me into the arsenal?"

"Sure! I work there. You could be my assistant today," she said with a laugh. "No, the arsenal is open to tour buses from the space center. There's only access into certain areas, and I won't try to slip you into any restricted places. There shouldn't be a problem."

Sometime later, Jenny pulled up to the gate at Redstone. The guard stepped out of his booth and greeted her.

"Good morning, Dr. Riddle. Did you call for your team to come in today?"

"No, Wayne. I'm just going in for a while; I won't be here all day."

"Fine. Have a good day!" he said with a wave as he allowed them to drive though.

Jenny proceeded into the secure area of the arsenal.

"Dr. Riddle?" Raleigh asked with a puzzled expression on his face.

"Jenny to *you*!" she said.

"But... but you never told me anything about that."

"You just weren't listening, Raleigh. The first day we met I told you that I got as much education as I could get. A PhD was as far as I could go."

"And what is this about your team?"

"Well, I do have a responsible position here. I suppose that's why I get so uptight at times. I'm in charge of our design team, but I have a group of capable coworkers that could hold the same position. It's no big thing; it just makes my work more of a challenge. I assume this is one time that my being a Native American has worked to my advantage. Management likes to promote minorities whenever possible. There are others on my team who are just as qualified to lead the group as I am. It requires teamwork to accomplish our goals, and I try to ensure that our team functions with that in mind."

Jenny gave Raleigh the grand tour of the arsenal. There were certain areas, however, into which she could not take him.

"I would like to show you my workspace, but it's off-limits to unauthorized personnel," she advised. "Much of what we do is classified, and the rules just don't allow visitors."

"I understand. I would expect that, Jenny. I've seen more than I could've hoped for, and it has definitely been interesting."

"When I visit *you* at work, I guess I will have to refrain from insisting that you take me to jail. You won't have to give me the grand tour of the jailhouse. How's that for a trade-off?"

"Agreed! But you don't know what you'll be missing. You'd have lots of admirers!" Raleigh laughed.

"I think I'll be able to survive a while longer without the attention that I might get during *that* visit."

Before leaving for home, Raleigh invited Jenny to come to Jasper the next weekend.

"You gave me a tour of the arsenal today; I will give you a tour of the county courthouse next week. Since we won't be including the jail, it'll only take about thirty minutes. After that, we'll find something else to do."

The offer was immediately accepted.

When they returned to the parking lot of Jenny's apartment, she walked with Raleigh to his car. She did not invite him back inside. Her goodbye kiss, however, did signal that she would be eager to see him again the following weekend.

During the week, Raleigh attempted to get a perspective of recent events that had profoundly affected his life. In a very short time, his world had been turned upside down. Little did he know, their relationship was having the same effect on Jenny—and she was a person of action, which he would soon come to realize. Saturday they would be back together again.

Raleigh's phone rang on Thursday night, and he picked it up, expecting it to be a jailor informing him of the arrest of one of his parolees. Instead, he was surprised to see Jenny's name on the caller id.

"Is it too late to change our plans for the weekend?" he heard her ask after he answered the phone.

Raleigh's heart sank. He had been looking forward to seeing her during the coming weekend, and now she wanted to cancel out, or so he reasoned.

He hesitated before giving his simple answer. "No."

"Good! Could I suggest a trip then?"

"Sure."

"Are you familiar with the old Cherokee town in Georgia called Echota?"

"That is part of our tribal history. Every Cherokee should be familiar with the story of that place. Some people call it New Echota."

"Yeah, I know. But the new part of the name may be redundant. The E in Echota means 'new' in the Cherokee language, or so I have been told. I don't speak the language, but I believe the actual meaning of the word is New Chota.

"In the early 1800s, the old capital, Chota, was taken and later flooded by water that backed up after the

construction of the Tellico Dam. The Cherokee moved
their capital to a beautiful piece of land located between
two small rivers, where they laid out their capital town
and called it Echota, or New Chota. But I suppose you
know the history as well as I do."

"Of course I know a little of that history, Jenny.
The Cherokee's old capital they named Chota was in
Tennessee. They left it to go into Cherokee lands in
Georgia. There they started what they first called 'new
town' but later christened the capital with a new name,
which was borrowed from the title of the previous
capital. Thus the name Echota."

"I see that you are up on your knowledge of the
history of the Cherokee."

"Well, Jenny, you know this history too. I think
it's interesting to consider the great accounts of the
struggles and battles our forefathers waged before they
lost everything in this section of the country. They
were determined to persevere, but the opposition was
too great for them to succeed. In 1822, at the annual
Cherokee council meeting, Echota was designated the
new capital of the Cherokee. The next October they
met there to talk about the action taken by the state
of Georgia to kick them out of the land that had been
promised them by a worthless treaty. Georgia was
determined to see that all of them were separated from
that state by the wide waters of the Mississippi River."

Jenny responded by including, "Ten years after
Echota was declared the new capital, they were forced
by the State of Georgia to vacate the prime piece of
property on which they had chosen to establish their
new seat of government. They then moved back to
Tennessee and established their last capital town at
Red Clay, Tennessee, in 1832. They were fast headed
toward the Trail of Tears, and this occupation lasted

only a short while before it too became a part of the Cherokee's past history."

"What prompted your interest in this trip?" Raleigh inquired.

"I have always wanted to go to Echota, Georgia! That's not far from the interstate that connects Atlanta to Chattanooga, and points beyond, of course. It is now near Calhoun. Echota is only a rural area but a place of historical value to the Cherokee. I noticed an article in the paper about a cultural event scheduled there for this weekend, and I thought it might be interesting to go and check it out. "

"That's a great idea! I recently re-read, for the third time, John Ehle's book, *The Trail of Tears—The Rise and Fall of the Cherokee Nation*, in which he discusses the history of the place. I promised myself that I would go there someday, and this weekend seems like the perfect time!"

"Will you be able to pick me up around nine on Saturday morning? We'll go to Scottsboro and cross the Tennessee River there. We can go the scenic route through Fort Payne and over Lookout Mountain to Rome, Georgia, then on to Calhoun. Echota is on the other side of the interstate. I've already placed the route on my GPS, so there won't be any problem getting there."

"I'll be looking forward to being with you on the trip. It sounds so much more exciting than a trip to the Walker County Courthouse, and we were going to forego the jail tour anyway. I'm glad you called."

"I'll pack for an overnight stay, and you can do the same. Maybe even for a couple of nights if you can spare the time. I hope for an exciting weekend."

CHAPTER 23

───────◆───────

Raleigh was at Jenny's apartment at around 8:30 Saturday morning. She opened the door before he reached it. Although he was thirty minutes early, she was dressed and appeared with a large piece of luggage in one hand and a cooler in the other. Raleigh moved to relieve her of the luggage, putting it in the trunk of his car.

"Food!" Jenny exclaimed as she positioned the cooler beside the luggage. "We'll have a picnic."

As they drove away, they headed east on U.S. 72 toward Scottsboro. Jenny had done her homework. The GPS immediately started issuing directions, even though they already knew the route to Fort Payne.

"The course we're taking goes through the Little River Canyon area." Raleigh remarked. "I've hiked there a few times; it's one of the most scenic places in Alabama."

Jenny showed how much she had already thought ahead when she spoke. "I have already made lodging reservations for the night, so there's no need to get in any hurry. I was able to find a vacancy at a nice location."

The conversation then turned to the events surrounding the establishment of the town that was to be the new capital of the Cherokee Nation.

Raleigh said, "Major Ridge envisioned a grand city to be the capital of the Cherokees. In New Echota, he laid out one hundred one-acre lots on ground that was reported to be as level as the floor of a house. In addition to the one hundred houses he planned for the new town, he also planned for a national academy with a library full of books from this country and from England. There was a council house, buildings for the supreme court and administrative offices, a museum modeled after the Smithsonian to display articles of the Cherokee culture, a printing office, and there was a two-acre central square, with the main street being sixty feet wide. It was a grand vision for a doomed society."

"But this wasn't a pretty time in our nation's history," Jenny continued the conversation. "The grand dreams of the Cherokee quickly became nightmares. What the white man wanted, the white man got—which soon was everything."

"Except what might have been hidden away, as your grandmother revealed about the lost cave. The Cherokee may have hidden as much as they possibly could, but their tribal homeland was their most precious possession, and it was taken away from them."

Before noontime, they stopped in Rome, Georgia, for a fast-food meal before traveling the short distance to Calhoun and New Echota. The old Cherokee capital had been located between the confluences of the Coosawatter and the Conasauga Rivers. These were not mighty streams, yet they provided the water and drainage that the settlement needed.

New Echota bore no resemblance to the bustling capital that was once the seat of government for the Cherokee Nation. The two-hundred-acre park was now on land that was still as flat as a cabin's floor. On the expanse of land, there was now a museum and welcome center, where an entry fee was paid to enter. Clusters of old log structures—a smoke house, corn crib, barn, and a log house—were situated only a short distance from the entrance. Scattered around the remainder of the park were reconstructed buildings, replicas of some of those that provided sheltered space for housing, recreation, business, and governmental affairs.

The Frontier Day celebration at the park featured various demonstrators depicting life as it would have been at the time of the Indian occupation. Raleigh picked up a copy of the self-guiding tour map of the resurrected New Echota. He took note that the tour was said to take from thirty to forty-five minutes to complete.

Starting at number one, a middleclass Cherokee house and outbuildings, they proceeded to tour the old capital's grounds. Going through the old town center, they observed the council house, the supreme courthouse, and a Cherokee cabin. The only original building still standing at the old town site was the Worchester house.

Samuel Worchester had been a scholarly Presbyterian missionary who had had printing and linguistic skills and had played an important role in the daily affairs of the Indian Nation. The old house was located off the large tract of flat land that constituted the town center. This choice plot of land had been taken from the Cherokee. The buildings had been destroyed, and it had become farmland for the white man.

Raleigh and Jenny crossed a small creek, walked up a slight incline, and soon reached the restored house which sat in a wooded section of the park. Leaving there, they made short stops at the Vann Tavern and the print shop before heading back toward the car. The tour had taken only about thirty minutes to complete.

As they walked back to the car, Raleigh thought of the reference that Eve had made in her journal about

Elias Boudinot and the Cherokee Phoenix newspaper. It had been printed here where they now visited. Jenny knew nothing about the journal, but Raleigh could not resist telling her about it.

"I recently read a document that mentioned a newspaper that was printed here at New Echota. It was edited by a guy named Elias Boudinot and printed by John Foster Wheeler. They built a house, twenty by thirty feet, to house the press, putting doors on each end for easy accessibility. The paper was printed in both the English and Cherokee language. The yearly subscription for the English edition was $2.50 if paid in advance. The Cherokee was $2.00 if paid in advance, $2.50 if paid throughout the year. The editor was paid three hundred dollars a year, but the printer demanded four hundred dollars a year because he had to have an assistant."

"Interesting!" Jenny replied.

"When they initially started to test the thousand-pound press, they realized that in their excitement to get started on the project, they had forgotten to order the paper they needed to print it on. After the printer's assistant, Isaac Harris, brought some paper from Knoxville, they printed their first issue on February 21, 1828. It was published weekly and had a wide distribution."

As they walked they passed the area where booths were set up by demonstrators to recreate a number of crafts and chores of pioneer days.

"Let's take in the demonstrations later," Jenny suggested.

They continued walking and reached the car.

"Okay—where to from here?" Raleigh inquired as they pulled out of the parking lot and onto the Trail of Tears highway. A sign pointing eastward advertised the "Vann House."

"The old Vann House is located at Spring Place. It's only about eighteen miles from here. It was the home of James Vann, one of the wealthiest of the Cherokee leaders. He was only half Indian but was a Cherokee Chief. He lived near the town of Pine Log before building the house in Spring Place. When he built the house, it was the finest house of any Cherokee. He was the son of a trader and had accumulated a lot of land, including a whole valley, where he had a great number of slaves planting and harvesting his crops. He was a drunk, but he was very influential. There's a lot of history there. Let's head that way," Jenny suggested.

"To the Vann House it is," Raleigh said as he turned eastward.

"After we tour the Vann House, we could go check into our room if you like," Jenny said.

This was also approved by Raleigh, and they continued on their trip.

The journey to Spring Place had taken them east, away from Calhoun and Interstate 75. Raleigh had assumed that the reservations Jenny made had been at one of the many sleeping accommodations along the I-75 corridor.

After completing a tour of the Vann House and while leaving the parking lot, he turned his wheels in the direction of the interstate. Before he could pull out, however, Jenny corrected him and motioned for him to continue traveling further in an easterly direction.

"Where did you make our reservations?" he asked.

Jenny gave him a little smile before answering. "We may have to travel a little ways further. There is a neat little place in the Chattahoochee National Forest where I was able to find an available cabin. I think we'll like it."

"You wanted to come here for the events happening at New Echota. Will it be convenient to return to the park from there?"

"We'll worry about that when the time comes. I have a computer printout of the route that we need to take. It looks so simple that I didn't bother to program it into my GPS. We go over to Ellijay and head north on U.S. 76. It's not that far."

The scenery was beautiful and the trip altogether enjoyable. They stopped briefly in Ellijay at a roadside stand and bought apples, as the town was known for its fruit orchards. They arrived at their destination before nightfall.

The lodging was not at all what Raleigh had expected when Jenny informed him that she had made reservations. This place was a retreat of extreme beauty. Their assigned cabin was secluded in a wooded area, and although there were a number of others there, each cabin offered a privacy that left the impression that there was no one else around. It was a place that had to be popular with the honeymooners.

After registering, they were soon unloading their bags. Jenny lifted the cooler from the trunk of the car and carried it inside.

"Seems like you really trust me, Jenny. I had no idea that we would be spending the night together in the woods—not that I'm complaining!"

"Don't forget that I'm a country girl. I can take care of myself—not that I think I need any protection!"

After they finished unloading and closed the cabin door behind them, Jenny put her arms around Raleigh's waist and pulled his body to hers.

She held him tight, looked into his eyes, and then began speaking again. "How do I say this?" She paused. "I too have read John Ehle's book. On the third page, he made a statement that I can quote. This is what he has to say, '*A Cherokee woman had more rights and power than European women. She decided whom she would marry, and the man built* a *house for her, which was considered her property, or else he came to her or her mother's house to live.'"*

She continued looking Raleigh in the eye. "Well, I am a Cherokee woman, and I know what I want." She pulled him tighter against her body. "Raleigh, I love you!"

He was speechless for a moment. This sudden revelation had come unexpectedly. It didn't take long, however, for him to reply. "And I love you, Jenny!"

That was all that was said before their lips met, and the expression of their admissions was made manifest by their embrace. Neither left any doubt that the words that had just been exchanged between them had been spoken with all sincerity.

After their embrace, Jenny spoke again. "I have always been a person who says what I think. Maybe that's good, maybe not. But Raleigh, I have to tell you that this week has been like no other in my lifetime. Last Sunday morning when you were asleep on the couch, I looked at you and had feelings that I had never had before. I wanted to lie down with you and have you take me. I have never wanted anything in my life as much as I wanted you to be intimate with me.

"It took great restraint for me to limit my emotions to the kiss that woke you up. I could tell that you had the same feelings for me and that it was hard for you to hold back as well. It took all the effort that I could muster to suggest that we eat breakfast instead of making love. That was the reason I suggested that we go to the arsenal for the day. I didn't trust myself alone in my apartment all day with you. I trusted *you*; I just didn't trust this Cherokee woman here.

"Remember what John Ehle said about us? I suddenly became aware of the meaning of that statement, and of the fact that I am truly a Cherokee at heart! I wanted you so much that it was necessary for me to divert my thoughts elsewhere. The arsenal was the first alternative I thought of. It was also why I didn't invite you back into my apartment, because it was all a strange experience for me. I suppose I just didn't know how to handle the situation."

Raleigh said nothing. He could sense that Jenny had more to say, and he did not want to interrupt her.

She continued.

"I've made no secret about the fact that I'm a country girl. I was not raised around many boys, except at school where I had to fight them off. They were interested in me, but I had no interest in them. This had a negative impact on me, as I considered them all to be predators that were out for a good lay on any consenting female who would fall into their trap.

"From a child, I was always taught the value of good morals. This teaching included the lesson that premarital sex was not the best choice for a rewarding lifestyle. Consequently, I made a pledge that I would be a virgin when and if I married. I have honored that commitment, not that I am trying to brag or sound high and mighty, but I am proud of my decision and that I have held firm to it.

"Actually, however, to be truthful, I have always been more interested in books, studies, and my work than in the opposite sex. It's not hard to say 'no' when you don't put yourself in a position to be asked. That's just about the way it has been with me, and I thought that I was happy with that—until Raleigh Walker showed up at the council meeting..."

Jenny looked up at Raleigh, her words trailing off as she reached up to place both hands on the side of his face and kissed him.

Still looking him in the eyes, she added, "Yes, Raleigh Walker. You are responsible for turning my world upside down!"

Raleigh kissed her and replied, "Sorry."

"You have nothing to be sorry about. Besides my family, you are the first meaningful person that I have allowed to enter my life. And it is bliss! But, I still plan to honor the pledge that I have grown up with. Now, here is the problem. We are together in a romantic setting, we are going to spend the night together, and I want you even more than ever."

Raleigh was not sure how he should respond to that statement. He soon realized that he did not need to as Jenny began speaking again. It was obvious that she still had a whole lot more to say.

"If you feel for me the way I do for you, then I'll go on. If you think that I am out of order in my expressions toward you, please let me know so that I won't make a fool of myself."

"Jenny, I have loved you from the day we met. I have thought of nothing but you since that time. This is all new to me too. No other girl has ever appealed to me, and I was no predator of women. I have always felt that I would not be with a woman until I knew it was the right thing to do. The University I attended was definitely not a party school. Those who attend Harding are there for an education. Outdoor pursuits have always been my passion. And then I saw you sitting alone on the bleachers at Oakville. You will never know how much I hoped that you were not there with another man, and how relieved I was to learn that you were not. Each time we have been together since then, my love for you has grown to the point that I could not conceive of being with anyone else in a romantic way. Jenny, I love you with all my heart!"

"If I had thought otherwise, Raleigh, we would not be here in the woods today. I will confess, this week I have allowed my Cherokee spirit to rule my actions. I took the liberty to plan this weekend for us. I have a whole lot more to say, and I realize that you may not agree to the things I might suggest. Feel free to interrupt me at any time to voice your thoughts. I have always been a take-charge person, and I do go after what I want."

Jenny sat on the bed and reached for Raleigh's hand, pulling him down beside her. After reaching her side, he placed his arm around her back and pulled the two of them together.

Jenny continued voicing her thoughts. "I have always been an individualist—I will admit that. Even though we did not talk about it outside our family when I was young, I was told of my Cherokee heritage, and it has always been an important part of my life. I have admitted that I was not that big on history, but Cherokee customs, for some reason, were significant to me. I have studied the Cherokee way of life and learned Cherokee traditions. This involves a lot of things."

Again she hesitated before continuing her talk. "Maybe this is a feminine thing, a girl's thing, but I am telling you this so that you can better understand me. When I began my menstrual cycle as I reached maturity, I separated myself in the traditional way of the Cherokee woman, for seven days, and considered myself unclean. No one touched me, and I did not handle my own food. A mature woman was chosen to feed me. After the seven days, I returned, bathed myself, washed my clothing, and then resumed my normal life." She looked at Raleigh. "Maybe I shouldn't be telling you this."

"I want to hear what you have to say," Raleigh quickly replied. "It's important to me."

"I want to make sure that you understand me. I did not do this purification ritual in order to be weird or different. I was not trying to make a statement. I did it because I wanted to live my life as closely as possible to the ways of my ancestors. They did it this way for generations. This ritual prepared them for the purity of marriage. This would cleanse them, and they could present a pure body to their marriage partner. I considered that I owed this to my future husband, that his bride be clean and pure. Through the years, I have not defiled my body after this act of commitment. A pure marriage is that important to me!"

She looked at Raleigh. He remained silent.

"Until this time, I have kept myself clean and pure. And now I know that it was for you, Raleigh Walker! I greatly desire that you be my life partner. Mr. Ehle says that the Cherokee woman decides whom she will marry. I would like very much to have this be you. I am asking you to marry me—if I may be so bold."

"Jenny, the answer is YES. Yes! Yes! And you too will be my first love. We have kept ourselves for one another."

"The reason I committed myself to being a maiden until after marriage is because I think I owe it to myself, my creator, and to my husband. It has always been my conviction that a true Cherokee woman should go to her marriage bed for the first time as a virgin. I am a true Cherokee woman.

"I know that there were plenty of Cherokee girls who did not hold this belief, like the mother of the crippled boy that my grandmother told us about. Maybe their desire for sexual activities was so strong that they could not resist. I also know that some writers of Indian history comment on some young Cherokee girls who were rather generous with sexual favors to young braves, and even the early white men, but this was not the path that I wanted to follow. Most writers are in agreement that Cherokee tradition emphasized that couples should be faithful to their marriage partner. Whatever, I had my own convictions about the matter, and I think they were worthy of my commitment to this purity. Well, that's enough said about that!"

"You can trust me to honor your wishes," Raleigh assured her. "I respect and admire that commitment. We should wait until after our wedding to share that marriage bed."

"I have more to say. Now, I repeat—you may not agree with me about this—and if you don't, just let me know. I realize that I have taken the initiative here, and I may be out of order, but here again, it is my Cherokee way. Will you consider another proposal?"

"Sure!"

"Okay! But maybe I should begin this proposition with an explanation as to the reason I make it. The invaders of our land and culture have taken everything away from my ancestral people—their land, their possessions, their hunting and burial grounds, their customs—everything. However," she hesitated, "there are some things that are beyond their reach. One of those things is *ME, Jenny Riddle*—my body, my virginity, my will to do things the Cherokee way, not the way that the newcomers to this land would want to dictate for me. I refuse to let foreigners dictate to me what I should do and how I should do it. I will do things the way of the Cherokee, not the white man's way!"

"You lost me there, Jenny. What are you saying?"

"The white man says that when I marry, it is proper that I set a date, buy an expensive wedding dress, hire a photographer, spend a small fortune on the wedding, get a preacher, and sign their documents. I say *Bull!* I want to get married Cherokee style. That was the way my ancestors started their families long before the white man screwed everything up. I refuse to let Europeans come here and dictate that I must do personal things their way. This is my body; it is my virginity that I have saved for my marriage, and I intend to do it my way—the way of my ancestors.

"If their ritual of entering into a lifelong family relationship was legal then, why would it not be legal now? I seek to replicate only the moral values of my heritage and my creator. The almighty white men can take their new laws and customs and march them to Oklahoma, or wherever they want, but I refuse to bow to them or follow their dictates in my marriage. There may have been a few illegitimate births in my family's history, but they were not all bastards because their parents didn't go to some courthouse and sign some legal papers. They married, legally I might add, following their own customs and traditions. I can marry the same way, and it is just as legal in the eyes of those whom I seek to please. It is to the traditions of the Cherokee, my commitment, and my husband, that I offer the gift of my virginity—and to no one else!"

"I think I followed what you were saying, Jenny. What are you proposing to do?"

"Would you marry me the Cherokee way?"

"Jenny, I want to marry you and do it the way that pleases you."

"Great! I was hoping that you would accept that proposal. Now I have another question. Will you marry me tonight?"

"What do you mean? Can we do that? We don't have a marriage license!"

"You don't understand, Raleigh. Did you not hear what I just said? A marriage license is the white man's way. It has nothing to do with the institution of marriage as the Cherokee or my creator would recognize a valid marriage. I have studied the way my ancestors entered into their family relationships, of which I am a product, and there was no license required. Theirs is the manner that I intend to use to enter into my marriage relationship. I came prepared, hoping that you would agree."

"I must admit that this is unexpected, but I do agree. I want nothing more than to please you, and to be married to you." Raleigh kissed Jenny as he allowed her to continue talking.

"There were several types of marriage ceremonies that the Cherokee used. I chose a simple one, and we will have to modify it slightly to meet our circumstances here. The Cherokee were never sticklers for precise methods of doing things anyway, the same way they were with time. As you are aware, Indian time means 'anytime.' The way that I have chosen requires two blankets, a leg of venison, and an ear of corn to finalize the marriage. I brought two Cherokee blankets that have been passed down to me. They have been in the family for generations. I have an ear of corn and yes, a leg of venison."

"Where did you get a leg of venison?"

"A co-worker is a deer hunter, and in the past he has offered to give me some deer meat, which I politely refused. As I was preparing for this weekend, I remembered that he normally had a stock of meat in his freezer, so I asked him if he had a leg of venison. He did and gave me one. He didn't know why I wanted it, and I didn't tell. I guess he thought it would be cooked. I have it in the cooler."

Jenny removed the blanket and the ear of corn from her luggage. She then went to the cooler and removed a piece of meat that had been packed in ice. She dried it with a towel and placed it on the table.

"Are things moving too fast here? I must acknowledge that, in order to make everything we do legal with our government, we must later sign their papers and play their games. For now, I am only interested in fulfilling my marriage commitment to you, to myself, and to a higher power."

Jenny arranged the items she had chosen to be used in her marriage ritual on the table. After the layout suited her, she again addressed Raleigh.

"I must ask you again—Raleigh Walker, will you marry me, Jenny Riddle, in the tradition of the Cherokee people, and by its authority?"

"I will."

"Are you willing to do it tonight?"

"I am—more than willing—anxious!"

"Normally, these items would be presented by family members. As there are none present, we will do it our way. Are you ready?"

"Ready!"

"Let us go to the center of the room and join our blankets. This is to symbolize the mutually supportive roles of the man and woman in marriage."

Jenny encircled half of her blanket around her body and waited for Raleigh to do the same with his. She then moved to him and encircled the other half of her blanket around him. He did the same with his blanket. They did not speak and they did not kiss; they stood in silence, joined together by the blankets, until Jenny felt that this aspect of the ceremony had been adequately executed. There was sufficient time for the warmth of their bodies to blend between themselves, underneath the old blankets, thus unifying them as one.

When she was satisfied, Jenny continued the proceedings with a statement. "The blankets are joined! Now we must take the corn and venison and complete another part of the ceremony."

Jenny gave Raleigh the leg of venison, and she took the ear of corn to the center of the room.

"You are the hunter and provide the meat; I am the farmer who grows the corn for our family. We are now to exchange our gifts to one another."

Jenny handed the ear of corn to Raleigh, and he passed the leg of venison to her. They tapped them together, as if making a toast to one another.

"This is to symbolize the mutual supportive roles of the man and woman in our marriage. The blankets are for comfort; the venison and corn for sustenance. With warmth, meat, and bread, may our needs always be filled. May this union be perfect and last forever."

All the activities of the ritual were initiated by Jenny. Raleigh willingly followed her leads. She felt compelled to make a brief statement before proceeding.

"As you are aware, it was the Cherokee women who did most of the work in the fields where they raised their agriculture products for the tribe. They prepared the food and cared for the children. The men hunted and fought battles against their enemies. Their role was to provide security for their people and meat for the table. Our marriage will be a relationship of mutual support and understanding for one another's needs."

With the blankets removed, Jenny placed the leg of venison on the table. Raleigh placed the ear of corn beside it. Jenny stood facing Raleigh. Both remained silent until Jenny spoke.

"We now face each other as two separate individuals. We must become as one. Now we must open our bodies to each other to be seen as we truly are, with no clothing to conceal any imperfections we might have. This is not to be done lustfully or passionately but as assurance that we do not enter into a relationship that we will later regret."

Looking at him for a brief second, she commented, "Clothing is another thing that our ancestors did not take seriously. The human body was on display while the young Cherokees roamed the country. As individuals matured, a loin cloth or animal skin may have been worn, but nudity basically was commonplace and not considered to be indecent. In marriage, the couples were familiar with their partner's body and without shame. This was the way of life for the early Cherokee."

Beginning at the top of Raleigh's head, Jenny slowly moved her eyes down his body, stopping at his feet. She then moved to him and loosened the top button of his shirt. Following that, she did the same with her blouse, moving Raleigh's hand to the second button. She proceeded to move down until she had his shirt unbuttoned. He had followed each move with the buttons on her blouse, gradually revealing a little more flesh.

After the last button was loosened, her blouse fell open, revealing her bra. Jenny removed Raleigh's shirt, and he likewise removed her blouse. Jenny took them both, folded them together, and placed them on the table beside the corn and venison. She then moved her hand to his jeans and removed his belt. Unloosening the top button of her slacks, she proceeded to do the same with Raleigh's jeans. Slowly, she slid the zipper of his pants down as Raleigh unbuttoned her slacks. After sliding their partner's garments down to their feet, each finished the act by stepping out of their clothing. Only their underwear concealed their naked bodies. Jenny immediately began to finish her task of unclothing him.

Raleigh attempted to do the same, but was not familiar with the workings of a bra. He fumbled with it for an instant before she quickly unsnapped it and moved for him to remove the loose article. She then reached to remove his briefs and Raleigh grasped the top of her panties. The last pieces of clothing were removed quickly, and Jenny collected them, folded them, and placed them on top of the blouse and shirt.

They then faced each other, revealing the perfection of each body. Neither detected a single flaw in their partner's appearance.

"Our clothing and our guilt has now been removed. We now present ourselves to each other the same way the first man and woman appeared in the garden in which they were first placed by their creator. Adam and Eve were naked in the garden, and they were without shame or guilt. This is the original and purest form of life here on this earth, and we should start our lives together in this fashion. It should be our daily goal to remain devoted to this high standard of living and always do that which will enrich our relationship together. Our actions now will be those intended for the bonding of a family, as our creator intended from the beginning of time. We will unite as one body and continue as one for as long as we shall live. Our conduct will be pure and motivated by the love that we share together."

Jenny again began at his head and moved her eyes down his body. Raleigh did likewise with her figure. Looking at Jenny's body had aroused in him the natural desires and passions that he had experienced in her apartment the weekend before. He stood there with his cravings for intimacy with her, uncertain of himself and the newly aroused feeling that he was again experiencing.

This was all new to her also, but she was pleased with what she saw. She moved closer, looked at his physique, and then continued speaking her thoughts.

"If we could only create something this marvelous at Redstone, we would..." She struggled for words that could adequately complete her assessment of the body she had just claimed for her own. She was unable to complete her evaluation for lack of suitable words. However, she was not finished with her comments.

"My desire for you is great, and you obviously feel the same toward me. We now see each other as we are; there is nothing concealed from our outward appearance. Our restraint signifies that we can also get a look at our inward self, which is of great importance. I detect no flaw in what I see of you, and I hope that you can say the same of me."

"I view perfection, Jenny."

"We are not yet one. We must now know one another as husband and wife." Jenny remained standing before Raleigh. "I am Jenny Riddle, you are Raleigh Walker. When our bodies unite as one, so will our names. I will take your name, and we will join ourselves together to create a new family. This is the way of the Cherokee— the glue that kept our people strong before the white men arrived to impose their way of life."

They stood in that position for a few moments in silence before Jenny continued with her remarks.

"The desire we have for one another has been the same with male and female from every generation since the beginning of time. It is the force that has populated the world. The creator designed it to be so overwhelming that there would be no danger that his creation would become extinct. This desire is a raw act of procreation in most animals, but he made mankind to be different. It is meant to be an act of love and devotion between partners which will create a strong family bond for a lifetime. It is designed to enhance the quality of the lives of both partners."

She paused again, briefly, and Raleigh continued his silence. He was listening to her, but his yearnings for her still overwhelmed him.

Jenny continued, "My desire is so great that I want you to take me immediately. I know that you must feel the same. We both have shown great restraint in that we have not allowed our passions to rule our actions. We must now make our decision. It will be the most important one of our lives. It will be the difference in our living a full and complete life together or one that will lead to heartache and turmoil. We must make a sacred vow to each other. If we come together as one, it will be a commitment for life. For either of us to dishonor this oath would violate and defile the body of both. After today we will be one body; we shall become as one. Do you understand what I am saying?"

"I understand and totally agree," Raleigh answered.

"Good! The Cherokee Nation has traditionally considered that marriage commitments are to be faithfully honored. We have joined our blankets together, which united us as one. For us to fail to be faithful to one another would be a parting of the blankets and a disgrace to our families. The Cherokee people condemned adultery and divorce. They believed in maintaining strong families among their people. This promoted strength and unity throughout the tribe. We must be completely sure that we follow their example and resolve that our commitment shall be for a lifetime."

Jenny paused to allow Raleigh time to respond to her comments, but he said nothing. When she realized that he was not going to speak, she prompted a reply.

"I have been doing all the talking. Our marriage shall also be one of mutual consideration and respect for the thoughts of one another. Even though we will be one, we must consider the wants and needs of the other. I have had my say, now you can have yours."

"Your comments have reflected my values so completely that I can think of nothing to add to it. Jenny, I love you so deeply that this love would prevent me from having any desire that would cause me to be unfaithful to you. I want you, and only you, to be my companion, partner, and friend for a lifetime. I am confident of that fact!"

Although unclothed, there had been no physical contact between them while they talked. Jenny moved to Raleigh and wrapped her arms around him, moving their bodies together. Raleigh pulled her tightly against himself and they kissed. The shared commitment flowed through their lips and throughout their bodies. They both knew that they were destined to have a beautiful life together, in sickness and in health!

Love, not passion, had ruled as Jenny had voiced her thoughts. The restraint they had shown, however, was now almost depleted. Desires were quickly gaining an upper hand. They could not wait much longer to enter into this lifetime relationship together as one.

"We must know one another as lovers now. According to Cherokee customs, what we do with the other's body is now honorable. We should first make our lifetime commitments to one another. Shall we go further?"

"All the way, Jenny. All the way!"

"Raleigh, I want you, and only you, to be my companion for the remainder of my life. If you do not feel the same way that I do, or you feel that you may not be able to fulfill this lifetime commitment, tell me now, and we will go our separate ways. If you detected anything about my body that displeases you, let me know. This is the reason we had to face each other, appearing as we did when we came into this world, with nothing concealed. Your nakedness has created an even greater desire for me to have you. My body aches for the final act that will join us together forever. There is no turning back after that point. We will then be as one flesh."

"Jenny, I love you and will do so forever. There could never be anyone else for me but you. My desire for you is obvious, and I could not hide it if I tried. But my love for you is more than this desire. It is in every aspect of my being."

Jenny took his hand and led him toward the bed. She lay down and pulled him down beside her. Turning on her side toward him, she pressed her naked body against his. Their lips met, and there was no turning back. They would unite as life partners the Cherokee way, the way their ancestors had begun their families for centuries before the Europeans and Scandinavians contaminated their long-established customs. It was not ugly or dirty; it was the uniting of purity to form a beautiful and lasting relationship the way the creator of mankind designed it from the beginning.

Their marriage was consummated. Their commitment was for a lifetime.

It was as if Jenny had completed a space project, and it was time to fly away together into a new world for both of them. Body parts merged as they were designed to do by the supreme engineer. The snug grasp of this intimacy ignited the rockets, as was devised from the beginning to ensure procreation. They fired flawlessly, and it was a beautiful ride into space, unlike anything either of them had ever experienced. All systems were 'go' as Jenny carried her new companion into orbit with her.

The long wait had been well rewarded. The festival at New Echota was forgotten. By the end of the weekend, they had made additional journeys into space with all systems continuing to work perfectly. They were well above "cloud nine" and were contented to float among the stars where their voyage into marriage had launched them.

CHAPTER 24

Jenny was able to get an extension on their stay in the cabin through Sunday night. Neither of them wanted to interrupt their new dream world together. They had both waited their entire lives for this experience, and they had a lot of catching up to do. The fact that everything had happened so abruptly only seemed to enhance the occasion.

Jenny felt it necessary to offer an explanation for her strange actions on Saturday night. It was undeniably the most bizarre experience that Raleigh could ever have expected to encounter. Jenny wanted to assure him that he had not fallen into a trap and married a "weirdo."

"I have always been married to my schoolwork or my job. I put everything I had into whatever I was doing, and I have been contented with my life—to some extent. I enjoyed school, and I love my job. I considered myself to be the luckiest person in the world. I actually thought that I would never marry. I had never met a man who appealed to me, and I reasoned that I never would." Jenny looked at him and gave him a passionate kiss before continuing.

"Then I met Raleigh! When I first met you, I wanted to consider you as just another admirer like the others before you." She placed her finger lightly on his nose. "Although an extremely good looking one." She ran her hand over his body as if to emphasize the remark. "That first meeting began to stir a strange emotion within me, and it was obvious to me that you were different from the others, but I would never have called you. I considered it a fleeing sensation that would quickly pass.

"I was surprised by your first call, and it was my initial reaction to reject any invitation for a date with you. The emotion that you first stirred in me was so powerful that I could not refuse the temptation to be with you again. When you called inviting me to meet you in Huntsville, I was very busy that week. But I also initially refused your invitation because I was not sure of myself. After I told you no, I had trouble concentrating on my work, and by the end of the week, I was sorry that I had not accepted your offer.

"I then hesitated to call, thinking that you had made other plans for the stay in Huntsville, perhaps with another woman. It weighed on me heavily as I considered that my refusal might end all communication with you. I felt compelled to call and ask for a second chance to meet you there. I felt a great relief when you were still so eager to meet with me. From that moment on, I knew that I might be in for the ride of my life, and I was eager to see where it would take me.

"Little did I realize that the journey would lead through the Chattahoochee National Forest, in a quaint little cabin, where I would truly enter the land of enchantment! I am just as eager to continue the excursion into the future when our love will grow even greater. It's so exciting..." she trailed off, apparently thinking about her comments.

"I'm getting a little carried away! I'm still living a dream. Does this interest you at all?"

"It is very interesting to me. I'm still trying to figure out how it was possible for me to get the girl of *my* dreams! Your explanation is intriguing. I want to hear more."

"Repeating what I just said, before accepting your offer in Huntsville, you seemed to be the person who could help me let my hair down and give romance a try. Still, it was a bad time for me, in that I was pressured to meet a deadline at work. But I could always come up with a legitimate excuse to turn down a dinner offer, so I thought, '*what the heck—do it, Jenny.*' When I left you that Friday night, I knew that I had not made a mistake."

"As for me, Jenny, I can remember thinking at the time of our first meeting that you stood out among the other tribal members. Even though they all can rightfully be proud of their Indian ancestry, they have to document it in order to be in the Echota tribe. Your appearance and physical characteristics were immediate proof that you belonged there. My first impression of you was that a dream catcher had brought you there. Your Indian features were unmistakable, and your beauty was startling."

He looked at Jenny lying beside him, now in a sheer, seductive nightgown with only her gorgeous figure visible beneath. "Your outer beauty is strikingly appealing, and your inward beauty is even greater. You are everything that I could ever hope for in a wife." Raleigh turned to get another kiss. It didn't stop there. The nightgown was soon on the floor. They had yet to catch up after years of suppressing their passions. They were beginning to realize that they probably never would.

Sometime later, Jenny called the office of the lodge to inquire if it would be possible to extend their stay through another night. They had to face a bit of reality, however, when informed that the cabin had already been booked for the night by a couple coming in for their honeymoon.

"We have to be checked out by noon today," Jenny said to Raleigh as she hung up the phone. "I guess it's for the best. I would never leave here if they didn't throw us out. Before now, I have never missed a scheduled work day. I have worked holidays and vacation days when I thought that I was needed. My co-workers were surprised when I called them and told them that I was going to take a leave today. Since I'm the person in charge, I didn't have to get approval. I gave them no explanation—if they only knew!"

Jenny returned to her comments regarding her actions and the events that had landed her in a Georgia forest, no longer a Cherokee maiden. She wanted to continue with the explanation because she felt that she owed Raleigh a clarification as to the reason she had plotted this whole weekend's activities without his knowledge or consent.

"Every time I was with you my interest increased, and there was nothing I could do about it. It soon became obvious to me that there was no way to ignore my emotions and desire for your companionship. More and more, you occupied my thoughts. Now, I know I said some of this before, but I have to say it again so that you will fully understand why I suddenly became so aggressive. I assumed that I had everything under control until last weekend. I thought that there would be no consequences to your spending the night in my apartment. You would be in one room and me in another."

She sighed.

"Was I ever wrong? When I undressed for bed, I could not shake the thought that you were so near and how nice it would be for you to be lying beside me in my bed. After you fell asleep, I could not resist the urge to go over and just look at you. You were lying there in your underwear; the sheet had slipped from your waist and legs. I admired your handsome body. Raleigh, you are so good looking! This was my first experience of this type, and it had a profound effect on me.

"It only took a moment for me to realize that I didn't want to remain a virgin for the rest of my life—or for the remainder of the night for that matter! I nearly lost all self-control. I am certain that I could not have avoided trying to lure you to my bed had it been a different time of the month. I was just completing my menstrual cycle, and I considered myself unclean at the time. I settled for a kiss on your cheek and returned to bed. My desires were so great that I could not get any sleep."

After a slight pause, she again began voicing her thoughts. "After you left on Sunday, I could think of nothing but you. I wanted you. I couldn't concentrate at work. I couldn't sleep. I am not a patient person. I had to do something! On Tuesday, I started to think about changing plans for the weekend. I saw the newspaper article about the cultural event at New Echota, but I wanted more than that. I was convinced that you had to have the same feelings for me as I did for you, so I started making plans.

"I went to the computer and found the cabins in the forest. They're normally fully booked this time of the year, but there had been a cancellation, and this cabin was available. I considered it to be by divine providence that this happened, and I proceeded to put this package together. I realize that I should have cleared everything with you, and I was continually tempted to call to explain and get your approval, but things were falling into place so smoothly that I decided to go ahead and make the arrangements. You would later have the option to refuse to go along with it. And don't forget what Mr. Ehle says about us Cherokee women—we like to take charge."

She stopped talking and looked into his eyes. "I hope you understand. I am just that type of person. I could never have inner peace if I did not do as I did. I know that a week is a short time for all of this to be planned and carried out. To be completely honest with you, Raleigh, I don't think that it would have been possible for me to have spent another weekend with you without begging you to take me—and my virginity. I was that desperate! My desires had been bottled up for so long, and the lid was about to blow—I had to have you! My menstrual period had just ended, and I reasoned that I wouldn't have a strong chance of getting pregnant until later in the month. I had to have you raw and untamed, the Cherokee way. Condoms and birth control pills are the white man's way. I would have none of that for our first marriage night together.

"The solution, in my mind, was for us to finalize our sacred marriage vows to one another and enter into our new relationship as one. It was extremely hard for me to refrain from having you take me immediately after we undressed and saw each other naked for the first time. In my planning, I considered how we should first become intimate, and I composed those comments. I promised myself that I would relate my feelings to you before we consummated our marriage. I wanted you more than I have ever wanted anything before, yet I was determined to carry through with my prepared comments. I strongly believed in their importance. It was hard, but I am happy that things occurred the way they did. It came together perfectly."

Once again, Raleigh reassured Jenny that everything had met with his approval. They continued their conversation, and love-making, until morning.

"I guess we should make this legal according to the ruling authorities" Jenny suggested. "Why don't we leave early enough so we can travel to the Madison County Courthouse in Huntsville? We should be able to get there before closing time. We can get a marriage license and let a justice of the peace make this whole thing legal by Alabama law.

"We made it legal in the way of the Cherokee and our creator, but Alabama officials may balk in accepting that. I'm happy to have the satisfaction of knowing that they couldn't steal my maidenhood and dictate how I was to become a bride. I suppose that getting their papers and recording it in their books is a necessary evil."

"We missed out on the tour of the Walker County Courthouse this weekend, so I guess we owe some courthouse a visit," said Raleigh. "And by working in one, I do know what kind of stickler they are about getting those papers signed and collecting your money for doing so. The sooner we get that done, the better. It may keep the talk down too.

"Although, there's no reason why we should explain anything to anybody, other than the fact that we fell in love and we married. It's as simple as that. People do it every day, we just happened to do it differently than others. As you said, we did it our way, the way of the Cherokee. Did we have a premarital affair? No! We did have a pre-marriage-license affair, but a license wasn't required for the way we chose to marry—the way of our ancestors."

They checked out of their cabin and headed back toward Alabama. The week had been perfect, and events had happened so fast that it all seemed like a beautiful dream. Now they were headed to a courthouse where they would make their marriage official.

Raleigh still had unfinished business. He and Jenny were now one. They were partners for life. Their future would be one of mutual respect and common interest.

They would share their possessions and their thoughts, but he still had a secret that he had not shared with her.

Jenny knew nothing about the journal or Raleigh's quest for answers to the mystery it created. As Raleigh drove back toward Huntsville, Jenny closed her eyes and rested. This silence provided him with the time to assess the future.

Eve and her journal had not entered his mind during the busy weekend. He even considered the fact that since he had met Jenny, the journal investigation had been relegated to the cold-case files. He had done practically nothing to solve the mystery. His request of Jenny to help provide information had been vague, the purpose of the inquiry not stated.

Raleigh was beginning to come back to earth long enough to realize that the weekend had been a marvelous adventure, but the real world was where they were headed, and there were many plans and decisions that had to be made for the future. One of these was that Jenny must be included in his future efforts to learn more about the family that had inhabited the cove in order to escape the Trail of Tears.

When Raleigh left the interstate to travel U.S. 72, Jenny opened her eyes and began speaking.

"I realize that I took the initiative this weekend, and I probably came across as a dominating female. However, I want us to plan our lives together with mutual respect and agreement. It will take time, and we will live apart for a while. It will not take too long for it all to come together. They say that absence makes the heart grow fonder, but I am not anxious to verify that. We'll be together as much as possible as we prepare for our future."

The trip to Huntsville went swiftly, and they arrived at the courthouse with ample time to get their marriage license. There was a justice of the peace available for courthouse marriages. Jenny had dressed in a simple dress before leaving their cabin, but Raleigh had not packed clothing for the weekend suitable for a wedding outfit. He wore the finest he had available, but clothing was not an important factor at this ceremony. There would be no pictures. They were only going through the motions to make it right with the state.

They said, "I do," signed the documents, and left the courthouse hand in hand, as was expected of all newlyweds. Raleigh had seen this ritual repeated daily at the courthouse where he worked, yet never would he have imagined himself being in that picture. Hands together, they returned to his car, now in the record book as Mr. and Mrs. Raleigh Walker, officially united as one.

"Too bad we couldn't get an extra night in Georgia," Jenny said as Raleigh pulled out from the parking lot at the courthouse. "How about tonight we go back to my apartment? This time we can share my—no, our—bed. There will be no more sleeping on the couch."

Jenny examined the legal papers the state required for them to legally back up their lifetime commitment. "We could have started with these papers, but they would have done nothing to improve on our weekend. I was determined to do it the Cherokee way. That was my dream, and it worked to perfection. I am convinced that the Indians had a better way before the foreigners came over to impose their ways and tear down our sacred traditions. I feel that we are the last of an endangered species."

CHAPTER 25

---◆---

Raleigh left Jenny's apartment early on Tuesday morning. In the process of returning to the real world, it had occurred to him that he was scheduled to be in court at 9 a.m. He had probation hearings on the docket, and the judge would be unhappy if he failed to appear in court as scheduled. Fortunately, he had completed all of his pre-sentencing reports and had already made them available for the judge to review. He could pick up his files and go straight to the courtroom.

Raleigh and Jenny had slept very little on Monday night. When they were not making plans for the future, they were enjoying their new liberties together as a married couple. They were in agreement that their marriage would remain a secret to coworkers and friends until they had the opportunity to sit down with family and give them the news. They also agreed that during the week, Jenny should first contact her family to arrange a weekend visit. They didn't want to delay the announcement of their marriage any longer than necessary. Raleigh's family also needed to be informed, but they would wait until a later date when they could meet them together with the news.

Raleigh was at his office before eight. He had called on Sunday night and left his secretary a message that he would be out of the office on Monday, saying that he would be taking a day of leave time for personal reasons.

When he entered the office, his secretary was waiting with questions.

"Where were you yesterday? Something must have come up that was mighty important."

"Yes, it was unexpected. If I had known on Friday, I would have told you."

"I hope there is no sickness in your family."

"No. It was nothing like that. I just went on a little weekend trip and decided to stay an extra day. That's all. I have the maximum amount of leave accumulated, and I thought it would be a good time to take a day of it."

"Yeah, I know; you never take your leave days. Sounds like you had a nice weekend. Where did you go?"

"Georgia. I went to New Echota—the old capital of the Cherokee Nation. They had a weekend festival, and I wanted to see what it was all about. I decided to hang around an extra day."

"Did you go by yourself?"

"I drove my car, but a friend went with me."

Raleigh had not mentioned his friendship with Jenny to her because he didn't want the questions she would be continually asking about the status of their relationship. She was the type who would want a full report after each date, and he chose not to share this information with her. She had heard nothing about Jenny Riddle, and now was not the time to introduce his new companion to her. He immediately changed the subject.

"Well, we have work to do. I suppose you were busy yesterday?"

"I was covered up in work! The phone rang constantly, and most of the calls were about today's hearings. There were several people who came by to talk with you too. The judge had a few questions, but I told him you would get with him before court time today. I made it through the day okay, but you need to go to the judge's office before the court proceedings begin."

The workday began on a busy note, and nothing else was said about his absence from the office on Monday. He had been truthful with the information he had given to his secretary, even though he did omit some of the finer details—a few items which might have been of interest to her. He was ready to get on with the day. At 8:35 he went to the judge's office, where they briefly reviewed the cases that were on the docket. He had officially plunged back into the real world.

The docket was long, and as usual, the attorneys challenged every negative aspect of their client's investigative report. Offenders generally did not fully level with their lawyer's request for background information regarding past arrests and criminal records, as well as their reputation and their relationships with others. When the truth appears on the pre-sentence report, the attorneys always demand documentation of those negative allegations. Raleigh was always careful to keep detailed documents on his findings and was able to verify the information he had submitted to the court.

It was a long day, but it was a day closer to the time that he could be with Jenny again. After work, he called her.

She answered on the first ring. "I already miss you, and it hasn't even been a day since we were together. Did you have a good day?"

"It was busy," he answered.

"I was bombarded with questions about my absence yesterday," Jenny said.

"So was I. All I told them was that I went to the old Cherokee capital in Georgia."

"That's basically what I did too. I had a pile of work waiting for me when I went in this morning."

"I know what you mean. I spent the day in the courtroom. I thought those lawyers would never shut up and let me get away so that I could call you. I love you, Jenny."

"And I love you. There's nothing like hearing it time and time again. I love you, Raleigh, and I always will."

With unlimited calling hours on their phones, their conversation continued into the night. Neither one of them wanted to say goodbye. Had it not been for their loss of sleep over the long weekend, they would have talked longer. Eventually, they reluctantly said goodnight and went to their separate beds.

On Wednesday night, Raleigh called again. Jenny informed him that she had contacted her mother, who said they had no weekend plans and would be delighted to have them visit. They were eager to meet Jenny's boyfriend.

"*Boyfriend*," Jenny reiterated. "If they only knew! We'll give them the news when we see them Saturday. Boy, will they have the surprise of their lives! Their little Jenny is a maiden no more! I bet they've given up on their daughter ever being the romantic type, and now I'm about to tell them that they have a new family member—a handsome young man. Maybe I shouldn't say anything and just hand them a copy of our marriage license so they can read it for themselves. We can provide them with certain selective facts but no details. We'll just inform them that we decided to get married and didn't want to make a big, expensive issue of it, so we had a justice of the peace hear our vows and proclaim us to be husband and wife."

"Jenny, we'll let them know what you want them to know. You will do most of the talking; I just hope they'll accept me. I have taken their daughter without asking them for her hand in marriage, and without your father giving you away to me. They may not take too kindly to that."

"They'll love you, Raleigh. How could they do otherwise? It will all be perfect."

"I hope so. This is all very important to me."

"Don't worry. We'll also go tell Grandmother. She will adore you, and I know you'll love her too. I'll probably have difficulty getting a word in edgewise when you two start talking."

"And let's not forget that we must also inform my parents. But I would like to meet with your family first if you are willing to wait another week to break the news to my mom and dad."

"I haven't forgotten them. We'll take this one step at a time."

Before ending the phone call, Raleigh had an additional request. "Would you object to my coming up there tomorrow after work? One night without you is about all I can take for now. Then I can come back Friday night for the beginning of the weekend. We can have four straight nights together before the weekend is over."

"I would love that. I'll expect to see you here tomorrow after work. I'll prepare dinner, and we can eat by candlelight. How does that sound?"

"Great! I can hardly wait."

They signed off with the anticipation of being together again before the end of another day.

Raleigh had a secondary motive for wanting to see Jenny before making the trip to meet her family. He wanted to share with her the story of Eve's garden, and he thought the next day's visit might provide him the opportunity to include her in his quest for answers. He felt that he should involve her in any future efforts to solve the puzzle regarding the fate of Gray Fox's family. After all, it was this pursuit that had brought them together.

As he attempted to fall asleep, he contemplated again the irony of the sudden turn of events. The journal was now secondary. Before meeting Jenny, it had been an obsession, but now everything was different. There was still that persistent wish to complete his investigation, but it had been trumped by an even stronger need— the one that Jenny had stirred within him. Yet, Raleigh reasoned, the desire for more information in his search would not disappear just because he was now married. Therefore, he would tell his wife everything, and perhaps the knowledge of her family could help tie the loose ends of the story.

This, however, created another problem. He had an agreement with Kurt that no one else would have knowledge of the journal without good reason. He had a good reason, but he also had an agreement with Jenny that they would not tell friends of their marriage until later. He wanted to inform Jenny of the journal now, so he decided to call Kurt.

He dialed and heard his friend's voice answer.

"Hello, Kurt, this is Raleigh. I thought I would call to see how you're doing. I haven't heard from you in a while."

Kurt and Raleigh had talked occasionally, and only about the status of the investigation. Raleigh had told Kurt nothing about Jenny. Kurt knew that   Raleigh had reached nothing but dead ends in his search for additional insight into the questions raised by the journal. His reply reflected that knowledge.

"I'm doing fine. Do you have any good news to report?"

"Well, I'm not sure. I've met a young, Cherokee woman who has a grandmother with knowledge of the ancient Cherokee people. I hope to be able to talk to her this weekend."

"Sounds good, Raleigh. Say, this young woman wouldn't possibly be a single girl, would she?"

Raleigh stammered with his answer. She had been single when they met. "Well, that was one of the first things I found out about her. I met her at the Echota tribal meeting, and she came alone. I sat with her when I learned that she was there unescorted. While we talked, she informed me that she wasn't married. I went there to try to learn more or find someone that might be able to assist me in getting some of the answers we're looking for, and she appeared to be a person who might be able to help. I haven't mentioned the journal to her, but if I'm successful in enlisting her for help, I think it may become necessary to let her know about it. I've gotten to know her well enough to be assured that she's trustworthy."

"Who is this girl?"

"Jenny Riddle. She lives and works in Huntsville."

"So, she's a city girl. Do you think she'll be able to help you?"

"She lives in Huntsville, but she was raised a country girl."

"Aha! A single, Cherokee, country girl. Hey now, Raleigh, is she pretty?"

"Beautiful."

"So, what we have now is a *beautiful*, single, Cherokee, country girl. You'd better watch out, Raleigh. That gal will soon have you tied up in a knot so tight that you won't be able to squirm out of it."

"Thanks for the warning."

"Well, I know that you had just better watch those Cherokee women. They can tend to have an appeal that you won't find with most other females—or so I've been told."

"I called to find out if you would have any objections to my including Jenny in on the journal investigation. I might think it necessary in order to get answers."

"It's your journal! You found it and toted it out of that canyon. Do whatever you like with it. I just hope you can make some headway in solving the puzzle."

They talked a little while longer before hanging up the phone. Raleigh had honored his commitment to Kurt that allowed him to have input in the fate of the journal. He had also informed him of the woman who entered his life. His answer to the inquiry regarding her marital status had been truthful—he just didn't tell the whole story. Kurt was certainly on target about the appeal of the Cherokee women though. Raleigh just happened to think that Jenny was a notch above any of the rest of them.

After leaving work on Wednesday, Raleigh went by his house and got the box containing the journal. It was the first time he had handled it since he and Kurt had examined its contents. Setting it in the trunk of his car, he thought of the cooler Jenny had placed there only five days ago, containing a leg of venison. He now wondered what had happened to that piece of meat after it served its purpose in their marriage. She didn't have the customary piece of wedding cake to freeze. Perhaps the leg of venison made a suitable substitution. It suddenly occurred to him that he still had a lot to learn about women.

Jenny met Raleigh at the door of her apartment, giving him a long, passionate kiss. The table set with candles provided the only light.

"I grilled some steaks. How does salad, baked potatoes, french bread, and T-bones sound?"

"Perfect! You shouldn't have gone to such trouble."

"No trouble! I want to cook for my husband. What is a wife for anyway?"

After Jenny spoke, she placed her hand over Raleigh's mouth to keep him from replying.

"Don't say it, Raleigh. I know what you're thinking. We'll get around to that later. But now, we are going to enjoy a romantic, candlelight meal to celebrate our five-day wedding anniversary."

"I guess there is some merit to the old adage, 'the way to a man's heart is through his stomach,' but you are already there. This is just icing on the cake."

Jenny grinned. "Now that you mention it, I did bake a cake for dessert—coconut icing."

"My favorite!"

They ate their dinner in the romantic atmosphere and took their time. After finishing, Raleigh assisted in clearing the table and placing the dishes in the dishwasher.

"I have to do this at home," Raleigh said. "There's no reason why I shouldn't be able to help you."

Raleigh was anxious to bring up the subject of the journal, but he didn't want to rush it. He found his opening when Jenny mentioned her grandmother.

"I'm looking forward to meeting her. She sounds like an extraordinary person."

"She is. She really is!"

"On the video, she told a story that was of great interest to me. They were all interesting stories, but one really caught my attention."

"Which one was that? She told several stories."

"The one about the mother and her disabled son. Their secret hiding place is similar to a story that I have. Would you be interested in hearing it?"

"Of course I would!"

"This story is known only to me and a friend of mine, Kurt Marshal. Now that you're my wife, I want to share it with you. I trust that you will consider this our secret until we might decide to involve others. I have something in the car that I want to show you, but I'll explain first so you won't think you have married some whacko. I have the box in the car. Would you like to see it?"

"After an opening like that, you have me hooked! Go get it!"

As Raleigh walked to the car, a thought suddenly occurred to him. He said it silently to himself, and it was sobering.

I am now officially a member of the family. Could it really be that I could be designated to be the new keeper of the treasure? Might it be that my appointed angel has instigated all these events—from finding the journal, hearing Grandmother's story, and then the wedding—all for that purpose? Could it be?

Raleigh retrieved the box and returned to the apartment. Jenny assisted him in opening it. They sat at the table as she looked into it and carefully removed the journal. She opened it to the first page and started reading. Before she could turn the page, Raleigh stopped her.

"If you get started reading this tonight, you will still be reading in the morning. I'll just leave this with you, and you can start reading it tomorrow after work. I didn't drive up here to watch you read. I think we can find something better to do with our time tonight."

Jenny closed the journal and placed it back in the box.

She looked at Raleigh and winked. "Just what did you have in mind?"

CHAPTER 26

◆

"This is unbelievable!" Jenny expressed when she met Raleigh at the door the next day.

She had been so engrossed in her reading that she hadn't even notice when he pulled into the parking lot outside her apartment. He'd had to ring the doorbell in order to get her attention.

She greeted him with a kiss but quickly turned her attention back to the journal.

"I have read Reverend Stone's part of the journal, and the person who is writing now has just gone into hiding. I'm afraid there'll be no T-bone tonight. How hungry are you?"

"I ate a late lunch. I'll go out and get a light dinner. What would you like?"

"A couple of chicken snacks from the Delightful Deli sounds good to me. They have good chicken, and they're close. Get me white meat, please, and make my side orders green beans and mashed potatoes."

"You got it. I'll have the same, except maybe I'll go with fries instead of mashed potatoes. I'll be right back."

"Don't get into any big hurry. I'm going to finish this before I eat. I don't think I can put it down."

The chicken was cold when Jenny finished reading Eve's last entry. After reading it, she closed the journal and placed it back in the box.

"What can I say? This is unlike anything I have ever seen or read! It is interesting, to say the least."

"I have tried everything I know to find out what happened to those people, but I have turned up absolutely nothing. Truthfully, however, I never had any illusions that it would be easy to learn about that family. "

"What have you done so far?"

"I've checked every Cherokee Roll that I could find. I've pursued every plan that I could come up with, which included inquiring at a few courthouses about old records—all to no avail. I've talked to tattooed Indians and anyone else that I thought might be able to shed some light on this family. I've even attended tribal meetings and powwows.

"Maybe our meeting at Oakville was by divine providence—the scheme of someone higher up. As I reflect on that gathering, I seriously doubt that there would have been anyone there who could have had the information I was seeking. We were guided to that assembly to meet and make everything worthwhile."

"You know, Raleigh, if there is anyone who might be able to provide some clues to all this, I suspect that my grandmother may be just that person. She knows more about the history of the Cherokee people than anyone I know. The problem is that the journal begins around 1838. That's a long time ago. Add that to the fact that those who were truly of Cherokee blood that escaped removal didn't talk about their heritage. There's not much left to work with. It doesn't surprise me that you haven't had much success in your search."

Raleigh realized that he knew very little about Jenny's family. She had talked about her grandmother, but very little about her parents. She had hardly ever mentioned her father.

"Tomorrow I'll meet your family. I really don't know a whole lot about them. I'm not sure what to expect."

Jenny thought for a minute. She smiled when she answered. "Don't worry, dear! You know more about them than they do about you."

"Are you quite sure that this is going to be safe for me?" he asked half-jokingly.

"I will protect you. I'm their only child. If I stand between you and them, they won't attack me to get at you. Actually, I think they always wanted a son, and now they have one!"

"It may not work that way. They may perceive that I've stolen their only child."

"You'll like my parents, and they will like you. I think they feared that I would never marry. When they get over the initial shock, they'll be pleased. And just think of the money we've saved them on the expense of a wedding."

"True, but your dad didn't give you away. Your mom didn't help plan your wedding. Those things are important to parents of a lovely bride."

"Raleigh, you just don't understand. My parents are the quintessential country folk. They didn't have a big church wedding. Fact is they basically married the same way we did. They never talked a lot about it, but I understand that they had a simple ceremony where they repeated the necessary words to be married. They can't say a whole lot about what we did."

"How much do you plan to tell them about our weekend? I think we had better be on the same page. As I said before, I expect you to do most of the talking."

"Basically, I'm going to let them know that we met, fell in love, and married. That is exactly what happened.

Maybe at some later time I will tell them more."

"I don't even know where they live. I wouldn't know in which direction to head without your guidance."

"Head west, young man. Head west. But not all the way to Oklahoma! Go toward Mississippi, but don't leave Alabama. They live near the Mississippi State Line in a rural area. That's where I grew up. I told you when we met that I was just a country girl. Well, my home is just a country place. We'll get some rest and head that way in the morning."

They got very little rest.

Jenny cooked breakfast early the next day, with homemade biscuits again. After eating, they packed some luggage in Jenny's car and headed west on Alternate U.S. 72. The route took them through Decatur, the old towns of Courtland, Town Creek, and Leighton, to the quad cities of Florence, Sheffield, Tuscumbia, and Muscle Shoals. This alternate route traveled south of the river, but it never strayed over a few miles from it.

The rich soil of the Tennessee Valley had been farmed from the time it was seized from the Indian tribes, who themselves had argued and fought over the same land. Native Americans had first populated the area because of the abundant food source. The land and the river had provided game, fruit, berries, fish, and shellfish in a plentiful supply. Now the highway passed through large fields of cotton, corn, and soybeans.

After passing the quad city area, Jenny continued west toward the Mississippi State Line. After passing through a small town named, aptly enough, Cherokee, she turned north on the Natchez Trace Parkway in the direction of the Tennessee River.

"Colbert's Landing is to our left." Jenny took on the role of a tour guide. "There's a lot of history there. I heard all of this as I was growing up. George Colbert was known as 'The Ferryman.' He was also called 'Tootemastubbe' by the Indians. The Chickasaws and the Cherokees both laid claim to this land. James Logan Colbert came to America in January of 1736 and married three Chickasaw women. Two were pure Chickasaw and the third was only half. James was a trader who conducted business with both the Chickasaw and the Cherokee. He had a number of children with these wives. I don't remember all of their names, but I do know that three of the boys were named George, Levi, and James. It was George who operated the ferry here.

"I could tell you more about the family, but I'll save that for a later date. George was born in 1744 near the Tennessee River, and he grew up here. He served as chief negotiator of treaties with the white government, and he served as chief of the Chickasaws for about twelve years, or so I was told."

As they crossed the long bridge spanning the Tennessee River, Jenny continued. "George operated a ferry across the river here and also a stand, a hotel/café of sorts, and a tavern. It was quite a prosperous operation, especially after he charged the federal government a small fortune to ferry Andrew Jackson's troops and equipment across the river when they were headed down to New Orleans to fight the British Army. I think he claimed that the government reneged on a promise to help him in his investment to locate the ferry there, and he saw the opportunity to get his payment in tolls. This is where the ferry crossed the river."

After crossing the river bridge, Jenny left the parkway on the first exit and headed left toward Mississippi. They then traveled a distance on a farm to Market Road; rich farm land bordered both sides of the narrow roadway.

"I warned you," she commented as she continued

driving. "My folks live in the boonies. They really are country people."

Eventually, she turned left on a long, winding, tree-lined driveway. After traveling a short distance, a large, white-columned plantation house appeared in the distance. It was surrounded by fields of cotton. Jenny stopped in the circular brick driveway in front of the house.

"Here we are!"

"Your parents live here?!" Raleigh exclaimed.

"This is where I was raised. This place has been in our family for generations. This is home!"

The house had been built on a small hill facing south toward the Tennessee River. The driveway, coming from the north, had made a winding approach through a grove of stately oaks, curving to make its entrance in the front of the residence. It was obvious that this had been a pampered piece of real estate for a very long time. The sparkling waters of the river could be seen in the distance. Cultivated fields stretched all the way to the tree line that abated the river. There was too much foliage to hamper the view of the water.

Raleigh was almost speechless. "This is all fertile, river-bottom land. Does some of this land belong to your family?"

Jenny laughed. "Yes. All this around here is family land."

"There is a lot of land here!"

"There are close to six thousand acres, I think. Dad has some more at other places—a bunch in Mississippi too. He also leases a lot of land. He has a big farming operation, maybe ten or twelve thousand acres. I don't keep up with that sort of thing."

Jenny proceeded to get her luggage from the car. Two black men who were doing yard work saw her and called her name.

"There's Miss Jenny! Do you need any help?" one inquired. "We can tote those bags in for you."

"That won't be necessary, Jacob. We can get them ourselves. Thanks for the offer."

Jenny looked at Raleigh. "Get your bag, and we'll go in and see Mom. Dad is out in the fields. I called him last night to tell him that I was coming. He'll be in for lunch; he's always busy."

Raleigh was still trying to sort everything out in his mind.

"Jenny, you never told me anything about this. This place is a plantation."

"Yeah, I know. But I didn't want you to marry me because of my family's money." She leaned over and kissed him on the cheek.

"All you said was that you were a country girl."

"Did I lie?"

"Well, no."

"I think this is about as country as a girl can get. There are no other houses for miles around."

The two men who were working in the yard had now approached the car, and Jenny gave them both a big hug.

"Raleigh, I want you to meet Jacob and Roosevelt. They were both here when I was born. They live here and are our gardeners. They keep the grounds around here neat and clean. Their wives helped raise me, and I grew up with their children; they are family."

Then she addressed the two men. "I want you to meet Raleigh Walker."

Raleigh offered his hand for a shake, but they hesitated.

The one she had introduced as Jacob spoke. "Our hands are nasty. We've been working in the dirt."

Raleigh extended his hand again. "A little dirt never

hurt anyone."

They shook hands.

"They have always kept this place looking good," Jenny said. "Everything looks great, doesn't it, Raleigh?"

He looked at the landscaping. The yard was immaculate, with flowering plants and shrubbery neatly worked and trimmed. The entire setting was a showplace.

His answer was simple. "Beautiful. Absolutely beautiful!"

Roosevelt and Jacob again offered to carry the bags into the house. Their offer was again rejected.

"We can handle this just fine."

Jenny picked up her luggage and headed toward the door. Raleigh followed.

They had walked only a few steps when Jenny turned to speak.

"Oh yeah! We won't say anything about our marriage until dad comes. I'd like for them to be together when we tell them."

"You do the talking," Raleigh reminded as they neared the door.

A middle-aged woman opened the door before Jenny had an opportunity to grasp the handle. She was strikingly attractive. There was no doubt that she was Jenny's mother; the resemblance was obvious. Her black hair was beginning to show a few strands of gray, but she remained trim and fit. Her face and body showed few signs of aging.

Jenny ran to her and hugged her tightly. Her mother hugged her in return, but her eyes soon focused on the man standing behind her daughter.

"Mom, I want you to meet someone. This is Raleigh Walker. Raleigh, this is my mother, Abigail Riddle."

"I'm happy to meet you, Mrs. Riddle."

This was all that Raleigh could muster as a greeting. He was meeting his new mother-in-law, but he did not want to say too much.

They stepped into an entrance hall and then into a large living area. The house was even more beautiful on the inside. Antique furniture, which Raleigh reasoned had been bought new, was tastefully distributed around the large, ornate room. He was sure these pieces had reached antique status where they had been placed a century or more ago. A crystal chandelier hung from the ceiling. There was nothing modern there to distract from the aura of old wealth.

Abigail led them to a sitting room located in the middle of the house. This room was nicely decorated but showed signs of use. A large, flat screen television filled a portion of one wall.

"I guess Dad will be in before long? It's almost noon, and he said he would be in for lunch," Jenny asked her mother.

"Yes. When you drove up he had just called to ask if you had arrived yet. He said that he would wrap things up for the morning and head in. They are working in a field near the river. It'll take him a few minutes to get here."

Abigail talked, but she continued to glance in Raleigh's direction. Jenny carried on some small talk but eventually thought it best to give a little explanation as to the reason she was not alone.

"Raleigh came with me today. I thought it would be a good time for you to meet him. I haven't said much because I would like for Dad to get here so you could both be together when I introduce him to you."

Abigail continued giving him the "once-over."

"I suppose you two work together?"

"No. Raleigh is a supervisor for the State Board of

Pardons and Paroles."

"Well, I hope you have not gotten into something we don't know about and he is your probation officer," Abigail commented with a grin.

"Well, now, he just could be," Jenny laughed. "No, Mom. You and Dad raised me right. I am not on probation—or parole."

A diesel engine could be heard in the background.

"Here comes Dutch now. I can hear his pickup coming up the driveway," Abigail announced her husband's arrival, unaware of the shocking news they were about to receive.

CHAPTER 27

◆

Dutch Riddle was an imposing figure as he entered the room. He removed a wide-brimmed work hat, exposing a full head of dark hair. His deep brown eyes glanced in Raleigh's direction. He was a bear of a man—muscled, trim, and seemingly self-assured. Exposure to the sun had tanned his already dark complexion. It wasn't hard to understand how he had been able to win the affections of a beautiful woman like Abigail.

Raleigh rose from the sofa where he had been seated next to Jenny. She stood with him and hastened to give her dad a hug.

She then motioned toward Raleigh.

"Dad, I want you to meet Raleigh Walker."

He and Raleigh shook hands—a strong, firm handshake.

"I met Raleigh at the Echota tribal meeting a couple of months ago. He lives in Jasper and is employed by the State Board of Pardons and Paroles, with an office in the courthouse. He's the officer in charge of that judicial circuit."

"Interesting work," Dutch said, observing Raleigh carefully. "I suppose it sure beats farming."

Raleigh laughed. "Oh, we still have to eat and wear clothes. There's nothing more important than providing the material for food and clothing. Your work is essential. I wish mine was not. We would all be better off without the criminals that I deal with. Everyone would be glad if I could work myself out of a job; but, regretfully, that will never happen."

Dutch took a seat in what was apparently his easy chair. Abigail brought him a large glass of iced tea, placing it on a small table beside his chair.

"Oh, I'm sorry!" she exclaimed as she served her husband his drink. "What is wrong with me? I forgot to ask our guests if they wanted anything to drink."

Jenny spoke before Raleigh had a chance to reply. "No, Mom. Don't bother now. We'll be okay until lunch. Dad has been out in the heat. He needs something to drink to cool him off."

"Lunch is ready now," Abigail said. "Dutch, bring your tea and let's move to the table. Angie has cooked a good meal for us."

Jenny explained to Raleigh, "Angie is the wife of Roosevelt. She does a lot of the cooking around here. Bessie, Jacob's wife, does most of the housekeeping chores."

Raleigh was introduced to Angie and Bessie, and Jenny got her big hugs from them. They both helped to serve the meat and vegetables that Angie had prepared. After serving, they called their husbands inside and served them also. They then prepared a plate for themselves and sat at the long table with the Riddles, sharing the common meal. Over the years, they had become part of the family. It had been this way during Jenny's entire lifetime.

Jenny inquired of her father about the status of the crops, and he reported that it was shaping up to be one of the best seasons ever. The rains and weather had cooperated, and it looked to be a good market year.

He had planted several thousand acres in corn, as it was bringing a premium price because of the increased demand of ethanol made from corn products.

Around the house, he still planted cotton because he owned a gin to prepare it for shipment, and he needed to utilize it as much as possible. Other farmers used it as well, but the price paid for cotton was not as high as he would like for it to be. He had also planted soybeans, but a lot of his crops were planted to maintain and preserve his government allotment, which he did not want to lose.

For dessert, Angie served a peach cobbler topped with vanilla ice cream.

"I picked these from our orchard this morning," she reported. "Both the early peach and apple crops are good this year. The workers have already hauled loads of fruit to the farmers market. I thought that I would get a few baskets for our own use. I'm going to can and freeze some for the winter. I'll also sun-dry some thin sliced apples so that I can bake some of those fried apple pies that Mr. Dutch likes so well. He's got to have some of them every once in a while. There are also lots of blueberries this year."

"This cobbler is delicious—as was everything else!" Raleigh assured Angie. "I would say that this is not the first time you have made and served peach cobbler."

Angie laughed. "I've made it a time or two. I've been making this recipe for a good thirty years. I should know how to fix it by now."

Dutch added, "And it's always this good, as is everything else that Angie cooks!"

Angie and Bessie cleared the table following their meal, and the Riddles and the Walkers returned to the sitting room.

Jenny wasted little time in giving them the news. She opened her overnight bag and handed them a copy of her and Raleigh's marriage license.

"I want you to see this," she said, waiting for their reaction.

Abigail and Dutch were both startled. They examined the document but said nothing. Jenny waited a while before speaking again.

"I know full well what a shock this is to you. To be truthful, to me it is still like a dream. I thought it best that you meet Raleigh as soon as possible. You can see the date on the license. I know that I have some explaining to do. That's why we're here."

Abigail and Dutch remained silent. They were obviously trying to digest this latest news that their child was bringing to them.

Jenny continued, "I think you should know right off that I was the one who proposed marriage. It was entirely my decision for us to marry the way we did. The Cherokee woman in me took the initiative when I realized that Raleigh was the person I wanted for my lifetime companion. When I met Raleigh and got to know him, I realized I didn't want to live without him. He felt the same way towards me. I saw no purpose in planning an expensive church wedding when that was not what I wanted in the first place. So, I did it the Riddle way! I asked him to marry me, and he accepted. You raised me. You know what an independent person I am."

Dutch nodded slightly as his daughter spoke, and he and Abigail continued to listen as Jenny spoke.

"You're aware that when I was young I made a commitment to save my body to be pure for my husband. I honored that commitment. I have reached the age where I realize that there are desires in my life which need to be fulfilled, and I have determined that Raleigh is the one who will make my life complete. I wanted a quiet, Cherokee ceremony, and that is what we had. If I have hurt you, I apologize, but please place the blame on me, not on Raleigh. I hope you understand that we wanted to do it our way."

Dutch spoke first. "Wow! This is quite a surprise. Your mother and I can't be too critical; this sounds a lot like our marriage, and we have absolutely no regrets. The important thing is for you to be happy, just as your mother and I have been."

Abigail added her thoughts, "To be truthful, Jenny, I never envisioned that you would have a big church wedding. Fact is I had my doubts that you would ever even marry. You never showed any interest in any of the boys around here." She paused before speaking again, still trying to process the news that her daughter had just presented.

"Ever since you were small, you have been your own person and seemed quite satisfied with your personal life. Your dad was right. Obviously this comes as quite a surprise to us. However, I trust your judgment. You and Raleigh have my blessings. I am sure that we will learn to love him as our only son." Abigail looked at Dutch. "I think your dad agrees with what I said. This is just so sudden." Then she took a long look at her new son-in-law. "Jenny, I must compliment you on your taste. Raleigh, you are quite a good-looking young man!"

Raleigh responded, "Thank you! I must say that you have a beautiful daughter—in every way."

Dutch did not return to the fields for the afternoon. After a brief chat on his cell phone, he announced that his foreman had everything under control in the fields. He wanted to become better acquainted with his new family member. The four of them talked until the early evening hours. Raleigh felt at ease with his new family, and they readily accepted him as their son.

The sun was barely beginning to set when Dutch rose from his chair.

"Please excuse me for the night. I always go to bed early—because I also get up early. I'll see you in the morning. Tomorrow is Sunday, so I won't be out working."

Jenny took Raleigh's hand. "Let me show you to my—uh—our bedroom." She smiled at the thought. "Follow me."

She headed up a wide staircase to the second floor of the house and opened the door of a large bedroom. It was decorated to please a feminine taste.

"I hope you don't mind pink," Jenny said with a laugh. "I'm going to tell Mom good night. You can bring the luggage up; I'll be right back."

Jenny soon returned with a small bag and headed toward the adjoining bathroom. She showered and emerged a few minutes later wearing a pink nightgown. She went to Raleigh, pulled him tight against her body and gave him a long, affectionate kiss.

"The bathroom is yours."

He took a short shower, brushed his teeth, and put on a splash of cologne. He returned to the bedroom in his pajamas.

Jenny was lying on the bed in a most provocative position.

"I have never had a man in this room before." She reached her arms toward him. "How exciting!"

She pulled him down onto the bed and held him tightly against her body. "A good looking man in my bed, with my parents right downstairs—wow!"

It was not long before the sexy gown was lying haphazardly on the floor, a pair of pajamas on top.

After another exciting ride into space, they lay in each other's arms and talked. They did not bother to slip back into their night clothes.

"In my wildest dreams, I never expected that marriage could be this good," Jenny said happily. "I grew up sleeping in this room, and it has always been a special hideaway for me. Now you have made it even more special. I can now lie in this bed in the arms of a gorgeous man, and it's all real."

"I'm glad it's me, Jenny. I would hate for it to be some other man."

"And I'm happy that we found each other. But I think that there could not have been anyone else. We were destined to be together."

"You didn't tell me about this house, Jenny. This..."

Jenny interrupted, "It wasn't important, Raleigh. The financial status of our families has nothing to do with our love for each other. If I had nothing, would that make you love me less? I hope not. Our marriage is based on love, not on material things."

Jenny considered the question that she had just asked. "As you considered me to be that country girl and had no knowledge of my financial situation, I know the answer to that question. You didn't care whether I came from riches or poverty. I could have had nothing, and it would have made no difference. I didn't want to spend a lot of money on an elaborate wedding ceremony. Perhaps you thought that I could not spare the expense. You married me because of your love for me; I married you for the same reason."

"But why me? You probably could have named your husband. Your parents are obviously well-off financially."

"That's exactly what I did, and his name is Raleigh Walker. I am now Jenny Walker. I have already told you that you are the only man that I have ever wanted."

She looked at Raleigh lying in the bed beside her. "And I have you exactly where I want you!"

They kissed before she spoke again. "And I bet we can make some beautiful children."

"We can if they look like their mother!" Raleigh again admired his attractive wife lying beside him.

Jenny snuggled closer and continued the conversation regarding finances. "And yes, Mom and Dad *are* quite well-off financially, and they're certainly able to pay for a wedding. They have never wasted money though, and to pay for a wedding that I didn't want would have been a waste. Money isn't really that important to them. They have no idea how much they are worth; it is much more than they could spend in a lifetime. The money is just one result of their good fortune, hard work, and sound management."

Jenny kissed Raleigh again. "I think Dad is pleased to have another man in the family."

Raleigh still wondered about his new family. "Where did all this come from? Has it been in the family for a long time?"

"Yes, on my mother's side of the family. She was raised in this house. At one time, this was her room. I bet that she and dad had a night similar to this when she brought him to her bed for the first time. I might have even been conceived right here. I think they moved out of this room shortly after I was born."

"The day went a lot better than I thought it would. You have very nice parents."

"Yes, I do! Dad always goes to bed early, but I'll bet he's not asleep tonight. He and Mom are probably trying to figure out what has happened to their poor, innocent daughter."

"Probably so!" Raleigh grinned. "I'm not sure I have everything figured out myself. The one thing that

I am sure of is that I love you and want to always be with you."

"I love you," Jenny replied simply.

They lay silently together for a while, enjoying just being together.

Raleigh broke the silence a few moments later. "It might have been a good thing that I didn't know your background. If I had known that you came from a place like this, it might have given me cold feet. I would have assumed that I was automatically disqualified from having any chance of winning your love. I came from a loving family and a comfortable home. We always had plenty, but there was never much excess. We certainly weren't rich people. You are probably accustomed to getting anything you want. That was never the case with me."

"That's not exactly true. It's obvious that I have rich parents. However, I never got everything I wanted—everything I needed, yes. Mom and Dad have always been quite conservative."

After considering what she had just said, she added, "I'll put it this way—my parents never spoiled me."

"How did your family acquire such a large holding of land and property?"

"It goes back to my great or maybe great-great-grandparents. As you already know, I never kept up with that kind of stuff. Well, anyway, the way that I understand it, somewhere back there, my ancestors began accumulating property, made some wise decisions, managed well, and progressively got more and more."

She ran her hand over Raleigh's body as if she was making sure that he was still there. "I think one thing that was in their favor was that they never trusted the white man, while always contending that they were as white as the next person." She paused for emphasis. "Black Dutch. That is what they always claimed to be.

"You've heard this from many of our people. Not only regarding my mother's family, but also with my dad's; that's how he picked up his name. He has the name Kerry Theodore Riddle on his birth certificate. When he was young, he was branded as being a mixed-blood Indian, which he was. He denied it, though, saying that he was Black Dutch, which his parents had taught him to say. His mother was full Cherokee, and his dad was three-quarters. A white person had slipped in there a few generations back, but both his parents were considered to have been Cherokee.

"His playmates started calling him 'Dutch,' and the name stuck. My mother is not quite a full Cherokee either, but it has been generations since anyone kept up with the bloodline in our family, so we just say that we are Cherokee and that speaks for itself. It was her family that accumulated the wealth. That is not to say that Dad didn't bring anything into their marriage. He came from a prosperous family also. He just didn't have as much as Mom did."

"How did your great-grandparents manage to hold on to everything and not lose it through the years?"

"Because they never trusted the white man! They insisted on dealing in things of real value. They accumulated gold and silver instead of paper money. That was back when there was a gold and silver standard. They never trusted banks or their paper money. Their bank was a large, hidden, underground cellar, which served as a safe and secure hiding place.

"They never flaunted their money but instead always pretended to be on the verge of financial ruin. They wanted people to believe that they had nothing, and that was the case when it came to having a bank account. A lot of this land was bought in the days of the Great Depression. When the banks collapsed, it never affected them. In fact, it actually helped them! They had all this gold and silver, and they could buy every available acre of land.

"There were a lot of people who lost everything in the crash of the financial institutions. This allowed my great-grandparents to acquire a lot of land, and they got it cheap. For many, it was a matter of survival to sell their possessions, and they were happy to have someone who could provide the money to meet their asking prices on their lands.

"For my great-grandparents, it was good business for them to buy whatever they could find that would be of value to them. They reasoned that the white man had taken away everything that the Indians had rightfully owned, and they wanted to get back all they could in a legitimate way. They bought land, got deeds, and increased their farming activities, thus making more money.

"I'm given to understand that they were quite generous with their garden produce when there were those in need. This gave them a favorable image in the area. They also hired a lot of people to work in the fields and paid them good wages."

"I think I'm beginning to realize why you insist on doing everything the Cherokee way. It has served your family well in the past," Raleigh said.

"Yes, it has. Perhaps I shouldn't say this, but you are now in the family, so I think you should know. Our family still has boxes—well, orange crates to be exact— full of silver and gold coins. They're stored in a vault built into the wall of an underground cellar somewhere on this property.

"You have to understand that it is extremely important that you do *not* mention this to anyone. I have never told another soul about it. I know you didn't marry me for my money, because you didn't know the financial situation of our family. So, I know that I can trust you when telling you this."

"You can trust me, Jenny. *You* are my treasure, not something stored somewhere in a cellar vault."

"When I was a teenager, I was made aware of this because my dad said that if something were to happen to him and my mom, someone needed to know about it. I was given a stern warning that it was not to be mentioned outside our family. It's worth millions—no telling how much in today's dollars. It has been put back and basically forgotten. The hiding place is cleverly concealed. Perhaps one of these days Dad may want to show you where it is. That's his call. I'm sure he'll have to get to know you better before he fully trusts you. That day will come eventually."

Jenny suddenly seemed to have second thoughts about what she had told him. "I don't know why I'm telling you about this now. Well, I do know. I trust you completely. Dad doesn't need the money from the sale of those coins, so they are left undisturbed. It would be my guess that it has been years since anyone has even entered that vault, but the contents are still there. Dad did spend money on an elaborate alarm system, which he installed himself so as not to reveal its location. I'm convinced that no one would ever be able to find the place."

"I can understand why no one should even know about this," Raleigh reassured her. "The fact that I work with criminals makes me more cautious than most people. A lot of people can't be trusted. I give you my word that I will never tell anyone."

"Dad makes good money on his farming operations. Not only do his federal subsidies amount to a few million dollars a year, but if he has a good crop year and the markets are good, that adds a few million more. My parents are not hurting financially to say the least. Dad still doesn't trust the stock markets or the banks. He has no money in any unsecured plan, and he limits his saving deposits to the maximum amount which is covered by the FDIC. He has money in half the banks in the state. I would also guess that he may have a few million dollars in bills in that vault, maybe to keep company with the gold and silver he has stored there. He is all set for a rainy day."

It was late when the newlyweds began to drift off. Jenny made one last remark before falling asleep. "We'll go see Grandmother tomorrow. Her house is on the farm."

CHAPTER 28

◆

Mattie lived in a modest house a short distance from the plantation home. She had been reared in the large house, and she in turn had raised her family there. When she became a widow, Abigail and Dutch were sharing the house with her, but she wished to have a smaller place where she could do her own housekeeping. She had the smaller house built for her needs and turned the mansion over to the Riddles. She also deeded all the property to them, as Abigail was her only heir.

Mattie was a descendent of a prosperous family in the area. She had married into the wealthy Jackson family, which only increased her fortunes. Her husband was a good business manager, and the business prospered. In addition to the plantation property north of the river, he also inherited, and purchased, vast holdings of land on the south side of the Tennessee River, both in Alabama and Mississippi. This was the land that Jenny had referred to as being in other places.

Sunday was an off day for the domestic workers at the plantation. Abigail cooked breakfast with homemade biscuits and seemed to delight in her attempt to please her new son-in-law. She and Dutch treated Raleigh as they would a longtime family member.

After eating breakfast, Jenny left the table and informed her parents that she and Raleigh planned a morning visit.

"I would like for Raleigh to meet Grandmother and for her to meet him. We're going to her house this morning."

Abigail agreed that this was the thing to do. "Yes, I think you should give her the news. She will be quite surprised that her granddaughter is now a married woman."

"I am anxious to meet her," Raleigh assured them.

"Raleigh is interested in the history of the Cherokee, and Grandmother knows more about the tribe than anyone I know."

Abigail cleared the table as she responded. "The trick is to get her to talk about it. In the past, she has been tight-lipped with her Cherokee talk, at least to outsiders. She felt that there was always the risk of losing her possessions and being carted off to Oklahoma. I have noticed that more recently she has opened up somewhat to that kind of talk. Now that she has deeded her property to us, she recognizes that no one is going to take anything from her or force her to go anywhere. She realizes now that times have changed."

"Did she talk about family history with you when you were young?" Jenny inquired.

"I heard some of the old stories that were told by older family members. These things were talked about only when there was no one else around. Most of those stories had been passed down for generations. I admit that they were quite interesting, but I was more concerned about other things when I was young. As I get older, I wish that I had talked more and listened better when those who had all the knowledge were available for a discussion on tribal customs and history.

Most people don't realize the importance of that until it's too late."

"I have admitted the same thing, Mom. I realize now that I know very little about our family."

"I'm happy that you two plan to spend some time with Mother; she will like that. I know how lonely she must be sometimes, and we stay too busy to spend the time with her that we should. There is no one else around to keep her company." Abigail smiled at her new son-in-law. "Raleigh, you're going to get on her good side really fast if you spend some time with her." She paused and then chuckled. "And it pays to stay on her good side! That is a lesson I learned a long time ago."

It was a beautiful day in Alabama. It was warm and not unbearably hot, with a gentle breeze blowing in from the river. Jenny suggested they walk the short distance to Mattie's house. The road led past rows of cotton and soybeans. When they reached the house, Mattie was sitting on the front porch. Raleigh noticed that she was in the same chair she had been sitting in while being videotaped by Jenny.

"Hi, Grandmother. How are you feeling today?" Jenny greeted her as she and Raleigh stepped onto the porch.

"'Bout like usual." This was her typical response to that question.

"Grandmother, I would like for you to meet Raleigh Walker."

"Pleased to meet you," Mattie said, looking him over from head to foot.

"We came down to tell you that Raleigh and I were married last week in Huntsville."

Mattie looked him over again. "Well, Jenny, you got yourself a good-looking man there. I didn't have no idea you even had you a fellow."

"We had our own private ceremony. I wanted it that way. That's the reason you didn't know about it. No one did but us two."

"Honey, that's the way things are done around here. There ain't nobody ever gone in for that fancy getting married stuff. I did it that way. Your mother and Dutch did the same thing. They didn't let me know nothing until after it had happened. As I said to them back then, if'n that's the way you want it, then that's the way it ought to be. Saves money on an expensive wedding!"

Jenny and Raleigh sat in rocking chairs near Mattie.

"Grandmother, as you can tell by his appearance, Raleigh has Cherokee lineage. He is interested in the history of the Cherokee and of our family. I told him that you have more knowledge on the subject than anyone alive today."

"Well, hon, I don't know so much about that now!" Mattie paused and thought for a moment. "But I don't rightly know of anybody that is still alive who might know more. All the old folks have done died away, and they ain't telling no stories from their graves."

The trio sat on the porch for hours; Mattie did most of the talking. Jenny and Raleigh asked an occasional question, but Mattie seemed to delight in reaching far back into her memory and relating stories she had heard long ago.

"I showed Raleigh the video we made a few weeks ago. He is now a member of the family, and he needs to know as much about his new relatives as possible. As you said, most of the proud Cherokee history has already gone to the cemetery with our ancestors—or to Oklahoma. Those who were removed from their ancestral lands here and resettled in the new Indian Territory had to adapt to a different culture than what they had here in the east. Much of their old customs and the stories that go with them did not make it across the Mississippi River. Their ancient ways were soon only a forgotten memory. It didn't take the white man long to wipe out centuries of a proud culture; their traditions were soon forgotten. There is no one who knows this better than you, Grandmother."

"Shore 'nuff! Them white people didn't do our people right by stealing our land. On top of that, they made a lot of them walk to Oklahoma in the wintertime. They run them out of their houses so that they could freeze and starve to death."

"How much do you know about the Cherokee families who managed to stay around here and avoid the removal to Oklahoma?" Jenny asked.

"Not a whole lot, hon. That was not talked about when I was growing up. Nobody wanted to say or do anything that might cause them trouble. You young folks can't understand that now, but back when I was growing up, didn't no Indian trust the government because of the way they done us. They never kept a promise or honored any treaty they ever made. Wasn't nobody that had any red man's blood going to do nothing that might land them on the other side of the Mississippi River."

Raleigh asked the question that he was anxious to have answered. "When you were growing up, or at any time during your lifetime, did you ever hear of a family who used the names or talked about Gray Fox, Eve, or Sarah?"

Mattie thought about the question before answering it. "Gray Fox, no. Eve, no. Now, Sarah is a fairly common name, and there may have been family members with that name, but I can't place any right now."

"Another question," Raleigh spoke again. "I was interested in your story of the mother and her handicapped son that you told about in the video. Do you know the names of those people?"

"Lordy, honey child, I don't have a clue. I never heard no names. It all goes back to what I just said. They didn't talk names back then. Everybody was scared!"

"We understand, Grandmother," Jenny said. "It's hard for us to fully realize the anxieties of your generation. We live in a totally different world today."

"You shore do. See, back then most folks had Indian names they went by. That way, when they were talked about, them white people didn't know who they were. There were a bunch of kids in my ma and pa's family, and I don't know none of their real names. All I know is their Indian names cause that is what they were always called by.

"I remember one called 'Straight Arrow' and one called 'Black Bear' and 'Water Bug,' and there was one who was called 'Poison Ivy.' He was the mean one of the bunch. The girls had names like 'White Dove' and 'Little Fawn' and 'Song Bird.' They had that kind of names. But I didn't know any Gray Fox."

"So it would be real hard to find out what their full names on their birth certificates might be?" Raleigh asked.

"They didn't put any names on no birth certificates back in them days if'n a baby was born with Indian blood. There weren't no doctors around to write that stuff down. Them mothers dropped their babies with help from a woman that did that sort of thing, and they picked them out a name and that was it."

"We call them midwives today," Jenny said.

"Well, whatever. But you shore ain't going to get no record about that woman and her bastard kid. First off, she weren't even married, and they had wrote her off as dead. Now that daddy, he raised more kids, but I never heard nobody say his name.

"As I done told you, best that I remember, he married that boy's mother and had more kids by her. Somehow or another, our family is descended from those people. It was the grandkid of those people who I heard them talk about who was keeper of the treasure. To the best of recollection, they were relatives, but I don't know how many greats you would need in there to get that far back. This thing gets too complicated for my brain, so I just say that they were kinfolks."

Mattie paused for a moment. "Let me think about what I am saying here. It's been over seventy-five years since I snuck around and heard Pa and my uncles talk about this. My old head don't store stuff like it once did. You two will find out what I mean when you get old."

"You're doing fine, Grandmother. I'm following what you're saying. You have not forgotten a thing."

"Sugar child, I have forgotten a lot of things. I'm going to try to say what I recollect here. Where was I? Oh, yeah. The cripple got killed and didn't have no kids, so it would have been a brother or sister that I descended from. Now, I understand that it was probably his brother, because he was the one who knew about the things hid in the cave. Do you understand what I am trying to say?"

"I think I do. The cripple's father got his son involved in the secret of the hidden jewelry. In turn, the grandson was appointed as keeper of the treasure. As time passed, more treasure was stored there for safekeeping. A lot of valuables were stored there to prevent them from being taken from the Cherokee by the white man. However much of that remains hidden is unknown."

"That's about the way that I recollect it. Now, I ain't a going to swear to none of this."

"We understand, Grandmother. That does go a long way back! After that much time has passed, it's difficult to keep everything clear as to just what really did happen."

Mattie continued talking. "That was back when the Cherokee still did things like they wanted to, the way that was their customs. There wasn't any white men to order them around like they did later on. Well, anyway, another reason that I 'spect the dad took her to a distant settlement and marry the kid's mother is because of the way our family has always taken an interest in helping young kids with health problems and deformities. That characteristic is very prevalent among Dad's folks and goes back as far as anyone can remember.

"See, there weren't the kind of doctors back then that they have now. There were a lot of kids that died young or had all kinds of disfigurements that needed fixing. Now as I say, some of my folks were always interested in helping them poor kids, and I think that it all comes from them old ones knowing about that cripple boy who was hid out and couldn't get no help. Maybe later on some of them did not know about that boy but got interested in helping kids because of the influence of their parents."

"Tell me again, Grandmother. Who was it that showed such a great interest in helping those unfortunate children?"

"It was more my aunts and uncles on my dad's side. They were always interested in this doctoring stuff when it comes to kids. Now, I will level with you. My dad wasn't that way. He seemed to have had more interest in farming than in doctoring."

"One more question," Raleigh tried again. "Do you know anyone else who might be able to give any more information about the old Cherokee families in this area—someone who might be able to answer the questions that I had about Eve and Gray Fox?"

"Well, as I said, they are all dead now. That's where I will be before long. I got over ninety years on this old body, and it is about worn out. Graves don't talk. If'n it ain't wrote down nowhere, then I would say that you are out of luck finding that out. I don't know anybody who can tell you anymore than I can."

Raleigh resigned himself to the fact that he already knew as much about Gray Fox, Eve, and Sarah as he ever would. His search had turned up no clue.

CHAPTER 29

———◆———

Mattie had a pitcher of sweet tea in her refrigerator. She placed ice in two glasses and set them on the table in front of Jenny and Raleigh before filling each with tea. She then removed a quart-sized fruit jar from the cabinet and filled it with tea and a few cubes of ice. She also made ham sandwiches and served them on a platter with some sliced tomatoes and potato chips.

After finishing their snacks, they returned to the porch where Mattie was eager to resume the conversation. She had her fruit jar refilled with tea when she returned to the porch. She placed it beside her chair as she had done while being videotaped by Jenny.

Earlier in the day, Jenny and Raleigh had initiated the subjects they wanted to talk about. This time Mattie seemed to have a few things on her mind, and she hurried to get in the first word.

"Now, I don't mean to hurt your feelings none, but you young people today think that you have got to have the answer to everything. What you got to learn is that the past is the past, and most of that is history that lies buried forever in graveyards across the land. A lot of our old ancestral burial places are no more; they are permanently lost. Many of them have returned to the forest, and no one knows or cares where they are or who is buried in them. Probably, the majority of them are under roadways or buildings or were dug up and tossed aside like garbage because they were in the way of development.

"Those white men had no more respect for the dead Indian than they did for the living ones, and you know just how much that was! When they came in and stole our lands, the hallowed sites of the Indians meant nothing to them. When they disturbed our sacred burial places and dug up the bones of our forefathers, they practically tossed them to the dogs. You young people today have no idea how difficult it was during the removal and afterwards, up until the time I was born."

Raleigh was the first to respond to her statement. "Those are the words of someone who has walked that rocky path, Grandmother. We have it so good today that we never stop to consider the great sacrifices that have been made in order for us to live as comfortably as we do now. We should hang our heads in shame; but the truth is that to most people, the harsh treatment of the Native Americans and African American slaves had no negative consequences.

"It's sad, Grandmother, but you are absolutely right. Most of the history of those dark days is now almost completely ignored in our schools and society. Consequently, most of that history is now lost, and there is no way to recall it. It is gone forever."

Jenny felt compelled to say, "Today we think that we must know everything, and we expect to be able to find anything we want, even though we have destroyed the source where it originated. This is one of the products of the electronic age. We think that all things are possible, when in reality they are not. It would be wonderful if we could type our great-great-grandparents' names into a search engine and then have the desired information about them appear on the screen and printed out—complete with pictures. But this cannot and will not happen."

"Jenny," Mattie responded. "You got all that education, and you help send people off the earth out into space, but you got to remember that they can't dig no grave or bury anybody out there in space somewhere. This earth that God gave us to live on is what should be important to people, and we should have learned to take care of it by now. Our ancestors, my people who lived before the white man got here, did just that. They realized that they depended on this land to produce things needed for their livelihood, and so they were careful not to mistreat it.

"Now it seems that all people want to do is to tear it up, and they expect that it don't really matter how they treat it. They think that it is always going to be perfect, but one of these days they are going to wake up and realize that they have ruined the place, and then it will be too late."

"Right again, Grandmother!" Jenny said. "Elderly people like you can see the destruction, the changes, and realize the consequences if this abuse continues. You can sound a warning that this is happening, but it does no good. Let's face it. Your voice is weak, and no one is listening. Everybody is too busy doing their own thing—watching T.V. or videos, networking, talking on cell phones, playing electronic games, riding their four wheelers, and tearing up the planet. The list is long, but the cry of concern from those who can comprehend what is happening and care about the end results of these mindless actions is not heard. The voices of old people who have so much wisdom have been silenced, drowned out by worthless chatter. How sad!"

"I don't know nothing about that modern stuff you are talking about there, but I do know the difference

between good and bad and between right and wrong.
All these other recent gadgets don't mean nothing to
me—these thingamajigs that get all the attention today
and people think they just have to have them. Well,
tomorrow they will be in the garbage dump, and people
will be foaming at the mouth to get something new
in order to take their place. People today cannot be
satisfied!

"In the simpler days of our ancestors, they were
happy with a little food and the enjoyment and security
given them by their families being together—loving,
sharing, and passing down through generations their
heritage and its history. Those were the good old days.
I don't care to know nothing about all this other stuff
that people think is so important today."

Mattie paused and waited for someone else to take
up the conversation. No one did. After a lengthy pause,
she continued.

"Now, you came here asking about some people
who lived a long time ago. Way back then, there was
an established way to know about the past. Young
people would sit at the feet of their elders and listen to
them as they discussed the ways of their people. They
were taught to participate in the activities of the day.
They shared the workload, and in turn, they passed this
knowledge down to their children.

"That system worked for centuries. They did not
receive a written education from books, but a better one
taught by verbal instructions and visual examples. Their
everyday life was their school. Today, young people
go to a modern, climate-controlled schoolhouse, and a
teacher, who at first is a stranger to them, attempts to
teach them something. Lots of kids have no interest in
trying to learn something in school. All many of them
want is to get out of the classroom so they can get on

their cell phones or their games. Now Jenny, I know you weren't like this, and probably you too—now, what is your name again?"

"Raleigh," Jenny hastened to answer.

"Oh, yes. Raleigh. I remember now. Like that city in North Carolina. I'm sorry I forgot my new grandson's name. My memory just ain't what it used to be. Now, let's see. Just where was I?"

"You were talking about kids in school today, Grandmother."

"Now I remember. As I say, my memory ain't what it once was. Well anyway, as I was saying, most of these young people today just want the teacher to shut up and let them go so they can get to their cell phones to talk about nothing. With this madness, it is no wonder to me that our schools don't do no better than they do. It don't surprise me one bit."

She then paused for some type of reaction from Raleigh and Jenny, but still there was none. When Jenny realized that Mattie was not going to say anything else before something was added by one of them, she spoke.

"Go on with what you're saying, Grandmother. We're listening."

"Well, all these things that I am a saying, you already know. I was giving you my thoughts on how I feel about the disorder that the white man has created after they took over everything. It ain't good, and I don't like it, but there is nothing that I can do about it because nobody would listen to me anyhow. I don't understand what's got into people's minds now, but lots of it just ain't no good. I learned that the best thing a person can do these days is just to keep your mouth shut and try to accept whatever comes and just go on with your life. You are not going to live it but once anyway, and then you are forgotten, just like those people you are trying to find out something about. What they did while they were living don't mean nothing now."

"But, Grandmother, we know that they did live, and we were trying to restore some of the family history that would otherwise be lost. We just thought it would be worth a try," Jenny said.

"If you dwell on the old stuff, you will probably get nowhere, and then that will cause you to worry your head off because you didn't find out what you wanted to know. Now you two ought to just forget about this and go on and make a life for yourself. What you can do now is to leave a better family record for your children and their children's children. There is not any reason, with all this electronic stuff now, why future generations cannot only know their family's history, but also be able to see what they looked and sounded like as they spoke of the family. This would actually be an improvement on our old way, because we could only imagine what our ancestors looked and sounded like, but most people won't make this happen."

"I have just met you, Grandmother, but I can already see that you are a sensible person," Raleigh told her warmly. "I can understand why you have such a special granddaughter. Regretfully, many young people have very little respect for their elders, and they are not willing to spend their time with them. Customs have changed since the early inhabitants of this land sat at the feet of their elders, learning about their history and customs and then passing it down to the generations."

"Sad but true," Jenny added. "Today, we expect things to reach a finality where we can wrap everything up in a neat, perfectly clear package. In television shows and movies, we expect a perfect ending that answers every question and pleases everyone. This is what people want to see today. We may want every mystery to be solved and all romances to bloom, but this doesn't always happen, and we know that it doesn't. Yet, this is hardly ever addressed in books and movies. As I said, we want everything fully explained for us, completely solved and tied up in a neat little bundle."

"True again," Raleigh agreed.

Raleigh noticed that Mattie had begun to doze off. His next statement was directed toward Jenny.

"The same thing is true with us. In our quest for solutions to the puzzles created by Eve's journal, we think we must answer every question that has been raised. We expected those answers to come marching along in a neat little order with flags raised, announcing their presence, and arranging themselves in a way in which everything would become perfectly clear in the end. We thought that if we put enough effort into it, we could dissipate the fog and the answers to our questions would be made perfectly clear. Even though we thought we could make this happen, it was not to be."

Jenny responded, "We should be satisfied with the fact that we gave it our best shot. And who knows? Maybe in the future we'll stumble upon evidence that will reopen the case."

"Jenny, you're already beginning to sound like a criminal investigator. We won't consider this to be a closed case. It will stay in the cold case file where it has been since the time of the Indian removal. Detectives have offices that are filled with unsolved cases. Many remain unsolved even after countless man hours have been spent in an attempt to solve them, but none of them come as remotely close to being cold-cased as this one.

"Exactly what should we have expected? Such failures are unavoidable. I agree that the search has been challenging and exciting, but tomorrow will surely bring another test. Yellow brick roads leading to all the answers and fairylands where everyone lives happily ever after exist only in the imagination."

Jenny said nothing but nodded in agreement.

After a pause, Raleigh continued. "The journal may not have led to a fairyland, but it did lead me to something even more beautiful, you."

Jenny looked at him in that just-married kind of way, eyes full of love. He returned that same gaze to her.

"Ever since I met you, I have been living in that land of enchantment," she said.

She leaned over the arm of her rocking chair to place her lips on his in a long, slow kiss.

"Even though we gave it a good try with the journal, we've reached the end of the road. I'm ready to admit defeat. We can't always win," Raleigh said quietly after they pulled apart. "What really hurts me about the whole thing is that Eve made an attempt to pass some history down to future generations, but we can't deliver the message on this end of the line. To me, it's like we're leaving the journal in the box, and in a sense we really are. It was not the paper but the message on the paper that filled that box.

"With the exception of us, that message is still there. It cannot be shared because there is no one to share it with. Few people even endeavor to do what Eve did, to try to pass on a record of her activities as she did in that journal. And to think, she was able to do that only because she essentially inherited that blank paper."

Jenny nodded. "As I have already said, many times it is impossible to realize what a great literary treasure is lost when a grave is dug and a body is covered. With every death, another book is closed forever. Many of those manuscripts were not written on paper but only existed in the departed soul that has left the body. It's a shame, but it's true. Many of them were simple people who did not receive much recognition in this life, but their books would have been masterpieces of history— sound advice and interesting tales of lifetimes of love, family, successes, and disappointments. The writings of Eve reinforce this thought."

"Our thanks should go to Eve for the effort she made to help us realize the truth of your observation. Sitting in that rocking chair right there," said Raleigh, "is one of those very special souls whose masterpiece will never be fully recorded on paper or video. Thankfully, we are getting a few chapters while there's still time. When she wakes up, I'm sure she can write a few more pages about her long and rewarding life."

CHAPTER 30

◆

Mattie had taken a short nap while Raleigh and Jenny carried on the conversation. She had been left out of the discussion for a while as they had talked about their failures. The roar of a tractor passing the house startled her back awake. Realizing that she had dropped out of the interchange of thoughts for a while, she felt the need to respond and assure them that they were not being ignored. She re-entered the conversation at the point where she had last been involved in it.

"Honey, I know that you two are very disappointed, and I wish that I had been able to help you out. I know you were hopeful when you came here that I would be able to answer your questions and give you the information that you wanted. Well, I just don't have it. I'm afraid that I came along too late to know those sorts of things."

"I understand, Grandmother," Jenny said. "Mom and Dad would occasionally discuss those hardships that were placed on the Native Americans who were forced from their ancestral homeland. As we said, it is difficult for our generation to fully comprehend what our ancestors endured during that difficult time." She looked at Mattie, who appeared to have more to say. "It's your turn to talk again now, Grandmother. We came here to hear from you."

"What you two were talking about brings back old memories. Most of them are painful, but there are a few pleasant ones there in the mix. I recall that when I was young, the family would sometimes gather together for what we would now call a tribal reunion. This would always be done without letting people other than our families know about it. One of the things that I remember about these gatherings was that the men, women, and children would always separate after we ate. The men and women would talk and us kids would go play.

"The men, as I recall back to my young mind, would discuss serious things that had to do with family matters. Now, I know that they would talk about other things too, but the serious part is what I remember most. The women would talk about things that were of interest to them, and I suppose that there was a whole lot of gossip mixed into their gab. Us children had a great time playing, and we were too young then to have any interest in family matters. We cared nothing about gossip, so we just played and had a good time.

"As time passed and us young people grew up, and, because of the hardships surrounding our Indian ancestry, we drifted apart and lost contact with one another. As I already said, I no longer even remember the names of most of them. It's a shame, but it's true. One would just have to live through times like that to fully understand what I'm saying."

"We know that what you're saying is entirely true," Raleigh assured her. "Hopefully, that era is now over. I want to think that painful chapter has been written, and the book of those shameful days has been forever closed. In reality, however, some of our people have never been able to fully erase the mindset that caused all of this to happen in the first place. We are working on it, but we are not totally there yet.

"There are still those, and probably always will be, who cannot conceive of the principle of human equality. There are still too many who think only of their wellbeing and refuse to acknowledge that all men—red or yellow, black or white—have their own goals and aspirations, their own feelings and desires, and these people would like to fulfill dreams and nurture those feelings. There should be no obstructions placed in front of any person that would prevent them from reaching the highest plateau of their capabilities, knowing that the climb may be difficult yet rewarding.

"In reality, there are some who work hard and are blocked from getting to the top, and there are others who want to get to the top without making the necessary effort to do so. Add to that mixture those who just don't care. To them, life is just a delusion. With that attitude, they live for the day, indulge, do their own thing, and live life to the fullest because we only go around once. If someone gets in the way, they clear it by any means possible. They let others do all the work, but they want their share of the bounty, thinking they need it to continue to live their lives of leisure..."

Raleigh paused and then added, "Well, I guess I got on my stump and made my speech. That was totally unnecessary and completely irrelevant to what we were talking about. I suppose that some of my probation and parole experience started coming through—at the wrong time, I might add. This world has some very good people and some very bad ones. Always has, always will. They had them during the time of the Indian removal; we have them now. There were those who wanted to help the Indians; there were those who thought that the only good Indian was a dead one. Whoops—I'm getting back on my soapbox. I just need to let someone else talk."

"I understand how you feel," Jenny said. "I also believe you still want to vent some of your frustrations over being unable to achieve more in your search for answers."

"You are perceptive enough, Jenny, to see how difficult it is for me to close this unsolved case. It might take me awhile to let this go."

"Well, I guess we could still show the box around with the journal inside," Jenny jested, displaying a slight grin on her face.

"But I would like for a story to go with it, other than the fact that I found it in the canyon and brought it out. That's like leaving a plot unfinished in a book or telling a joke with no punch line."

Pausing a moment, a thought suddenly occurred to Raleigh. "Maybe something positive did come from all of this. I am now a member of the family, which could qualify me to be a keeper of the treasure. I just might have enough knowledge about the situation to claim that position. Perhaps that higher power, which has made possible all that has occurred, has been searching for a capable replacement for the last keeper of the treasure. If so, it is possible, considering all the circumstances, that I am the appointed one. If this is true, perhaps I was guided to the lost cove.

"I have felt, since that discovery, that my findings were not accidental. And all this led me to you. Then Grandmother tells of the position of the keeper of the treasure being left vacant. I think that cove holds a lot of mysteries and riches, which are too significant to be lost and abandoned. Perhaps even the rattlesnakes and rough terrain are all part of the plan to ensure the safekeeping of this treasure. This may be fantasy, but to me it makes perfectly good sense."

"That could be so," Jenny agreed. "But I suppose anything that we might speculate as to the reason for your discovery will never be known for certain. Perhaps it's time that we put this journal issue to rest and just enjoy Grandmother's company for a little while longer."

"You're right. The journal issue is dropped until further notice." Raleigh reluctantly admitted defeat—for the time being. "I would like for Grandmother to finish telling us her story about her younger days."

Looking at the old lady sitting there on the porch, Jenny inquired. "How much do you remember about those old family reunions you were talking about?"

"Not very much, honey. You see, the men would be talking in one place and the women in another. And as I say, us kids would be playing somewhere else, so I don't remember much. Except that I was always excited when I learned that we would all get together for a while. I am sure that it wasn't easy back then to get everything arranged in order for us to meet like we did. So when we did get together, the gathering would last for a few days before everybody went back home again."

"That makes a lot of sense. Do you remember any specifics that might be of interest now?" Jenny asked.

"I'm sorry, hon. I just can't think of a thing. I remember that the men would talk into the night about things that I suppose was man's business. As I have already confessed, sometimes I would sneak around and listen to them talk when they didn't know that I was there, but I don't remember nothing that they talked about. You have to remember, child; that was a long time ago."

"I realize that, Grandmother."

"About all I remember is that one night the men had an old notebook out there that they were reading from. I remember that because when they read it, sometimes they had serious talks, and sometimes they would be laughing about something they read from it. I thought at that time that I sure would like to know what was in that book, but they did not talk loud enough for me to understand them."

"An old notebook?" Jenny interrupted. "They were reading from an old notebook?"

"Yep, sure was. It was the first notebook like that I ever saw. It was of great interest to me then. I don't know where it came from or where it went, but I do remember that it was very old."

Raleigh and Jenny were stunned.

"Did you ever get to read any from that notebook, Grandmother?"

"Lord, no!" she answered hastily, and then paused with a grimace on her face before adding, "Well, you see, they wouldn't let us little kids touch it. That was stuff for the grownups to read. Best I remember, there wasn't but one or two of them that *could* read. My pa was one of them. They had to read it to the others. I suppose that is why I always saw it with my pa when he was around. He was about the only one that could read it."

"Did you ever hear them talk about what was in it?" Jenny wondered.

"Well, as I said, they talked about it among themselves but never when us kids or other young people was around. Not a word!"

"My gracious!" Jenny exclaimed. "I would wager, if I were a betting person, that there was a lot of history in that notebook. It could have contained something that might have offered us a clue as to what we might be searching for pertaining to another notebook—one that we have not mentioned to you, Grandmother. But I guess you're saying that just like everything else, over time, it has disappeared."

"I'm afraid so, honey. That's just the way it is."

Raleigh had suddenly become very interested in the new revelation made by Mattie.

"Well, if there was a notebook during your lifetime, and it was in the hands of the men in your family, then perhaps it still exists somewhere here. Jenny, do you think that your dad might know anything about its whereabouts? He would probably know more about it than Grandmother would. The men seemed to have been in charge of its safe keeping."

"I have never seen or heard anything about an old notebook," Jenny responded, and then looked back to her grandmother.

"What do you think, Grandmother?"

"Just as I said, honey, I haven't even thought about that book since I was a kid. I don't have any idea if it is around anywhere now. If your dad has it, it would probably be in that old cellar vault that was built to store his valuables in. To be truthful, I ain't never been in that thing myself and don't know nothing about what might be inside it, except I know that is where money and deeds and records that he didn't want to lose are kept.

"But all of that is men's business. Now, you know that your granddad did not want to put all his money in the banks for them bankers to take like when they did after the collapse. And he didn't want to leave it where thieves would know where it was at so they could steal it, so he used that cellar vault to put all that stuff in it and didn't tell but a few people about where it was at. I don't know if anybody except your dad knows anything about that—where it is and what's in it."

"So, it's possible that the notebook you mentioned could be in that cellar vault?" Jenny immediately inquired.

"Honey, you young people just don't listen! Now, you listen to me, child. I don't know where that vault is or what is in it!"

"Sorry, Grandmother. I just got caught up in the moment. I have heard of that vault, but I don't know where it is either or what might be inside. I do know that Dad does know all about it because one day he gave me some instructions regarding it. He showed me a hiding place in the house where he kept a key to a safety deposit box. He said that if anything happened to him suddenly that he had left instructions in this box as to the location of the vault and how to enter it.

"I'm sure that if he had a son these instructions would have gone to him. He stressed the fact that unless something did happen to him, I was never to use the key. He also made me promise that I would not talk about this to anyone. I only mention it now because of your statement.

"Of course, I would never go against his wishes, and I pray that nothing happens to him. I suppose that we could ask Dad if that notebook is there, but the chances are that it's not, and I would be very reluctant to request anything out of that vault. I never have, and unless there is a far more pressing matter than a notebook, I never intend to.

"As you said, Grandmother, that book only exists in your memory, and maybe we should leave it like that."

There was silence for a while. Everyone sat wrapped up in their own individual thoughts. Finally, a sound came from Raleigh. It was more of a mumble than anything else.

"Now wouldn't that be something?"

"Wouldn't what be something?" Jenny asked.

"Oh, I was just thinking to myself," Raleigh said.

"Okay, so what were you thinking about, Raleigh?"

"Well, I will admit that it is difficult for me to admit defeat after I have been so determined to find out something about the family of Eve and Gray Fox.

Now wouldn't it be something if one day we found that notebook in the cellar vault and it contained the answers to all of our questions?"

"Raleigh, you're dreaming now!"

"I am aware of that, Jenny, but just let me dream. Oh, what a rewarding dream that would be!"

"We don't live in the never-never land of dreams, Raleigh. We just talked about that a while ago. This is the real world, and in this world, there are disappointments that must be accepted."

"Jenny, you're the ultimate realist. Let me dream a little more!"

Jenny grinned. "Dream on, lover boy. It won't hurt anything."

She leaned over to him again and hugged him tightly. After brushing a kiss to his cheek, she settled back into her chair. "You can be my dreamer," she chuckled. "Tell me and Grandmother your dream."

"Maybe in this dream I would write a book. I would start by telling how I was determined to hike into that canyon just because it presented a challenge. I would embellish it as much as I could get by with to make it interesting. I would represent the hike as being more of a challenge than it actually was, but I would not have to exaggerate a whole lot because it *was* difficult.

"I would blame my dear friend Kurt of trying to talk me out of making the hike, which he actually did of course. I would write that the inherited warrior instinct in me dominated my actions and that I was determined to prove that I was no tenderfoot. I would complain that it was difficult at first and I soon found myself in big trouble. I would insist that it was my guardian angel that led me to those hidden steps and then revealed to me the entrance route to the cove. I would try to describe everything as best I could to give the reader a visual image of the place.

"Then, I would tell how I find the box and bring it out of the wilderness, not knowing what was inside. I would write how Kurt and I open it, find the journal, read it, and become mesmerized by Eve's story. I would be determined to get all the answers to the mystery surrounding this family and do a perfect job of recording the story for future generations." Raleigh stopped to ask, "How does that sound so far?"

"You really don't want me to answer that, Mr. Detective," Jenny said mockingly. "Notice I didn't mention the word 'author?' But go on!"

Raleigh didn't let Jenny's sarcasm faze him as he continued. "Then, I would tell how I met you and how I begged you so hard to marry me and you—"

"Hold up there, Sherlock Holmes-turned-Erle Stanley Gardner! *Now* you want to be Danielle Steele and go the romantic route? We want the truth in this crummy book! You better get yourself back on track."

"*I'm* writing this book, Jenny! You can read it when it's finished. Better still, I'll let you proofread it for me. This is my dream. The book will say whatever I want it to say!"

"Guess I'll just repeat it again—dream on."

"If you want truth, I'll give you truth. Maybe I should just tell the truth about our romance. Then there will have to be some steamy parts. If you want all of that written down for the world to know, then I'll do it."

"By all means, tell it like it is," she snapped back. "That'll be the best part. Everybody loves to read steamy romances. The juicier the better. If you want the book to sell, you can't leave that part out!"

"It's as good as done then. But there's a whole lot more to the story, and I'll put it all down. Eventually I'll come to the part where we are now, and I will write

that we thought we had come to a dead end and that
we would probably never know what happened to that
family that stayed in Alabama to escape the Trail of
Tears, only to stay here and cry a pail of tears. What do
you think about that for embellishing the story?"

"Weak! Woefully weak!"

Raleigh had not intended for his question to be
answered, but he got it from Jenny anyway. "Getting
back to my story where you interrupted me... Voila!"
Raleigh shot his hands in the air. "We find a notebook
in the cellar vault, we walk right through the impasse
that we have now reached, and the book ends with the
reader having a clear picture of the fate of that family.
Then, everything is tied up in a neat little package.
When the readers finish the last page, they jump up and
shout 'Halleluiah! What a good read that was!'"

"Well, your dream has it all figured out all right. But
you were mighty vague about that last part. Can you
tell me now what your little vision had to say about who
is related to whom and whether or not that family got
out of the cove, and if so, how and what can we know
about them now? Now you answer that for me, Mr.
Author-Man. When you can clear out all that fog, then
you will have this investigation all wrapped up, and we
will go and relive some of that steamy romantic stuff.
Otherwise, let's talk to Grandmother while we're here.
We are practically ignoring her."

"All right, Jenny. If you want me to shut up, I will. But
then you wouldn't know about my sequel to that book."

"Good heavens, Raleigh! Have you completely
lost your mind? I find out now that I have married a
complete airhead. You are further out in space than we
can send our rockets."

That comment did not affect Raleigh in the least.
"Yes. I can see it now— the cover of that book! I will

call it *Grandpa's Cellar Vault*. I'll bet there are some extremely interesting things in that vault."

"Hold it!" Jenny almost shouted. "Hold it, Raleigh. Maybe we should have never mentioned that vault to you in the first place. If you even breathe a word of it, Daddy wouldn't even need his ploughs, because there would be so many thieves digging the farm to try to find it. Probably half of your probationers and parolees would be right in there with them. You can't say anything to anybody that about that cellar vault— not even to Mom and Dad."

"Sorry, Jenny! I got just a little carried away with that story. I won't let it happen again, and I would never do anything to jeopardize your—uh, our—family's security or safety."

"I know that, Raleigh. We won't say anything else about your little pipe dream either."

Jenny turned to Mattie. "What did you think about all that nonsense, Grandmother?"

"What nonsense, honey?"

"That stuff that my beloved husband was just spouting off."

"Honey, I didn't pay no mind to what he was saying. You know that I am hard of hearing anyway, and sometimes I pretend to be listening, but I really ain't. My mind is just somewhere else. That comes with age."

Jenny looked at Raleigh. "Thank goodness! Maybe she won't think you're a complete fool, just a jabber mouth."

Raleigh laughed. "Maybe so. I'll try to leave a good impression on this dear old lady in the future. The journal will stay in the box, and I will turn my thoughts elsewhere. Your love has given me the motivation to do that."

Jenny looked back at Mattie. "It's your turn to talk again, Grandmother."

"Well, one reason I don't know nothing about what—uh—uh—" Mattie looked at Raleigh. "What's his name again?"

"Raleigh," Jenny answered then re-emphasized, "*Raleigh*, Grandmother, Raleigh. Remember, that city in North Carolina."

Jenny looked at Raleigh and whispered again, "Good! She can't remember your name. Maybe that's not so bad, after all that gobbledygook you just spouted."

"That's right. Raleigh—Raleigh!" She repeated it a few times to herself. "I just got to remember my new boy's name. Now where was I in that talking that I was a doing?"

"You were just starting to tell us the reason you don't know anything about what Raleigh was saying, Grandmother."

"Oh, yes. My mind is just about like my hearing—ain't much left! But I'm back on track now. Well, one reason that I didn't know what Raleigh was a saying is because I had my mind on something else, something I want to get off of it. Off my mind, that is."

"Go ahead, Grandmother. You have our full attention now."

"Well, I don't know just where to start this. What I had on my mind is that I may have told you a little lie a while ago, and I don't never want to lie. I told a lie about the same thing to my pa when I was young. It is about the only time that I ever lied to him, and it has always bothered me.

"Now, I swore that I would never tell this to a living soul because I know that what I did wasn't right, and I ain't never breathed a word of it to nobody. What I am saying is not going to help you find out anything you want to know, but I think that I ought to make things right. I ain't got much longer here on this earth, and I will feel better if I confess this bad thing that I did before I die. I want to tell this to you two young folks only if you won't hold it against me." She paused, rethinking her decision.

After a long silence, Jenny spoke. "We won't hold anything against you, Grandmother. You know that you and my mom and dad are the dearest people on earth to me..."

Jenny paused, looked at Raleigh, then added, "And now my dear Raleigh, of course. Nothing you say will change that. Grandmother, you have always been one of the most important people in my life. You probably helped deliver me when I was born, and I know you helped Mom change diapers on me when I was a baby. I know what a wonderful person you are, and I would never hold anything against you. Never in a million years."

"Well, I just made it out to you as being some big thing that I did, but it weren't much, except to me it was. Now I ain't killed nobody, I ain't stole nothing, nor had no babies 'cept your mom. No, it weren't anything big except to me. But I was ashamed of this afterwards because I had disobeyed my pa, so I never talked about it."

"We will understand, Grandmother. Tell us what you have on your mind."

"Well, you see, I mentioned that old notebook that the men were reading from. One time when that notebook was a laying out, he told me that I should never touch it, and I promised him that I would not do it. Well, he left it on the table, and I decided to see what was in it after I had already done told him that I wouldn't. I opened it and read some from it and then I heard him coming back. I closed it real fast like, but he almost caught me with it open.

"I remember this just like it was yesterday. He walked in and asked me if I had been reading from that book, and it scared me so that I lied to him, just like I lied to you a while ago. I told him that I hadn't touched it but was just looking at it lying on the table like it was. This is what hurt me afterwards. I never ever lied to my pa, and he had never caught me telling a lie because I never did. He believed my lie and didn't say nothing else about it. He forgot about it, but I didn't. I was ashamed of it afterwards, and I still am until this day.

"The truth is that I did get to read for a little while from that book. There ain't many things that I remember about what was in it, and that wouldn't do you a lick of good in helping you find out what you need to know."

"But you do remember a couple of things?" Jenny inquired.

"Yep, there was a couple of things that just stuck in my head, 'cause as a young girl I just found them interesting. There was nothing big. No names or nothing. As I say, it ain't nothing that would help you or that you would be interested in."

Raleigh made the request this time. "Would you mind telling us what those couple of things were?"

Mattie thought a moment before answering. "I think that I better not tell about anything that I read out of that book, because I wasn't supposed to read it to start with. That would be like Eve in the Bible, eating that apple and then talking about it to Adam what she had done. It got them both in trouble. It just wouldn't be right, and as I done told you, it don't mean nothing anyhow."

"We understand, Grandmother. We don't want you to do anything that you don't want to do. It would just be interesting for you to share that information with us. It would be a tidbit of history from that notebook which could be passed down to future generations." Jenny waited to speak so that Mattie could contemplate her last remark.

Finally, Mattie said, "At my age I know that I ain't going to live much longer, and since what I saw in that book don't amount to nothing no how, I suppose it wouldn't hurt none to tell what I remember. Since I have already told you this much, it won't hurt no more than to just tell you the rest. Now as I say, there weren't but two little things that I remember about what I saw before I closed it real fast. One of them I don't remember too well, but the other one interested me so much that I memorized it. It wasn't but one little saying. I can still quote it to this day." She paused for a long moment.

"Tell us about it," Jenny urged again.

"Well, honey, give me time to get it straight in my mind. I want to tell you just like it was. Give this old woman time to think."

"Us younger people get impatient sometimes, Grandmother. Just overlook what we say and take all the time you want."

"I was a gonna do just that anyway. Well, now that I think about it, there ain't much left in my head to tell you about that one. As I said before, that was a long time ago. Now what little bit of that I remember is what the woman who wrote it had to say about herself. I remember she said that she wrote in the notebook because her mother had taught her to read and write by using a notebook, which she wished that she had, but it was hid away where no one could get at it."

"Did she say where it was hid?" Raleigh asked.

"Now I done told you that I didn't read much, and I have done about forgot what it was that I did read."

"How was this person related to our family?" Jenny asked.

"I could be wrong about this part, but I seem to remember hearing that it was my great-great, maybe another great or two needs to go there, grandmother or something like that. This stuck in my mind because she said that she was married to the son of a preacher man. I did not know that there had been a preacher man in our family, and nobody ever said nothing about it before or since. All I know is what I read out of that notebook. Now, she told his name in there, but I forgot it. I do remember that it was a name that made me wonder. Give me a minute and let me think."

She stopped talking, and it was apparent that she was putting deep thought in her effort to come up with the name. After a while, she started talking to herself.

"Rock—Rock—Rock—seems like it was Rock. No, that don't sound just right." She shook her head before addressing her two listeners again. "It's been so long since I even thought about this. I knew that I could not remember this stuff."

She thought a while longer, and no one interrupted her. All of a sudden, she exclaimed, "Stone! That's it! Stone. That's the name I was trying to recall. She was married to the son of a Reverend Stone. The reason that I remember that is because this woman who was writing in that notebook was a telling how that her husband's daddy, who was this preacher man, had met a Cherokee woman who was said to be the most beautiful one around. I remember that she called her 'Sunbeam.' I guess they called her that because she was so pretty."

Mattie hesitated again before speaking. "You know that a Cherokee woman has always decided what man she wanted, and I suppose that this Sunbeam decided that she wanted a preacher man. When a beautiful Cherokee woman comes after a man, he is just about as good as caught. Preacher man or not!

"Preacher Stone. Yeah, I believe that was his name. Stone. He fornicated with her, and it wasn't long before she was going to have his child. At that same time, they were rounding up the Indians so as to take them to the new Indian Territory in Oklahoma. They found out that the guard men were about to come get Sunbeam, so the preacher took off with her so they could be together.

"Now he did not want nobody to know that he, being a man of God, had done this sinful thing of getting the woman, who was not his wife, pregnant. He made everybody think that he had died."

Mattie halted for a moment before continuing carefully. "Now, I want to tell this right to the best of my recollection. I don't want to say nothing that ain't right."

Raleigh and Jenny said nothing. They did not want to interrupt Mattie or cause her to lose her train of thought. This was too important.

"There is a reason as to why I remember what I am a saying to you. I thought, in my young mind, just what kind of a preacher man would do that? That is the reason I hadn't forgotten this cause that ain't no way a reverend should do—fornicate with a young girl and make a child by her. Seems like she said that he was a Methodist, but I am not real sure about that.

"Nowadays it don't seem so strange that some preacher would do something like that, or so I have been told. Word is that they even do worser things now; but as a little girl, that struck me as being a bad thing to do. Except he kept those people from taking Sunbeam to Oklahoma, which was good."

"Grandmother, are you saying that the son of a Reverend Stone, a Methodist preacher, was married to the woman who had written in the book?"

"Well, honey, I am not real sure about the Methodist part, but I do remember that he was the son of a preacher man, supposed to have been his love child. That was the reason the preacher man wanted everybody to think that he had died. He married her later, but not before they had made that child."

An audible gasp was heard from both Jenny and Raleigh. They were so astonished that neither of them could speak for a while.

Finally, Jenny regained enough of her composure to ask a follow up question. "Tell me again who that woman was, Grandmother. Do you remember her name?"

"How many times have I done told you that I don't remember no names? As I said, the word was that she was my pa's great-grandmother, or something like that. I'm not real sure about that either. I couldn't call her name if my life depended on it. I don't even recall seeing no name for her in that book. 'Course, as I said, I didn't read much out of it before I almost got caught."

"So you think that this was probably your great-great-grandmother that was married to this preacher's boy, but you don't know their names except the last name would probably be Stone. Is this a logical deduction from what you just told us?" Raleigh asked after regaining his breath.

"Well, I couldn't say for certain that he took the preacher's last name. He was a love child, you know. Back then they were real careful not to let people know too much about their family business. Wasn't no birth certificate that was going to be filed with the government to give them all the information that they wanted. I know that way back somewhere there was a little of the white man's blood that got mingled in with our family, and I imagine that this is when it happened. After that, all of the family went back to marrying Cherokee, but you understand that this is all just guessing."

Jenny looked at Raleigh. "What a turn of events! We were looking for ancestors from Eve's portion of the journal, and we never gave Reverend Stone's writings a second thought, making the assumption that he had died. Now look what turns up all of a sudden."

Raleigh nodded. Earlier he had been accused of being a jabbermouth. For once in his life, he was without words.

Finally, he managed to speak. "We got nowhere in the search for Eve's descendents, but surprise, surprise!"

Both Raleigh and Jenny spent a few more moments digesting the information Mattie had just given them.

Then Jenny spoke up. "We got so excited about this information, Grandmother, that I completely forgot that there was something else you said you remembered from that book and that you had it memorized. Tell us about that."

"Yes," Mattie responded. "You two got so wound up about that wicked preacher man and him marrying that Indian that he fornicated with, that I almost forgot about that myself. Well, you see, the reason that this caught my eye was that whoever had written it had wrote it in big capital letters like they wanted to print it. You couldn't miss reading it. When I read it, I thought that it was so good that I said it over and over, and I still remember it word for word."

"Did she say why she wrote it?" Jenny made the inquiry.

"I'm glad you asked that because what she said made a lot of sense, and it helped me later. She said that it was a special saying because her mother taught it to her when she was a young child and she never forgot it. She said that it helped her out many times when things got hard and she would think of it and it would help. She also said something about her mother teaching it to her younger brother who had it real hard when he was little. From what I read, I think they both did, but she didn't do no whining about it being so rough. I guess it was because things were much better when she was a writing in that notebook than they had been when she was smaller."

Mattie had drained her jar of tea. She picked up the empty jar and looked at Jenny. "It's getting a little warm out here. I need some more iced tea. Can you go fill my jar back up? Put a lot of ice in it, if you will. I make my tea strong so it will still be good when the ice melts. If you will do that, I will be much obliged to you. I would do it myself, but these old bones don't want to cooperate sometimes. You can get some for you and your new fellow too if you are so a mind."

Jenny hurriedly refilled all their glasses with tea and returned to her chair. She was anxious to hear the rest of the story.

Mattie continued talking. "Seems like there was something about them not being allowed to be around many people when they were little. Well, I don't know why I got off on that part about her and her brother. This ain't got nothing to do with this."

"Maybe it doesn't, Grandmother, but did she say anything else about her brother?"

"Jenny, you keep asking these hard questions like I just read that book yesterday. I keep a telling you that I was just a little kid when I did that. I'm not the smartest person in the world, you know."

"Well, I think you are, but that's beside the point. If you remember anything about her brother, we would like to hear it."

"There you go again. You are after me to give you a name, and I don't remember no names, and I already done told you that a bunch of times. Now, I am not saying that the book did not say his name, but that I don't remember it."

Raleigh entered the conversation next. "You don't have to give us names, Grandmother. Just tell us what you remembered, if anything, about her younger brother."

"I do remember she said that the little saying that I recalled had helped him about as much as it had her. She seemed to believe that it had helped him make real good in life and perhaps had caused him to take an interest in helping the crippled and sick or anybody that needed some help. Thinking about it as a child, I thought this might be the type of person for me to look for someday when I wanted to marry. You know, just childhood fantasies.

"Best I recall, she said that her and him were the only kids. No—wait a minute." Mattie paused for a second. "Now that I think about it, seems like she mentioned a little brother that had died. I think she said he got bit by a snake what killed him. You know, that happened a lot back then when the little ones didn't know any better than to try to play with a bad snake. She didn't say nothing else about the rest of the family."

"That's very interesting," Jenny said. "Do you remember anything else she said about him?"

"Well, now that I got to thinking about it, I do recall that there was something else she told about him that stuck in my mind, 'cept I hadn't thought about this part in a long time. That's what I was thinking about when I just quit talking for a while. I was just trying to get it straight in my mind again. I remember she said that her brother also had a little quote that he would say after he had helped somebody out. Yeah, now I recollect—they both had their own little saying."

Mattie took a drink from her replenished supply of iced tea, put her head between her hands, and thought for a few minutes without saying anything. When she did speak, she was not quite ready to jump back into the conversation.

"Let me think a minute more while I try to remember what that was. Now you just be quiet a minute while I go back over this in my mind." She hesitated again, giving some serious thought about what she wanted to say. She appeared to be satisfied when she spoke again.

"I think I got it right in my mind what that little saying was that her brother had. Best I recall, it was...

> *"Helpless we begin our life*
> *Dependent on a man and wife*
> *Nurtured then by love and care*
> *We must each our burdens bear*
> *Helpful then we must become*
> *Troubles will surely fall on some*
> *With the golden rule to guide*
> *Help is always by your side*
> *Always do unto others as you*
> *Would have them do to you."*

She then nodded in the affirmative. "Yep, that's it! She said that was her brother's little saying. Now that is a short one, but I thought it was something that everybody should think about."

Raleigh was too startled to speak. He had heard this quote many times before.

"You said there was a saying, Grandmother?" Jenny asked. "And you can remember it too?"

"Yep, I remember it because lots of times I would quote it to myself, and it always helped me a lot like it did that girl and her brother. Sometimes I would forget about it, then I would have some kind of trouble and that saying would come back to my mind and it would help me get through tough times."

"Quote it for us, Grandmother," Raleigh requested. He was tempted to ask her to repeat the last little saying she had quoted, but he had heard it plainly enough. He added, "Jenny and I are still young, and I am sure there will be times in our lives when we might need a little saying to give us a boost. If it helped the writer of the notebook and helped you through tough times, perhaps it can do the same for us."

"It won't be no problem for me to quote that! It may be that later you might want to get a pencil and write it down so you can remember it."

Little did she know that Raleigh had the original document from which she quoted, written in pokeberry ink.

Grandmother recited,

"Walk with the wind at your back
Whenever you can.
Face it whenever you must.
Be brave and strong
Hard times will soon be gone.
Tomorrow is the beginning
Of a whole new day.
We cannot know
What this day might bring
But the sky is not always gray.
Endure the storms
And soothe the pains.
Enjoy the sunshine
That follows the rains.

About the Author

Wheeler Pounds grew up in rural Alabama, and he has always possessed a deep connection to the outdoors and his Native American heritage. He is a member of the Echota Cherokee Tribe of Alabama, of which he is the chief of the Blue Clan. For thirty years he was employed by the State Board of Pardons and Paroles and was an adjunct instructor of Criminal Justice at Faulkner University.

Since retiring, he has been able to devote time to his favorite hobby of being an avid hiker. He has backpacked the majority of the National Parks in the United States but maintains that his favorite is Bankhead National Forest, which is near his home. He is also a committed husband, father, and grandfather and has dedicated a significant portion of his life to volunteer work.

Wheeler resides in Walker County, Alabama with his wife, Judi, where he spends time with family and friends and continues to foster his passion for nature.

Read more from the *Secrets of the Cherokee Hideaway*
by Wheeler Pounds

ISBN: 978-1934610244

ISBN: 978-1934610794

If you enjoyed this book, try these other titles from
Bluewater Publications

The Archer's Son
M. E. Hubbs
ISBN: 978-1934610947

Promises to Keep:
Southern Short Stories
Tom McDonald
ISBN: 978-1934610190

Hiking Sipsey: A Family's Fight
for Eastern Wilderness
Ricky Butch Walker
ISBN: 978-1934610930

Doublehead: Last Chickamauga
Cherokee Chief
Ricky Butch Walker
ISBN: 978-1934610671

www.ingramcontent.com/pod-product-compliance
Lightning Source LLC
Chambersburg PA
CBHW020530020726
47494CB00006B/1707